DANIEL WARREN JOHNSON

DO A POWERBOMB!

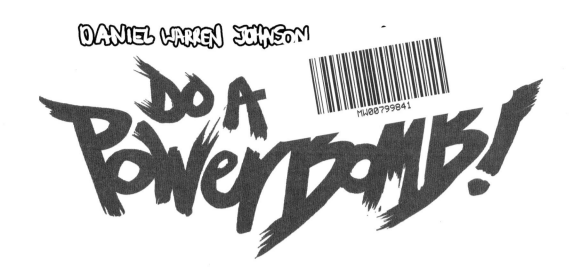

DO A POWERBOMB!

CREATED, WRITTEN, AND ILLUSTRATED BY
DANIEL WARREN JOHNSON

COLORS
MIKE SPICER

LETTERS
RUS WOOTON

DO A POWERBOMB. First printing. March 2023. Published by Image Comics, Inc. Office of publication: PO BOX 14457, Portland, OR 97293. Copyright © 2023 Daniel Warren Johnson. All rights reserved. Contains material originally published in single magazine form as DO A POWERBOMB #1-7. "Do a Powerbomb," its logos, and the likenesses of all characters herein are trademarks of Daniel Warren Johnson, unless otherwise noted. "Image" and the Image Comics logos are registered trademarks of Image Comics, Inc. No part of this publication may be reproduced or transmitted, in any form or by any means (except for short excerpts for journalistic or review purposes), without the express written permission of Daniel Warren Johnson, or Image Comics, Inc. All names, characters, events, and locales in this publication are entirely fictional. Any resemblance to actual persons (living or dead), events, or places, without satirical intent, is coincidental. Printed in the USA. For international rights, contact: foreignlicensing@imagecomics.com. ISBN: 978-1-5343-2474-9.

IT WAS THE SUMMER OF 2018,

and my daughter refused to sleep. She wouldn't cry when we held her, but the tears would begin as soon as we put her down to rest. My wife and I had our beautiful Fiona that February, and after months of solid sleep, we now suddenly had to take the night in shifts: first me for four hours, then Rachel, and so on. It was during this time that I found myself sitting on the couch or walking through our apartment, comforting her moment by moment, with the TV turned on to help pass the time. After watching every kind of show, movie, and documentary, I wanted something different. I remembered conversations I'd had with friends months prior, them talking about something called New Japan Pro-Wrestling. Pro-wrestling? You mean men in underwear? The soap opera for boys? I was never allowed to watch it growing up and I had missed out on the 90's glory days of the Attitude Era. But I loved the look of the wrestlers my friends had shown me, and I was intrigued. Also, I had a non-sleeping baby and a lot of time on my hands. So I gave New Japan a try. It was during the G1 Climax, a famous month-long tournament where some of the best matches of the year occur. And sure enough, I found myself getting drawn to the characters, to the physical feats, to the entire energy and production. It sucked me in. I had been watching for a few weeks with one toe in the water until I watched a specific match: Kota Ibushi versus Tomohiro Ishii. There was an intensity to both of those wrestlers. They had a look in their eye that said "we are going to give absolutely everything we have to this fight" and they did. As Ibushi did a moonsault off a fifteen foot balcony, I knew I was watching two people at the peak of their craft. It was magical. From there on I was hooked. It was the start to my loving this incredible art form, and the inspiration to what eventually would be DO A POWERBOMB!

I could go on for a long time on why I love pro-wrestling: The combination of real life sports with curated moments, the drama of seeing a person put their life on the line for a story, but honestly, if someone hasn't experienced wrestling intentionally, it's tough to explain why it's so great. Which brings me to comics. I believe that comics are inherently an inviting art form. From memes to newspaper strips, we connect with images and words together immediately. It makes, in my opinion, the perfect platform to introduce someone to new ideas and worlds. It's one of the many reasons why I love comics so much: It's so easy to share my passion with other people. And sharing things that I love brings me so much joy. I did it with Murder Falcon with heavy metal, and I'm doing it here too, with pro-wrestling. The goal is and always has been to invite people in, no matter where they're at. So if you are into pro-wrestling, welcome, old friends! And if you aren't into it, damn am I glad you made it this far!

-Daniel Warren Johnson

P.S. A special thanks to my daughter, Fiona Johnson, for helping me get inspired by something new. You are the best and I love you!

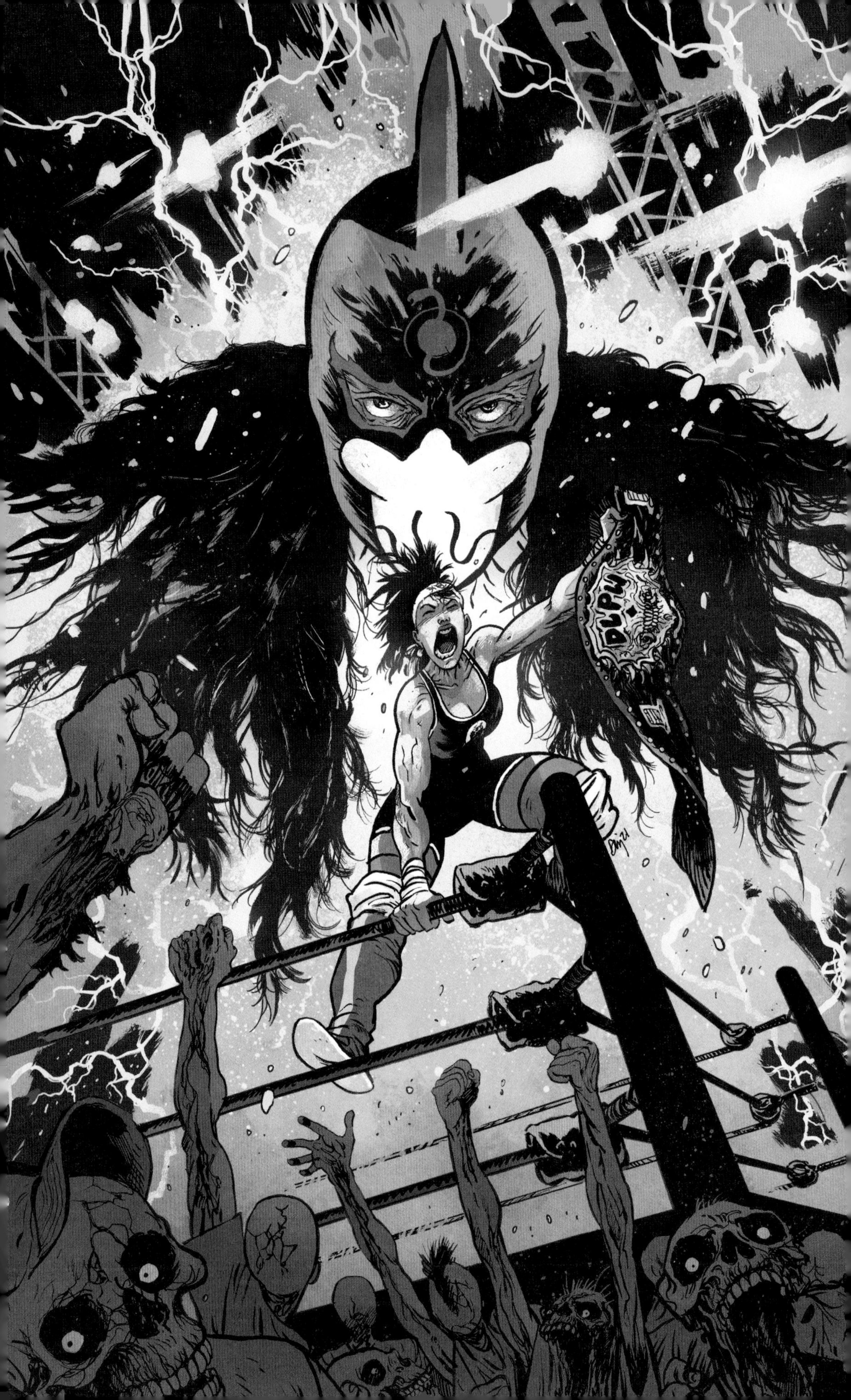
DLPW

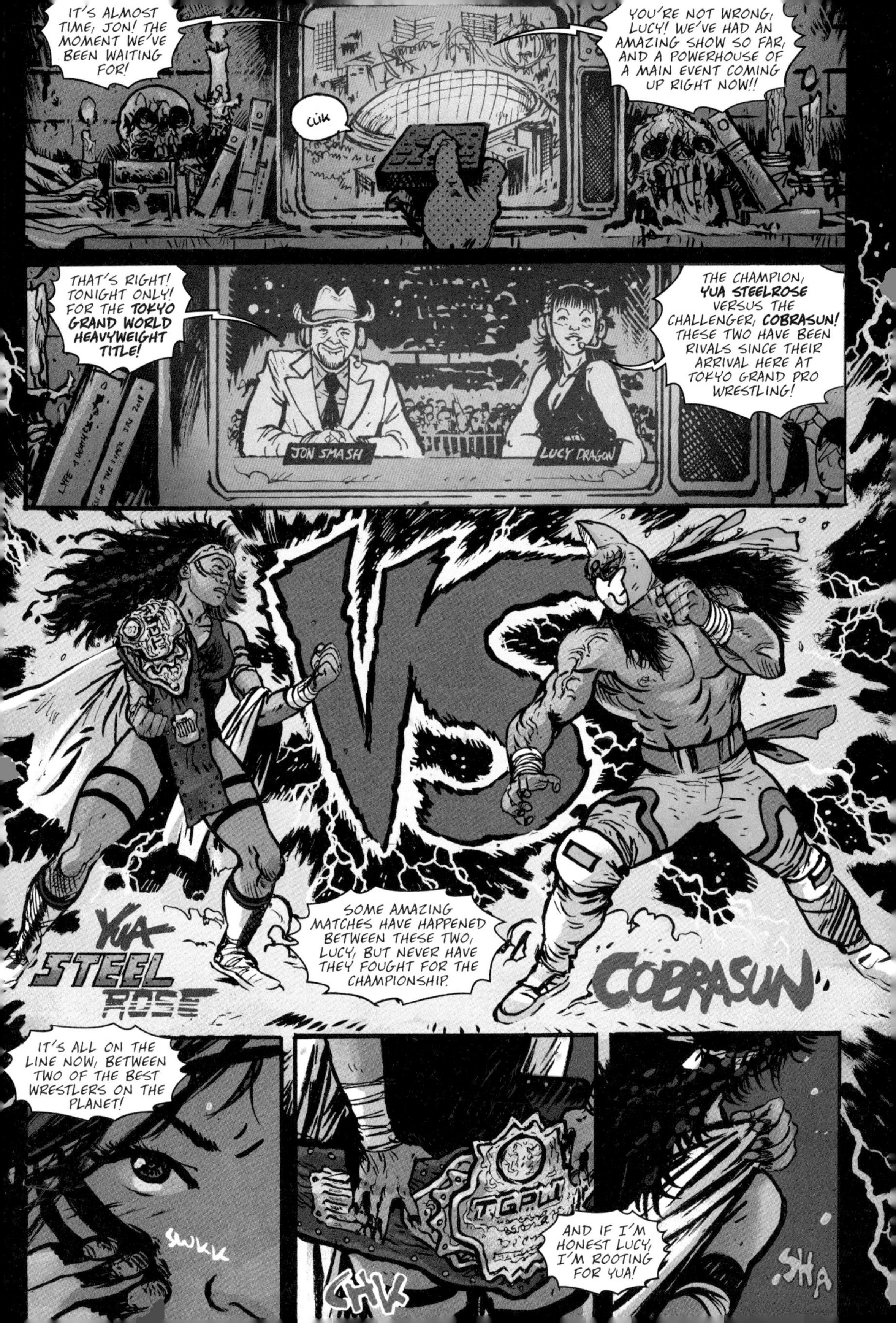
IT'S ALMOST TIME, JON! THE MOMENT WE'VE BEEN WAITING FOR!
YOU'RE NOT WRONG, LUCY! WE'VE HAD AN AMAZING SHOW SO FAR, AND A POWERHOUSE OF A MAIN EVENT COMING UP RIGHT NOW!!
CLIK
THAT'S RIGHT! TONIGHT ONLY! FOR THE TOKYO GRAND WORLD HEAVYWEIGHT TITLE!
JON SMASH
LUCY DRAGON
THE CHAMPION, YUA STEELROSE VERSUS THE CHALLENGER, COBRASUN! THESE TWO HAVE BEEN RIVALS SINCE THEIR ARRIVAL HERE AT TOKYO GRAND PRO WRESTLING!
VS
YUA STEEL ROSE
SOME AMAZING MATCHES HAVE HAPPENED BETWEEN THESE TWO, LUCY, BUT NEVER HAVE THEY FOUGHT FOR THE CHAMPIONSHIP.
COBRASUN
IT'S ALL ON THE LINE NOW, BETWEEN TWO OF THE BEST WRESTLERS ON THE PLANET!
SWKK
T.G.P.W.
CHK
AND IF I'M HONEST LUCY, I'M ROOTING FOR YUA!
SHA

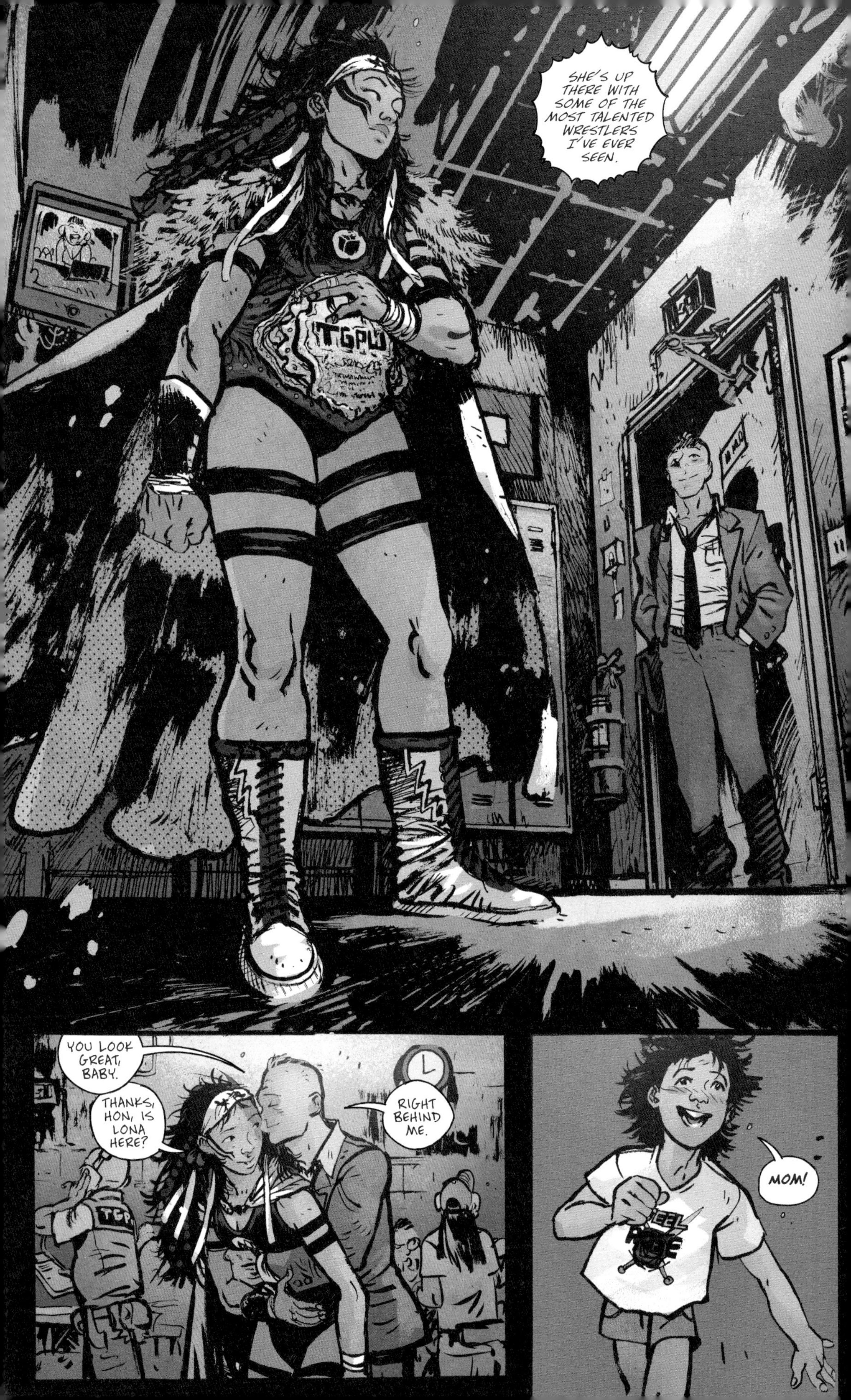
SHE'S UP THERE WITH SOME OF THE MOST TALENTED WRESTLERS I'VE EVER SEEN.
TGPW
YOU LOOK GREAT, BABY.
THANKS, HON, IS LONA HERE?
RIGHT BEHIND ME.
MOM!

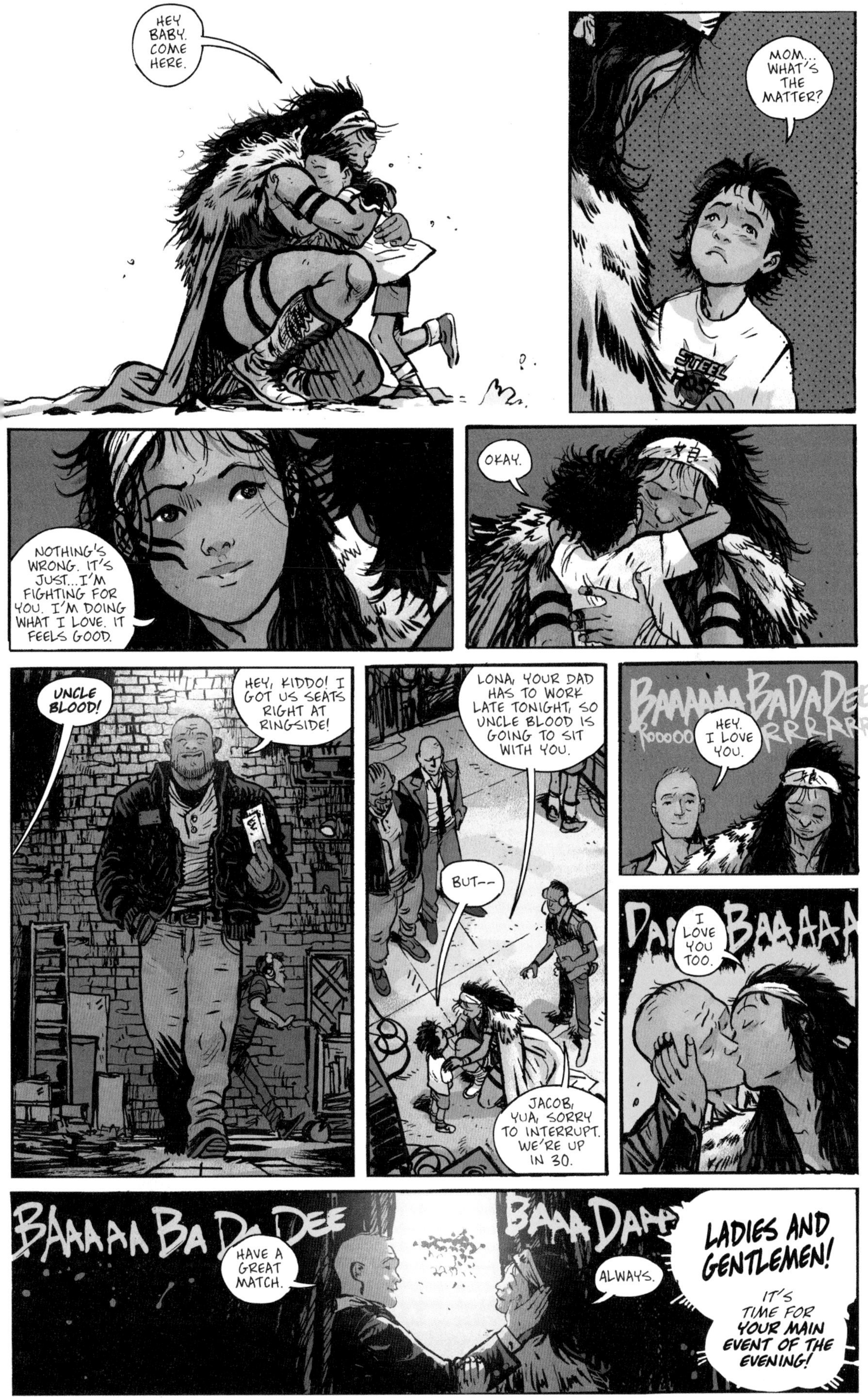
HEY BABY. COME HERE.
MOM... WHAT'S THE MATTER?
NOTHING'S WRONG. IT'S JUST... I'M FIGHTING FOR YOU. I'M DOING WHAT I LOVE. IT FEELS GOOD.
OKAY.
UNCLE BLOOD!
HEY, KIDDO! I GOT US SEATS RIGHT AT RINGSIDE!
LONA, YOUR DAD HAS TO WORK LATE TONIGHT, SO UNCLE BLOOD IS GOING TO SIT WITH YOU.
BUT--
JACOB, YUA, SORRY TO INTERRUPT. WE'RE UP IN 30.
BAAAAA BADADEE
ROOOOO RRRRR
HEY. I LOVE YOU.
DAP BAAAA
I LOVE YOU TOO.
BAAAAA BA DA DEE
BAAA DAP
HAVE A GREAT MATCH.
ALWAYS.
LADIES AND GENTLEMEN!
IT'S TIME FOR YOUR MAIN EVENT OF THE EVENING!

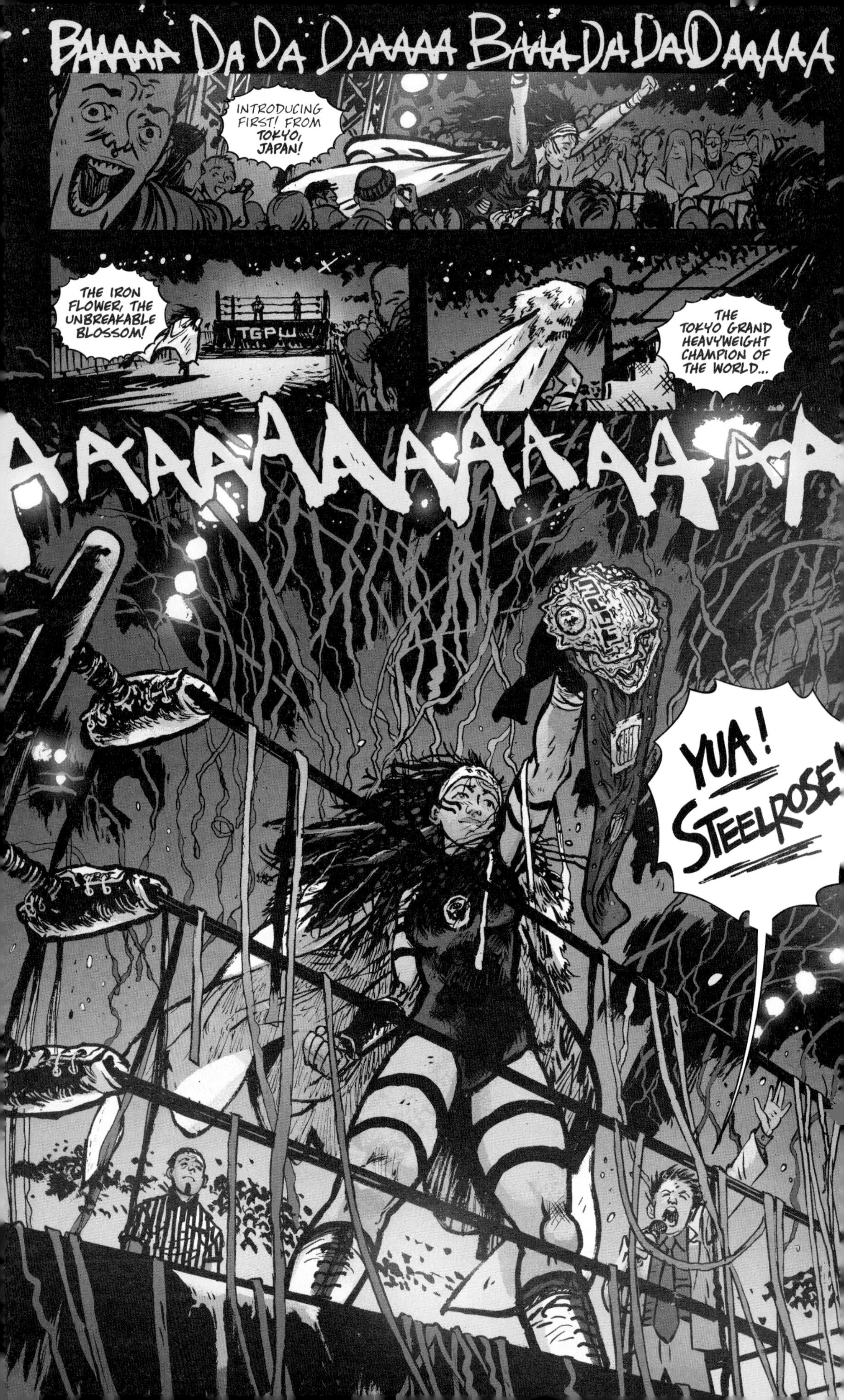
BAAAAA DA DA DAAAAA BAAA DA DA DAAAAA
INTRODUCING FIRST! FROM TOKYO, JAPAN!
THE IRON FLOWER, THE UNBREAKABLE BLOSSOM!
TGPW
THE TOKYO GRAND HEAVYWEIGHT CHAMPION OF THE WORLD...
AAAAAAAAAAAAA
YUA! STEELROSE!

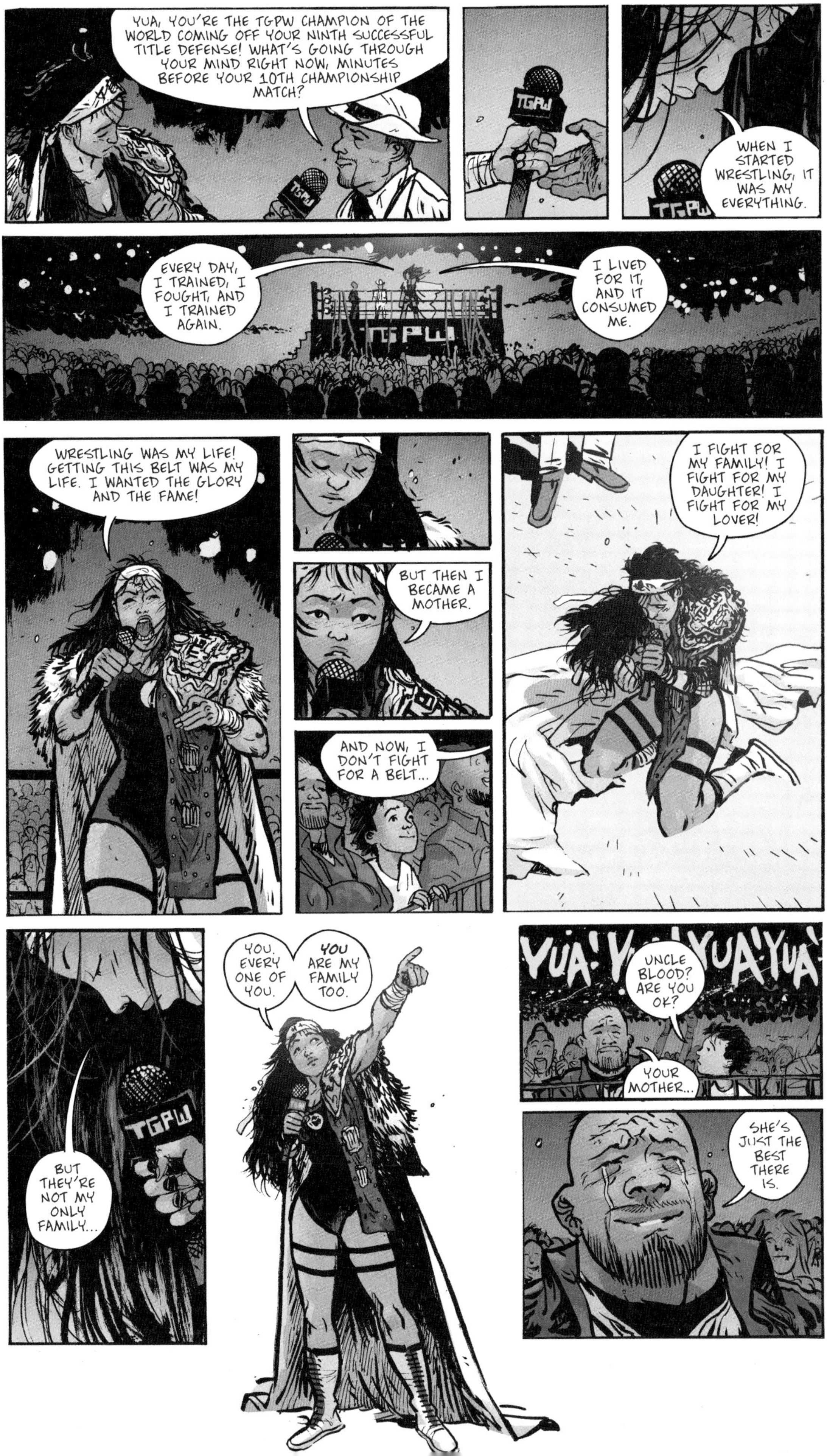
YUA, YOU'RE THE TGPW CHAMPION OF THE WORLD COMING OFF YOUR NINTH SUCCESSFUL TITLE DEFENSE! WHAT'S GOING THROUGH YOUR MIND RIGHT NOW, MINUTES BEFORE YOUR 10TH CHAMPIONSHIP MATCH?
TGPW
TGPW
WHEN I STARTED WRESTLING, IT WAS MY EVERYTHING.
TGPW
EVERY DAY, I TRAINED, I FOUGHT, AND I TRAINED AGAIN.
I LIVED FOR IT, AND IT CONSUMED ME.
TGPW
WRESTLING WAS MY LIFE! GETTING THIS BELT WAS MY LIFE. I WANTED THE GLORY AND THE FAME!
BUT THEN I BECAME A MOTHER.
AND NOW, I DON'T FIGHT FOR A BELT...
I FIGHT FOR MY FAMILY! I FIGHT FOR MY DAUGHTER! I FIGHT FOR MY LOVER!
BUT THEY'RE NOT MY ONLY FAMILY...
TGPW
YOU. EVERY ONE OF YOU.
YOU ARE MY FAMILY TOO.
YUA! YUA! YUA!
UNCLE BLOOD? ARE YOU OK?
YOUR MOTHER...
SHE'S JUST THE BEST THERE IS.

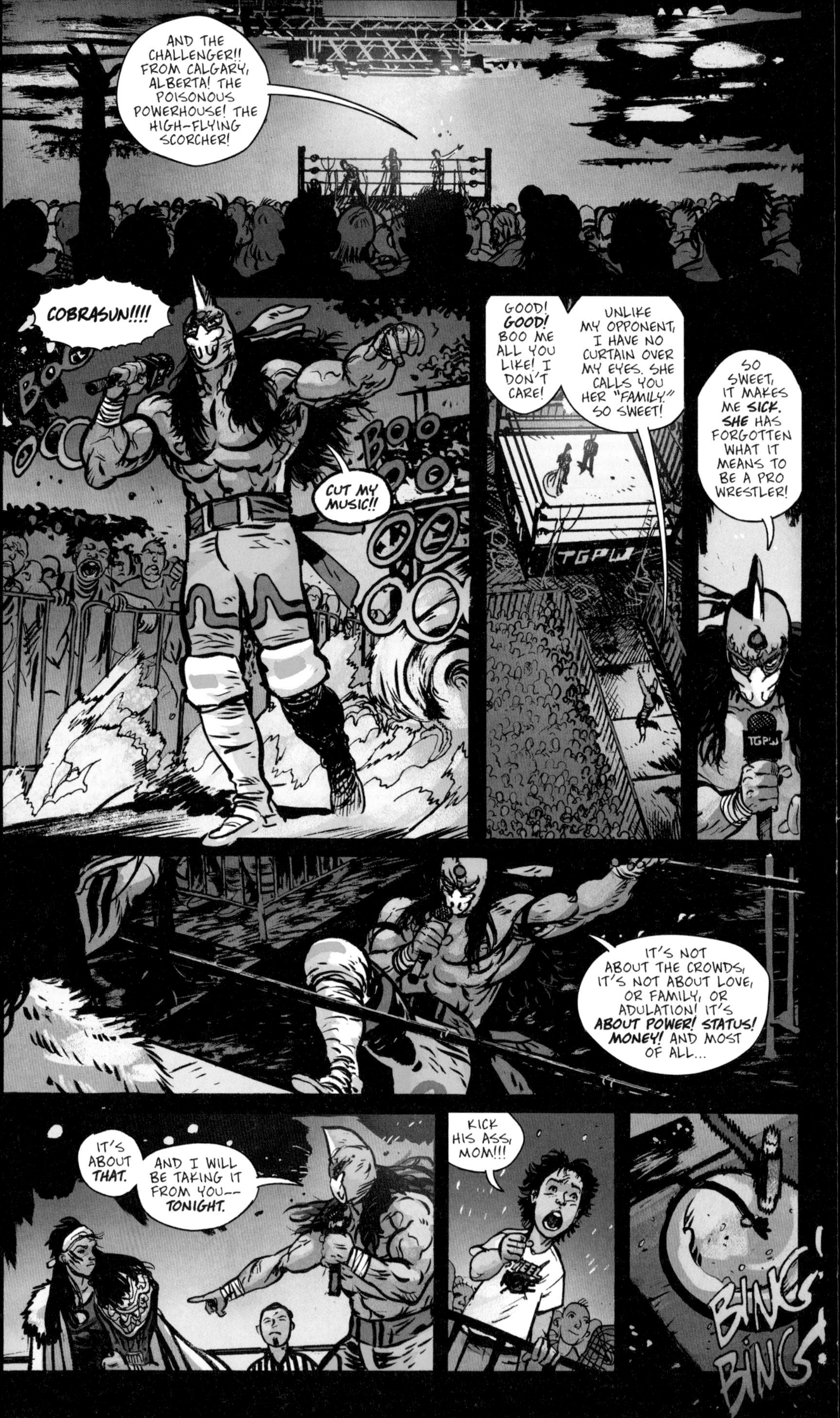
AND THE CHALLENGER!! FROM CALGARY, ALBERTA! THE POISONOUS POWERHOUSE! THE HIGH-FLYING SCORCHER!
COBRASUN!!!!
BOO
BOO
CUT MY MUSIC!!
GOOD! GOOD! BOO ME ALL YOU LIKE! I DON'T CARE!
UNLIKE MY OPPONENT, I HAVE NO CURTAIN OVER MY EYES. SHE CALLS YOU HER "FAMILY." SO SWEET!
TGPW
SO SWEET, IT MAKES ME SICK. SHE HAS FORGOTTEN WHAT IT MEANS TO BE A PRO WRESTLER!
TGPW
IT'S NOT ABOUT THE CROWDS, IT'S NOT ABOUT LOVE, OR FAMILY, OR ADULATION! IT'S ABOUT POWER! STATUS! MONEY! AND MOST OF ALL...
IT'S ABOUT THAT.
AND I WILL BE TAKING IT FROM YOU-- TONIGHT.
KICK HIS ASS, MOM!!!
BING!
BING!

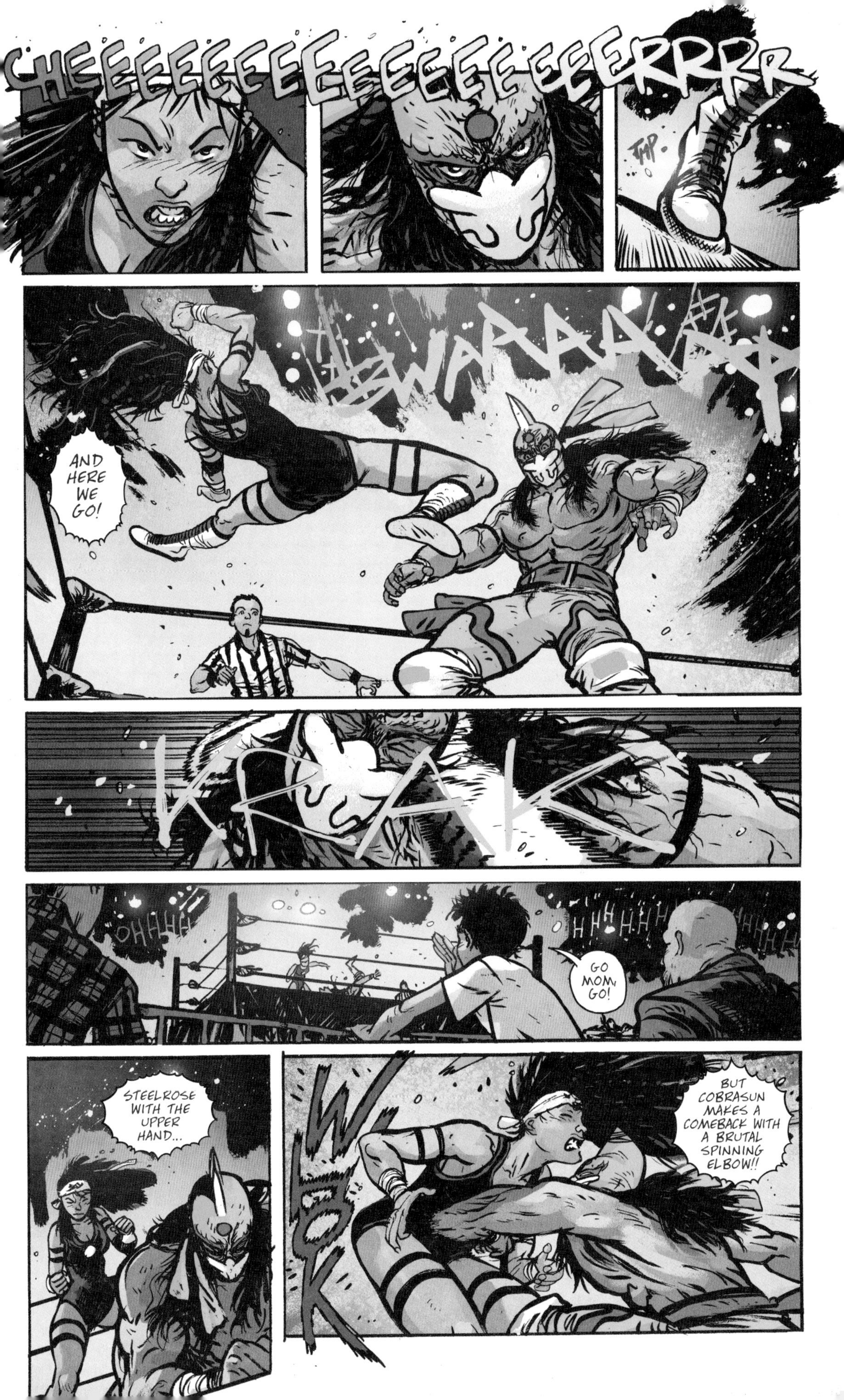
CHEEEEEEEEEEEEEEEEEERRRR
TMP.
AND HERE WE GO!
OHHHH
HHHHHH
GO MOM, GO!
STEELROSE WITH THE UPPER HAND...
BUT COBRASUN MAKES A COMEBACK WITH A BRUTAL SPINNING ELBOW!!
WOK

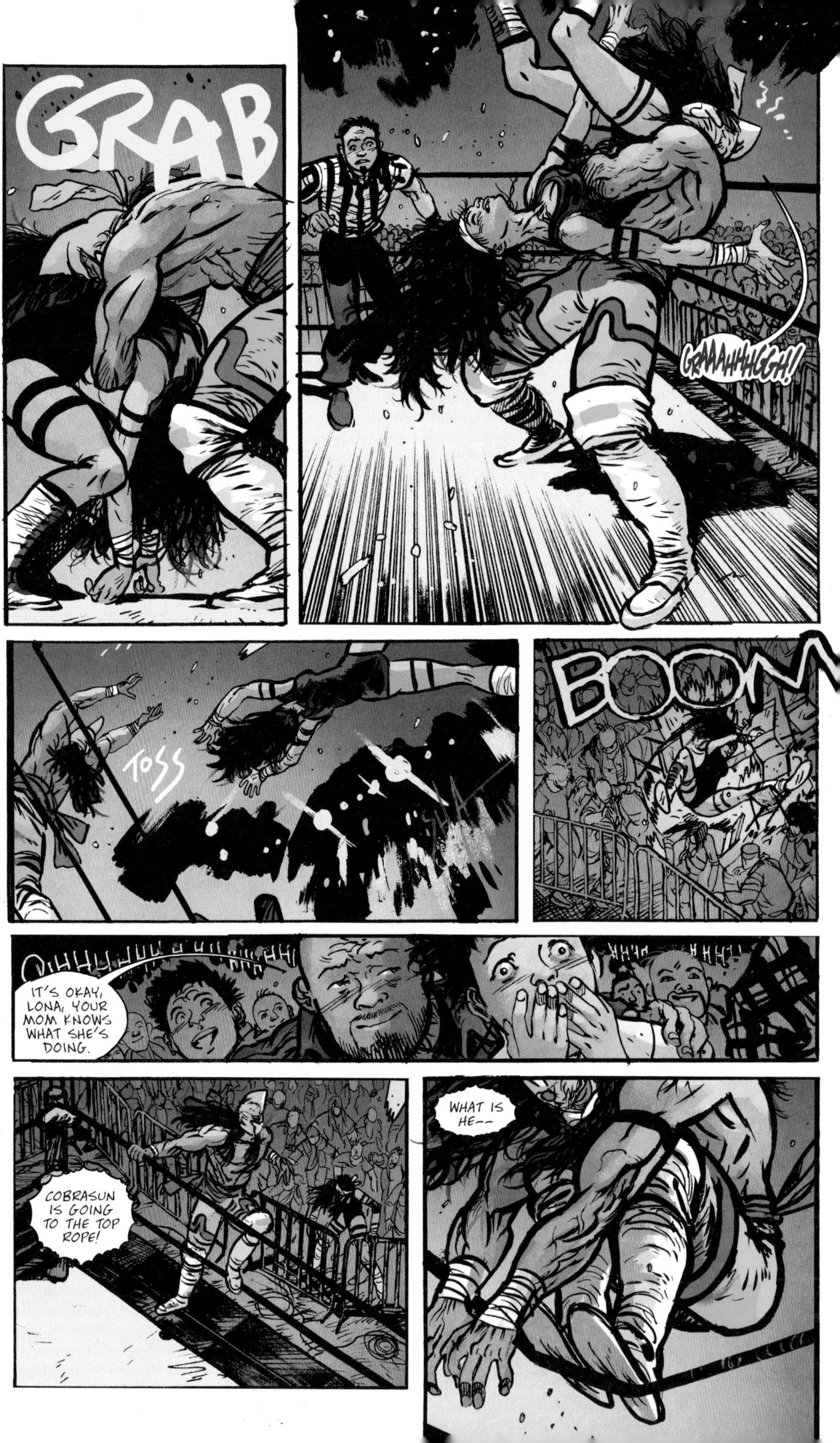
GRAB
GRAAAHHHGGH!
TOSS
BOOM
IT'S OKAY, LONA, YOUR MOM KNOWS WHAT SHE'S DOING.
COBRASUN IS GOING TO THE TOP ROPE!
WHAT IS HE--

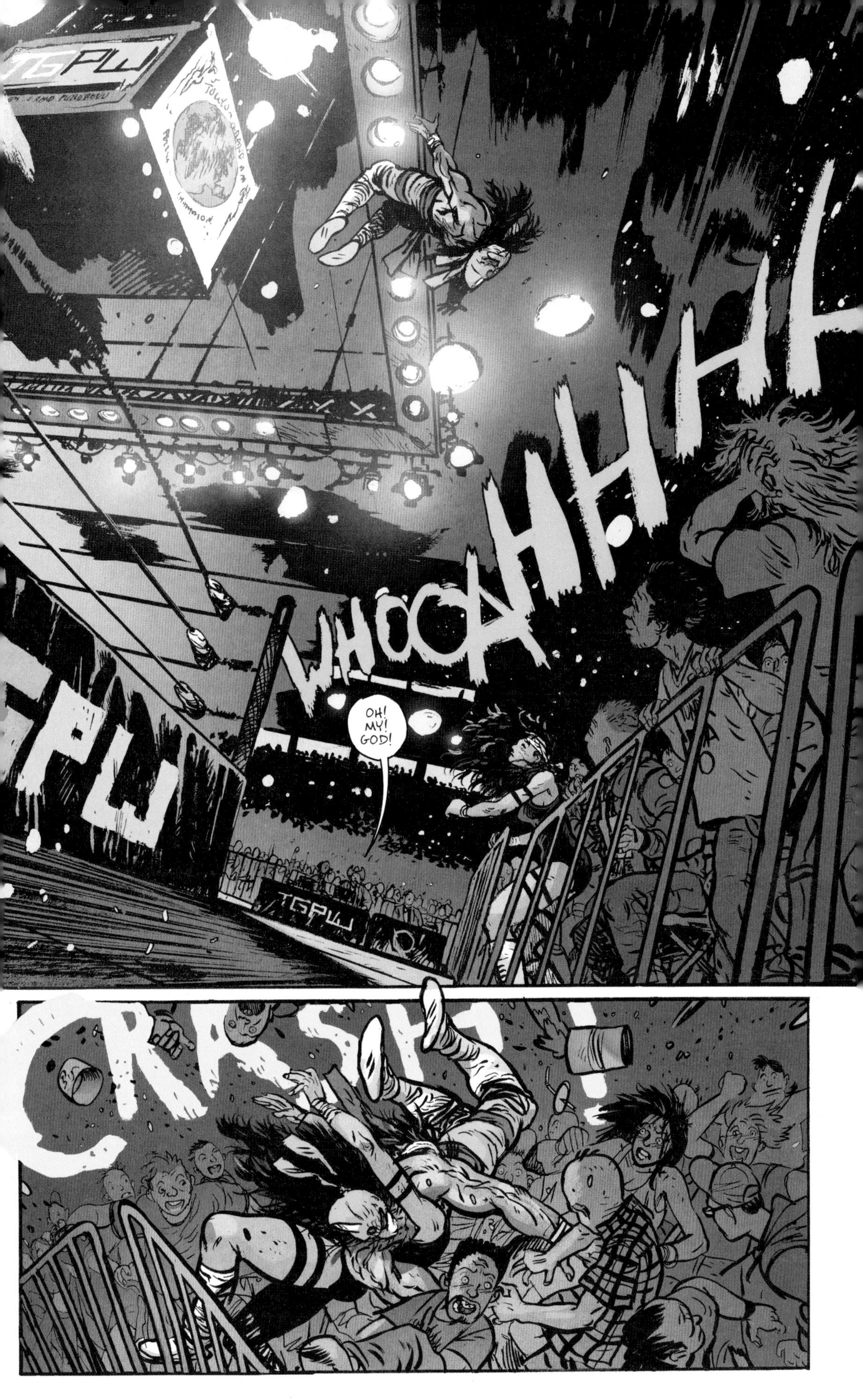
TGPW
WHOOAHHHHH
PW
OH! MY! GOD!
TGPW
CRASH!

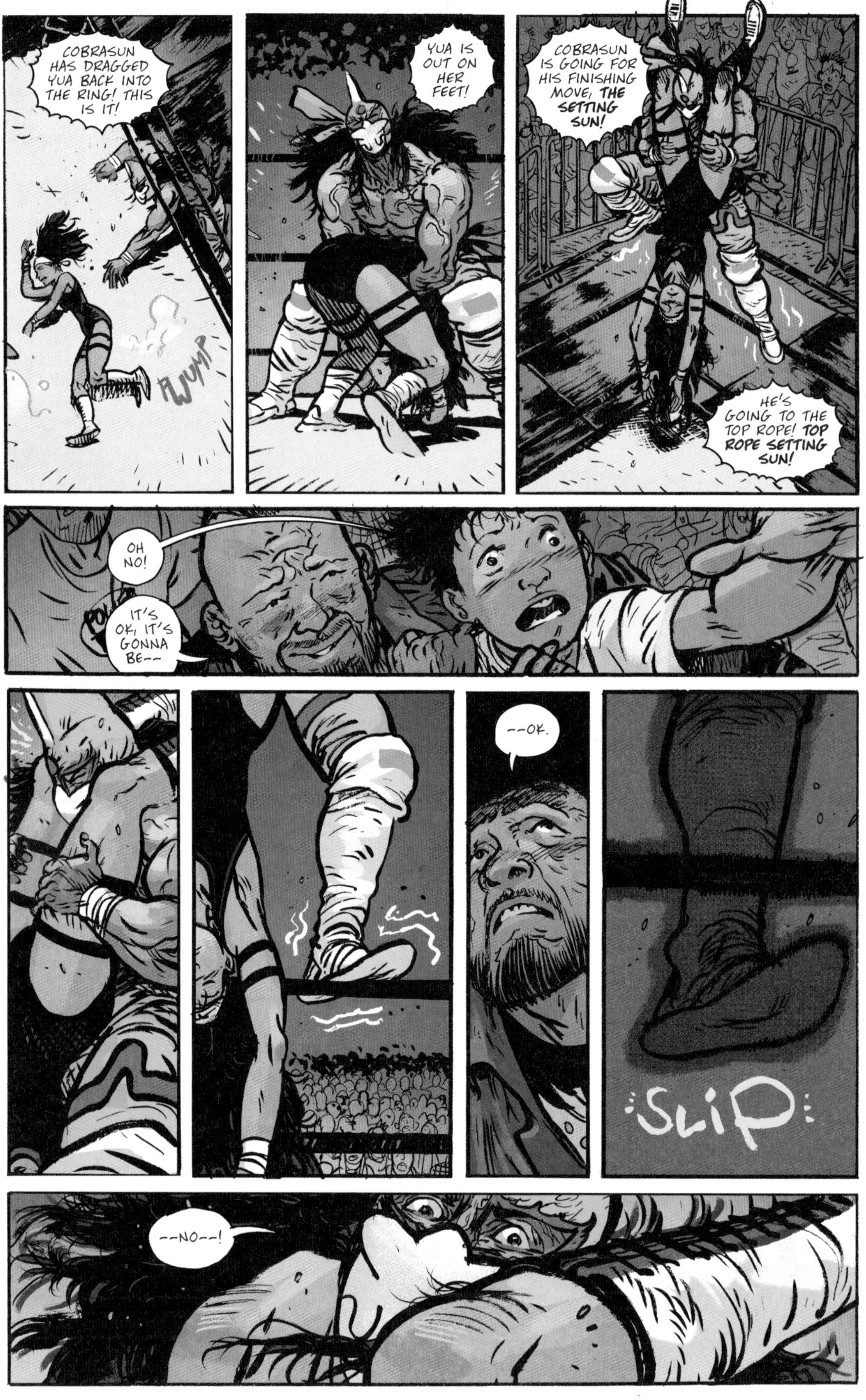

COBRASUN HAS DRAGGED YUA BACK INTO THE RING! THIS IS IT!
FWUMP
YUA IS OUT ON HER FEET!
COBRASUN IS GOING FOR HIS FINISHING MOVE, **THE SETTING SUN!**
HE'S GOING TO THE TOP ROPE! **TOP ROPE SETTING SUN!**
OH NO!
IT'S OK, IT'S GONNA BE--
--OK.
SLIP
--NO--!

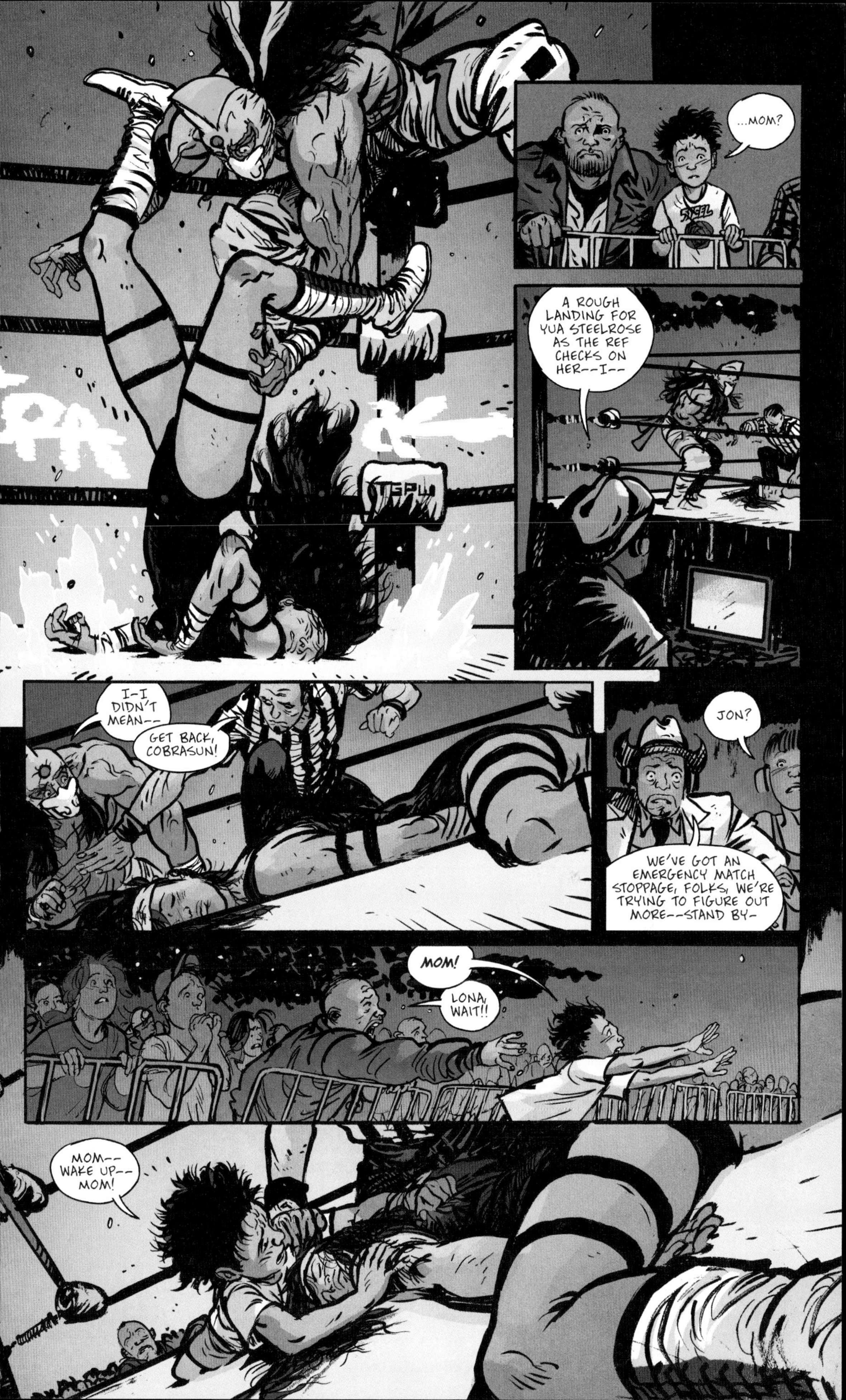
...MOM?
A ROUGH LANDING FOR YUA STEELROSE AS THE REF CHECKS ON HER--I--
I-I DIDN'T MEAN--
GET BACK, COBRASUN!
JON?
WE'VE GOT AN EMERGENCY MATCH STOPPAGE, FOLKS, WE'RE TRYING TO FIGURE OUT MORE--STAND BY-
MOM!
LONA, WAIT!!
MOM-- WAKE UP-- MOM!

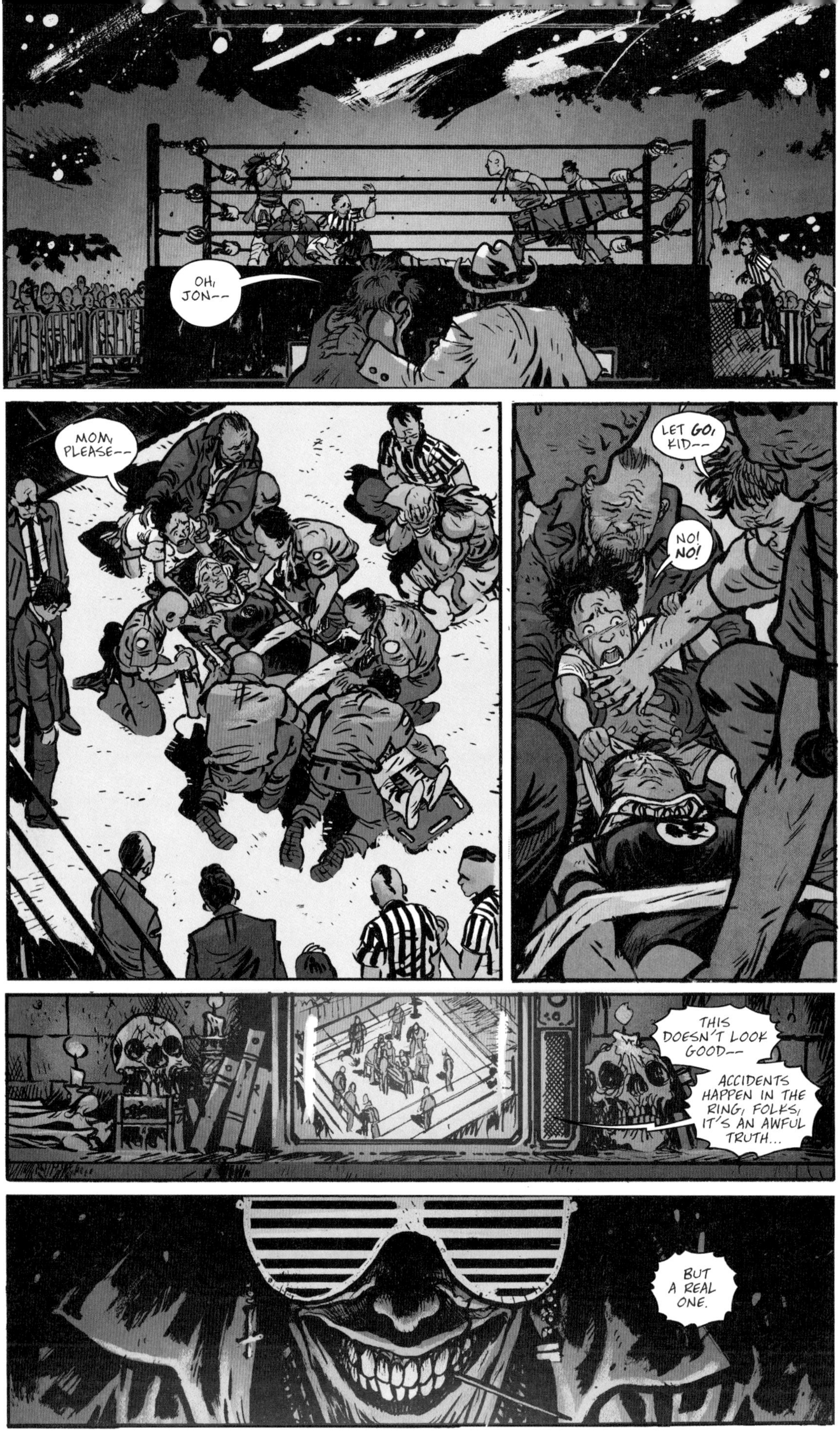
OH, JON--
MOM, PLEASE--
LET GO, KID--
NO! NO!
THIS DOESN'T LOOK GOOD--
ACCIDENTS HAPPEN IN THE RING, FOLKS, IT'S AN AWFUL TRUTH...
BUT A REAL ONE.

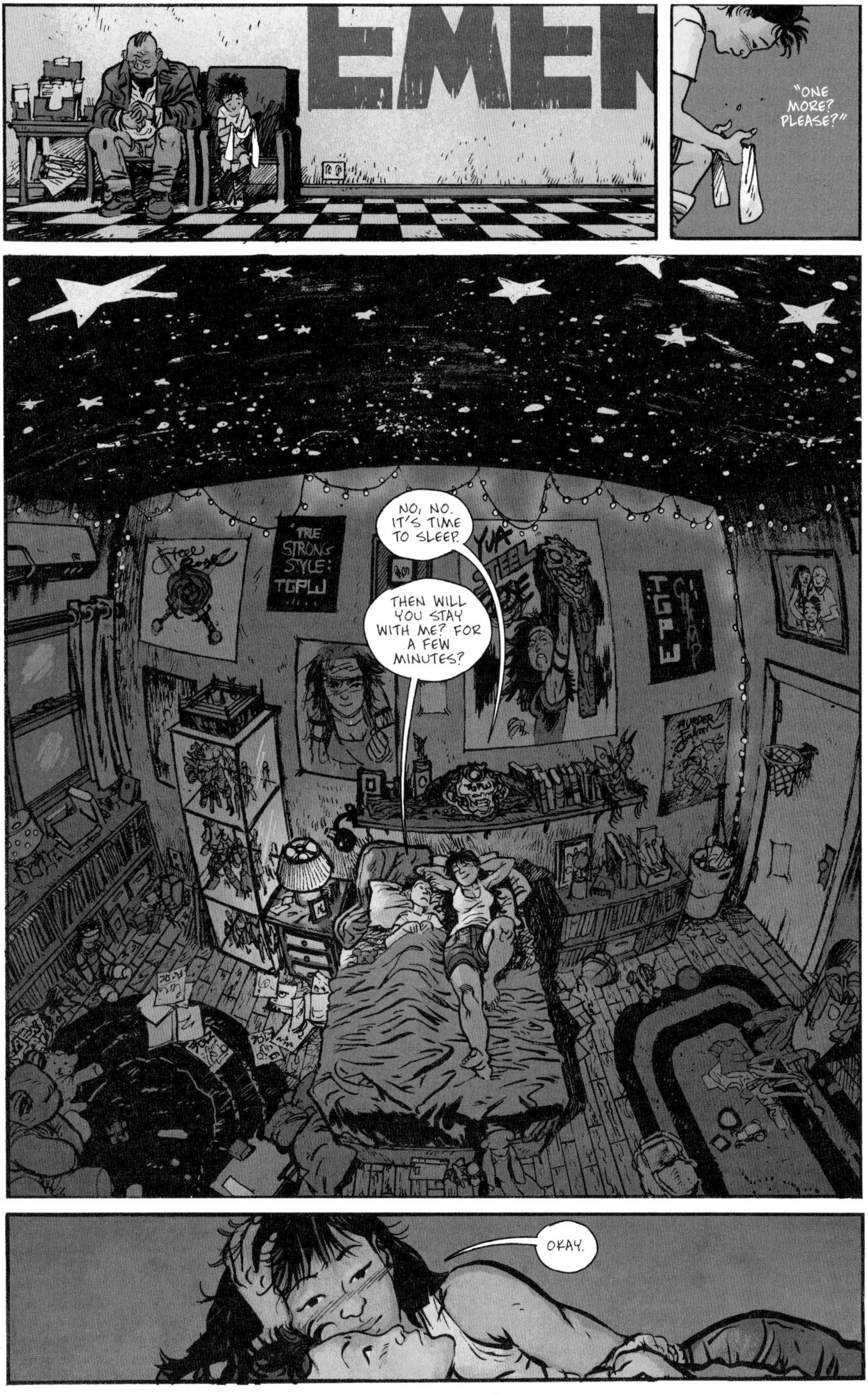
EMER
"ONE MORE? PLEASE?"
TRUE STRONG STYLE: TGPW
NO, NO. IT'S TIME TO SLEEP.
THEN WILL YOU STAY WITH ME? FOR A FEW MINUTES?
TGPW
OKAY.

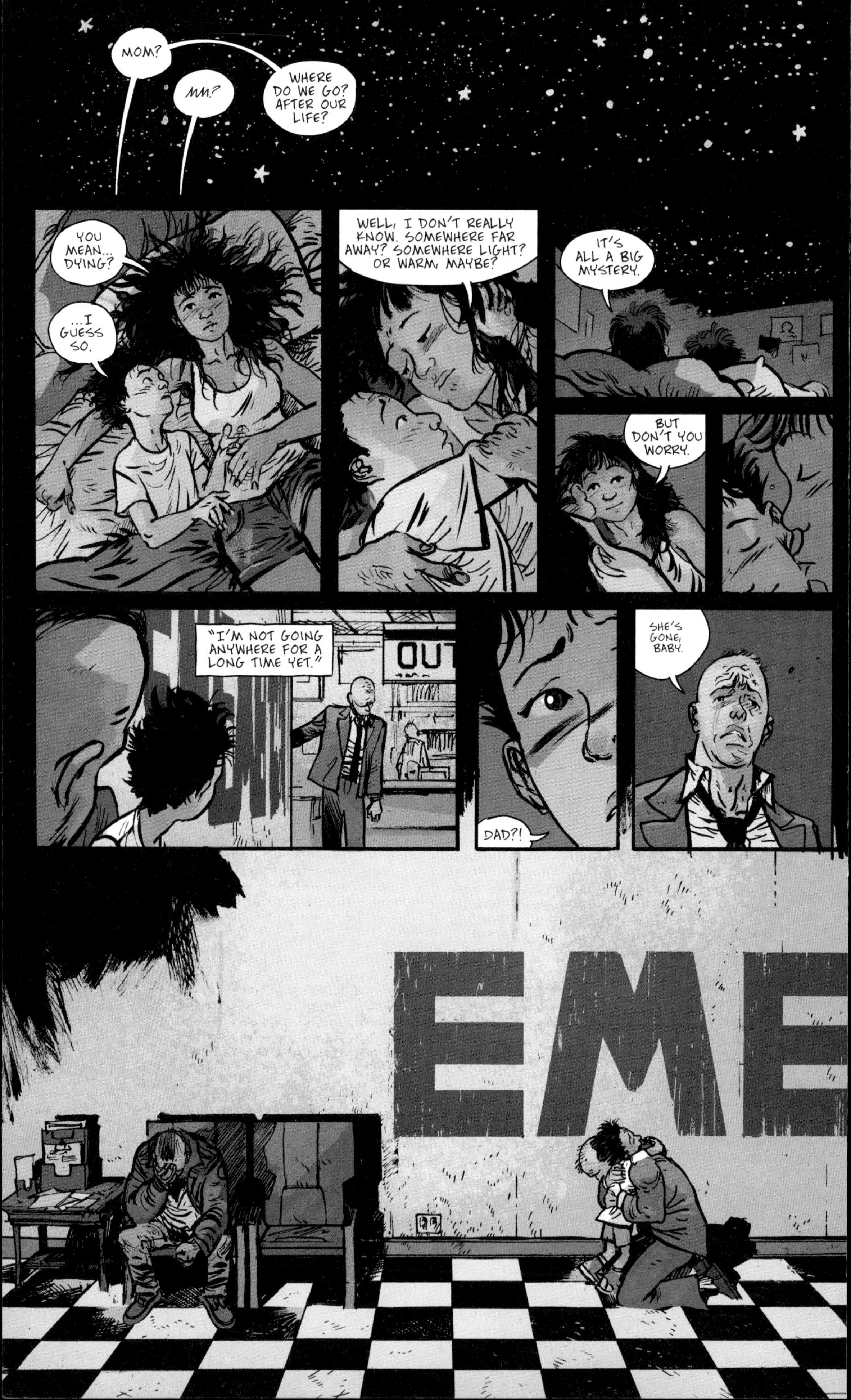
MOM?
MM?
WHERE DO WE GO? AFTER OUR LIFE?
YOU MEAN... DYING?
...I GUESS SO.
WELL, I DON'T REALLY KNOW. SOMEWHERE FAR AWAY? SOMEWHERE LIGHT? OR WARM, MAYBE?
IT'S ALL A BIG MYSTERY.
BUT DON'T YOU WORRY.
"I'M NOT GOING ANYWHERE FOR A LONG TIME YET."
OUT
DAD?!
SHE'S GONE, BABY.
EME

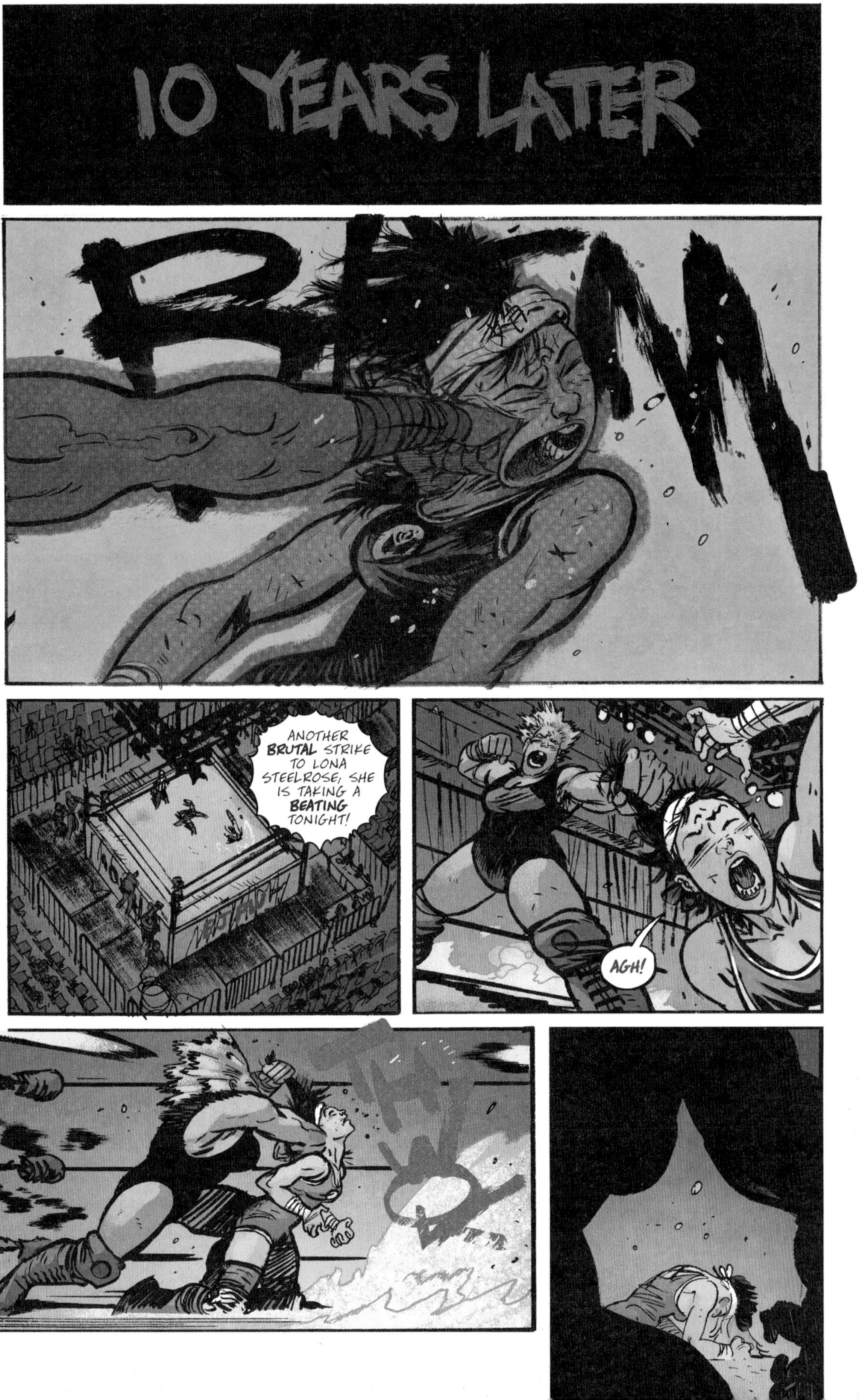
10 YEARS LATER
BAM
ANOTHER BRUTAL STRIKE TO LONA STEELROSE, SHE IS TAKING A BEATING TONIGHT!
AGH!

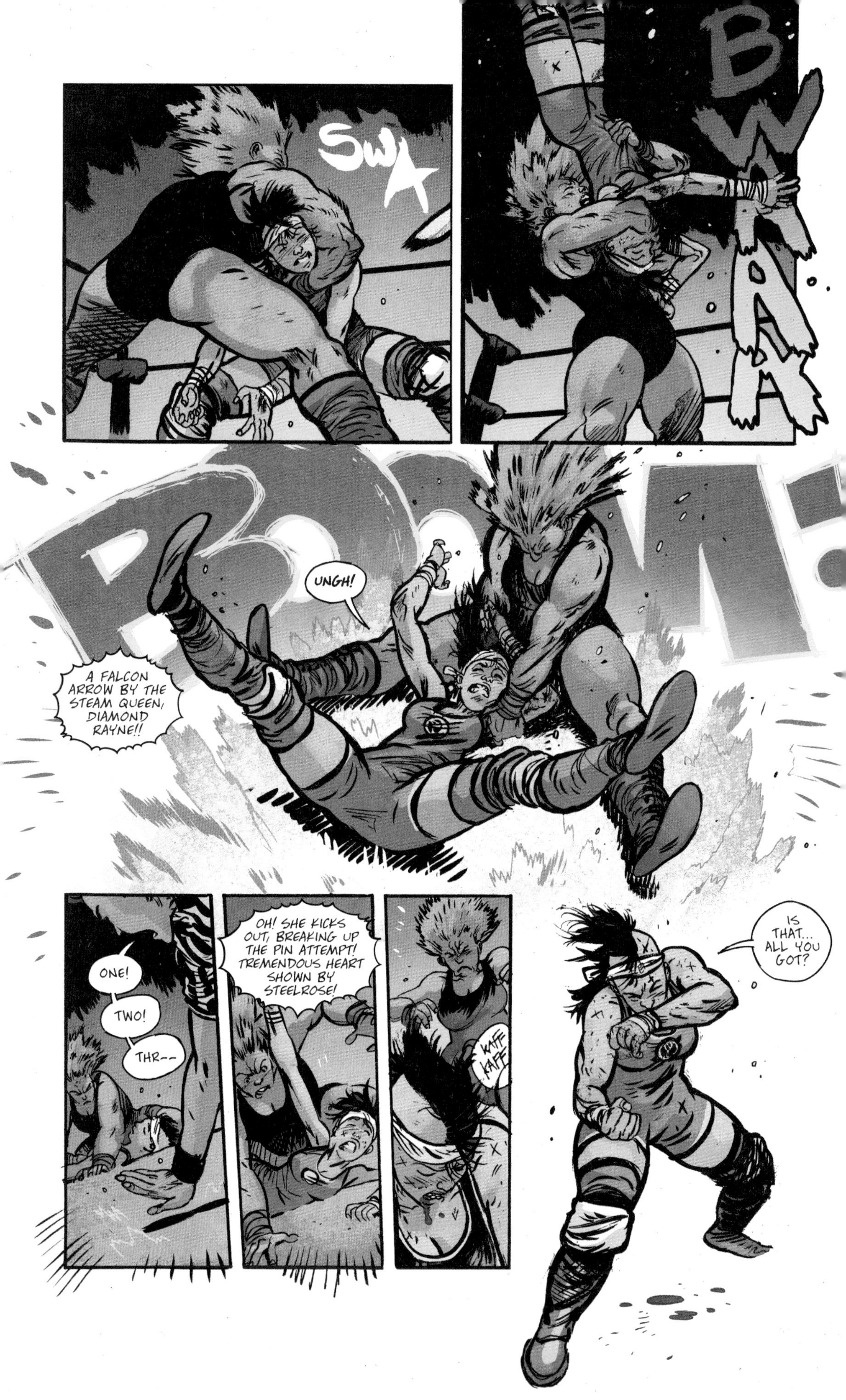
SWA
BWAA
BOOM!
UNGH!
A FALCON ARROW BY THE STEAM QUEEN, DIAMOND RAYNE!!
ONE!
TWO!
THR--
OH! SHE KICKS OUT, BREAKING UP THE PIN ATTEMPT! TREMENDOUS HEART SHOWN BY STEELROSE!
KAFF KAFF
IS THAT... ALL YOU GOT?

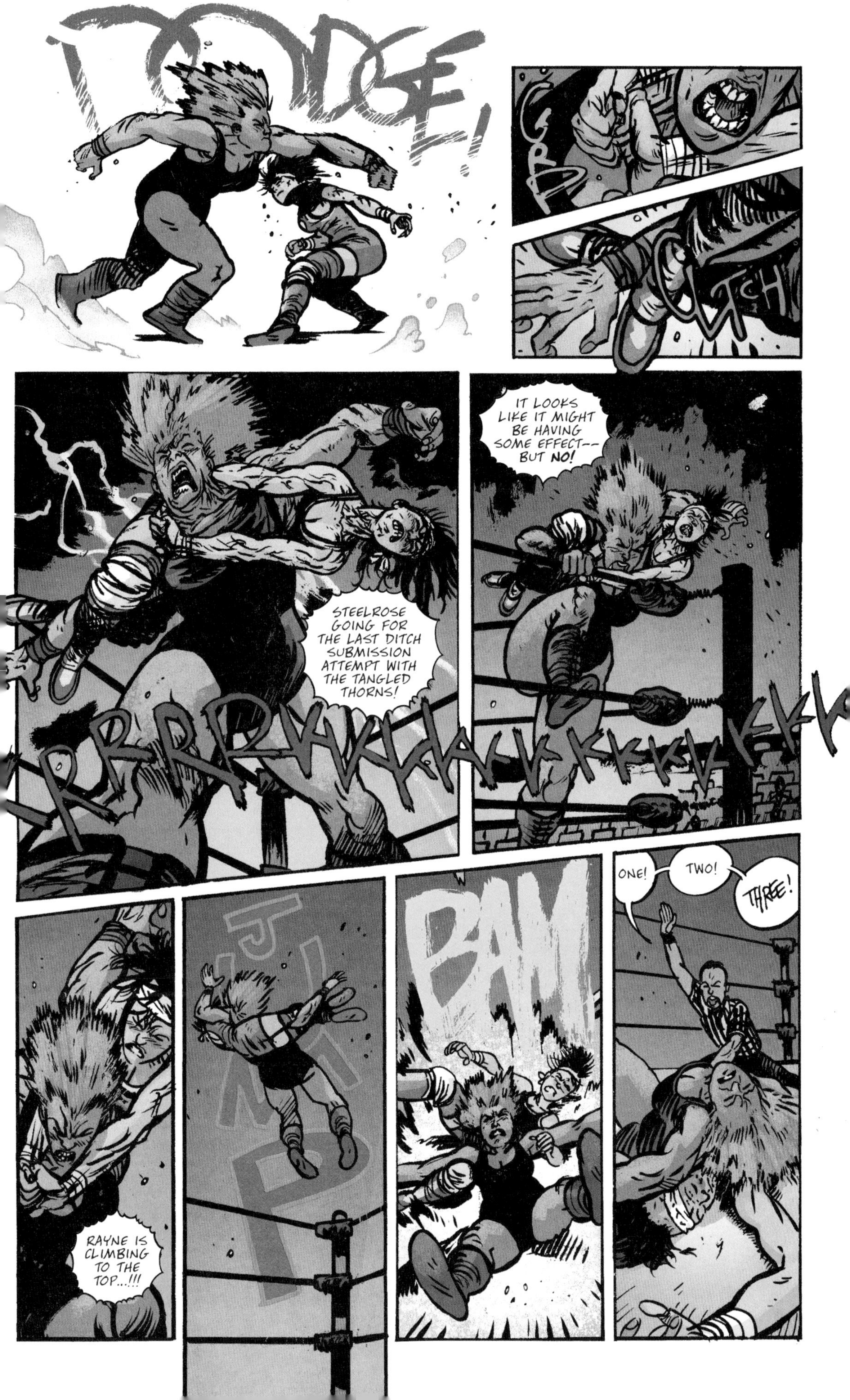
DODGE!
GRAB
CLUTCH
STEELROSE GOING FOR THE LAST DITCH SUBMISSION ATTEMPT WITH THE TANGLED THORNS!
RRRRRAAAAKKKKKKKK
IT LOOKS LIKE IT MIGHT BE HAVING SOME EFFECT-- BUT NO!
RAYNE IS CLIMBING TO THE TOP...!!!
JUMP
BAM
ONE!
TWO!
THREE!

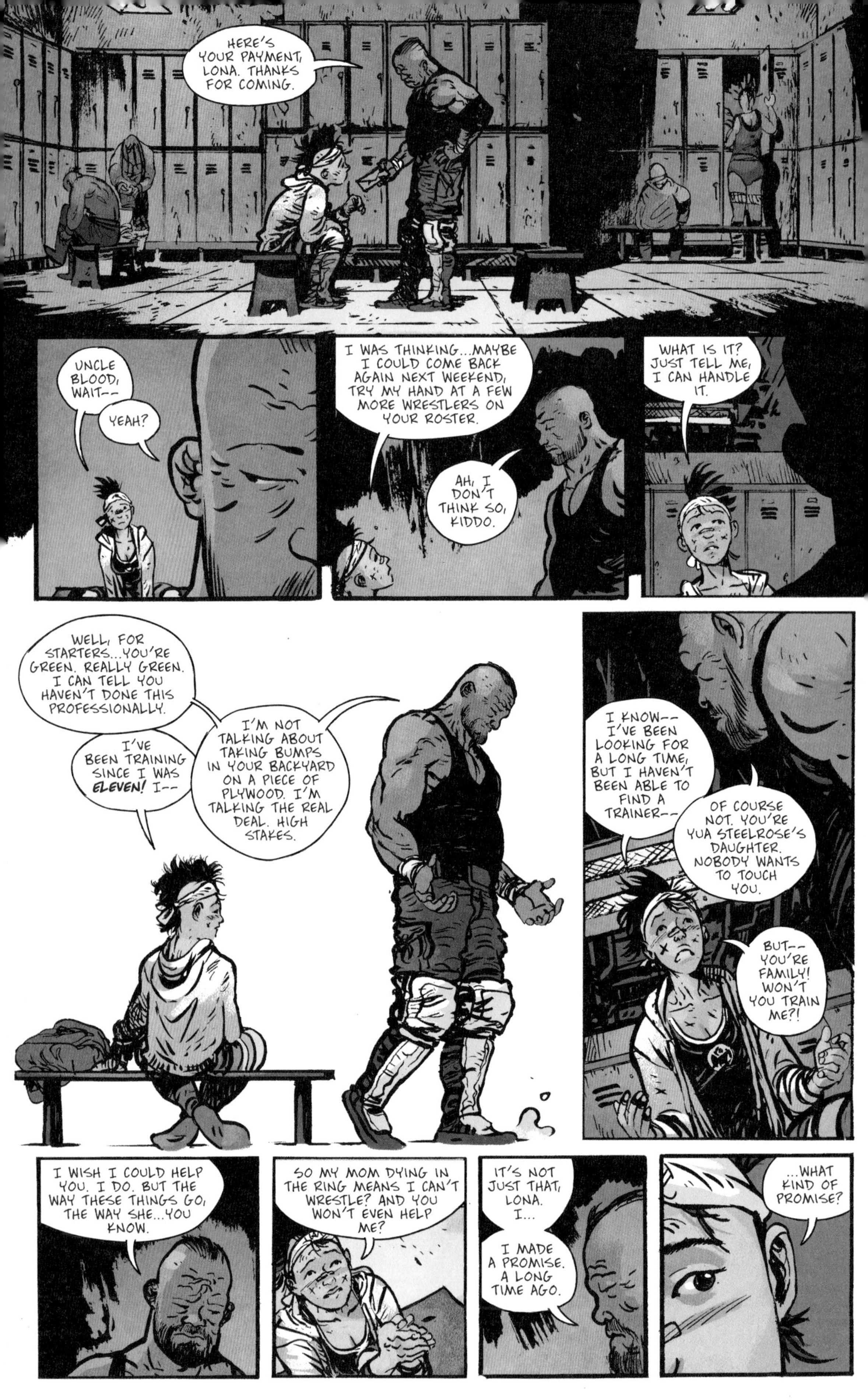
HERE'S YOUR PAYMENT, LONA. THANKS FOR COMING.
UNCLE BLOOD, WAIT--
YEAH?
I WAS THINKING...MAYBE I COULD COME BACK AGAIN NEXT WEEKEND, TRY MY HAND AT A FEW MORE WRESTLERS ON YOUR ROSTER.
AH, I DON'T THINK SO, KIDDO.
WHAT IS IT? JUST TELL ME, I CAN HANDLE IT.
WELL, FOR STARTERS...YOU'RE GREEN. REALLY GREEN. I CAN TELL YOU HAVEN'T DONE THIS PROFESSIONALLY.
I'VE BEEN TRAINING SINCE I WAS **ELEVEN!** I--
I'M NOT TALKING ABOUT TAKING BUMPS IN YOUR BACKYARD ON A PIECE OF PLYWOOD. I'M TALKING THE REAL DEAL. HIGH STAKES.
I KNOW-- I'VE BEEN LOOKING FOR A LONG TIME, BUT I HAVEN'T BEEN ABLE TO FIND A TRAINER--
OF COURSE NOT. YOU'RE YUA STEELROSE'S DAUGHTER. NOBODY WANTS TO TOUCH YOU.
BUT-- YOU'RE FAMILY! WON'T YOU TRAIN ME?!
I WISH I COULD HELP YOU. I DO. BUT THE WAY THESE THINGS GO, THE WAY SHE...YOU KNOW.
SO MY MOM DYING IN THE RING MEANS I CAN'T WRESTLE? AND YOU WON'T EVEN HELP ME?
IT'S NOT JUST THAT, LONA. I...
I MADE A PROMISE. A LONG TIME AGO.
...WHAT KIND OF PROMISE?

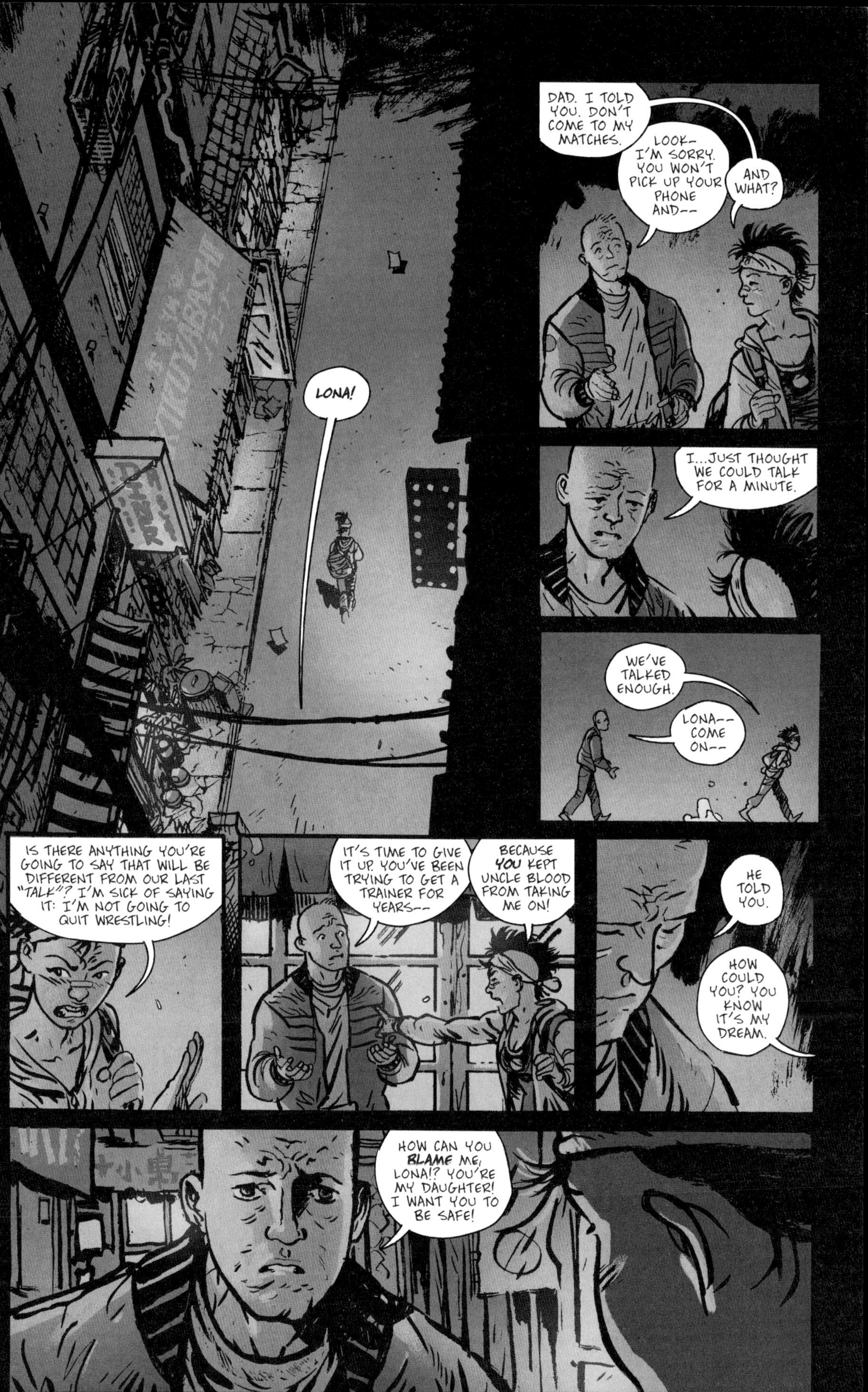
LONA!
DAD. I TOLD YOU. DON'T COME TO MY MATCHES.
LOOK– I'M SORRY. YOU WON'T PICK UP YOUR PHONE AND––
AND WHAT?
I...JUST THOUGHT WE COULD TALK FOR A MINUTE.
WE'VE TALKED ENOUGH.
LONA–– COME ON––
IS THERE ANYTHING YOU'RE GOING TO SAY THAT WILL BE DIFFERENT FROM OUR LAST "TALK"? I'M SICK OF SAYING IT: I'M NOT GOING TO QUIT WRESTLING!
IT'S TIME TO GIVE IT UP. YOU'VE BEEN TRYING TO GET A TRAINER FOR YEARS––
BECAUSE YOU KEPT UNCLE BLOOD FROM TAKING ME ON!
HE TOLD YOU.
HOW COULD YOU? YOU KNOW IT'S MY DREAM.
HOW CAN YOU BLAME ME, LONA!? YOU'RE MY DAUGHTER! I WANT YOU TO BE SAFE!

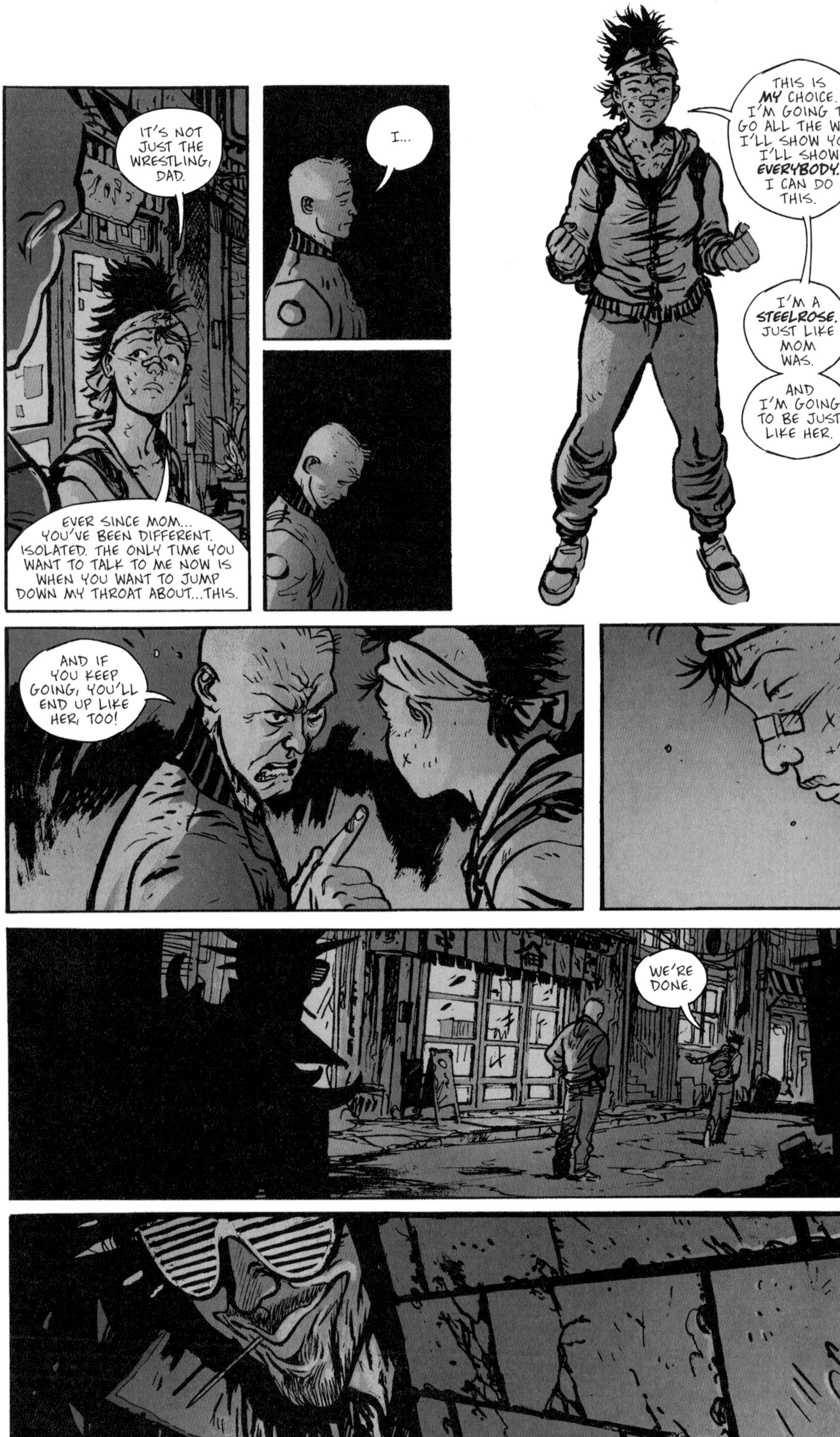

IT'S NOT JUST THE WRESTLING, DAD.
EVER SINCE MOM... YOU'VE BEEN DIFFERENT. ISOLATED. THE ONLY TIME YOU WANT TO TALK TO ME NOW IS WHEN YOU WANT TO JUMP DOWN MY THROAT ABOUT...THIS.
I...
THIS IS **MY** CHOICE. I'M GOING TO GO ALL THE WAY. I'LL SHOW YOU. I'LL SHOW **EVERYBODY.** I CAN DO THIS.
I'M A **STEELROSE.** JUST LIKE MOM WAS.
AND I'M GOING TO BE JUST LIKE HER.
AND IF YOU KEEP GOING, YOU'LL END UP LIKE HER, TOO!
WE'RE DONE.

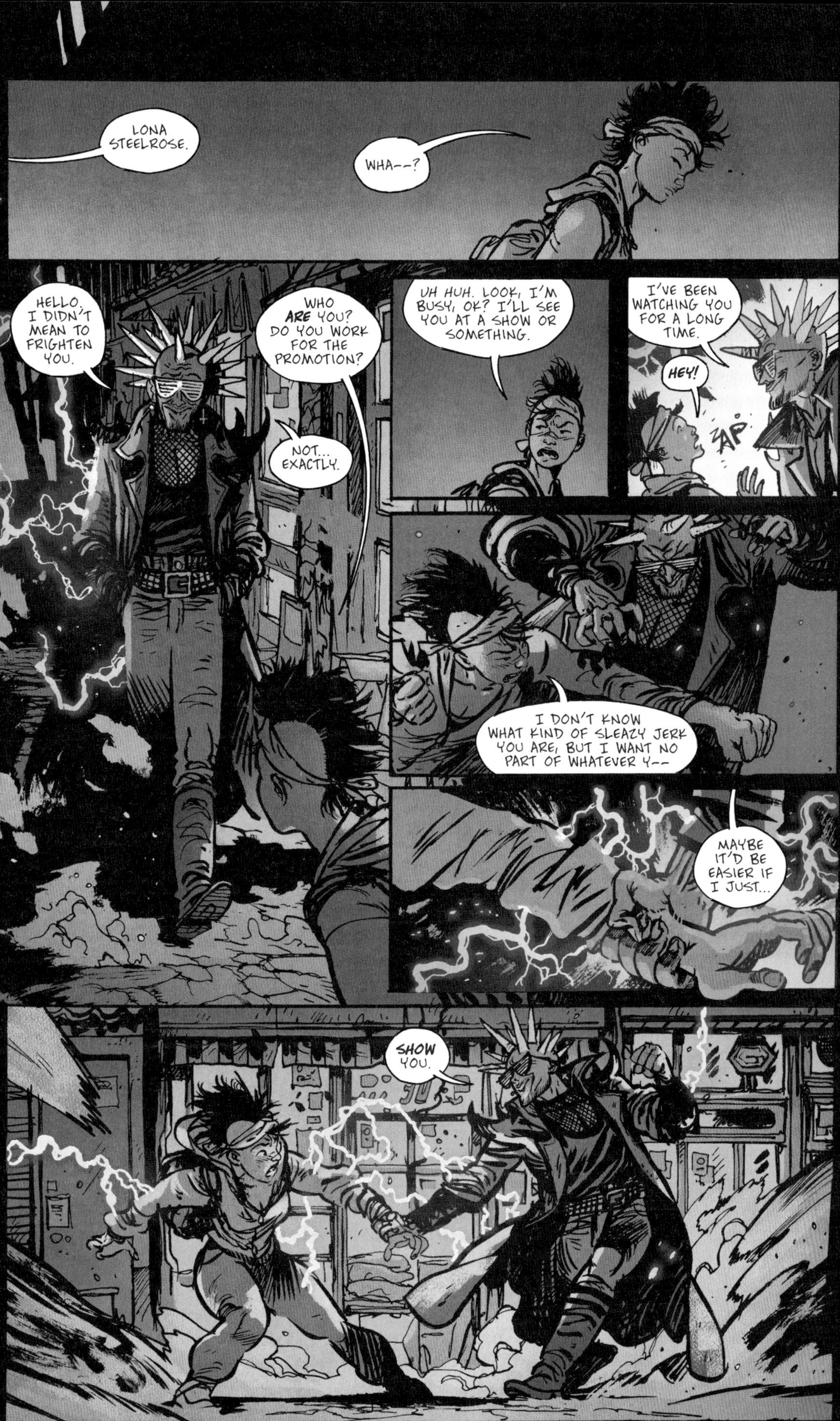
LONA STEELROSE.
WHA--?
HELLO. I DIDN'T MEAN TO FRIGHTEN YOU.
WHO **ARE** YOU? DO YOU WORK FOR THE PROMOTION?
NOT... EXACTLY.
UH HUH. LOOK, I'M BUSY, OK? I'LL SEE YOU AT A SHOW OR SOMETHING.
I'VE BEEN WATCHING YOU FOR A LONG TIME.
HEY!
ZAP
I DON'T KNOW WHAT KIND OF SLEAZY JERK YOU ARE, BUT I WANT NO PART OF WHATEVER Y--
MAYBE IT'D BE EASIER IF I JUST...
SHOW YOU.

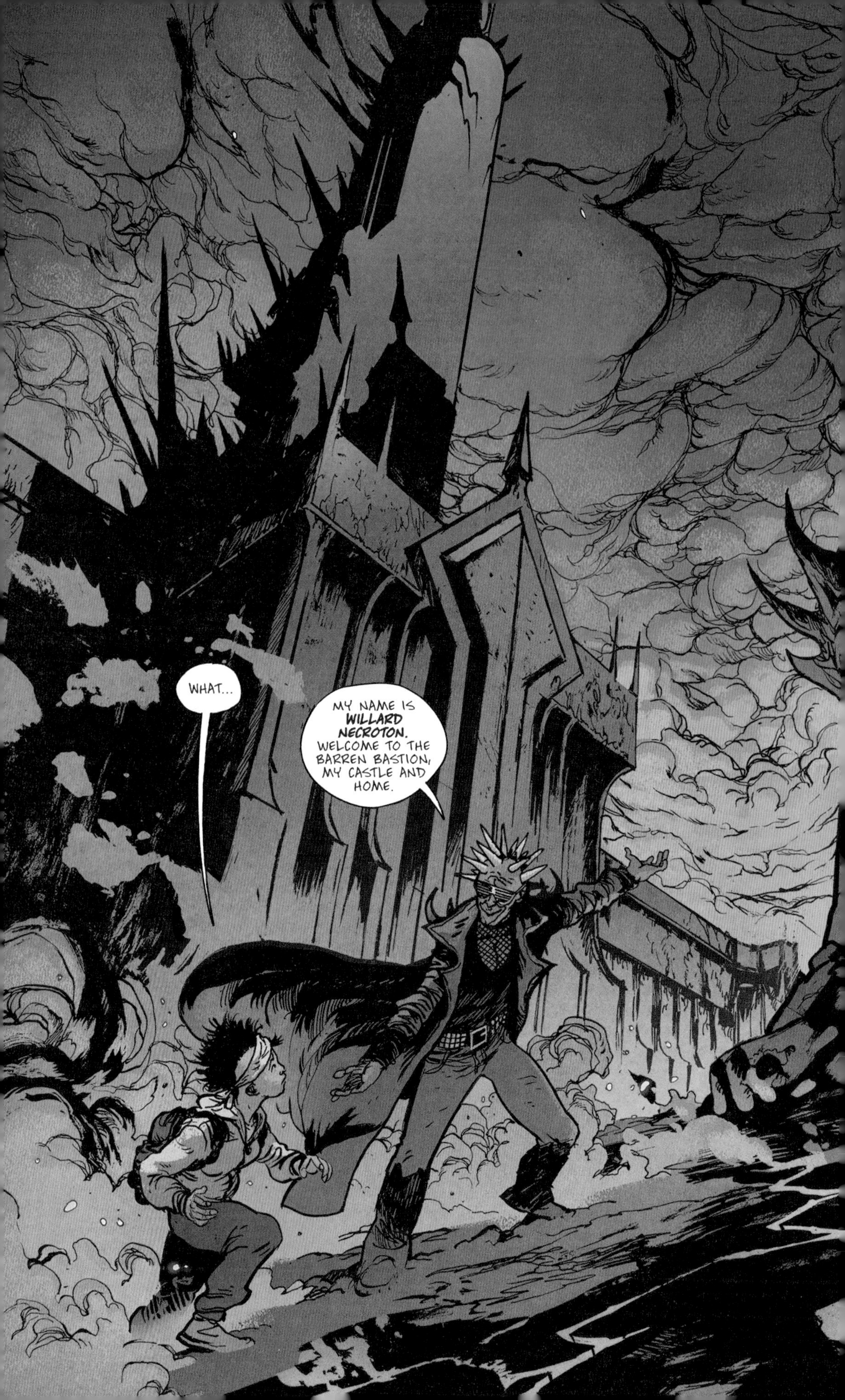
WHAT...
MY NAME IS **WILLARD NECROTON.** WELCOME TO THE BARREN BASTION, MY CASTLE AND HOME.

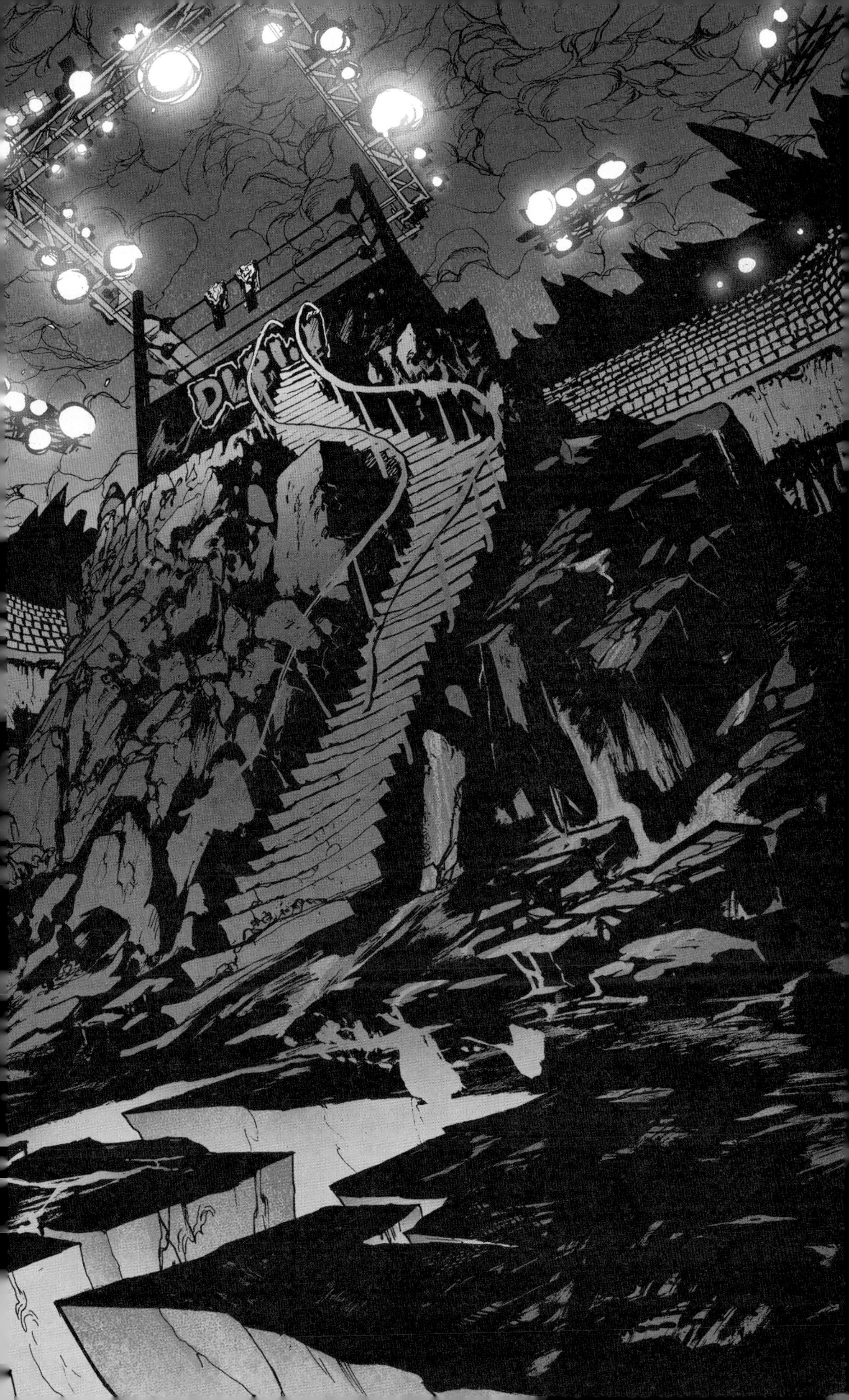

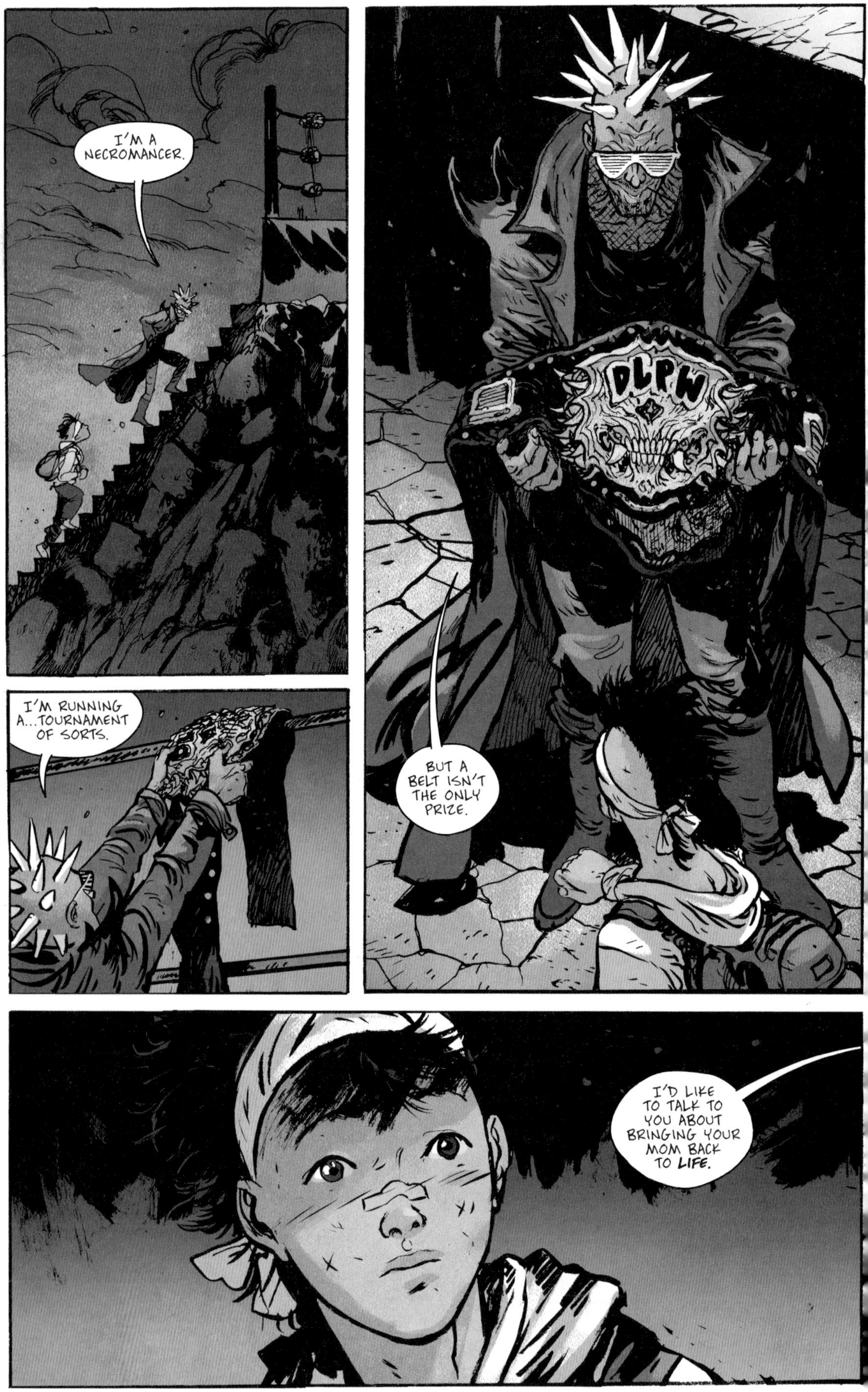
I'M A NECROMANCER.
I'M RUNNING A...TOURNAMENT OF SORTS.
DLPW
BUT A BELT ISN'T THE ONLY PRIZE.
I'D LIKE TO TALK TO YOU ABOUT BRINGING YOUR MOM BACK TO **LIFE.**

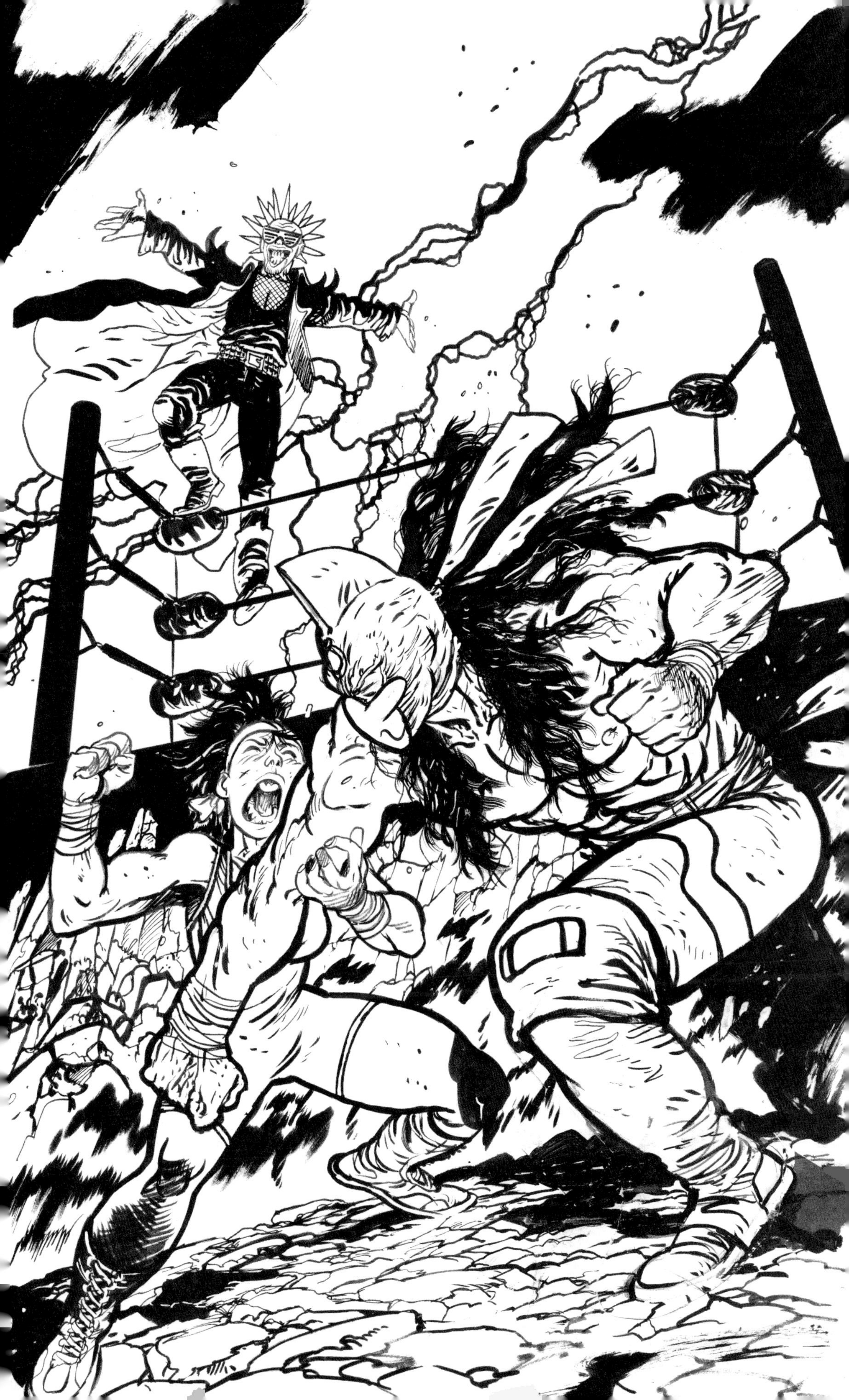

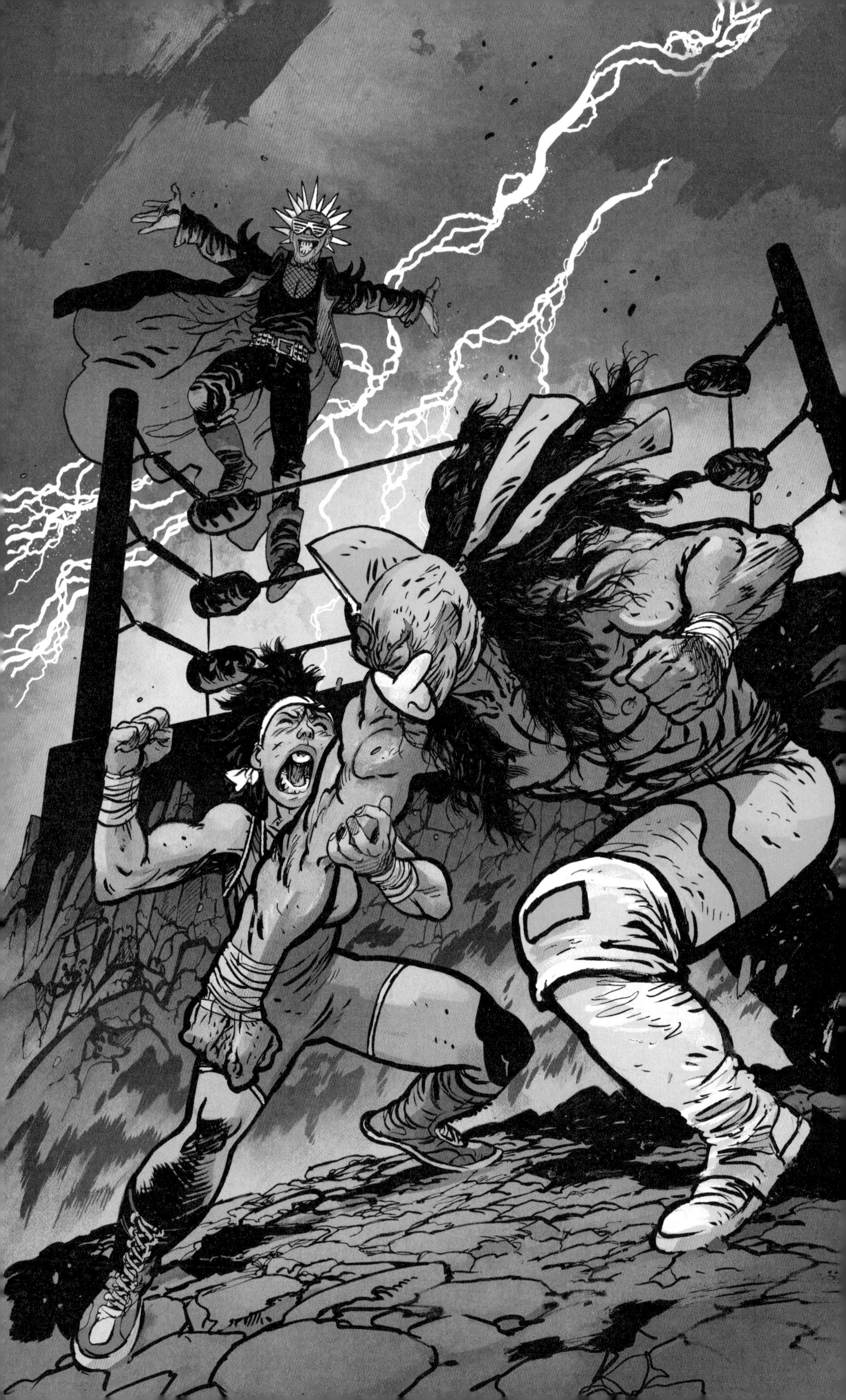

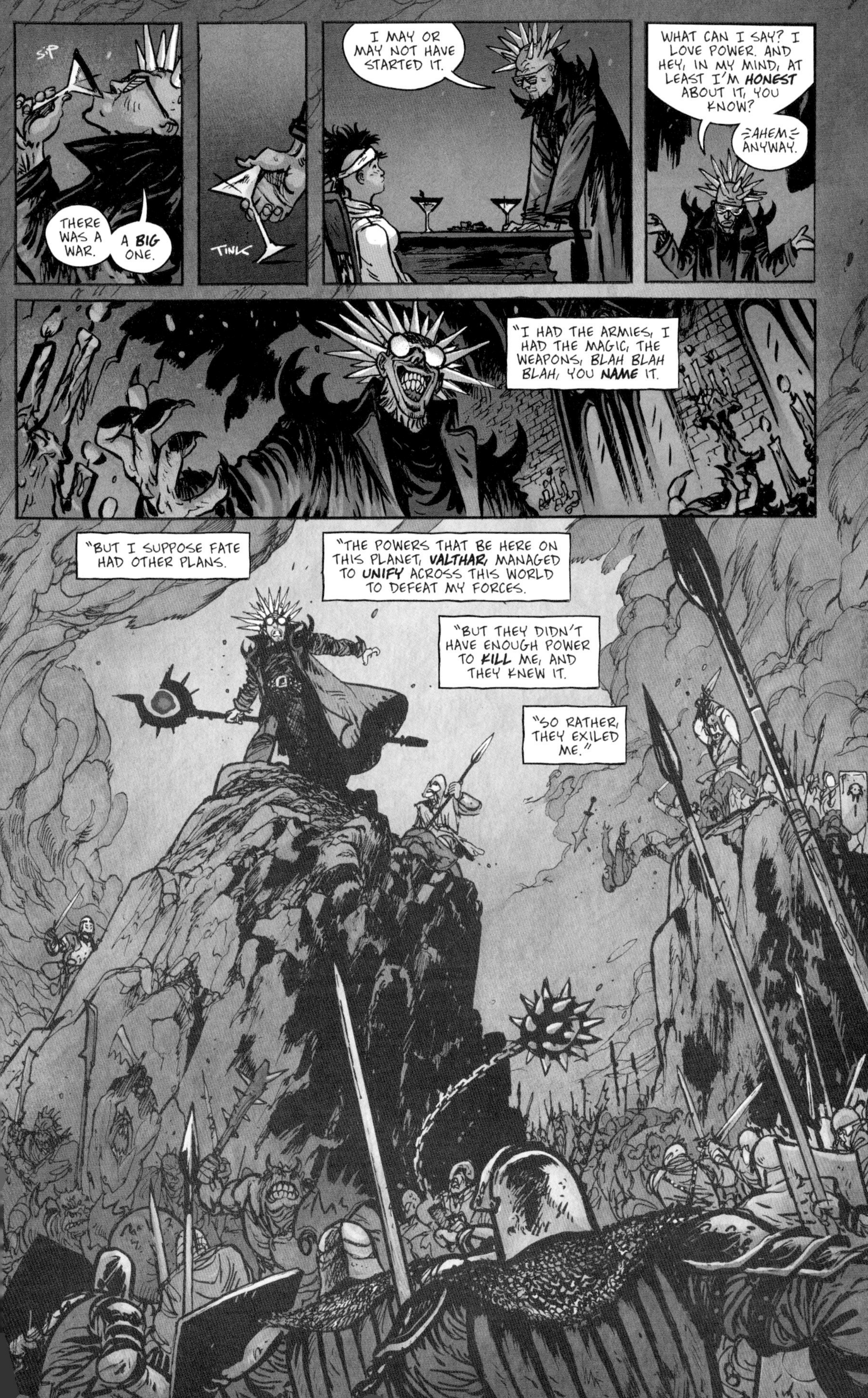
SIP
THERE WAS A WAR.
A BIG ONE.
TINK
I MAY OR MAY NOT HAVE STARTED IT.
WHAT CAN I SAY? I LOVE POWER. AND HEY, IN MY MIND, AT LEAST I'M HONEST ABOUT IT, YOU KNOW?
AHEM ANYWAY.
"I HAD THE ARMIES, I HAD THE MAGIC, THE WEAPONS, BLAH BLAH BLAH, YOU NAME IT.
"BUT I SUPPOSE FATE HAD OTHER PLANS.
"THE POWERS THAT BE HERE ON THIS PLANET, VALTHAR, MANAGED TO UNIFY ACROSS THIS WORLD TO DEFEAT MY FORCES.
"BUT THEY DIDN'T HAVE ENOUGH POWER TO KILL ME, AND THEY KNEW IT.
"SO RATHER, THEY EXILED ME."

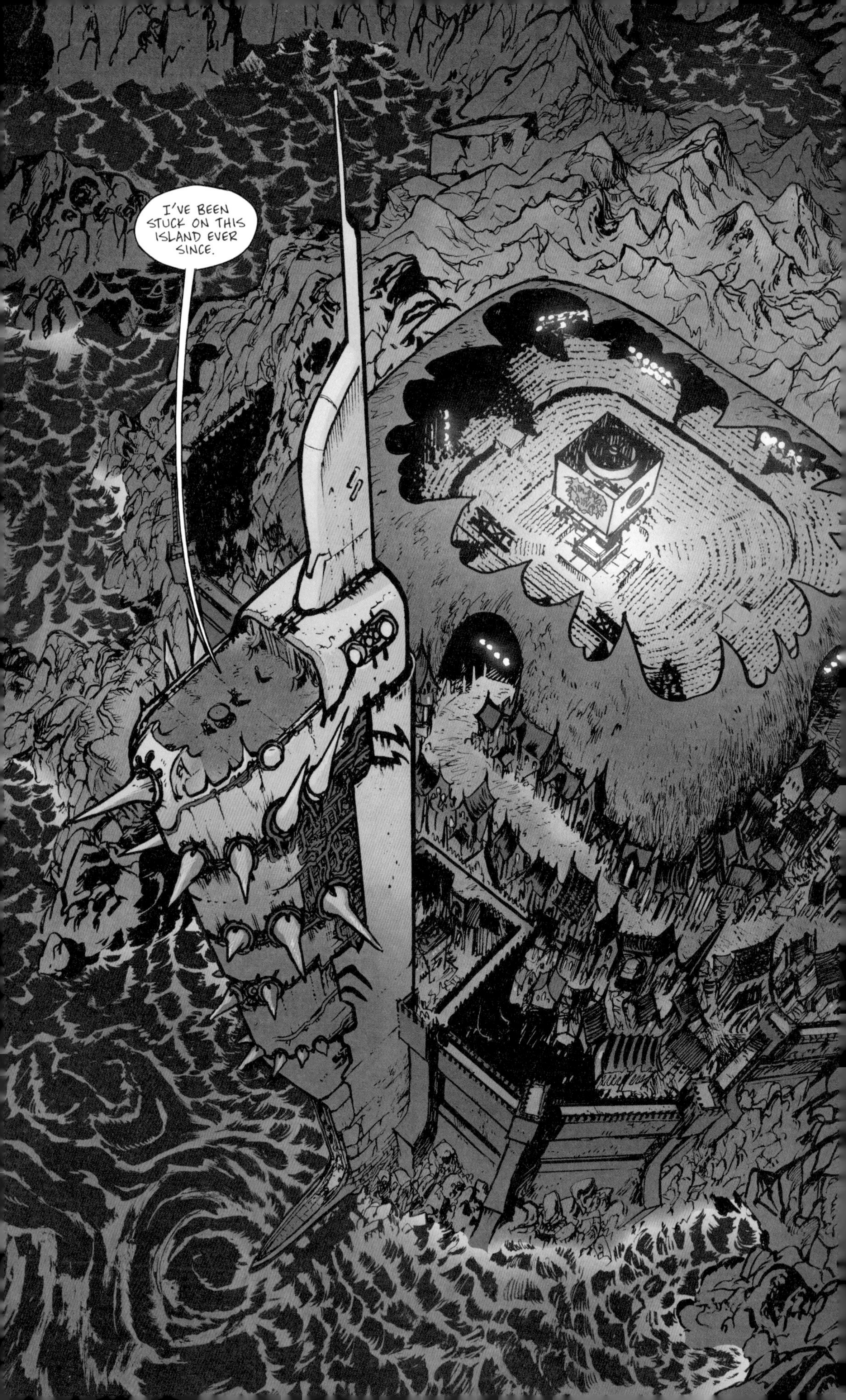
I'VE BEEN STUCK ON THIS ISLAND EVER SINCE.

WAIT. IF YOU'RE STUCK HERE, HOW DID YOU GET TO EARTH?

WHAT YOU SAW ON YOUR PLANET WAS MERELY AN APPARITION! I CAN COMMUNICATE AND BRING BEINGS HERE, BUT AWAY FROM THIS PLACE I AM ONLY A WHISPER OF MY TRUE SELF.

MY ESSENCE AND SOUL REMAIN TRAPPED HERE... FOREVER.

BOB!

MORE CHEESE.

OF COURSE, SIR.

NOW I KNOW WHAT YOU'RE THINKING: "NECRO, CAN'T YOU REGROUP? TRY TAKING OVER THE WORLD AGAIN?"

THOUGHT ABOUT IT. TRIED IT. FAILED. AGAIN.

HONESTLY, ALL THE WORLD-CONQUERING STUFF IS SO MUCH WORK. I JUST WANTED TO TAKE A BREAK AFTER ALL THAT KILLING, YOU KNOW?

WOOF.

SLUMP

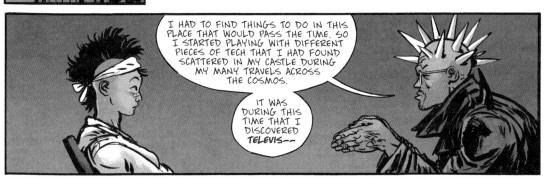

I HAD TO FIND THINGS TO DO IN THIS PLACE THAT WOULD PASS THE TIME. SO I STARTED PLAYING WITH DIFFERENT PIECES OF TECH THAT I HAD FOUND SCATTERED IN MY CASTLE DURING MY MANY TRAVELS ACROSS THE COSMOS.

IT WAS DURING THIS TIME THAT I DISCOVERED *TELEVIS--*

LOOK--ALL THIS IS...GREAT, BUT CAN WE PLEASE CUT TO THE CHASE?

I--

YOU TOLD ME YOU HAD THE POWER TO BRING MY MOM BACK. SO? WHAT DO I NEED TO DO? OTHERWISE, WHY AM I EVEN HERE?

VERY WELL.

THE REASON YOU'RE HERE...

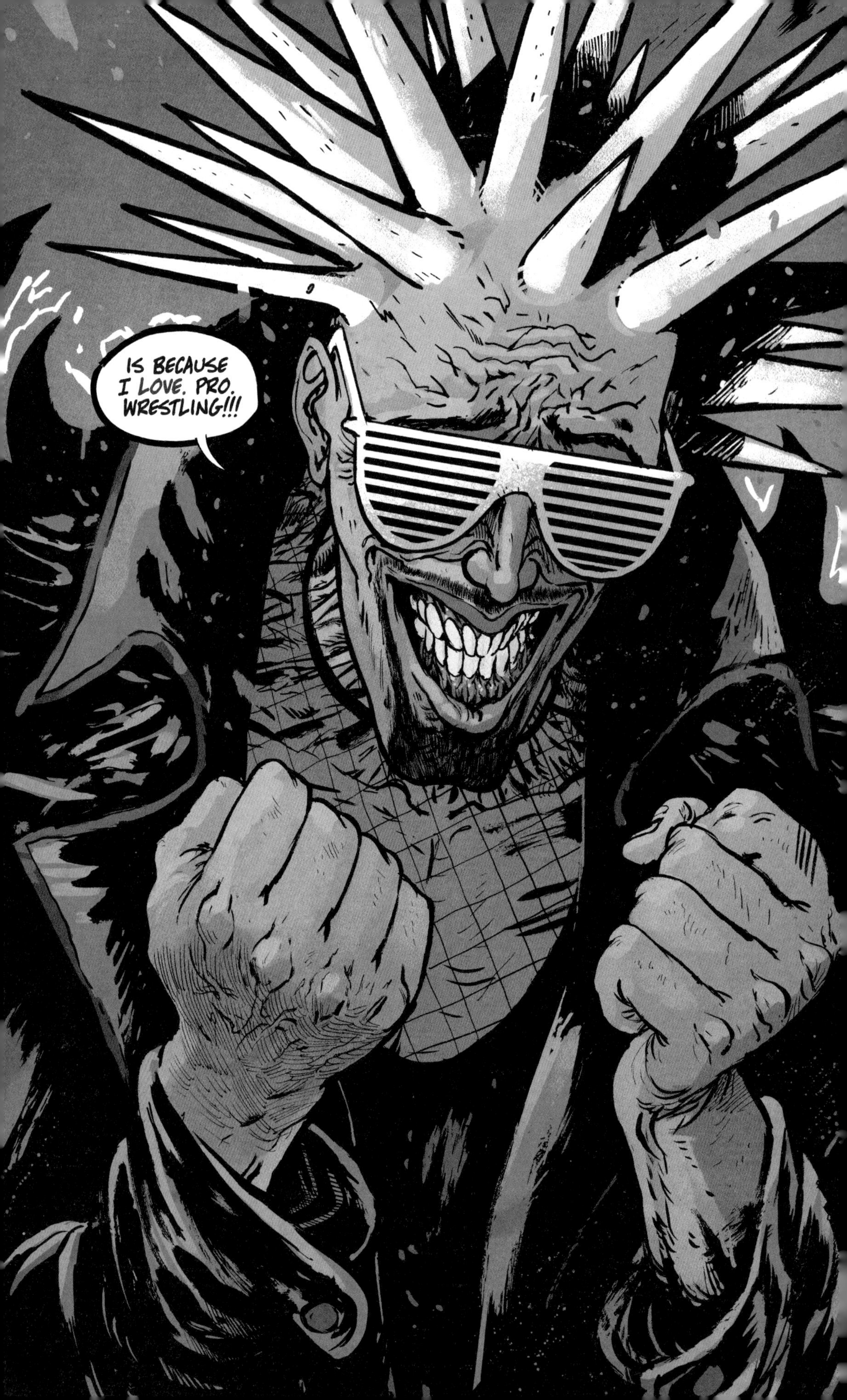
IS BECAUSE I LOVE. PRO. WRESTLING!!!

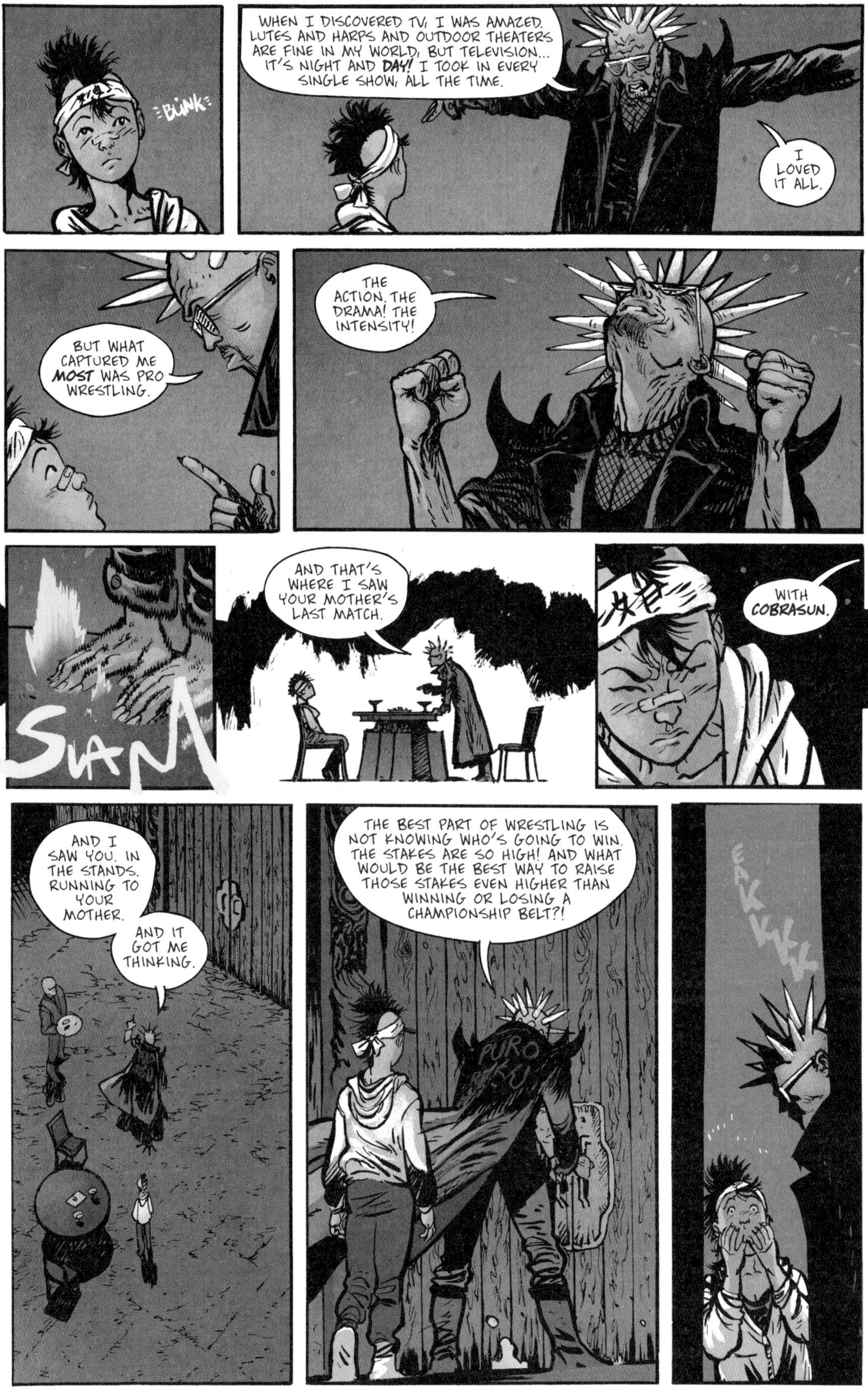
BLINK
WHEN I DISCOVERED TV, I WAS AMAZED. LUTES AND HARPS AND OUTDOOR THEATERS ARE FINE IN MY WORLD, BUT TELEVISION... IT'S NIGHT AND DAY! I TOOK IN EVERY SINGLE SHOW, ALL THE TIME.
I LOVED IT ALL.
BUT WHAT CAPTURED ME MOST WAS PRO WRESTLING.
THE ACTION. THE DRAMA! THE INTENSITY!
SLAM
AND THAT'S WHERE I SAW YOUR MOTHER'S LAST MATCH.
WITH COBRASUN.
AND I SAW YOU. IN THE STANDS. RUNNING TO YOUR MOTHER.
AND IT GOT ME THINKING.
THE BEST PART OF WRESTLING IS NOT KNOWING WHO'S GOING TO WIN. THE STAKES ARE SO HIGH! AND WHAT WOULD BE THE BEST WAY TO RAISE THOSE STAKES EVEN HIGHER THAN WINNING OR LOSING A CHAMPIONSHIP BELT?!
PURO

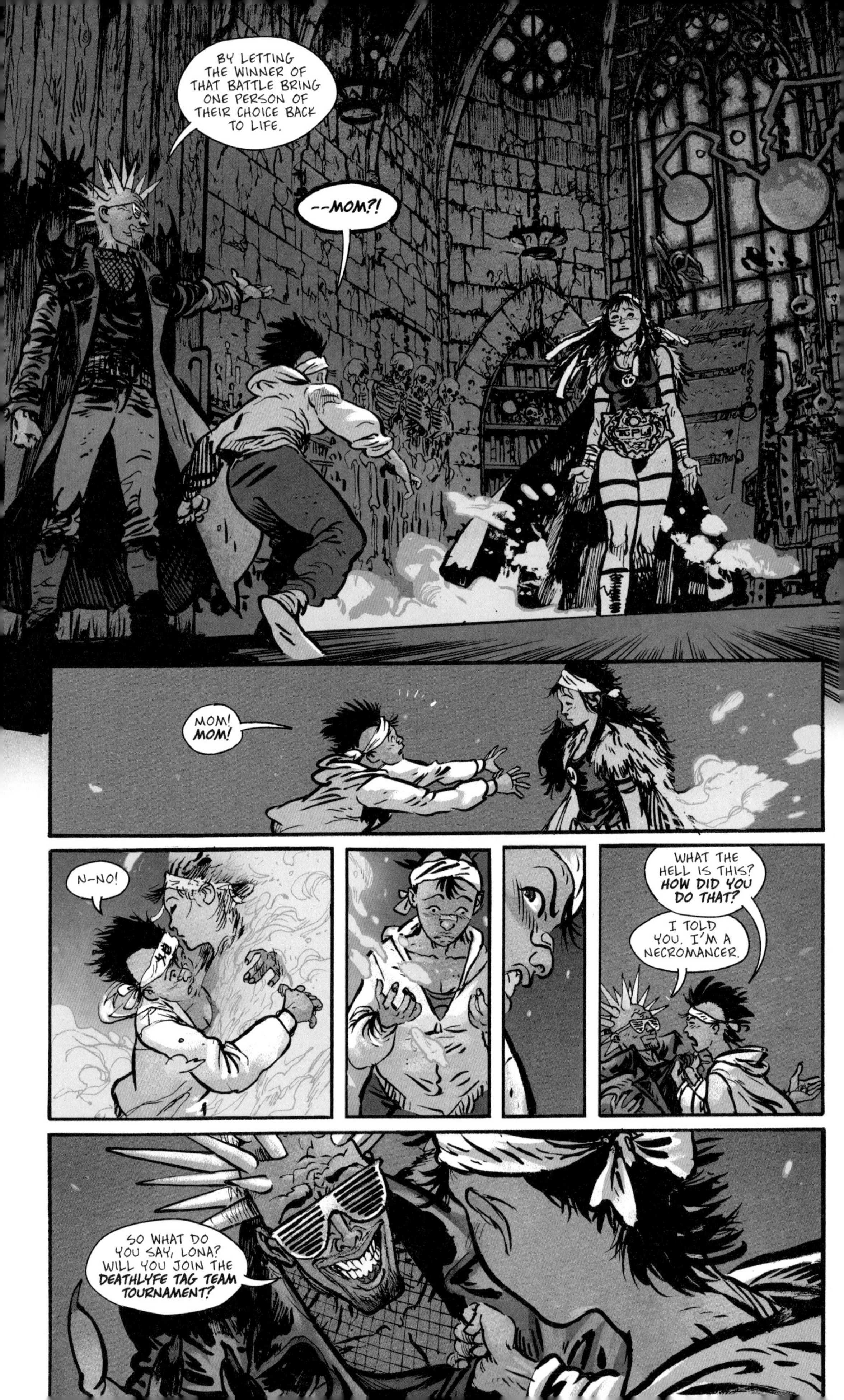
BY LETTING THE WINNER OF THAT BATTLE BRING ONE PERSON OF THEIR CHOICE BACK TO LIFE.
--MOM?!
MOM! MOM!
N-NO!
WHAT THE HELL IS THIS? HOW DID YOU DO THAT?
I TOLD YOU. I'M A NECROMANCER.
SO WHAT DO YOU SAY, LONA? WILL YOU JOIN THE DEATHLYFE TAG TEAM TOURNAMENT?

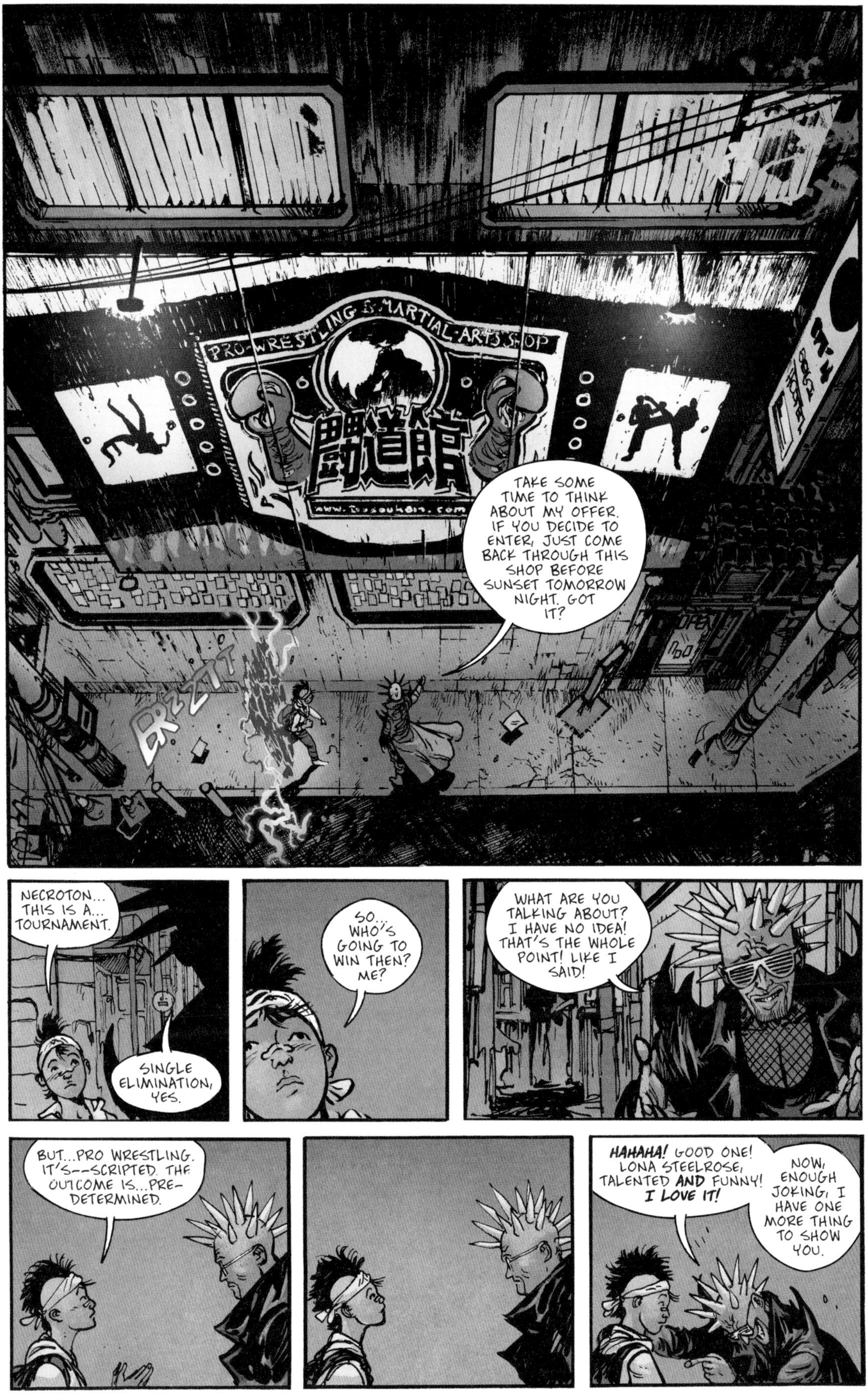
PRO-WRESTLING & MARTIAL-ARTS SHOP
闘道館
TAKE SOME TIME TO THINK ABOUT MY OFFER. IF YOU DECIDE TO ENTER, JUST COME BACK THROUGH THIS SHOP BEFORE SUNSET TOMORROW NIGHT. GOT IT?
OPEN
NECROTON... THIS IS A... TOURNAMENT.
SINGLE ELIMINATION, YES.
SO... WHO'S GOING TO WIN THEN? ME?
WHAT ARE YOU TALKING ABOUT? I HAVE NO IDEA! THAT'S THE WHOLE POINT! LIKE I SAID!
BUT...PRO WRESTLING. IT'S--SCRIPTED. THE OUTCOME IS...PRE-DETERMINED.
HAHAHA! GOOD ONE! LONA STEELROSE, TALENTED AND FUNNY! I LOVE IT!
NOW, ENOUGH JOKING, I HAVE ONE MORE THING TO SHOW YOU.

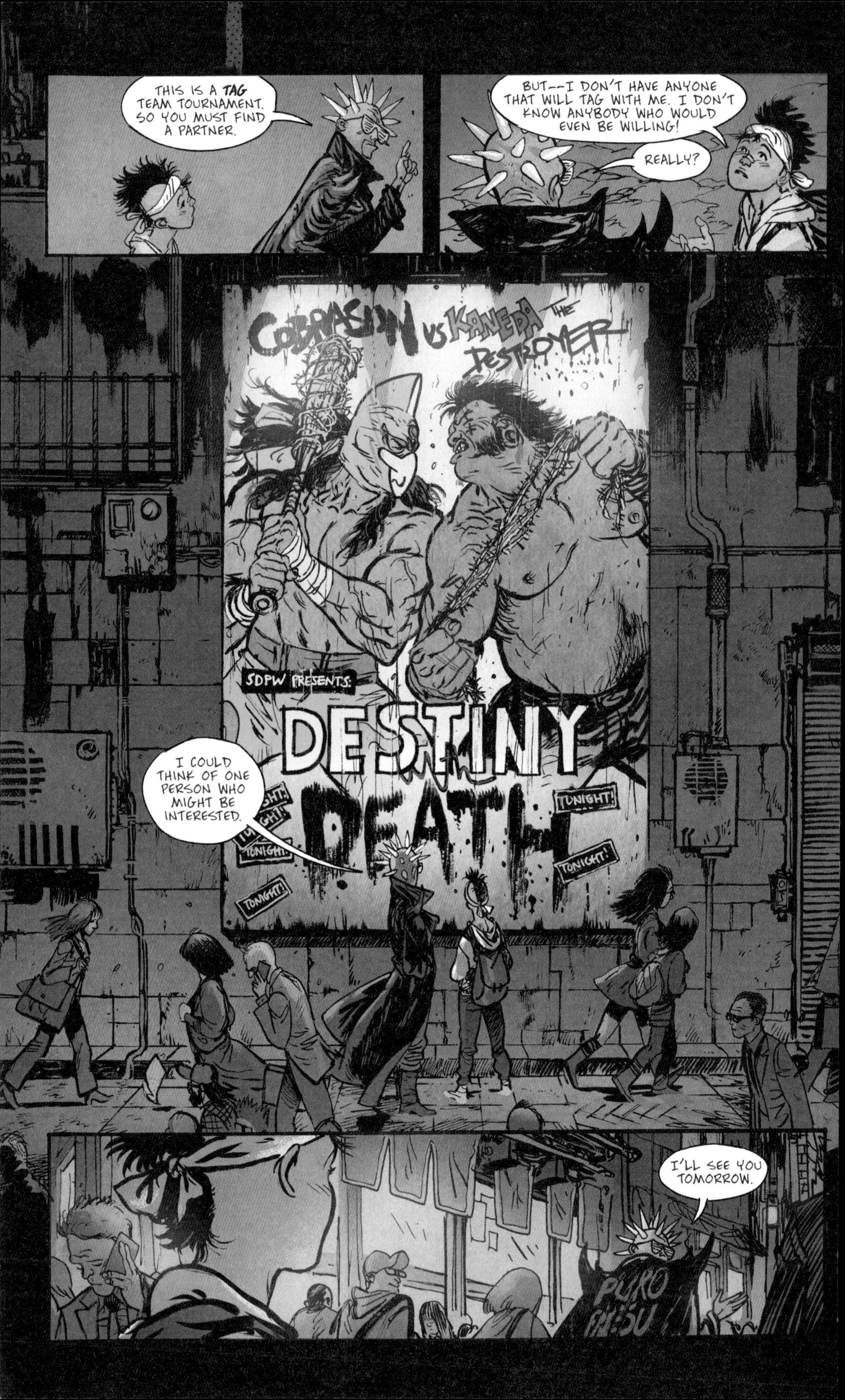
THIS IS A TAG TEAM TOURNAMENT. SO YOU MUST FIND A PARTNER.
BUT--I DON'T HAVE ANYONE THAT WILL TAG WITH ME. I DON'T KNOW ANYBODY WHO WOULD EVEN BE WILLING!
REALLY?
COBRASIAN VS KANEDA THE DESTROYER
SDPW PRESENTS:
DESTINY DEATH
TONIGHT!
TONIGHT!
TONIGHT!
TONIGHT!
I COULD THINK OF ONE PERSON WHO MIGHT BE INTERESTED.
I'LL SEE YOU TOMORROW.
PURO

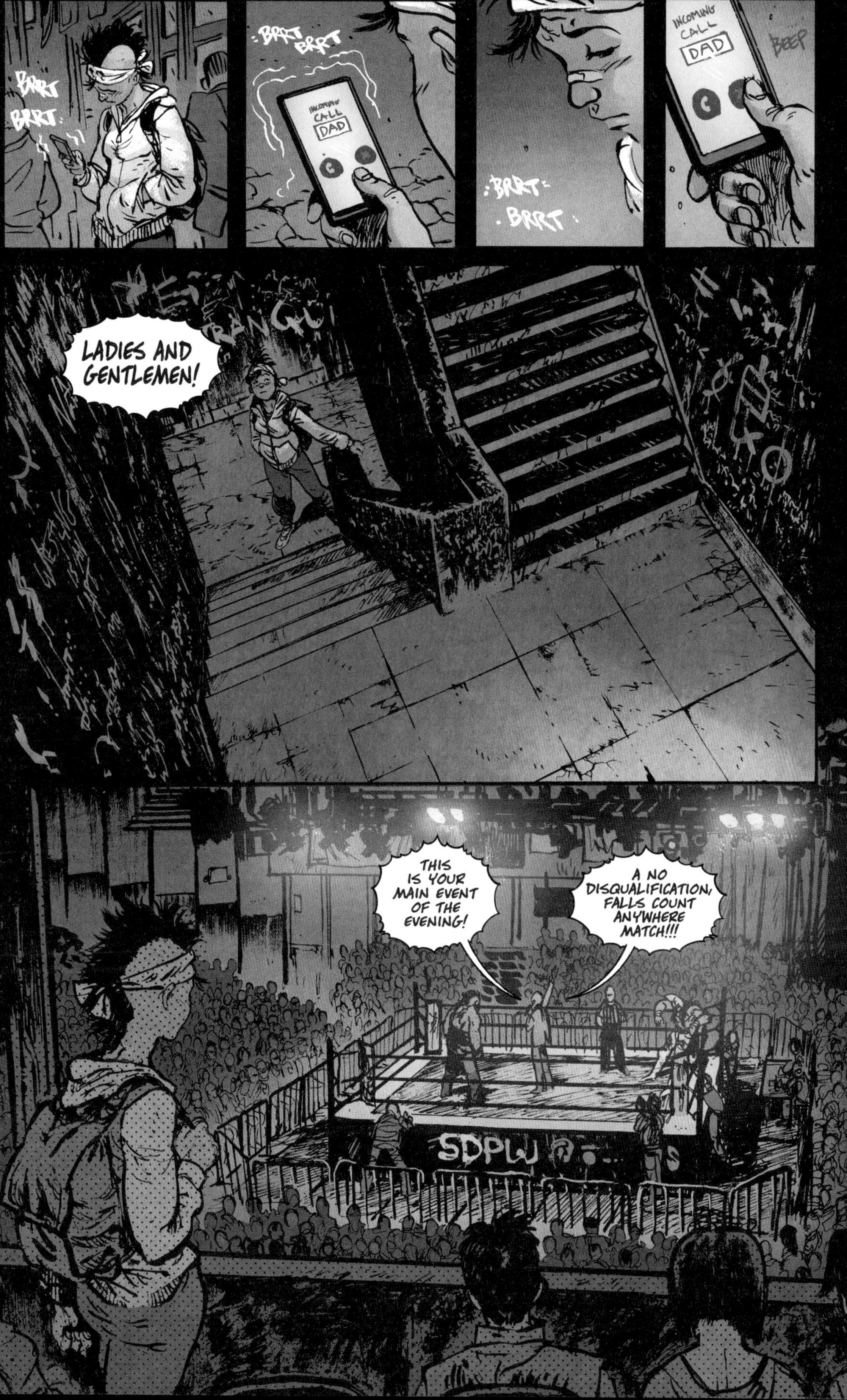
BRRT
BRRT
BRRT BRRT
INCOMING CALL DAD
BRRT
BRRT
INCOMING CALL DAD
BEEP
LADIES AND GENTLEMEN!
THIS IS YOUR MAIN EVENT OF THE EVENING!
A NO DISQUALIFICATION, FALLS COUNT ANYWHERE MATCH!!!
SDPW

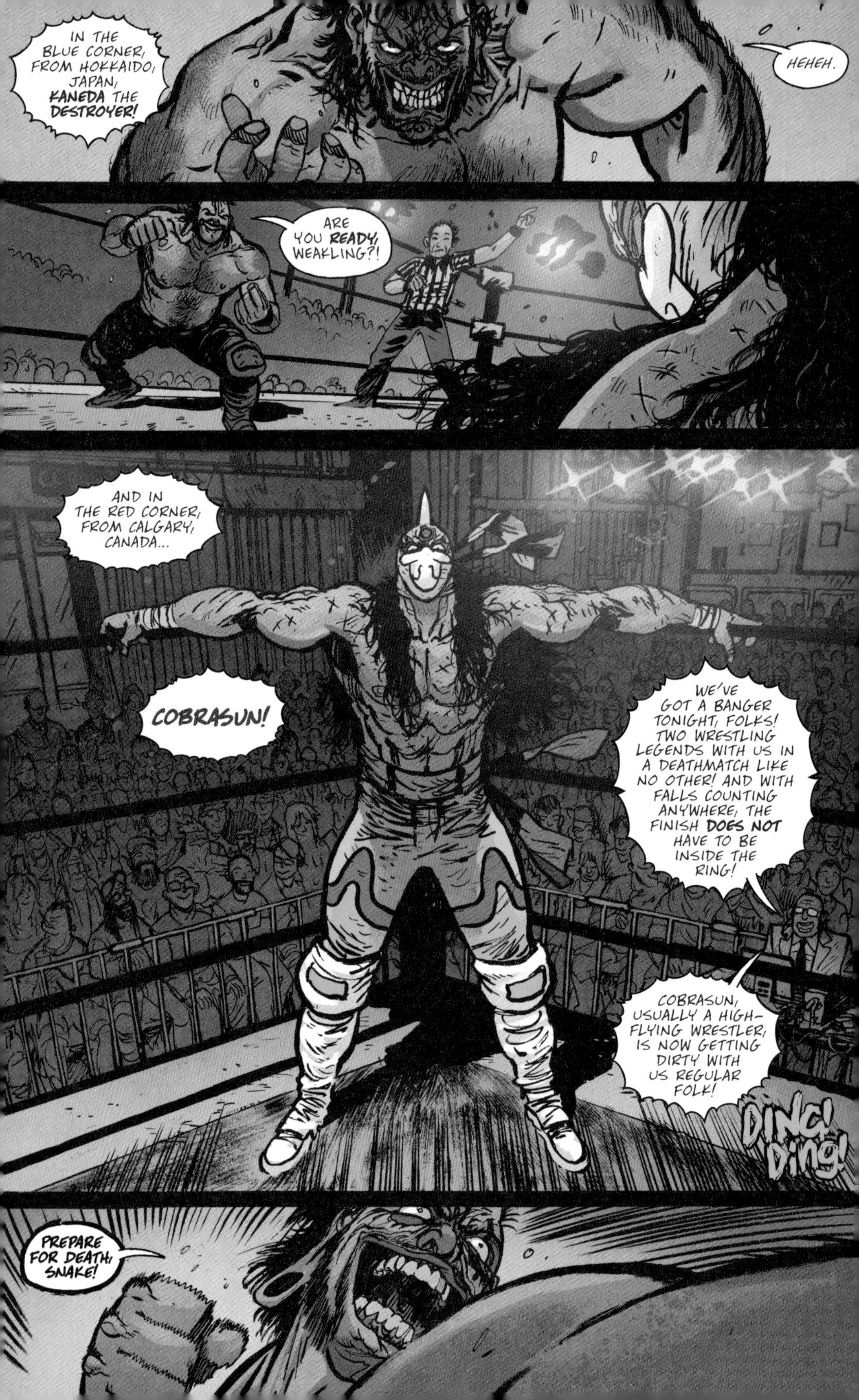
IN THE BLUE CORNER, FROM HOKKAIDO, JAPAN, **KANEDA** THE **DESTROYER!**
HEHEH.
ARE YOU **READY,** WEAKLING?!
AND IN THE RED CORNER, FROM CALGARY, CANADA...
COBRASUN!
WE'VE GOT A BANGER TONIGHT, FOLKS! TWO WRESTLING LEGENDS WITH US IN A DEATHMATCH LIKE NO OTHER! AND WITH FALLS COUNTING ANYWHERE, THE FINISH **DOES NOT** HAVE TO BE INSIDE THE RING!
COBRASUN, USUALLY A HIGH-FLYING WRESTLER, IS NOW GETTING DIRTY WITH US REGULAR FOLK!
DING! DING!
PREPARE FOR DEATH, SNAKE!

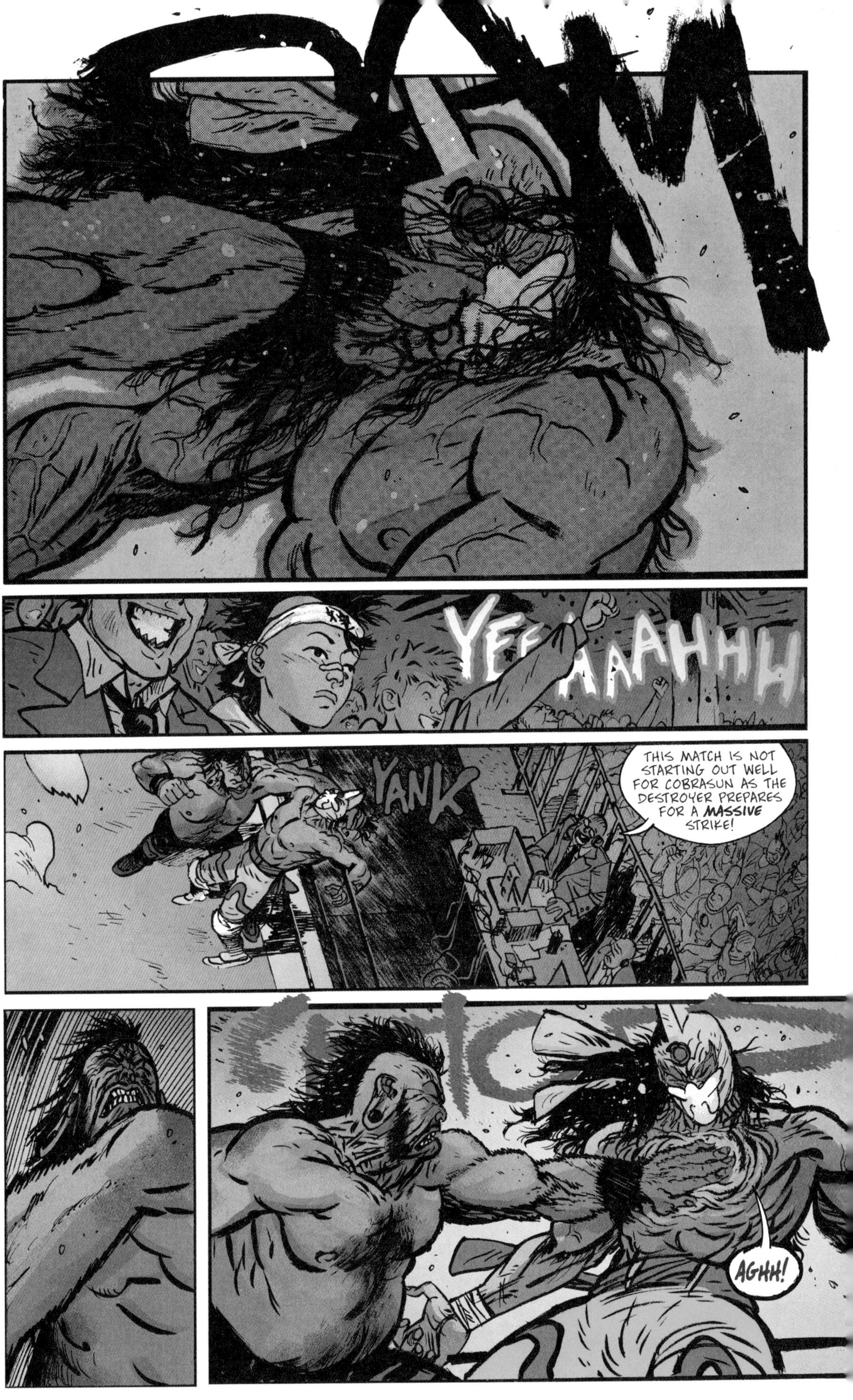
YEEAAAHHH
YANK
THIS MATCH IS NOT STARTING OUT WELL FOR COBRASUN AS THE DESTROYER PREPARES FOR A **MASSIVE** STRIKE!
AGHH!

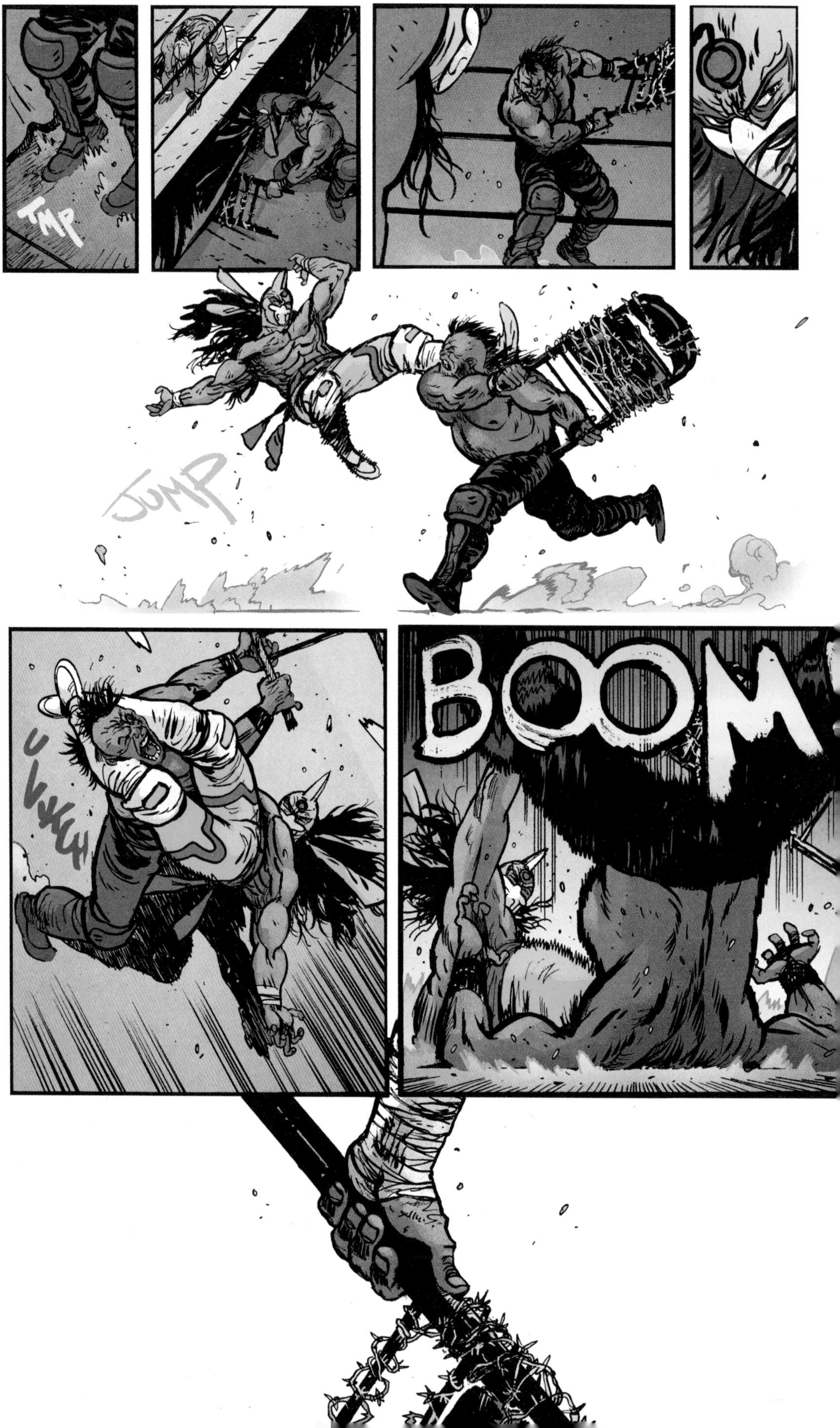
TMP
JUMP
BOOM

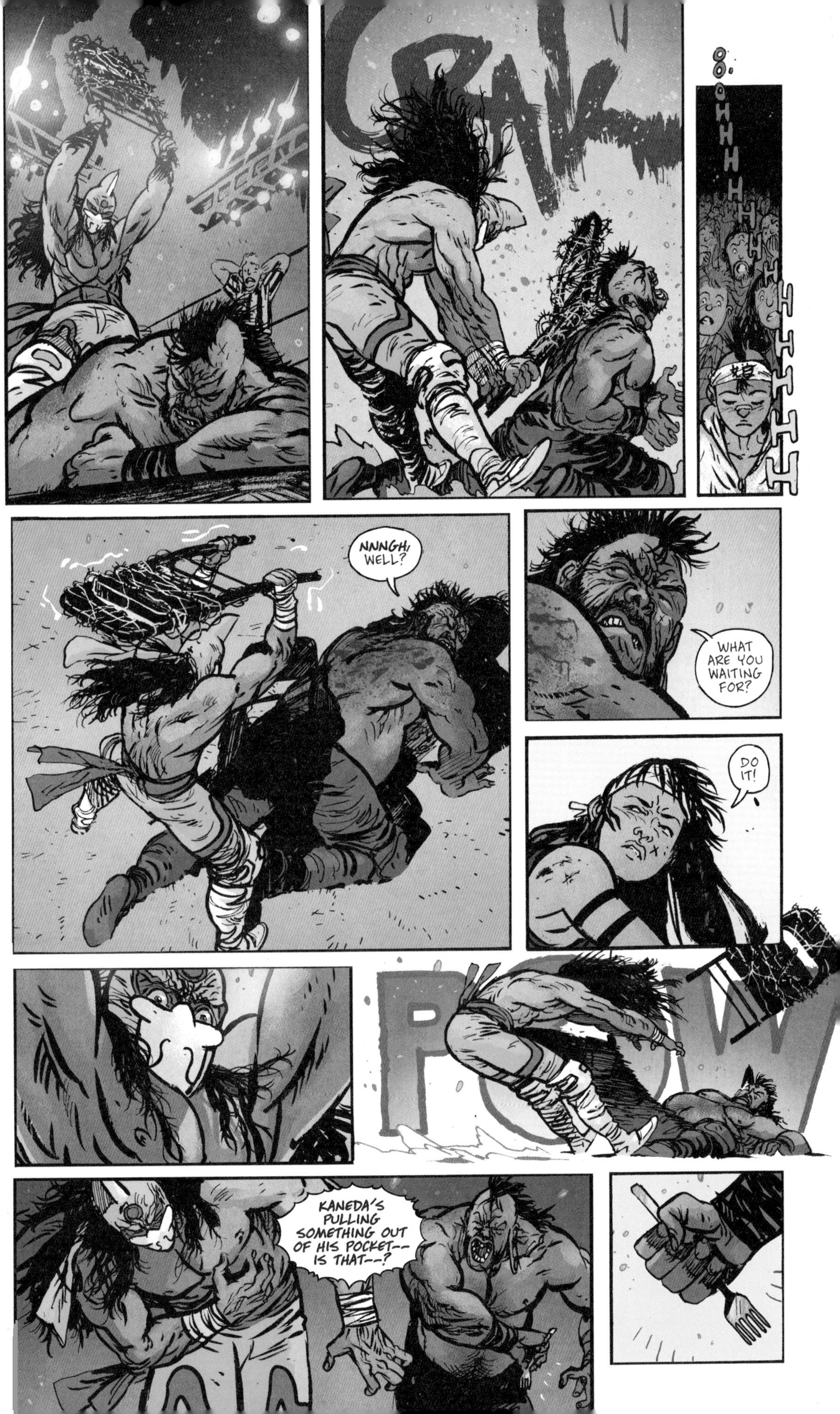
CRAK
OOOHHHHHHHHHHHH
NNNGH, WELL?
WHAT ARE YOU WAITING FOR?
DO IT!
POW
KANEDA'S PULLING SOMETHING OUT OF HIS POCKET-- IS THAT--?

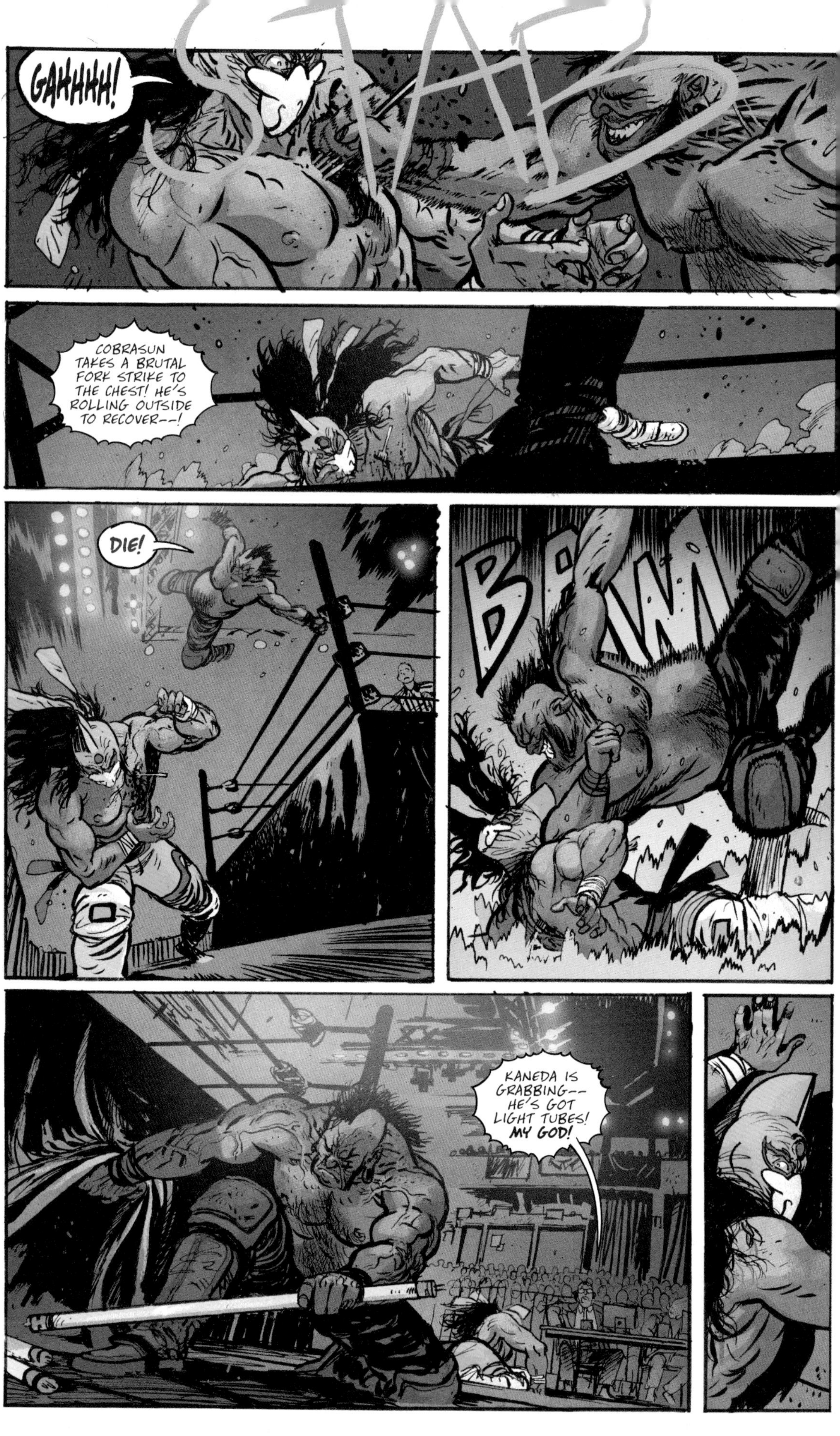
STAB
GAKHHH!
COBRASUN TAKES A BRUTAL FORK STRIKE TO THE CHEST! HE'S ROLLING OUTSIDE TO RECOVER--!
DIE!
BAM
KANEDA IS GRABBING-- HE'S GOT LIGHT TUBES! MY GOD!

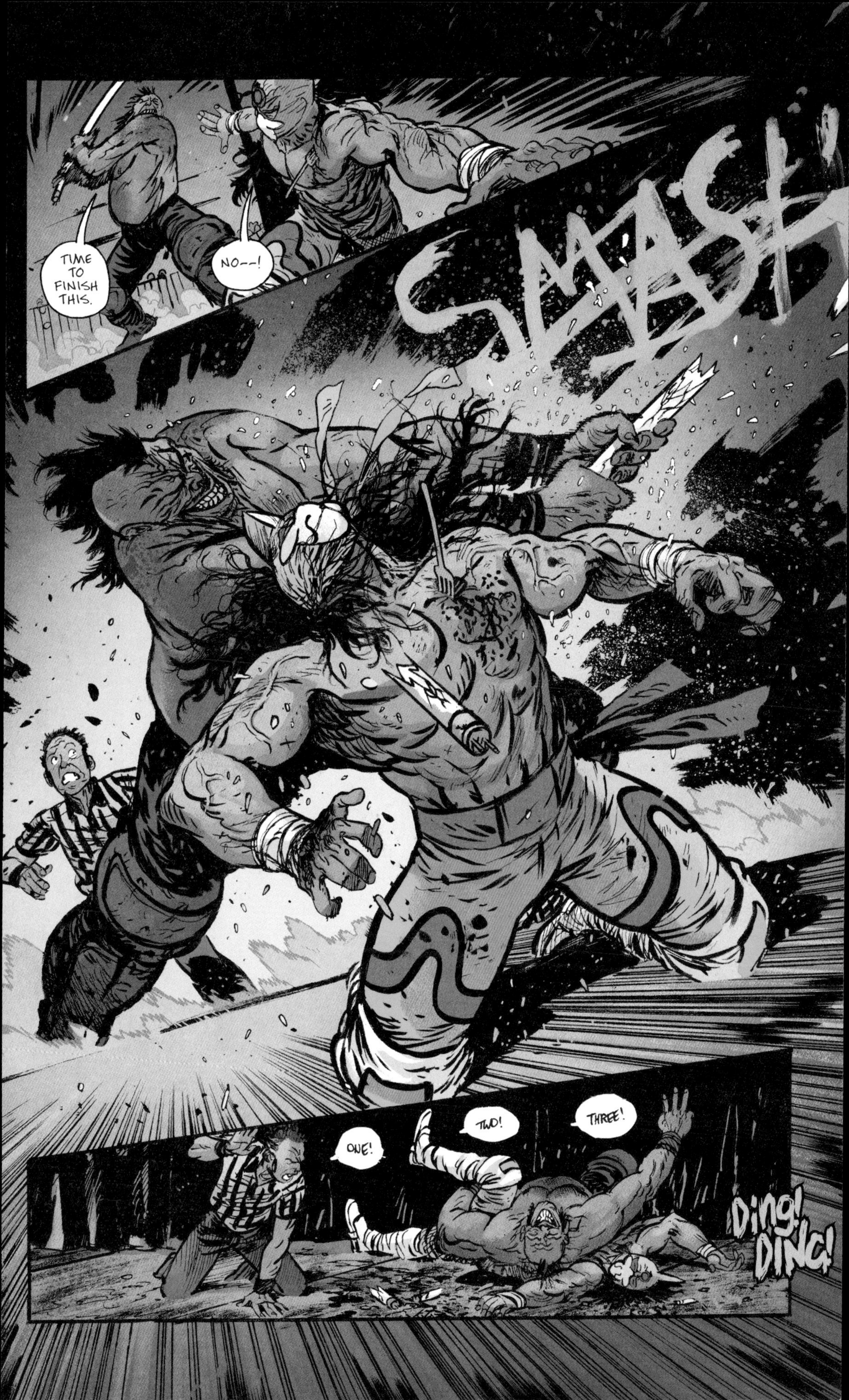
TIME TO FINISH THIS.
NO--!
SMASH!
ONE!
TWO!
THREE!
DING! DING!

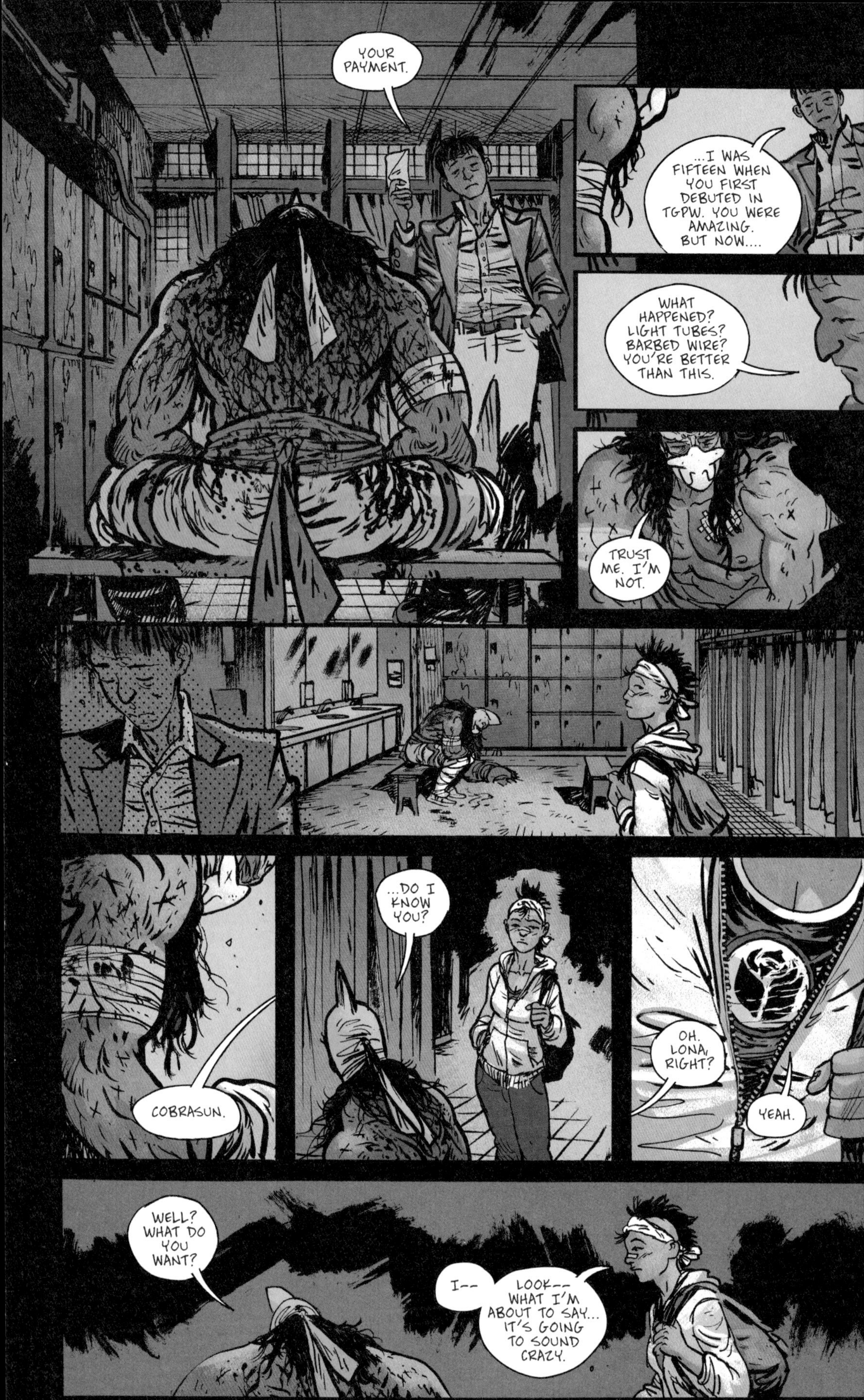
YOUR PAYMENT.
...I WAS FIFTEEN WHEN YOU FIRST DEBUTED IN TGPW. YOU WERE AMAZING. BUT NOW....
WHAT HAPPENED? LIGHT TUBES? BARBED WIRE? YOU'RE BETTER THAN THIS.
TRUST ME. I'M NOT.
COBRASUN.
...DO I KNOW YOU?
OH. LONA, RIGHT?
YEAH.
WELL? WHAT DO YOU WANT?
I--
LOOK-- WHAT I'M ABOUT TO SAY... IT'S GOING TO SOUND CRAZY.

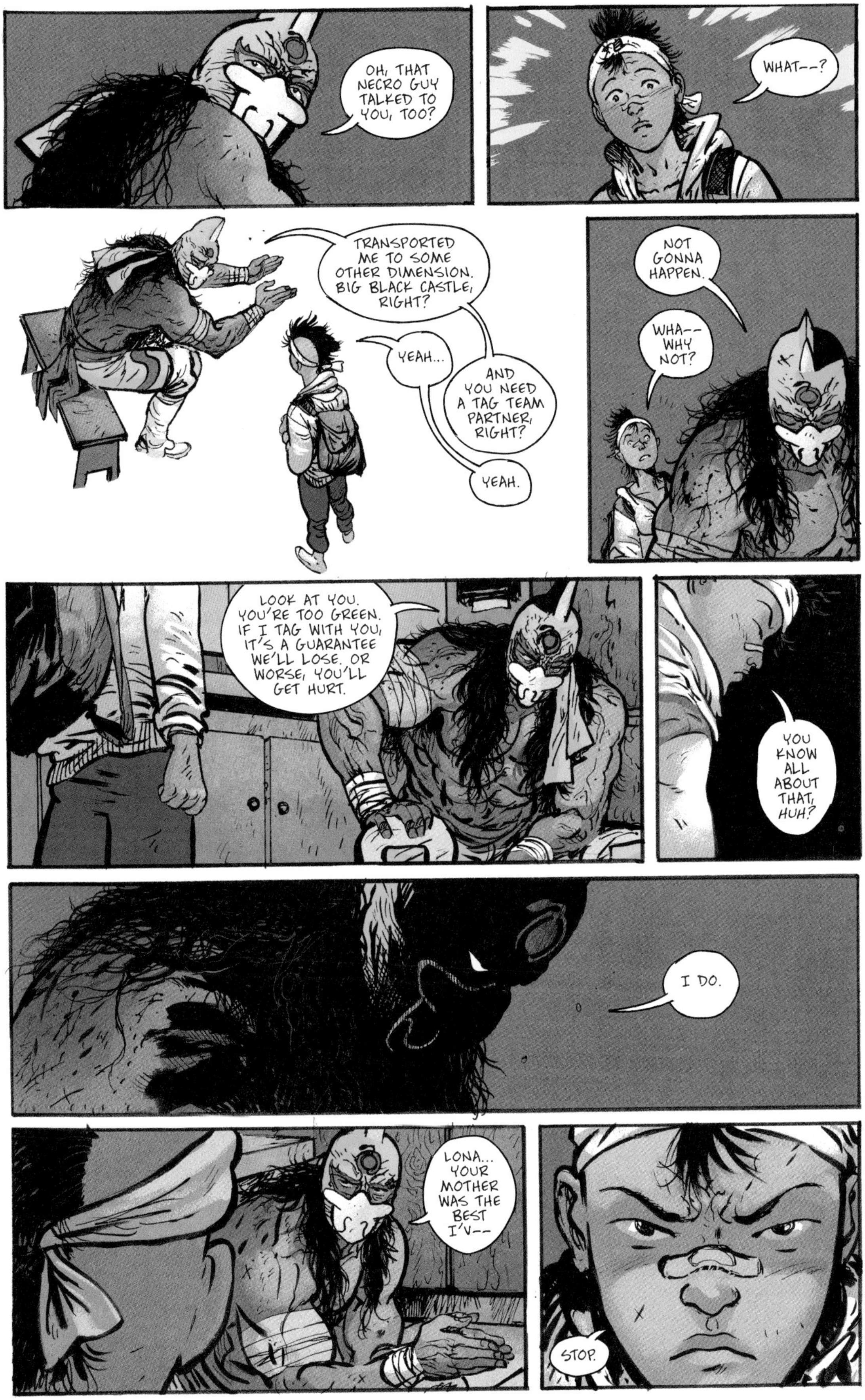
OH, THAT NECRO GUY TALKED TO YOU, TOO?
WHAT--?
TRANSPORTED ME TO SOME OTHER DIMENSION. BIG BLACK CASTLE, RIGHT?
YEAH...
AND YOU NEED A TAG TEAM PARTNER, RIGHT?
YEAH.
NOT GONNA HAPPEN.
WHA-- WHY NOT?
LOOK AT YOU. YOU'RE TOO GREEN. IF I TAG WITH YOU, IT'S A GUARANTEE WE'LL LOSE. OR WORSE, YOU'LL GET HURT.
YOU KNOW ALL ABOUT THAT, HUH?
I DO.
LONA... YOUR MOTHER WAS THE BEST I'V--
STOP.

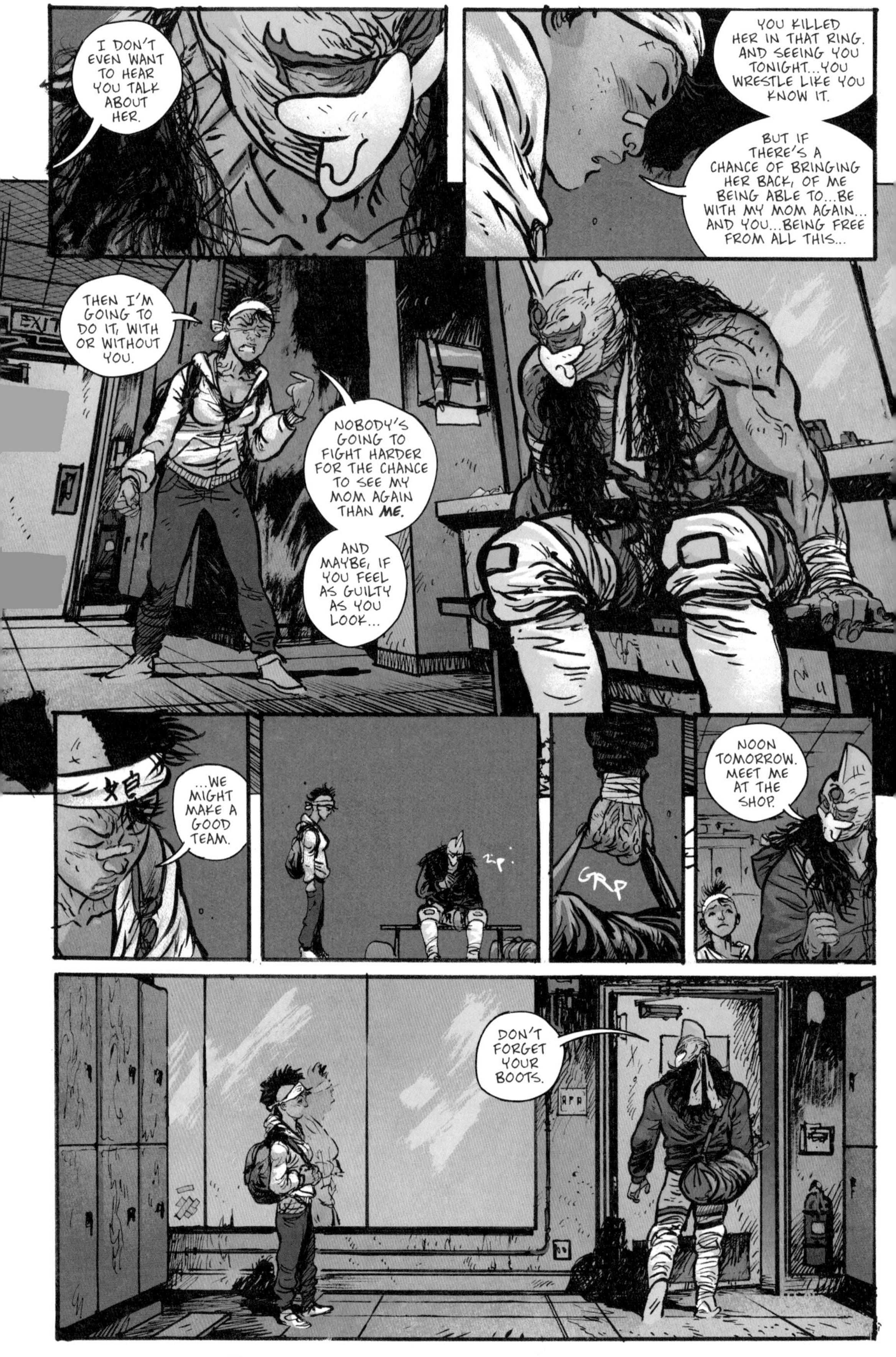
I DON'T EVEN WANT TO HEAR YOU TALK ABOUT HER.
YOU KILLED HER IN THAT RING. AND SEEING YOU TONIGHT...YOU WRESTLE LIKE YOU KNOW IT.
BUT IF THERE'S A CHANCE OF BRINGING HER BACK, OF ME BEING ABLE TO...BE WITH MY MOM AGAIN... AND YOU...BEING FREE FROM ALL THIS...
EXIT
THEN I'M GOING TO DO IT, WITH OR WITHOUT YOU.
NOBODY'S GOING TO FIGHT HARDER FOR THE CHANCE TO SEE MY MOM AGAIN THAN **ME.**
AND MAYBE, IF YOU FEEL AS GUILTY AS YOU LOOK...
...WE MIGHT MAKE A GOOD TEAM.
ZIP
GRIP
NOON TOMORROW. MEET ME AT THE SHOP.
DON'T FORGET YOUR BOOTS.

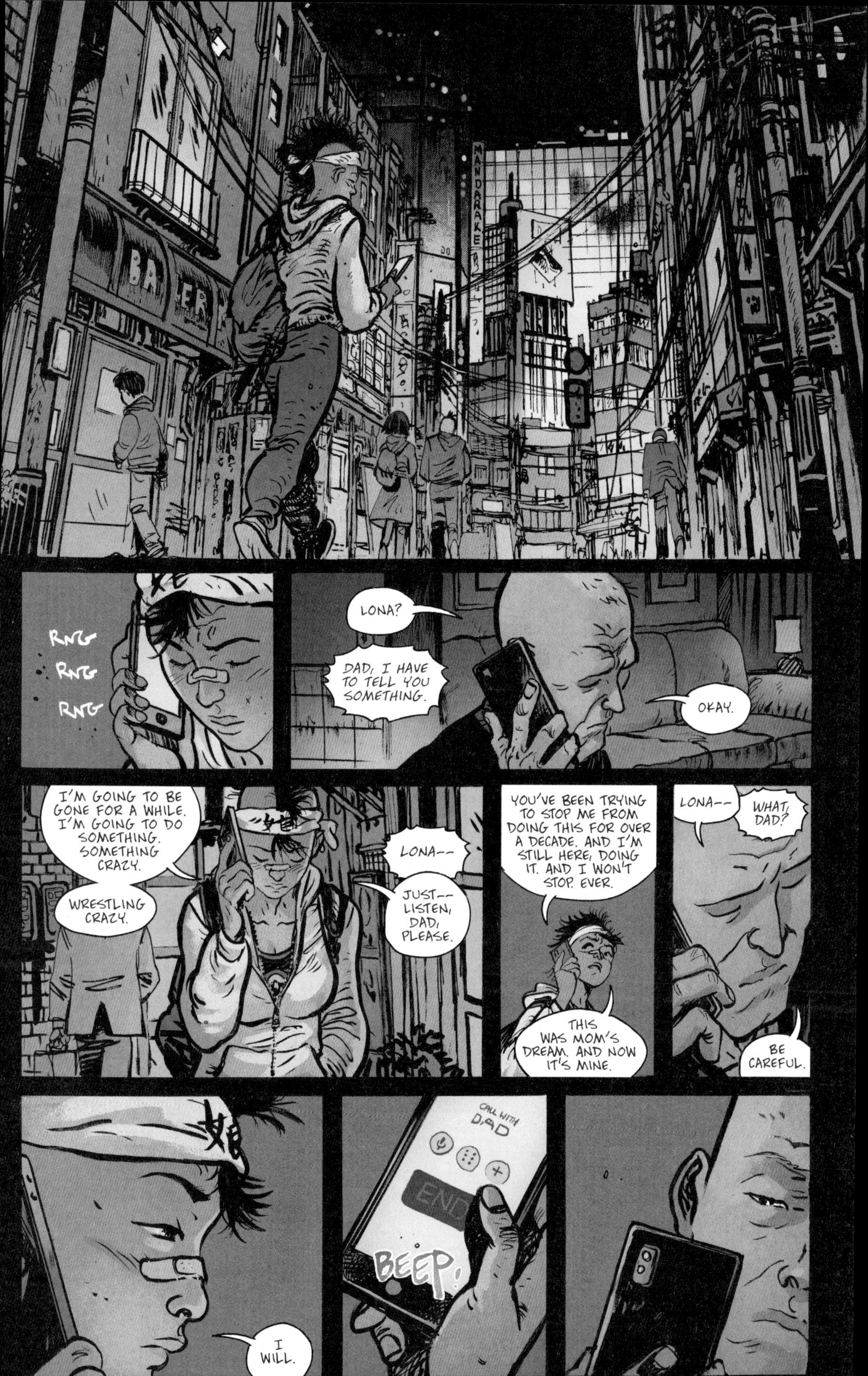
MANDARAKE
RNG
RNG
RNG
LONA?
DAD, I HAVE TO TELL YOU SOMETHING.
OKAY.
I'M GOING TO BE GONE FOR A WHILE. I'M GOING TO DO SOMETHING. SOMETHING CRAZY.
WRESTLING CRAZY.
LONA--
JUST-- LISTEN, DAD, PLEASE.
YOU'VE BEEN TRYING TO STOP ME FROM DOING THIS FOR OVER A DECADE. AND I'M STILL HERE, DOING IT. AND I WON'T STOP. EVER.
THIS WAS MOM'S DREAM. AND NOW IT'S MINE.
LONA--
WHAT, DAD?
BE CAREFUL.
I WILL.
CALL WITH DAD
END
BEEP!

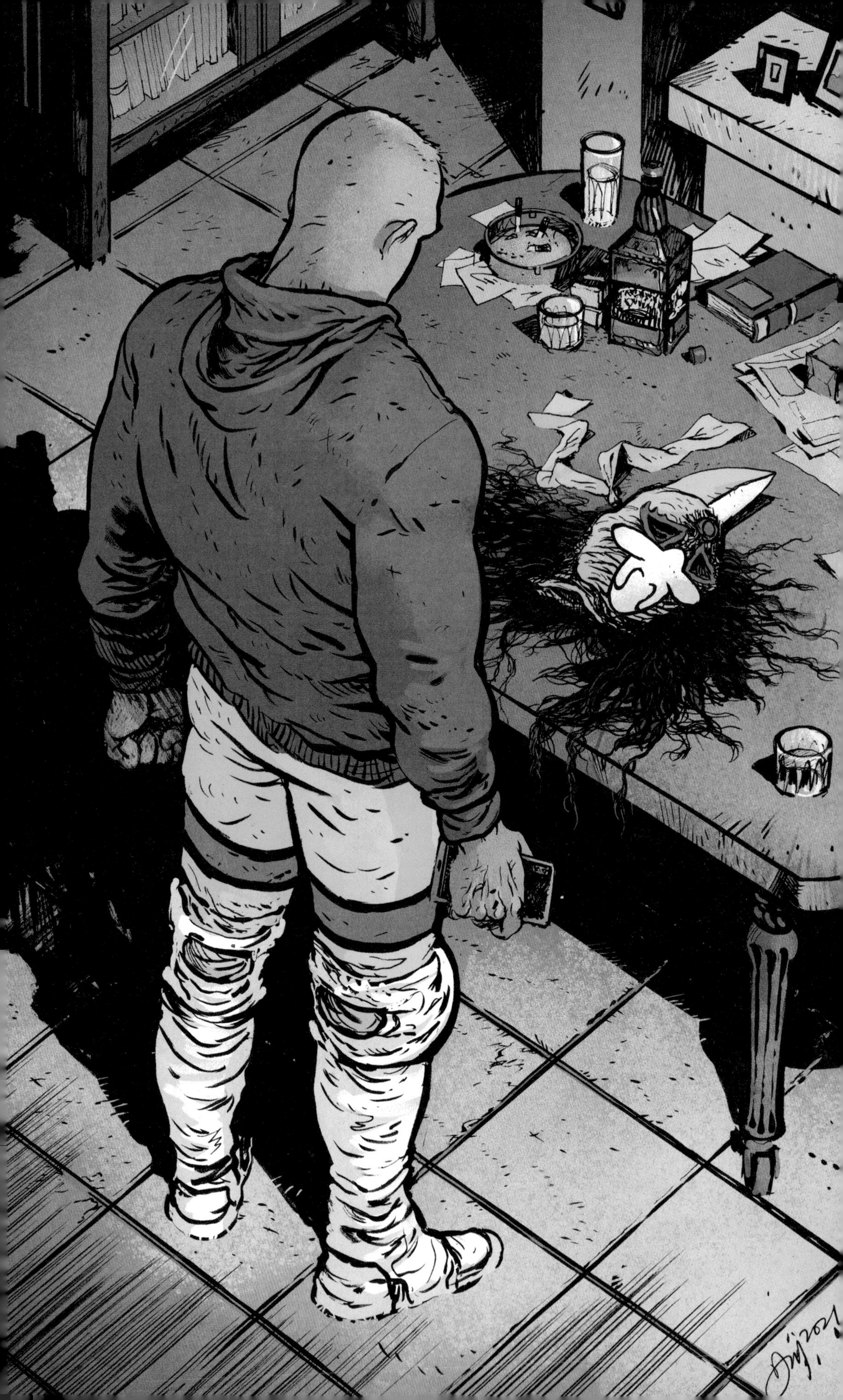

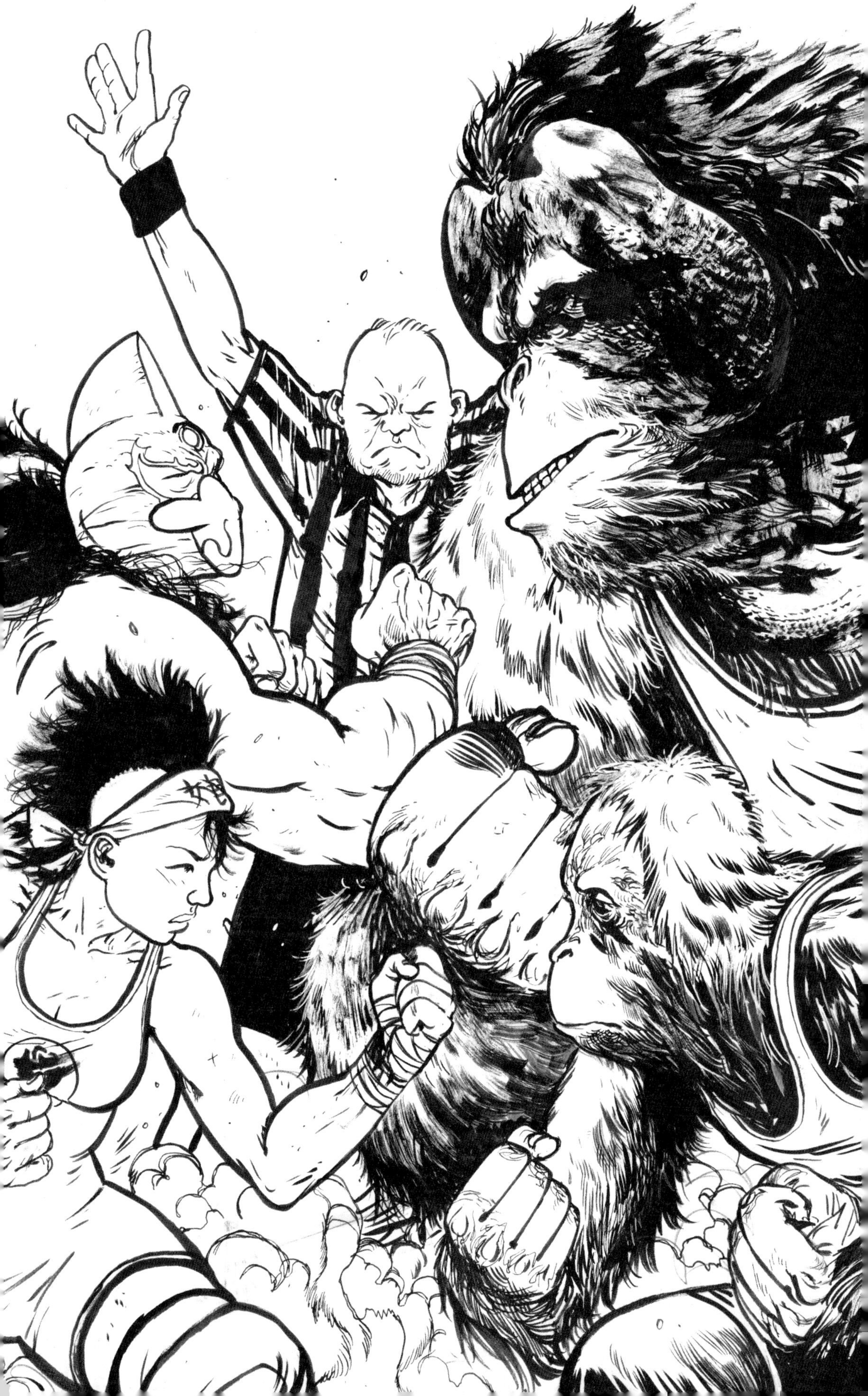

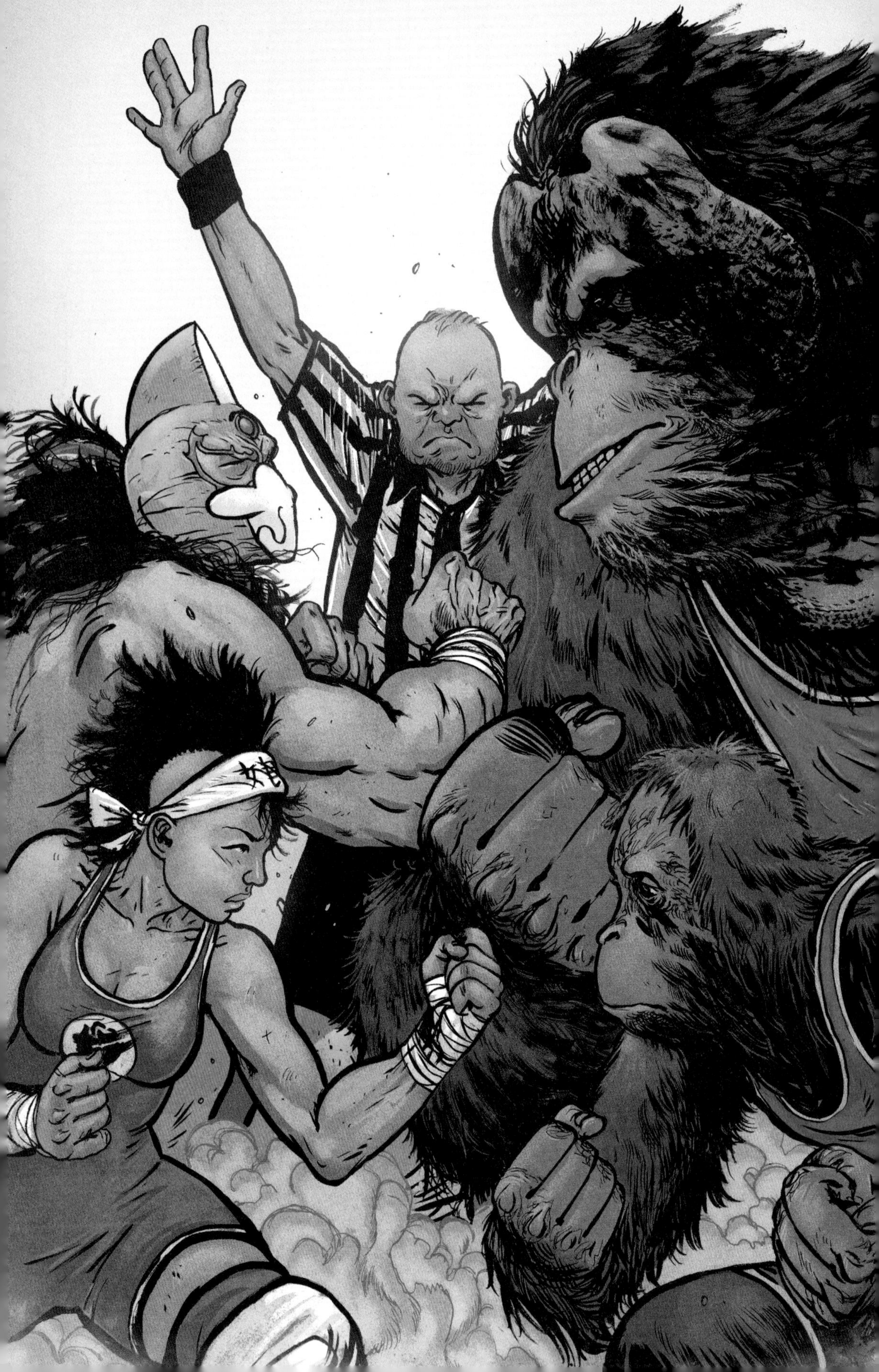

BLOOD.

JACOB.

WHAT ARE YOU DRINKING?

WHISKEY. ROCKS.

SAME FOR ME THEN.

WELL? WHAT IS IT YOU WANT?

YOU SHOULDN'T HAVE TOLD HER.

WHAT, THAT YOU MADE ME PROMISE TO NEVER TRAIN HER? I WAS SICK OF LYING.

SHE'S MORE DETERMINED THAN EVER NOW. THANKS TO YOU.

JACOB! YOUR DAUGHTER HAS THE FIRE! TRUE RAW, UNBRIDLED **TALENT!**

SHE'S GOT WHAT HER MOM HAD, AND YOU **KNOW** IT! SHE DESERVES THE TRUTH.

SP

YOU SHOULD HAVE TOLD HER IT WAS YOU UNDER THAT MASK SINCE THE FIRST TIME SHE WATCHED YOU WRESTLE. WHEN SHE WAS LITTLE.

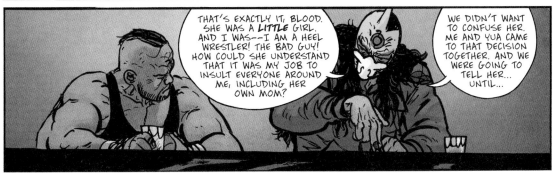

THAT'S EXACTLY IT, BLOOD. SHE WAS A **LITTLE** GIRL. AND I WAS--I AM A HEEL WRESTLER! THE BAD GUY! HOW COULD SHE UNDERSTAND THAT IT WAS MY JOB TO INSULT EVERYONE AROUND ME, INCLUDING HER OWN MOM?

WE DIDN'T WANT TO CONFUSE HER. ME AND YUA CAME TO THAT DECISION TOGETHER. AND WE WERE GOING TO TELL HER... UNTIL...

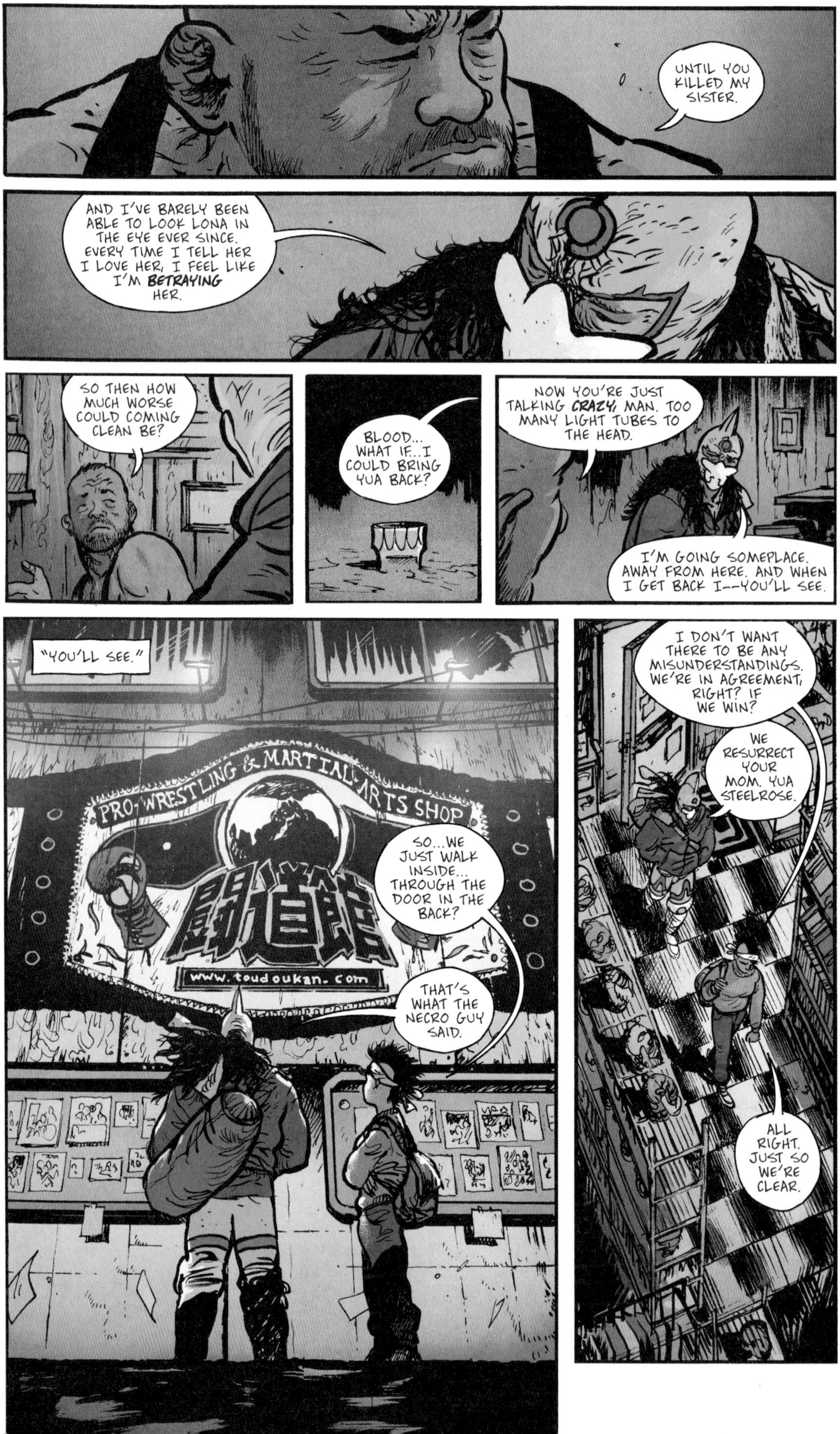
UNTIL YOU KILLED MY SISTER.
AND I'VE BARELY BEEN ABLE TO LOOK LONA IN THE EYE EVER SINCE. EVERY TIME I TELL HER I LOVE HER, I FEEL LIKE I'M BETRAYING HER.
SO THEN HOW MUCH WORSE COULD COMING CLEAN BE?
BLOOD... WHAT IF... I COULD BRING YUA BACK?
NOW YOU'RE JUST TALKING CRAZY, MAN. TOO MANY LIGHT TUBES TO THE HEAD.
I'M GOING SOMEPLACE. AWAY FROM HERE. AND WHEN I GET BACK I--YOU'LL SEE.
"YOU'LL SEE."
PRO-WRESTLING & MARTIAL ARTS SHOP
闘道館
www.toudoukan.com
SO... WE JUST WALK INSIDE... THROUGH THE DOOR IN THE BACK?
THAT'S WHAT THE NECRO GUY SAID.
I DON'T WANT THERE TO BE ANY MISUNDERSTANDINGS. WE'RE IN AGREEMENT, RIGHT? IF WE WIN?
WE RESURRECT YOUR MOM. YUA STEELROSE.
ALL RIGHT. JUST SO WE'RE CLEAR.

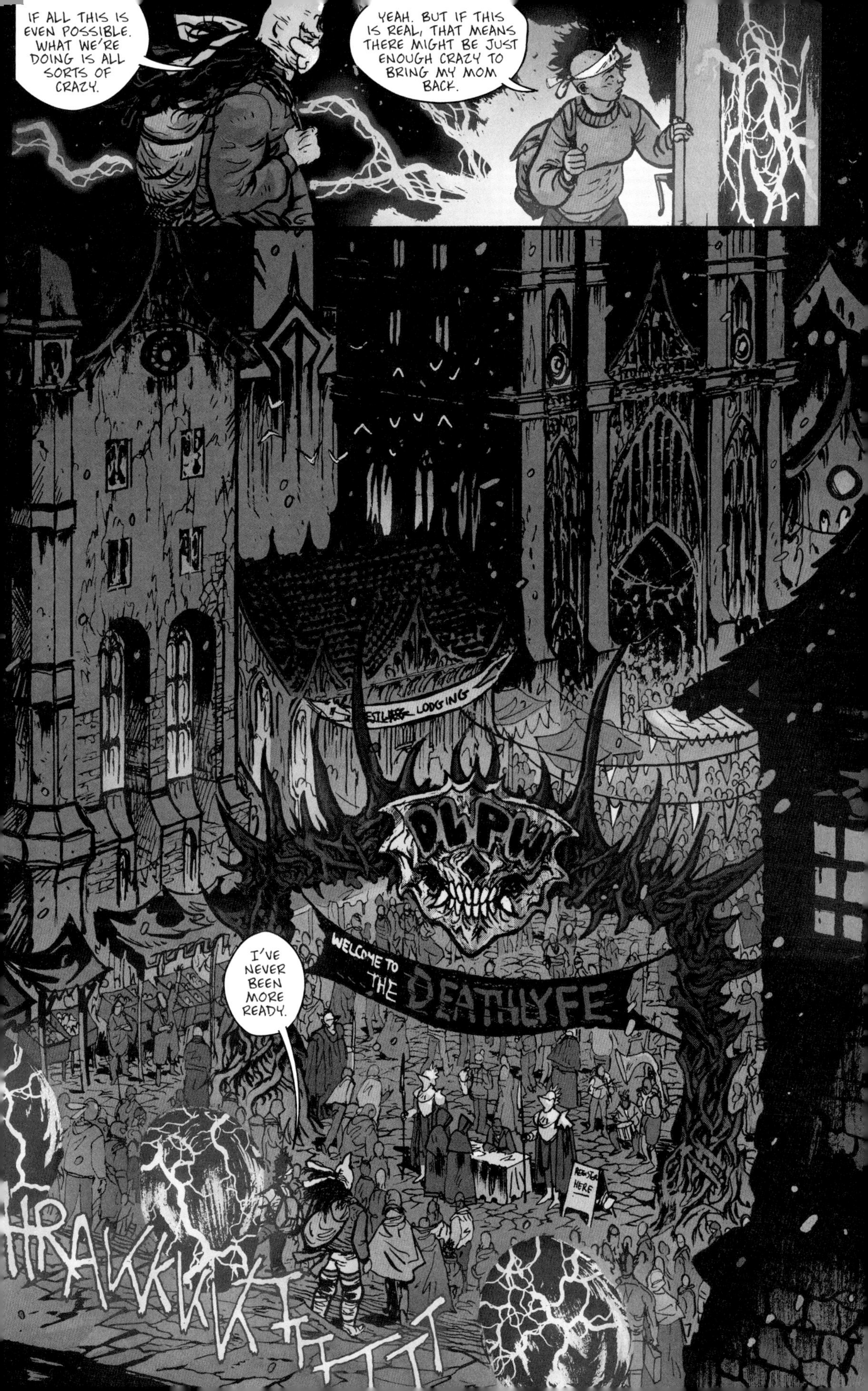
IF ALL THIS IS EVEN POSSIBLE. WHAT WE'RE DOING IS ALL SORTS OF CRAZY.
YEAH. BUT IF THIS IS REAL, THAT MEANS THERE MIGHT BE JUST ENOUGH CRAZY TO BRING MY MOM BACK.
LODGING
DLPW
WELCOME TO THE DEATHLYFE
I'VE NEVER BEEN MORE READY.
REGISTER HERE
HRAKKKKTTTTT

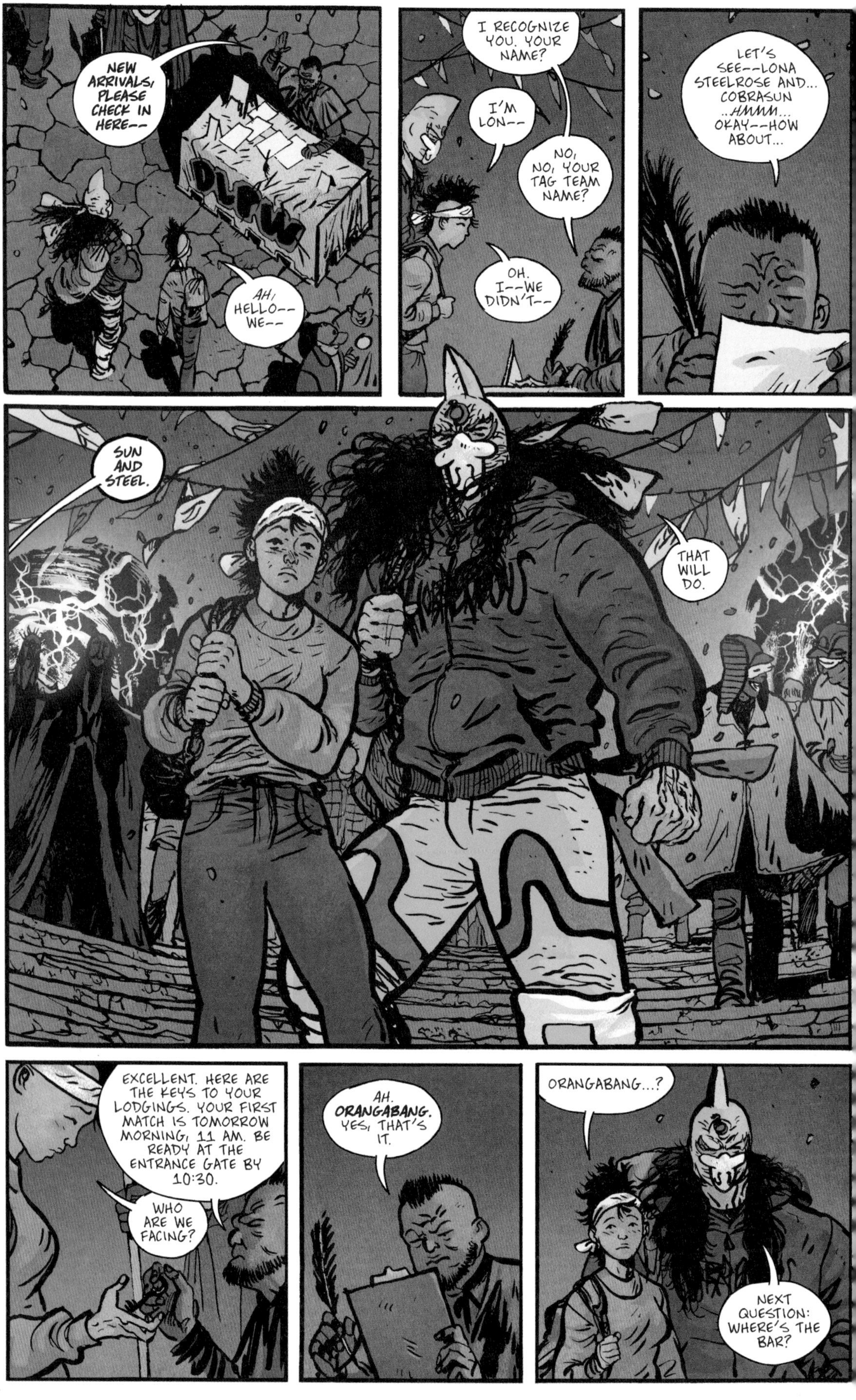
NEW ARRIVALS, PLEASE CHECK IN HERE--
AH, HELLO-- WE--
I RECOGNIZE YOU. YOUR NAME?
I'M LON--
NO, NO, YOUR TAG TEAM NAME?
OH. I--WE DIDN'T--
LET'S SEE--LONA STEELROSE AND... COBRASUN ...HMMM... OKAY--HOW ABOUT...
SUN AND STEEL.
THAT WILL DO.
EXCELLENT. HERE ARE THE KEYS TO YOUR LODGINGS. YOUR FIRST MATCH IS TOMORROW MORNING, 11 AM. BE READY AT THE ENTRANCE GATE BY 10:30.
WHO ARE WE FACING?
AH. ORANGABANG. YES, THAT'S IT.
ORANGABANG...?
NEXT QUESTION: WHERE'S THE BAR?

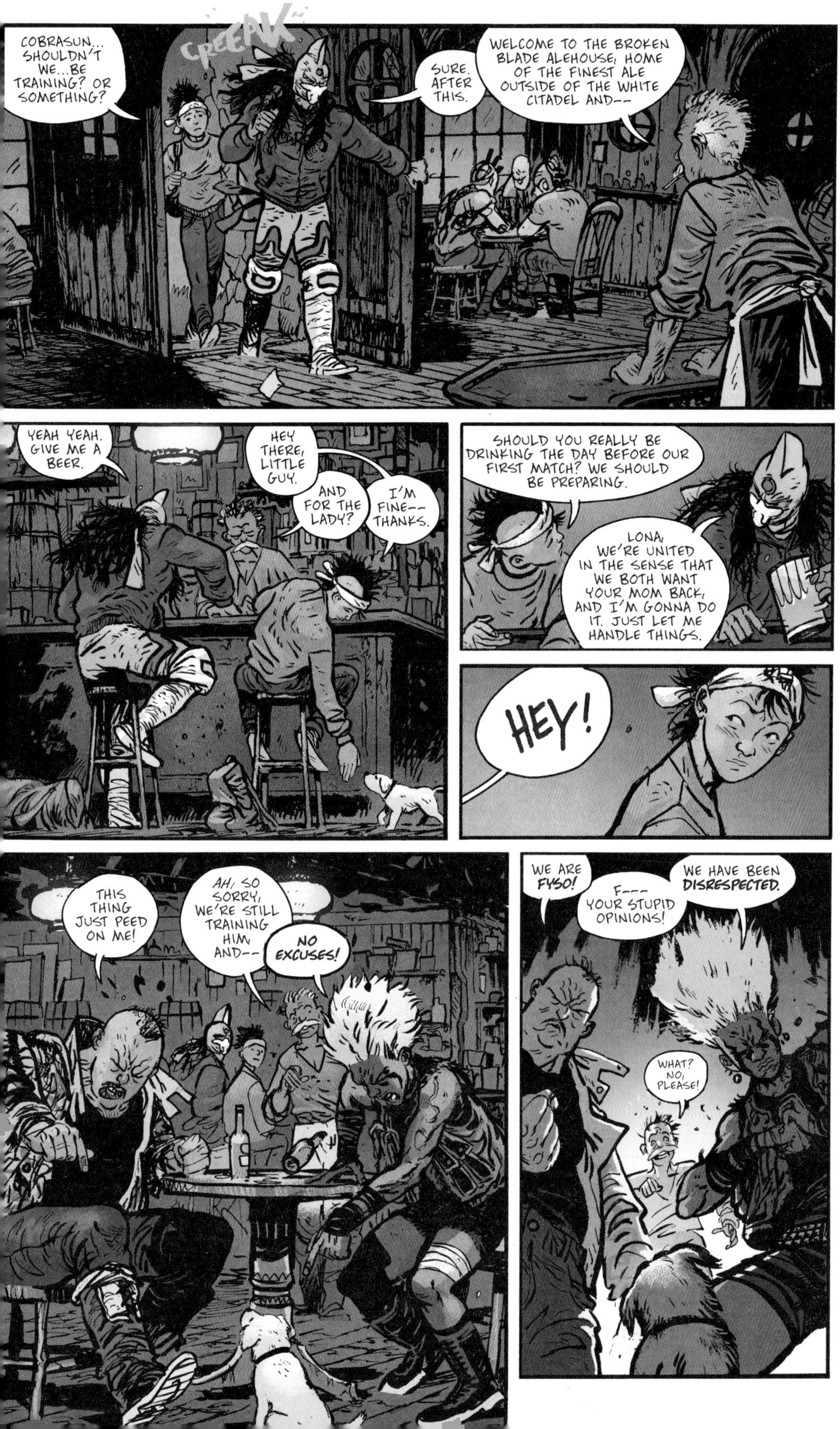
CREEAK
COBRASUN... SHOULDN'T WE...BE TRAINING? OR SOMETHING?
SURE. AFTER THIS.
WELCOME TO THE BROKEN BLADE ALEHOUSE, HOME OF THE FINEST ALE OUTSIDE OF THE WHITE CITADEL AND--
YEAH YEAH. GIVE ME A BEER.
HEY THERE, LITTLE GUY.
AND FOR THE LADY?
I'M FINE-- THANKS.
SHOULD YOU REALLY BE DRINKING THE DAY BEFORE OUR FIRST MATCH? WE SHOULD BE PREPARING.
LONA, WE'RE UNITED IN THE SENSE THAT WE BOTH WANT YOUR MOM BACK, AND I'M GONNA DO IT. JUST LET ME HANDLE THINGS.
HEY!
THIS THING JUST PEED ON ME!
AH, SO SORRY, WE'RE STILL TRAINING HIM AND--
NO EXCUSES!
WE ARE FYSO!
F--- YOUR STUPID OPINIONS!
WE HAVE BEEN DISRESPECTED.
WHAT? NO, PLEASE!

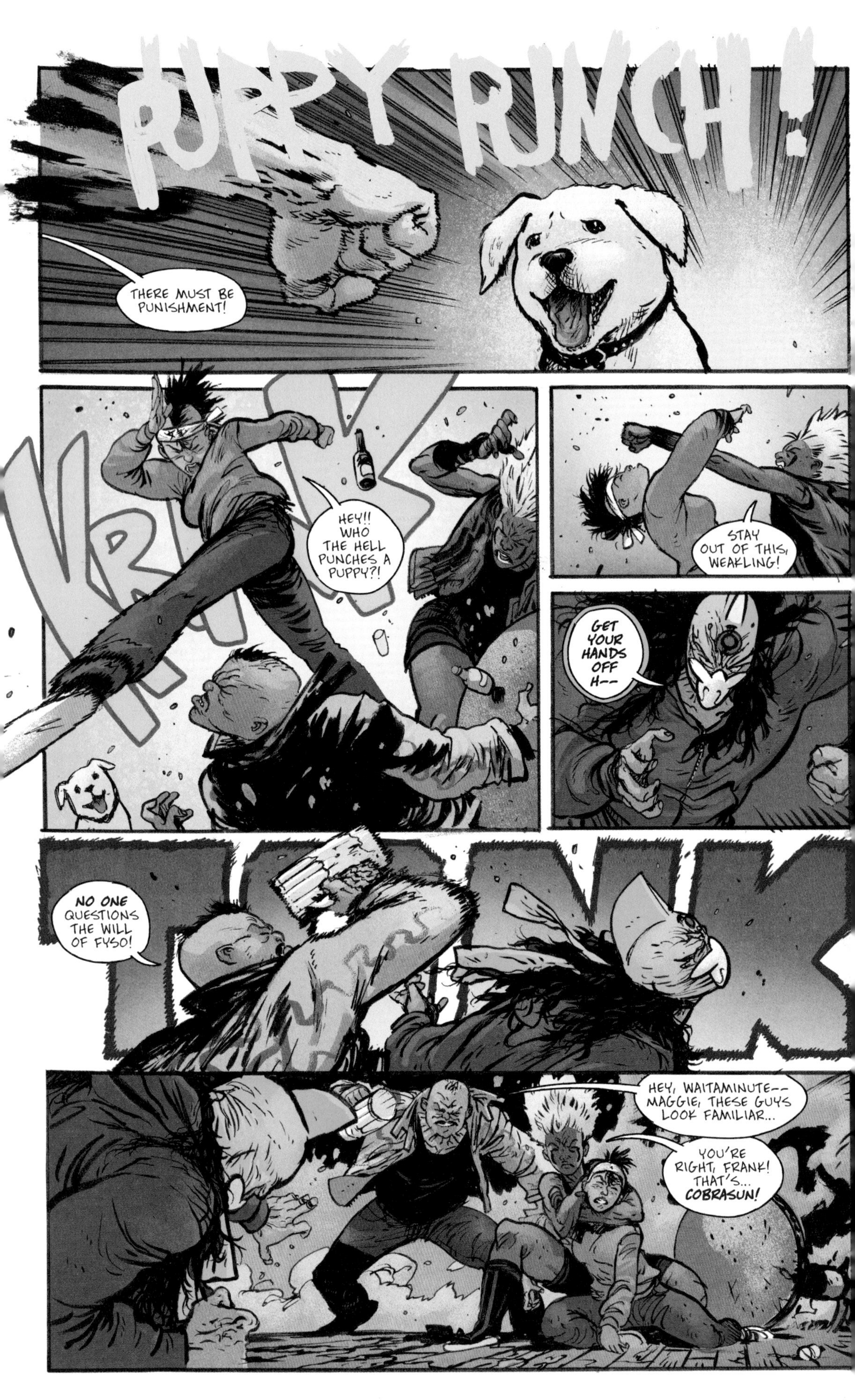

PUPPY PUNCH!
THERE MUST BE PUNISHMENT!
HEY!! WHO THE HELL PUNCHES A PUPPY?!
STAY OUT OF THIS, WEAKLING!
GET YOUR HANDS OFF H--
NO ONE QUESTIONS THE WILL OF FYSO!
HEY, WAITAMINUTE-- MAGGIE, THESE GUYS LOOK FAMILIAR...
YOU'RE RIGHT, FRANK! THAT'S... COBRASUN!

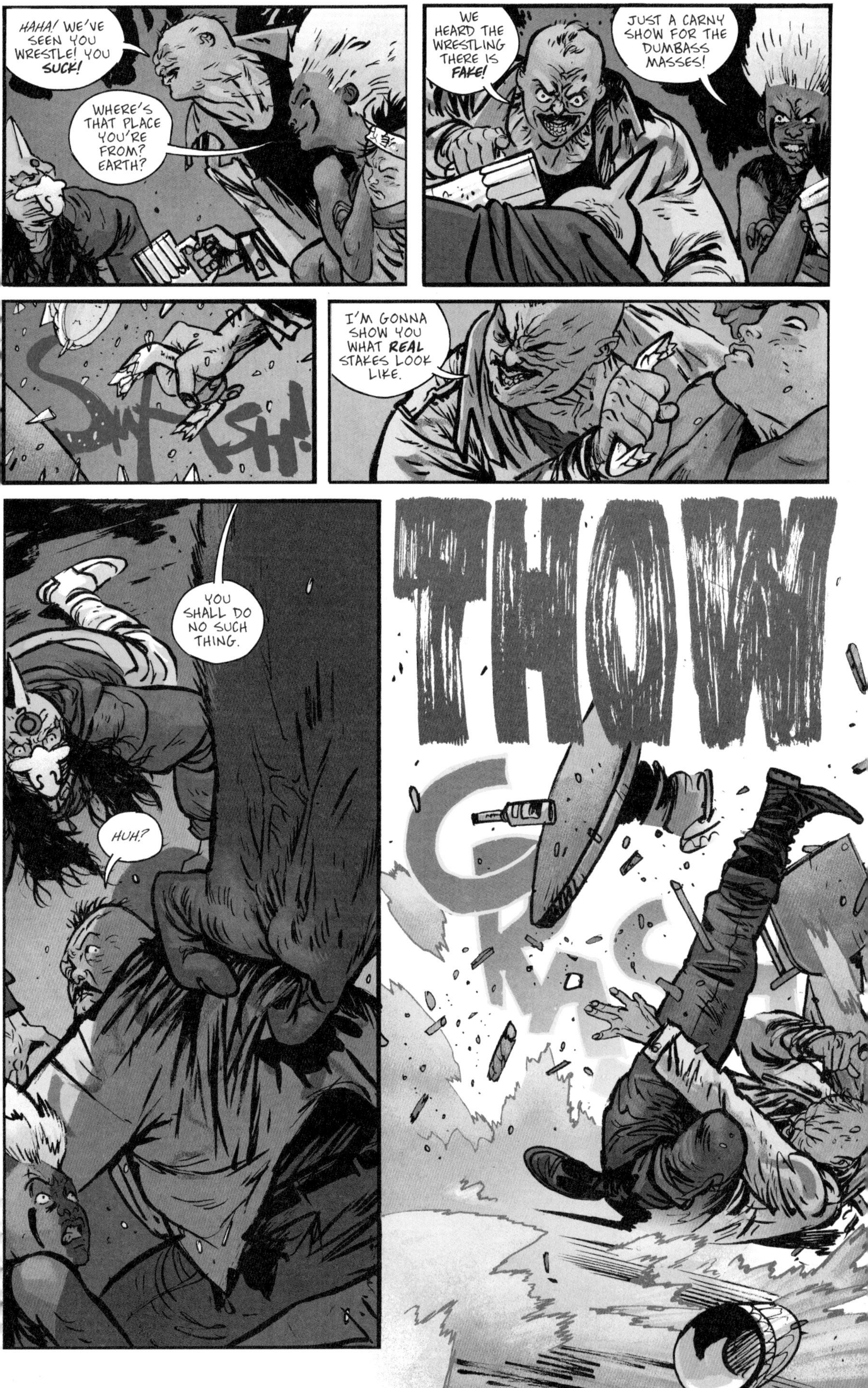
HAHA! WE'VE SEEN YOU WRESTLE! YOU SUCK!
WHERE'S THAT PLACE YOU'RE FROM? EARTH?
WE HEARD THE WRESTLING THERE IS FAKE!
JUST A CARNY SHOW FOR THE DUMBASS MASSES!
I'M GONNA SHOW YOU WHAT REAL STAKES LOOK LIKE.
YOU SHALL DO NO SUCH THING.
HUH?
THOW

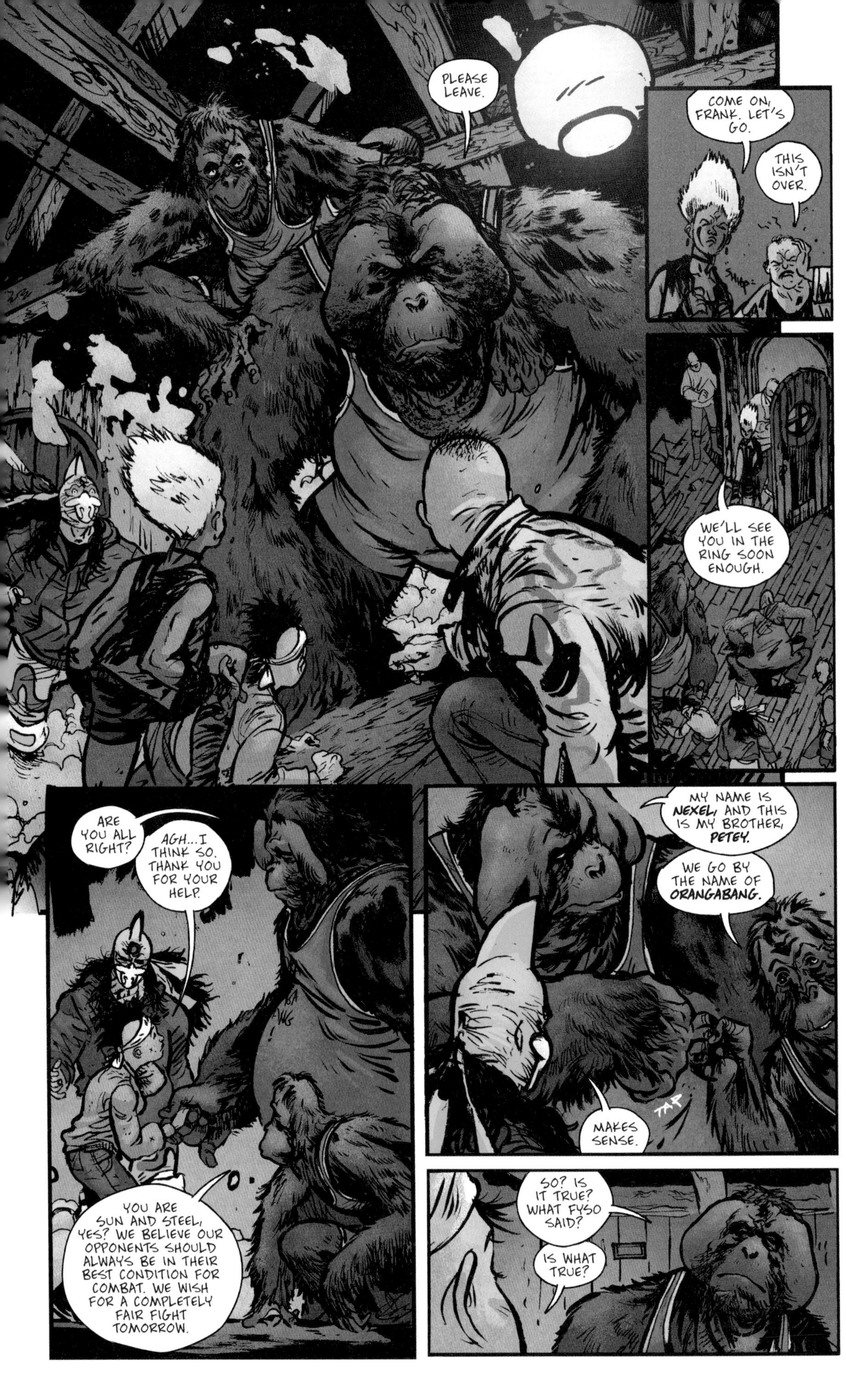
PLEASE LEAVE.
COME ON, FRANK. LET'S GO.
THIS ISN'T OVER.
WE'LL SEE YOU IN THE RING SOON ENOUGH.
ARE YOU ALL RIGHT?
AGH...I THINK SO. THANK YOU FOR YOUR HELP.
YOU ARE SUN AND STEEL, YES? WE BELIEVE OUR OPPONENTS SHOULD ALWAYS BE IN THEIR BEST CONDITION FOR COMBAT. WE WISH FOR A COMPLETELY FAIR FIGHT TOMORROW.
MY NAME IS **NEXEL**, AND THIS IS MY BROTHER, **PETEY**.
WE GO BY THE NAME OF **ORANGABANG**.
TAP
MAKES SENSE.
SO? IS IT TRUE? WHAT FYSO SAID?
IS WHAT TRUE?

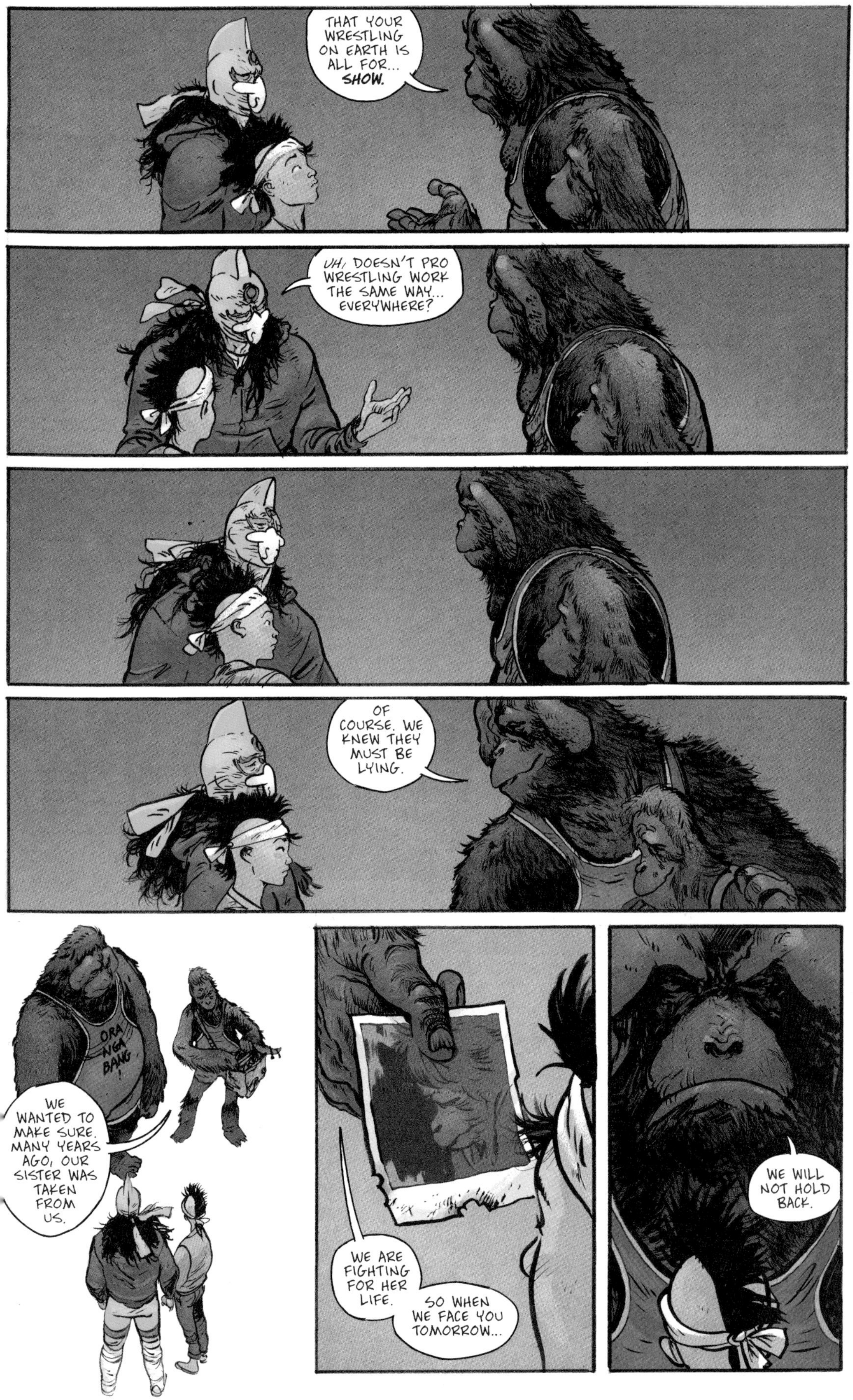
THAT YOUR WRESTLING ON EARTH IS ALL FOR... **SHOW.**
UH, DOESN'T PRO WRESTLING WORK THE SAME WAY... EVERYWHERE?
OF COURSE. WE KNEW THEY MUST BE LYING.
ORA NGA BANG!
WE WANTED TO MAKE SURE. MANY YEARS AGO, OUR SISTER WAS TAKEN FROM US.
WE ARE FIGHTING FOR HER LIFE.
SO WHEN WE FACE YOU TOMORROW...
WE WILL NOT HOLD BACK.

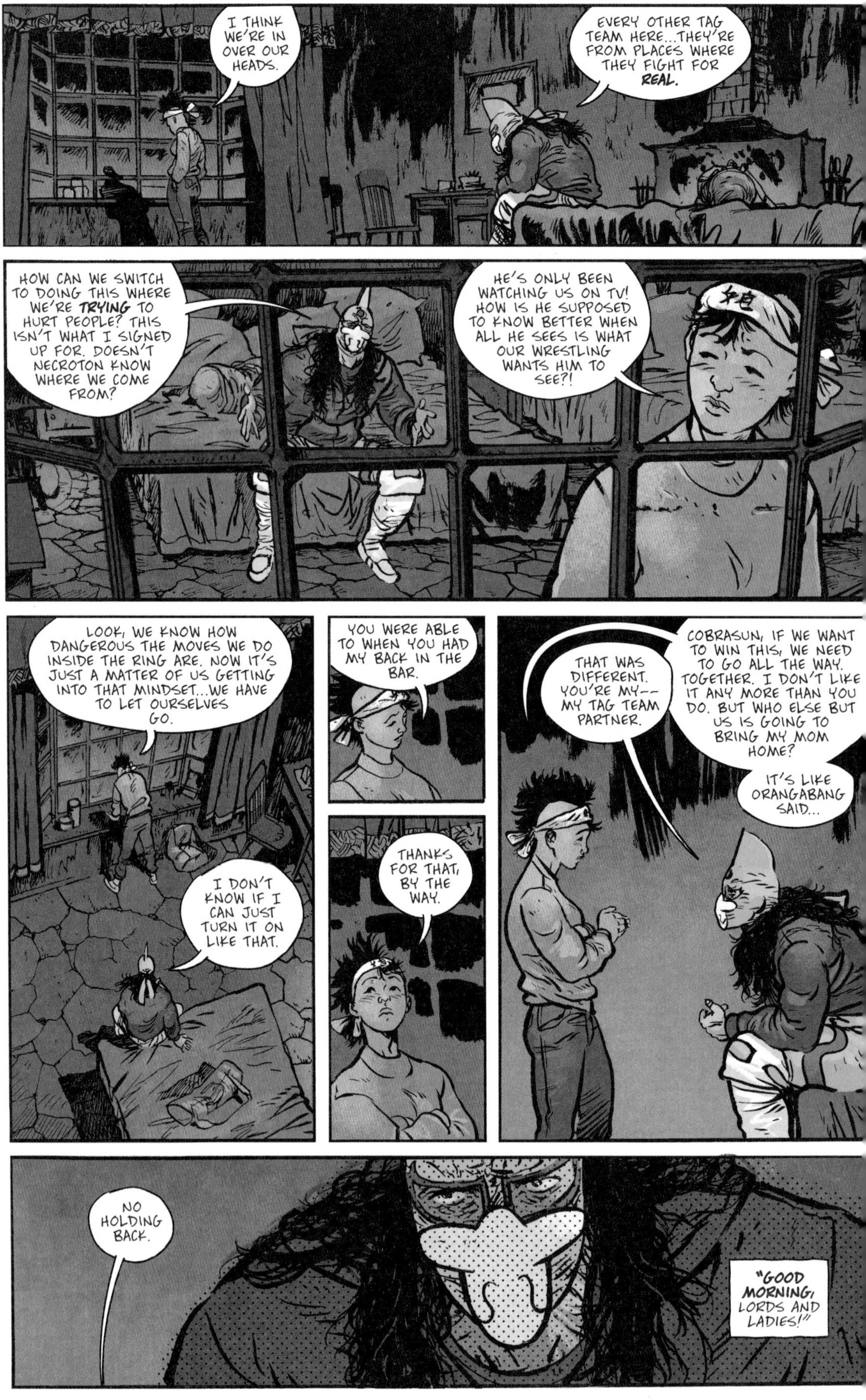
I THINK WE'RE IN OVER OUR HEADS.
EVERY OTHER TAG TEAM HERE...THEY'RE FROM PLACES WHERE THEY FIGHT FOR **REAL.**
HOW CAN WE SWITCH TO DOING THIS WHERE WE'RE ***TRYING*** TO HURT PEOPLE? THIS ISN'T WHAT I SIGNED UP FOR. DOESN'T NECROTON KNOW WHERE WE COME FROM?
HE'S ONLY BEEN WATCHING US ON TV! HOW IS HE SUPPOSED TO KNOW BETTER WHEN ALL HE SEES IS WHAT OUR WRESTLING WANTS HIM TO SEE?!
LOOK, WE KNOW HOW DANGEROUS THE MOVES WE DO INSIDE THE RING ARE. NOW IT'S JUST A MATTER OF US GETTING INTO THAT MINDSET...WE HAVE TO LET OURSELVES GO.
I DON'T KNOW IF I CAN JUST TURN IT ON LIKE THAT.
YOU WERE ABLE TO WHEN YOU HAD MY BACK IN THE BAR.
THANKS FOR THAT, BY THE WAY.
THAT WAS DIFFERENT. YOU'RE MY-- MY TAG TEAM PARTNER.
COBRASUN, IF WE WANT TO WIN THIS, WE NEED TO GO ALL THE WAY. TOGETHER. I DON'T LIKE IT ANY MORE THAN YOU DO. BUT WHO ELSE BUT US IS GOING TO BRING MY MOM HOME?
IT'S LIKE ORANGABANG SAID...
NO HOLDING BACK.
"GOOD MORNING, LORDS AND LADIES!"

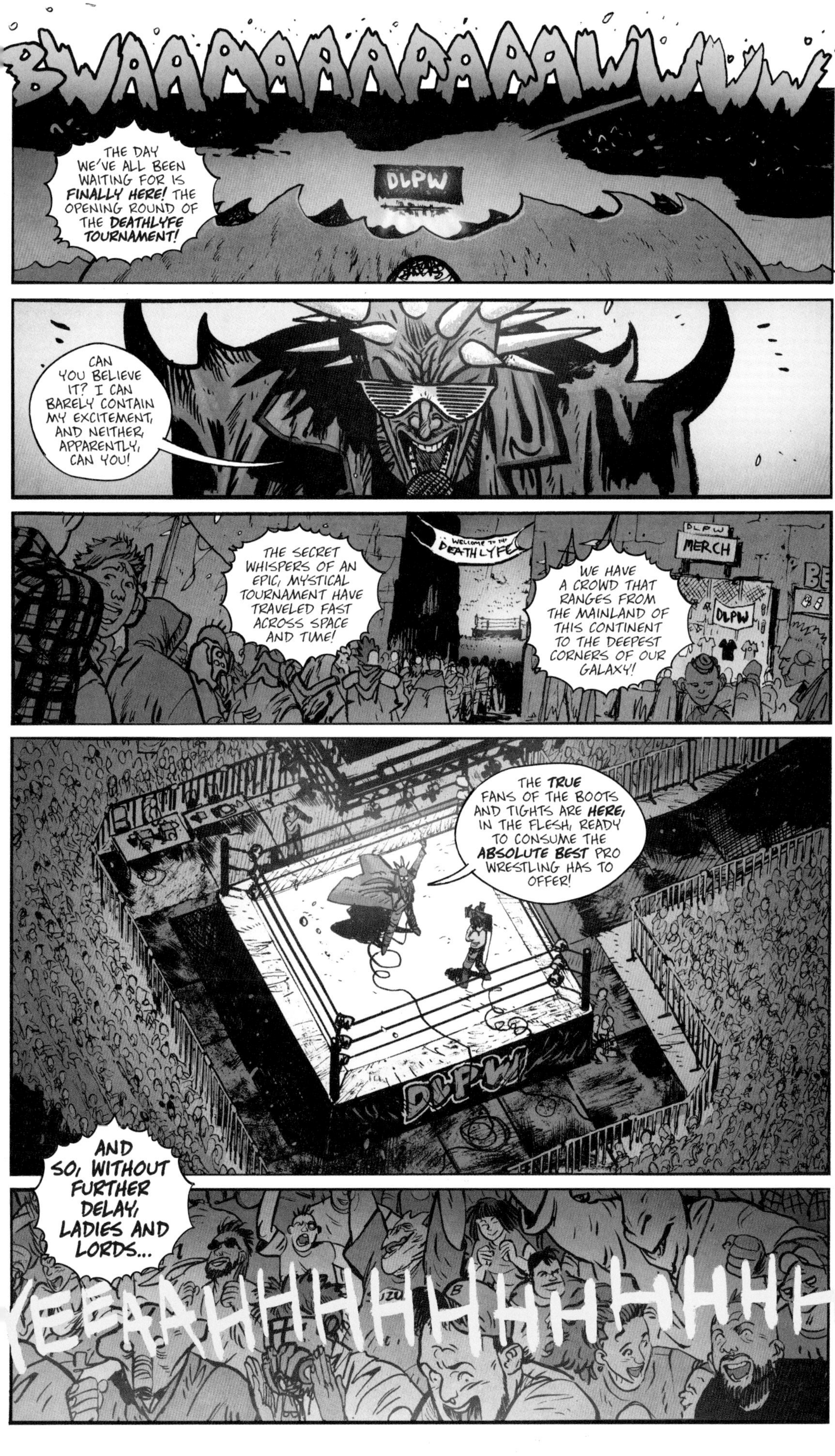
BWAAAAAAAAAAWWW
THE DAY WE'VE ALL BEEN WAITING FOR IS FINALLY HERE! THE OPENING ROUND OF THE DEATHLYFE TOURNAMENT!
DLPW
CAN YOU BELIEVE IT? I CAN BARELY CONTAIN MY EXCITEMENT, AND NEITHER, APPARENTLY, CAN YOU!
WELCOME TO THE DEATHLYFE
DLPW MERCH
THE SECRET WHISPERS OF AN EPIC, MYSTICAL TOURNAMENT HAVE TRAVELED FAST ACROSS SPACE AND TIME!
WE HAVE A CROWD THAT RANGES FROM THE MAINLAND OF THIS CONTINENT TO THE DEEPEST CORNERS OF OUR GALAXY!
THE TRUE FANS OF THE BOOTS AND TIGHTS ARE HERE, IN THE FLESH, READY TO CONSUME THE ABSOLUTE BEST PRO WRESTLING HAS TO OFFER!
DLPW
AND SO, WITHOUT FURTHER DELAY, LADIES AND LORDS...
YEEAAHHHHHHHHHHHH

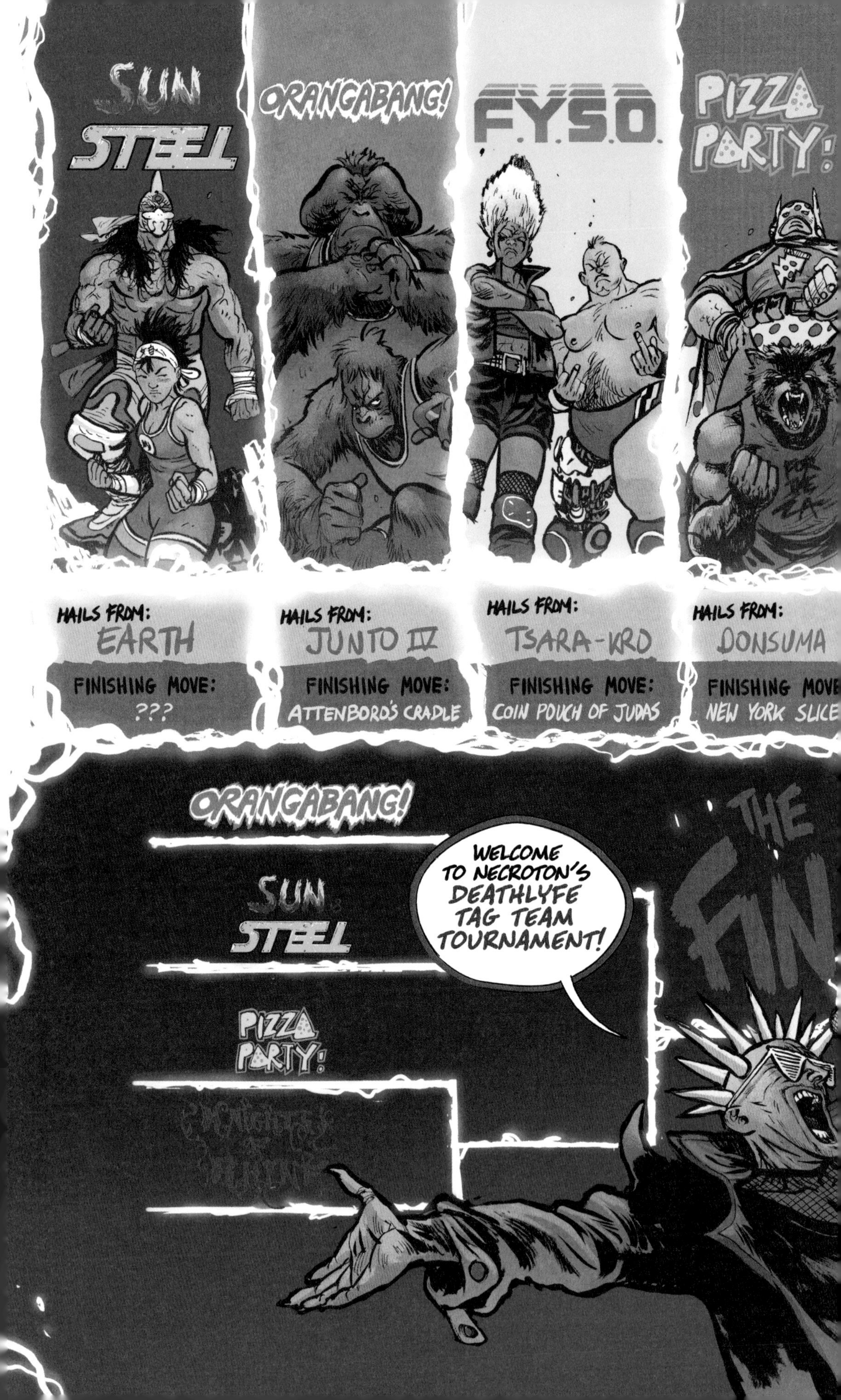

SUN STEEL
ORANGABANG!
F.Y.S.O.
PIZZA PARTY!
HAILS FROM: EARTH
FINISHING MOVE: ???
HAILS FROM: JUNTO IV
FINISHING MOVE: ATTENBORO'S CRADLE
HAILS FROM: TSARA-KRD
FINISHING MOVE: COIN POUCH OF JUDAS
HAILS FROM: DONSUMA
FINISHING MOVE: NEW YORK SLICE
ORANGABANG!
SUN STEEL
PIZZA PARTY!
THE
WELCOME TO NECROTON'S DEATHLYFE TAG TEAM TOURNAMENT!

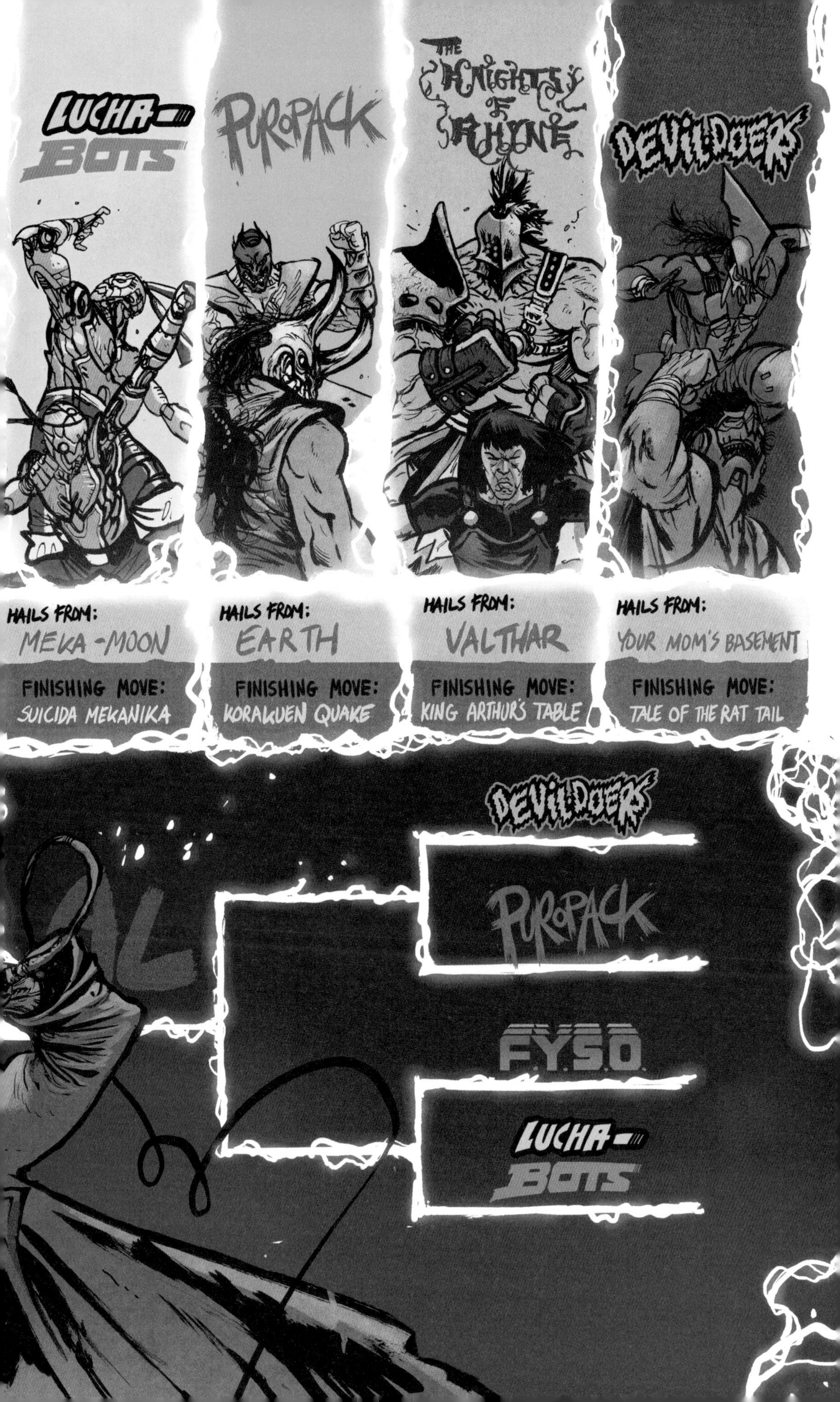

LUCHA-BOTS
PUROPACK
THE KNIGHTS OF RHYNE
DEVILDOERS
HAILS FROM:
MEKA-MOON
FINISHING MOVE:
SUICIDA MEKANIKA
HAILS FROM:
EARTH
FINISHING MOVE:
KORAKUEN QUAKE
HAILS FROM:
VALTHAR
FINISHING MOVE:
KING ARTHUR'S TABLE
HAILS FROM:
YOUR MOM'S BASEMENT
FINISHING MOVE:
TALE OF THE RAT TAIL
DEVILDOERS
PUROPACK
F.Y.S.O.
LUCHA-BOTS

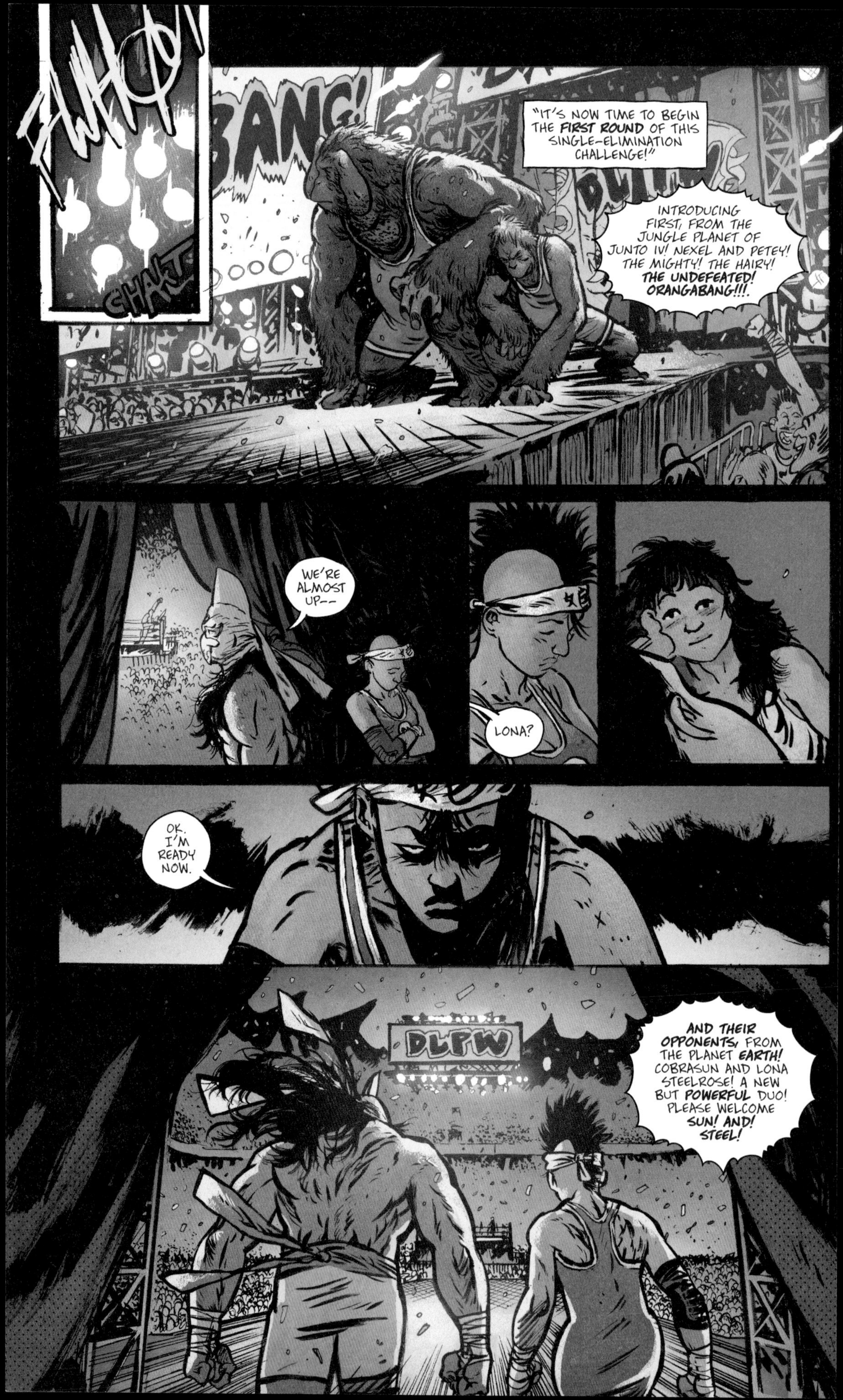
FWHOOM
BANG!
CHANT
"IT'S NOW TIME TO BEGIN THE **FIRST ROUND** OF THIS SINGLE-ELIMINATION CHALLENGE!"
INTRODUCING FIRST, FROM THE JUNGLE PLANET OF JUNTO IV! NEXEL AND PETEY! THE MIGHTY! THE HAIRY! **THE UNDEFEATED! ORANGABANG!!!**
WE'RE ALMOST UP--
LONA?
OK. I'M READY NOW.
DLPW
AND THEIR OPPONENTS, FROM THE PLANET **EARTH!** COBRASUN AND LONA STEELROSE! A NEW BUT **POWERFUL** DUO! PLEASE WELCOME **SUN! AND! STEEL!**

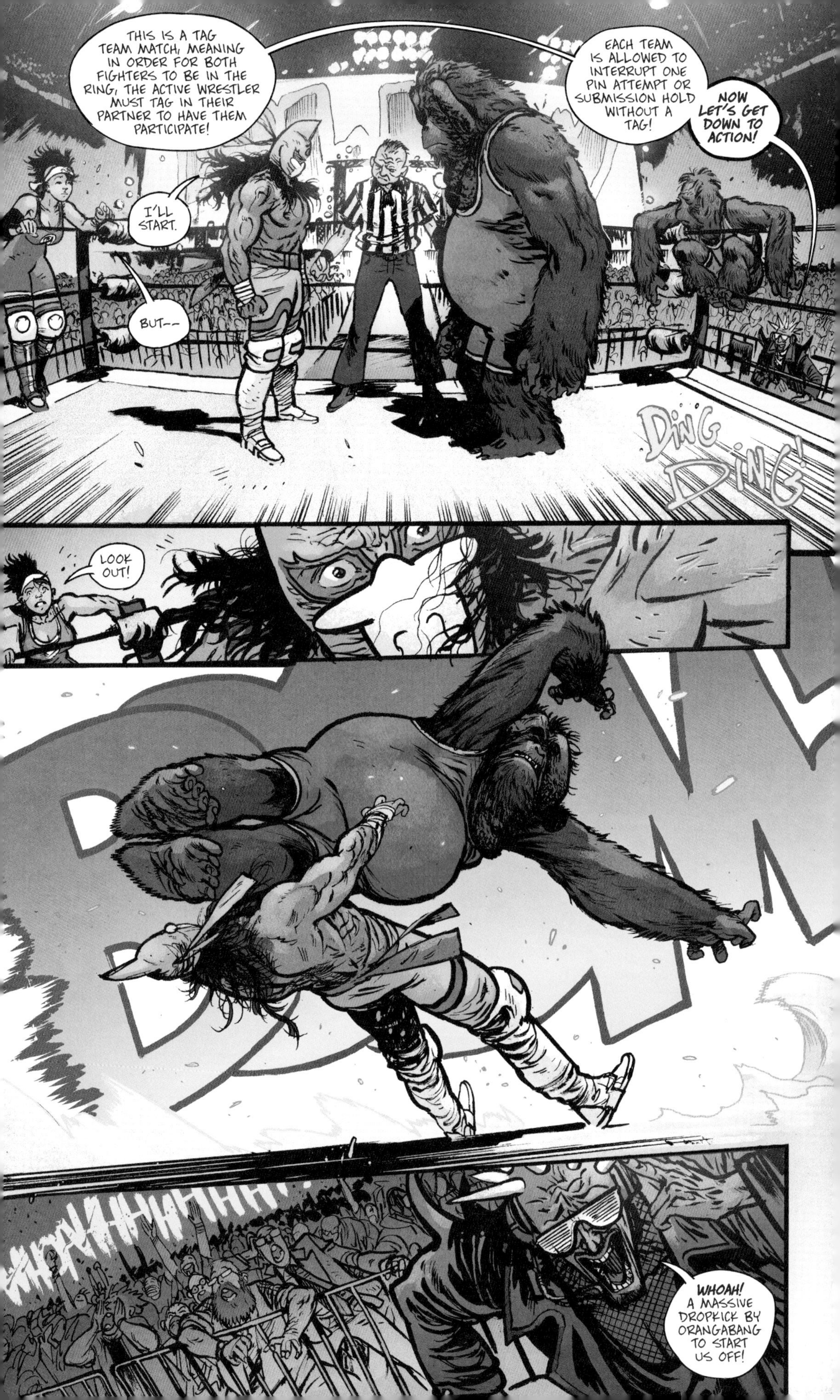

THIS IS A TAG TEAM MATCH, MEANING IN ORDER FOR BOTH FIGHTERS TO BE IN THE RING, THE ACTIVE WRESTLER MUST TAG IN THEIR PARTNER TO HAVE THEM PARTICIPATE!
EACH TEAM IS ALLOWED TO INTERRUPT ONE PIN ATTEMPT OR SUBMISSION HOLD WITHOUT A TAG!
NOW LET'S GET DOWN TO ACTION!
I'LL START.
BUT--
DING DING!
LOOK OUT!
WHOAH! A MASSIVE DROPKICK BY ORANGABANG TO START US OFF!

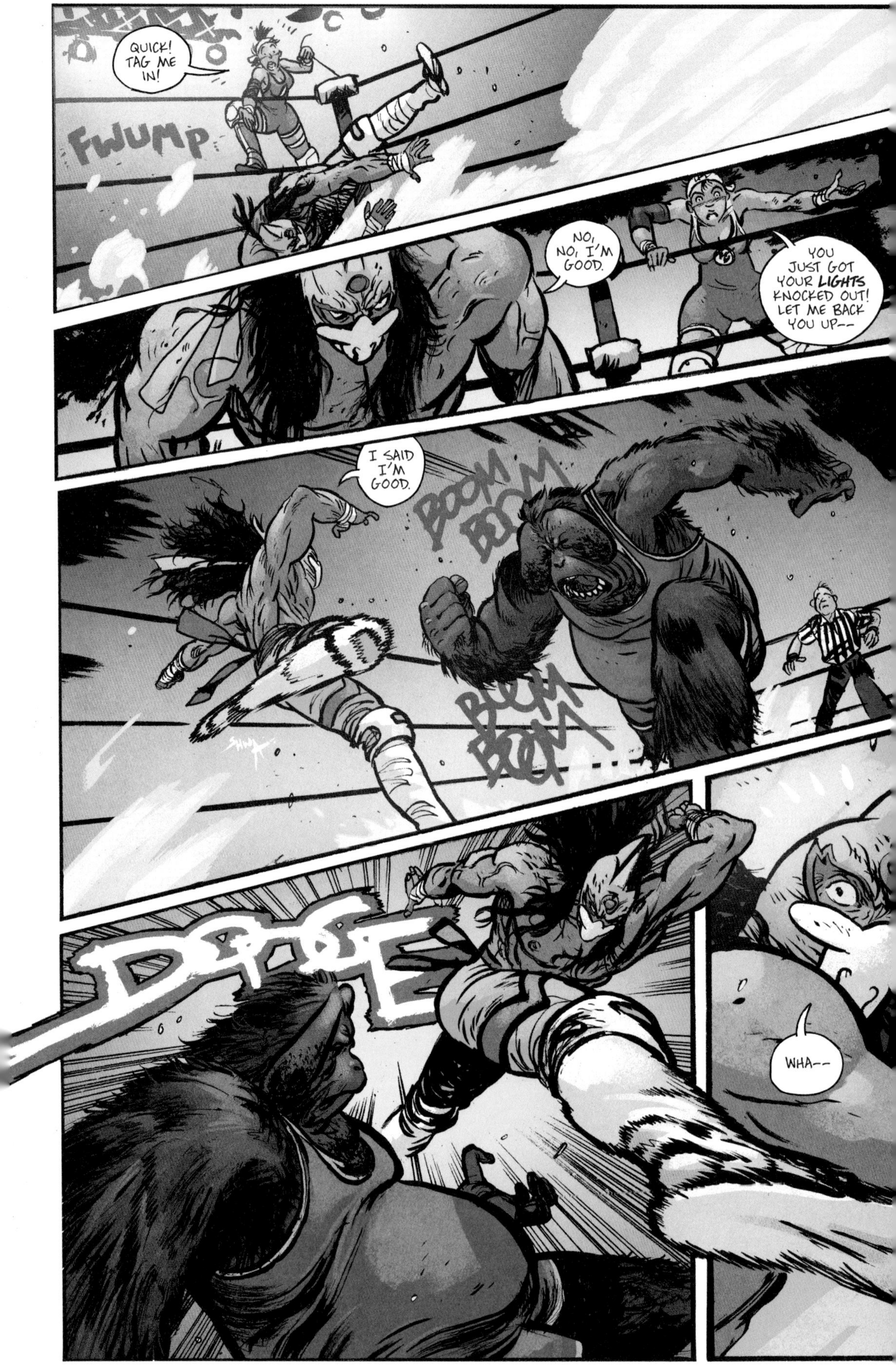
QUICK! TAG ME IN!
FWUMP
NO, NO, I'M GOOD.
YOU JUST GOT YOUR **LIGHTS** KNOCKED OUT! LET ME BACK YOU UP--
I SAID I'M GOOD.
BOOM BOOM
BOOM BOOM
WHA--

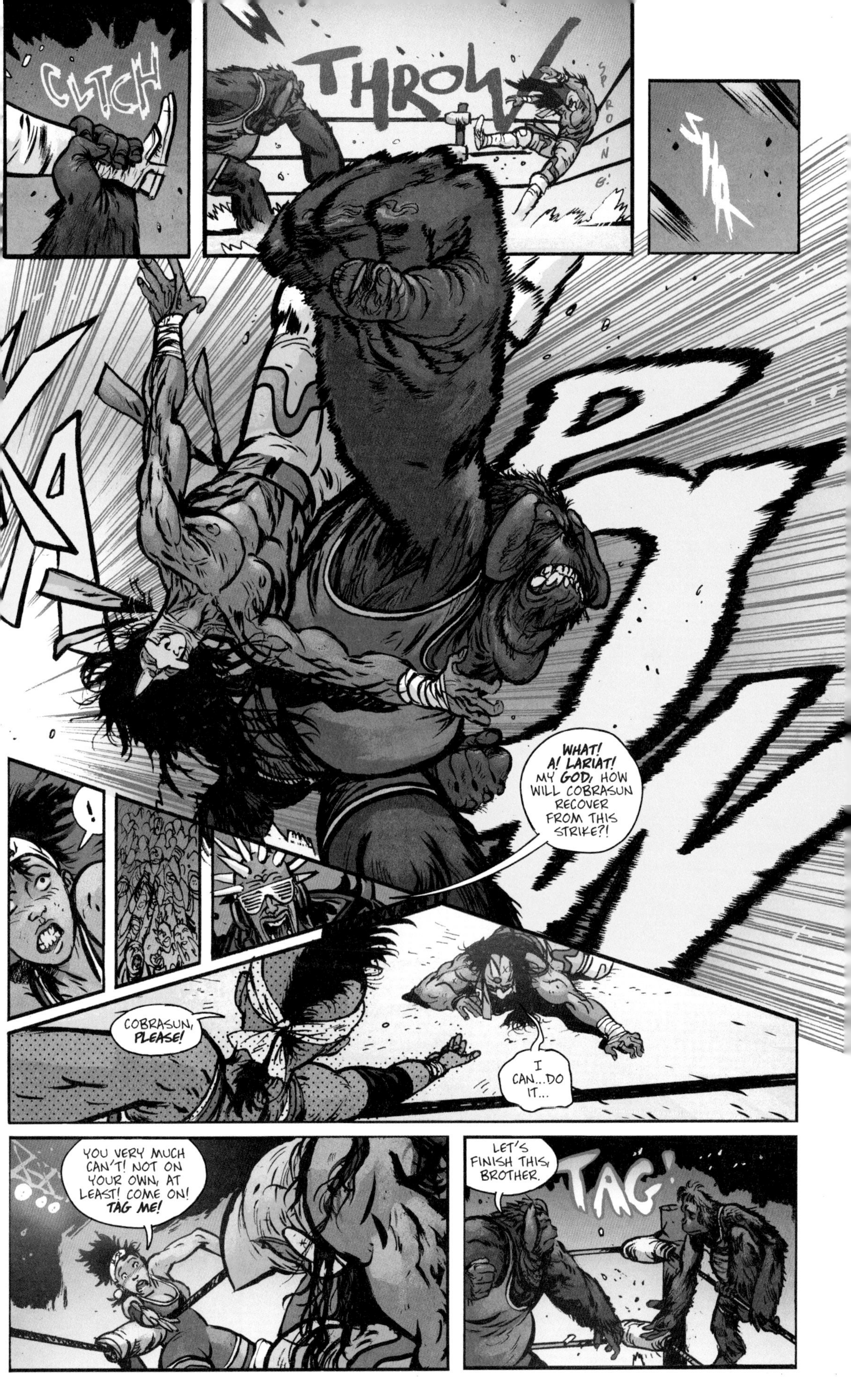
CLTCH
THROW
SPROING!
SHA
WHAT! A! LARIAT! MY GOD, HOW WILL COBRASUN RECOVER FROM THIS STRIKE?!
!
COBRASUN, PLEASE!
I CAN...DO IT...
YOU VERY MUCH CAN'T! NOT ON YOUR OWN, AT LEAST! COME ON! TAG ME!
LET'S FINISH THIS, BROTHER.
TAG!

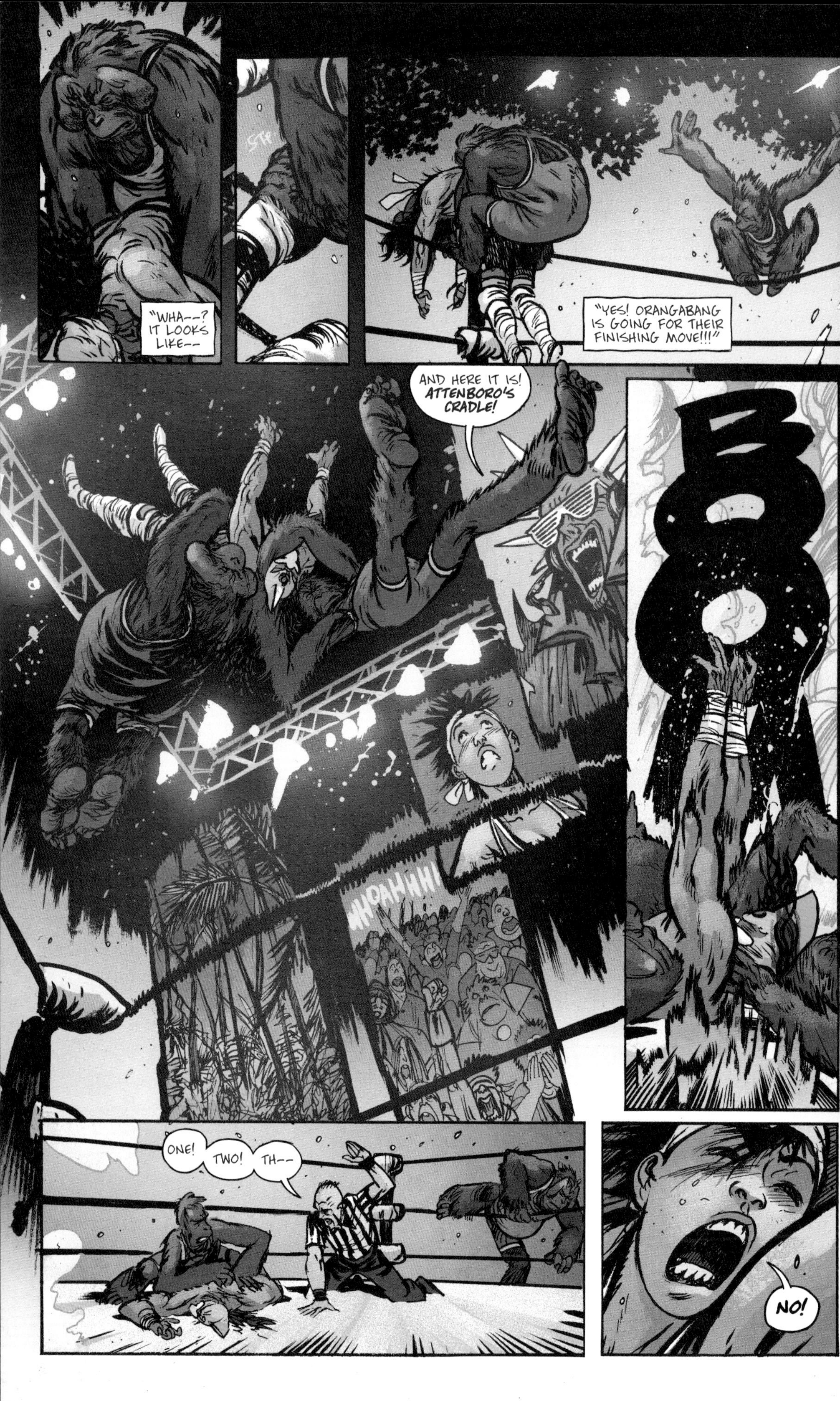
"WHA--? IT LOOKS LIKE--
"YES! ORANGABANG IS GOING FOR THEIR FINISHING MOVE!!!"
AND HERE IT IS! **ATTENBORO'S CRADLE!**
WHOAHHH!
ONE!
TWO!
TH--
NO!

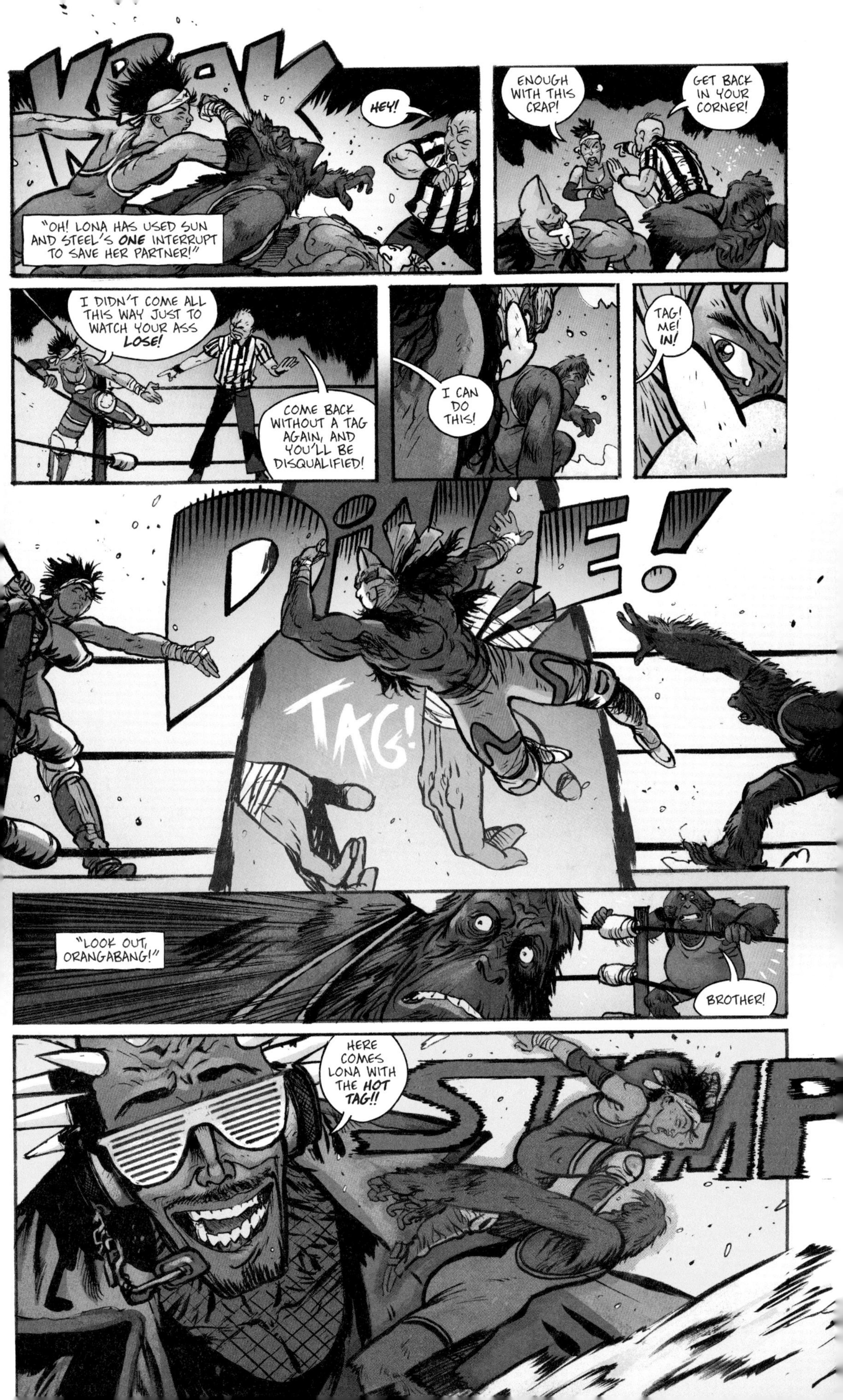
KRAK
"OH! LONA HAS USED SUN AND STEEL'S ONE INTERRUPT TO SAVE HER PARTNER!"
HEY!
ENOUGH WITH THIS CRAP!
GET BACK IN YOUR CORNER!
I DIDN'T COME ALL THIS WAY JUST TO WATCH YOUR ASS LOSE!
COME BACK WITHOUT A TAG AGAIN, AND YOU'LL BE DISQUALIFIED!
I CAN DO THIS!
TAG! ME! IN!
DIVE!
TAG!
"LOOK OUT, ORANGABANG!"
BROTHER!
HERE COMES LONA WITH THE HOT TAG!!
STMP

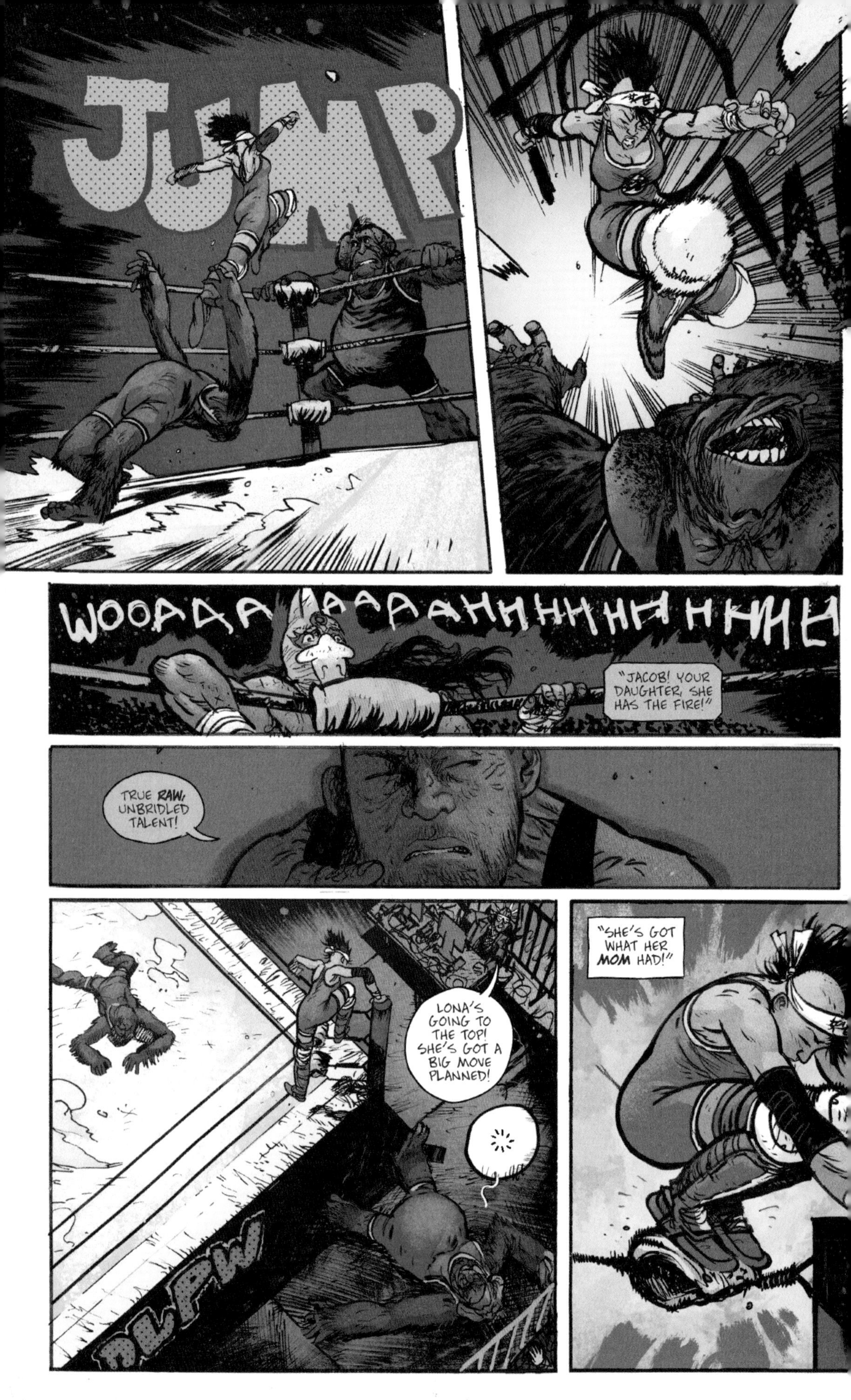
JUMP
WOOAAAAAAAAHHHHHHHHHHH
"JACOB! YOUR DAUGHTER, SHE HAS THE FIRE!"
TRUE RAW, UNBRIDLED TALENT!
LONA'S GOING TO THE TOP! SHE'S GOT A BIG MOVE PLANNED!
"SHE'S GOT WHAT HER MOM HAD!"
DLPW

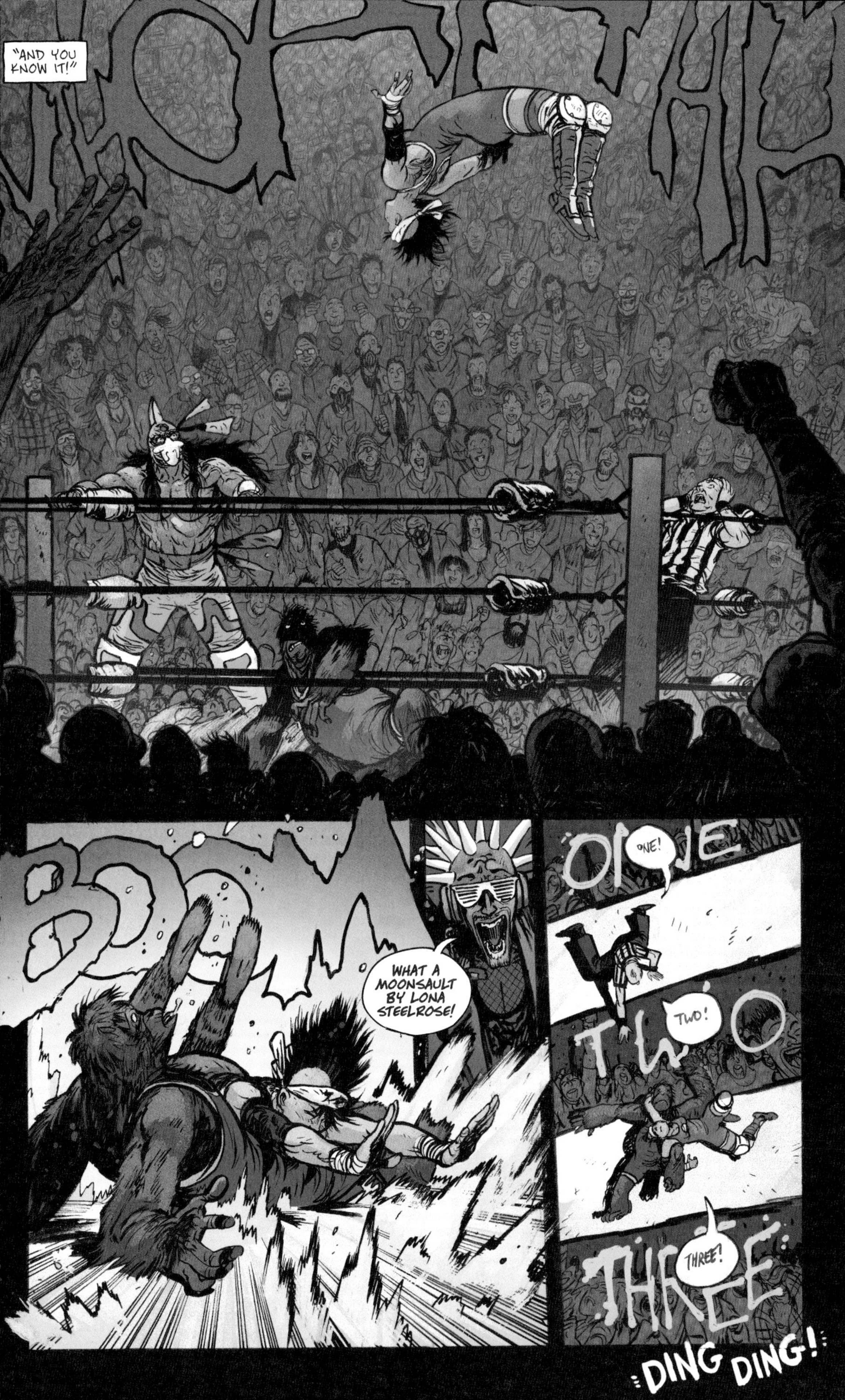
"AND YOU KNOW IT!"
WHAT A MOONSAULT BY LONA STEELROSE!
ONE
ONE!
TWO!
TWO
THREE!
THREE
DING DING!

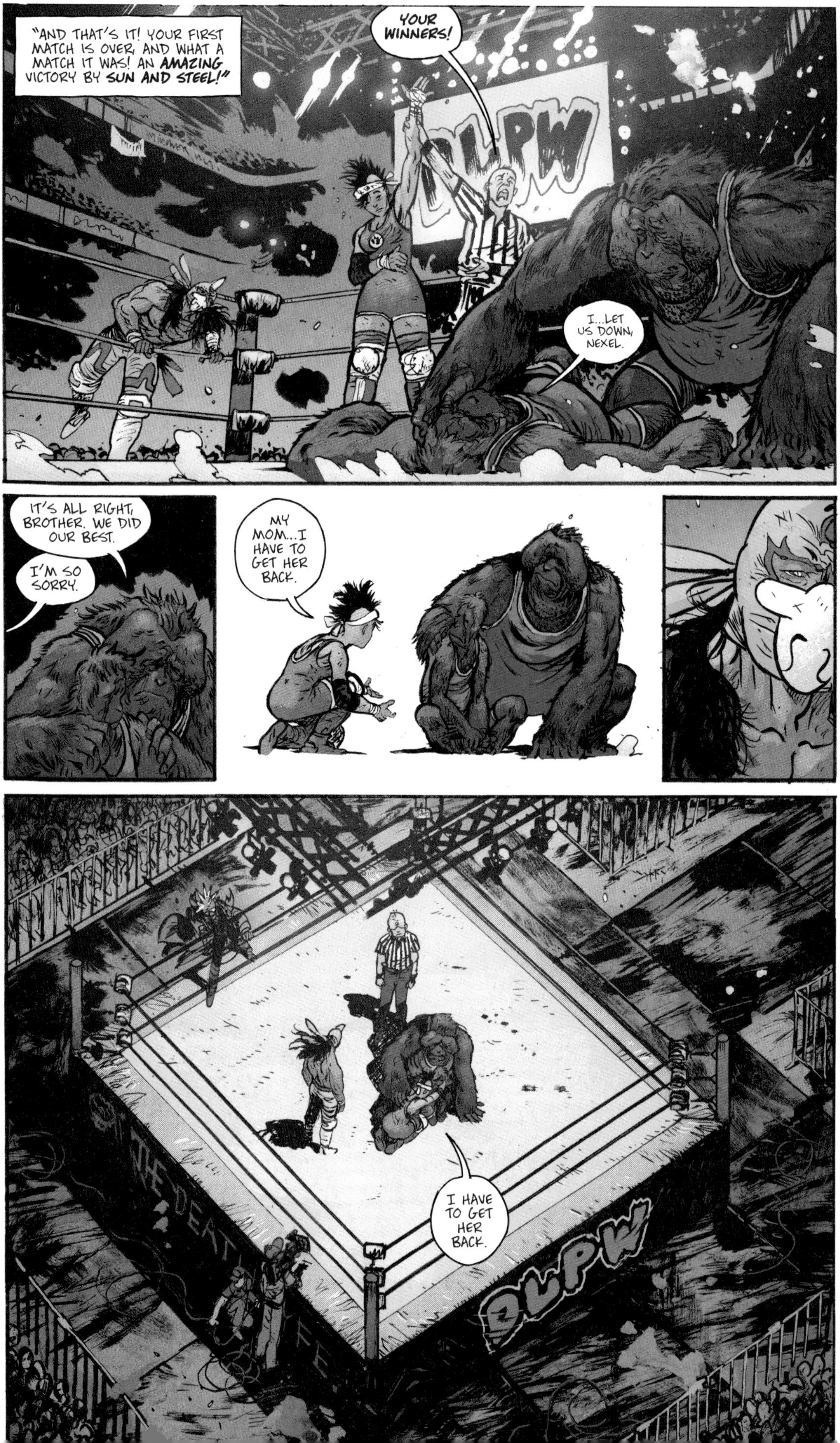
"AND THAT'S IT! YOUR FIRST MATCH IS OVER, AND WHAT A MATCH IT WAS! AN AMAZING VICTORY BY SUN AND STEEL!"
YOUR WINNERS!
DLPW
I...LET US DOWN, NEXEL.
IT'S ALL RIGHT, BROTHER. WE DID OUR BEST.
I'M SO SORRY.
MY MOM...I HAVE TO GET HER BACK.
I HAVE TO GET HER BACK.
DLPW

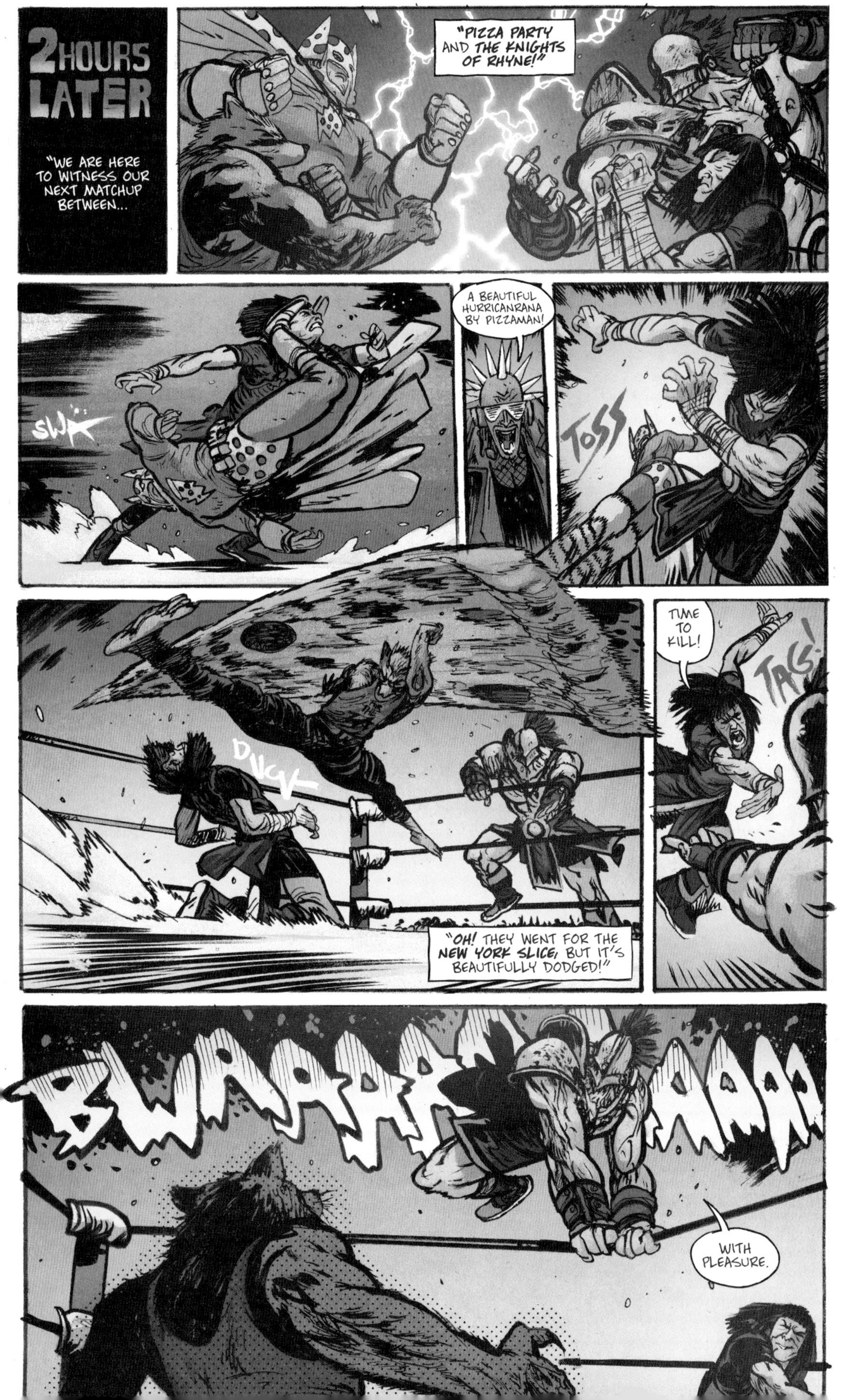
2 HOURS LATER
"WE ARE HERE TO WITNESS OUR NEXT MATCHUP BETWEEN...
"PIZZA PARTY AND THE KNIGHTS OF RHYNE!"
SWA
A BEAUTIFUL HURRICANRANA BY PIZZAMAN!
TOSS
DUCK
"OH! THEY WENT FOR THE NEW YORK SLICE, BUT IT'S BEAUTIFULLY DODGED!"
TIME TO KILL!
TAG!
WITH PLEASURE.

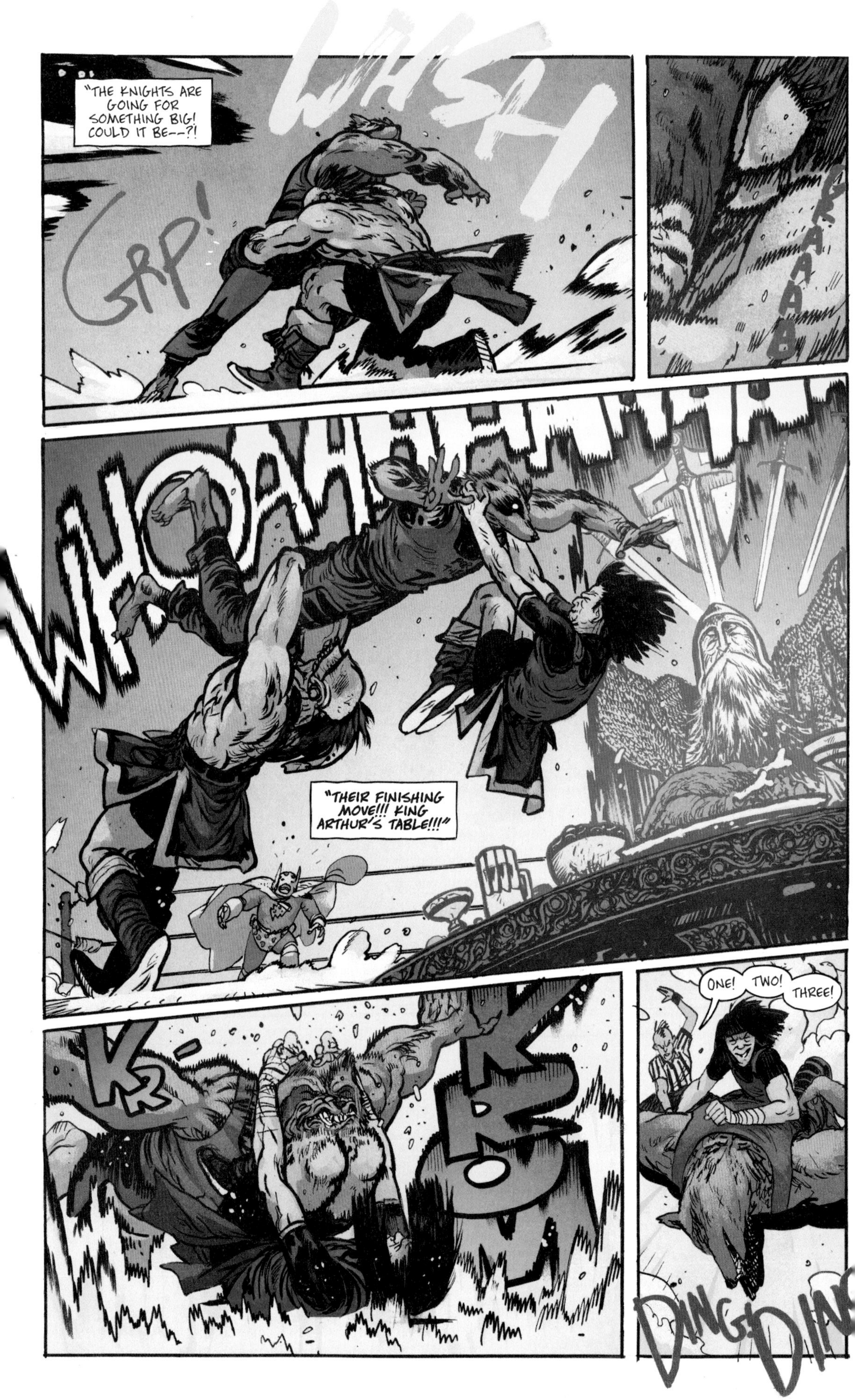
"THE KNIGHTS ARE GOING FOR SOMETHING BIG! COULD IT BE--?!
WHSH
GRP!
KRAAAAB
WHOAHHHHH
"THEIR FINISHING MOVE!!! KING ARTHUR'S TABLE!!!"
KR-
KROOM
ONE!
TWO!
THREE!
DING DING

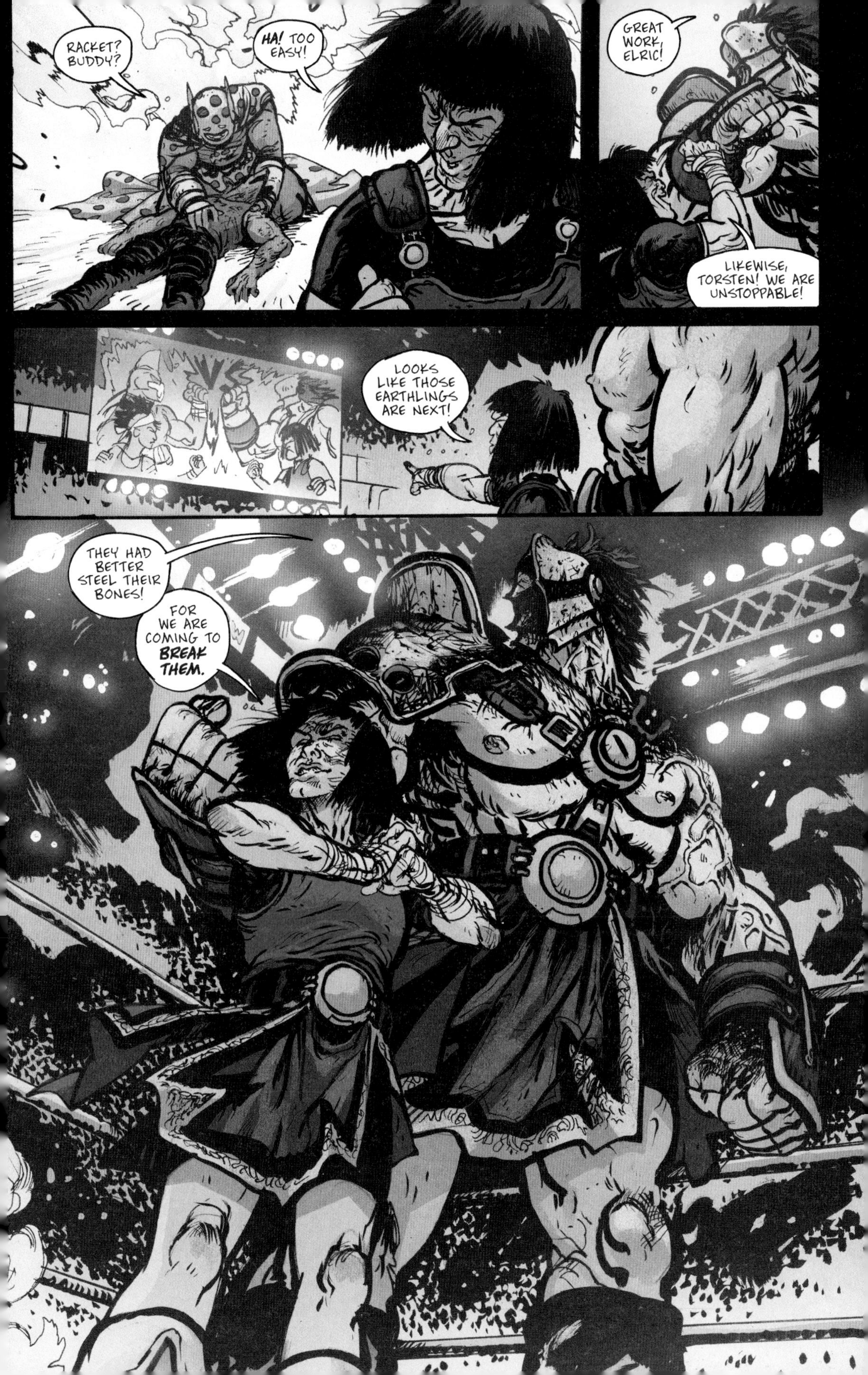
RACKET? BUDDY?
HA! TOO EASY!
GREAT WORK, ELRIC!
LIKEWISE, TORSTEN! WE ARE UNSTOPPABLE!
LOOKS LIKE THOSE EARTHLINGS ARE NEXT!
THEY HAD BETTER STEEL THEIR BONES!
FOR WE ARE COMING TO BREAK THEM.

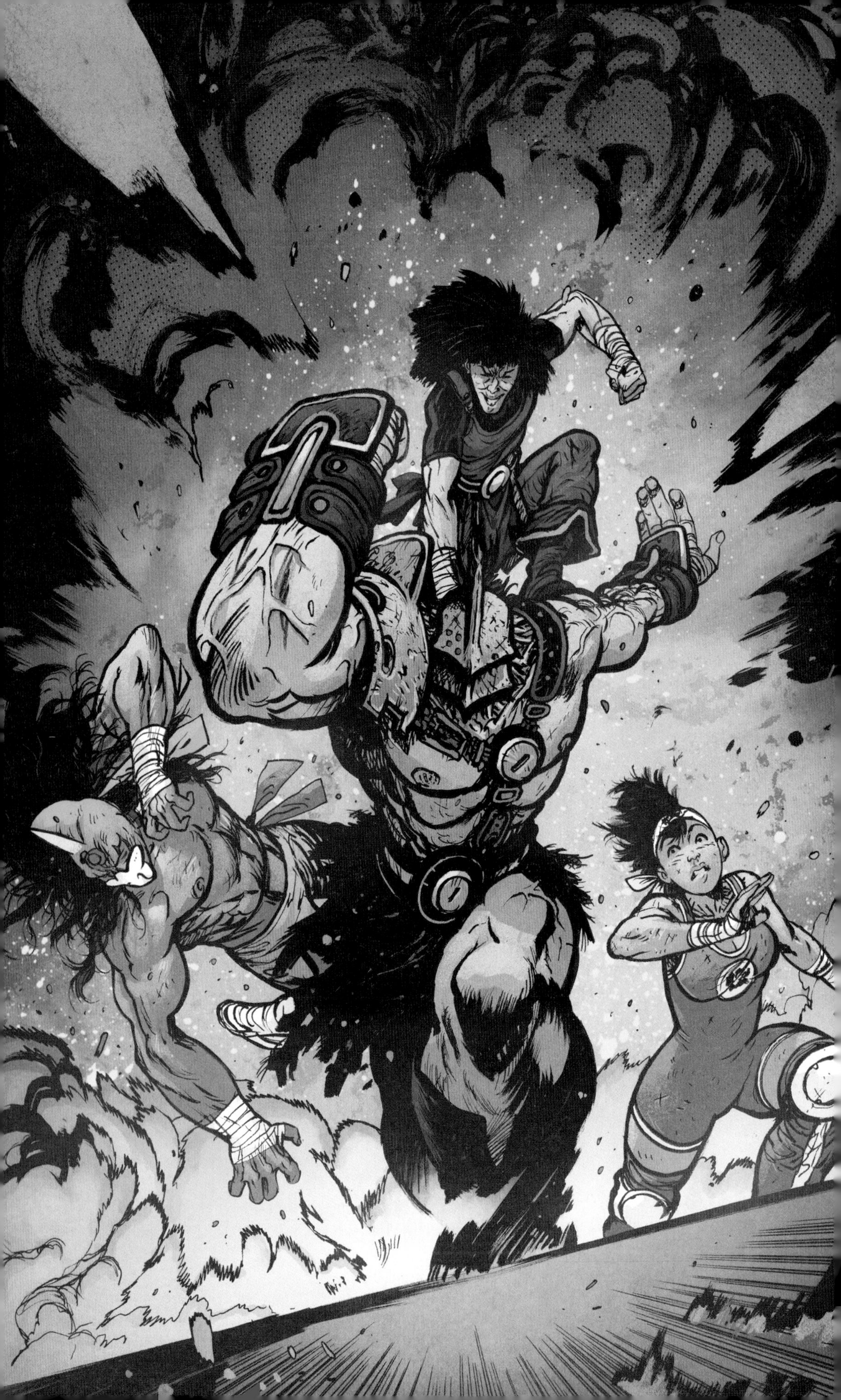

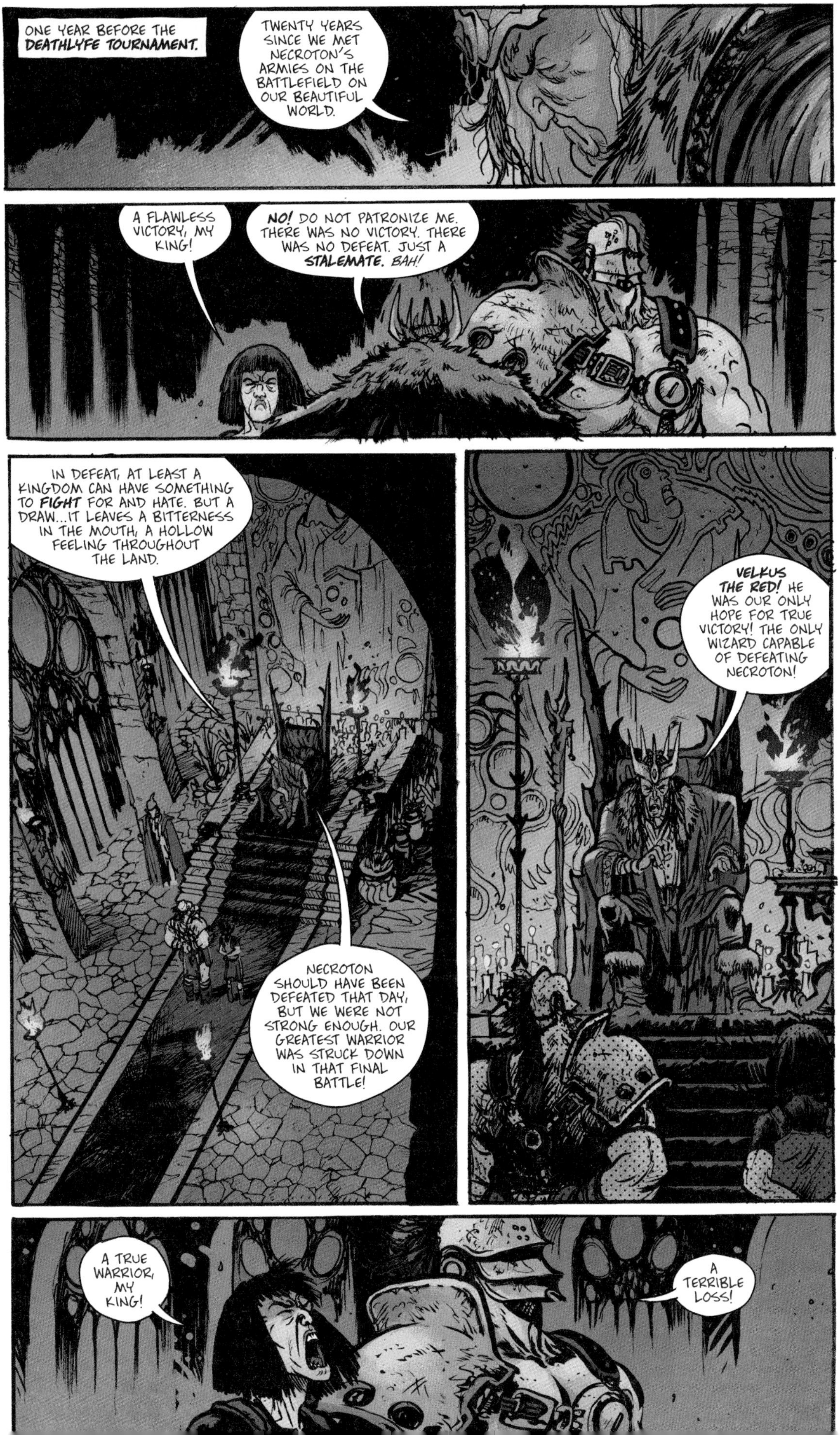
ONE YEAR BEFORE THE DEATHLYFE TOURNAMENT.
TWENTY YEARS SINCE WE MET NECROTON'S ARMIES ON THE BATTLEFIELD ON OUR BEAUTIFUL WORLD.
A FLAWLESS VICTORY, MY KING!
NO! DO NOT PATRONIZE ME. THERE WAS NO VICTORY. THERE WAS NO DEFEAT. JUST A STALEMATE. BAH!
IN DEFEAT, AT LEAST A KINGDOM CAN HAVE SOMETHING TO FIGHT FOR AND HATE. BUT A DRAW...IT LEAVES A BITTERNESS IN THE MOUTH, A HOLLOW FEELING THROUGHOUT THE LAND.
NECROTON SHOULD HAVE BEEN DEFEATED THAT DAY, BUT WE WERE NOT STRONG ENOUGH. OUR GREATEST WARRIOR WAS STRUCK DOWN IN THAT FINAL BATTLE!
VELKUS THE RED! HE WAS OUR ONLY HOPE FOR TRUE VICTORY! THE ONLY WIZARD CAPABLE OF DEFEATING NECROTON!
A TRUE WARRIOR, MY KING!
A TERRIBLE LOSS!

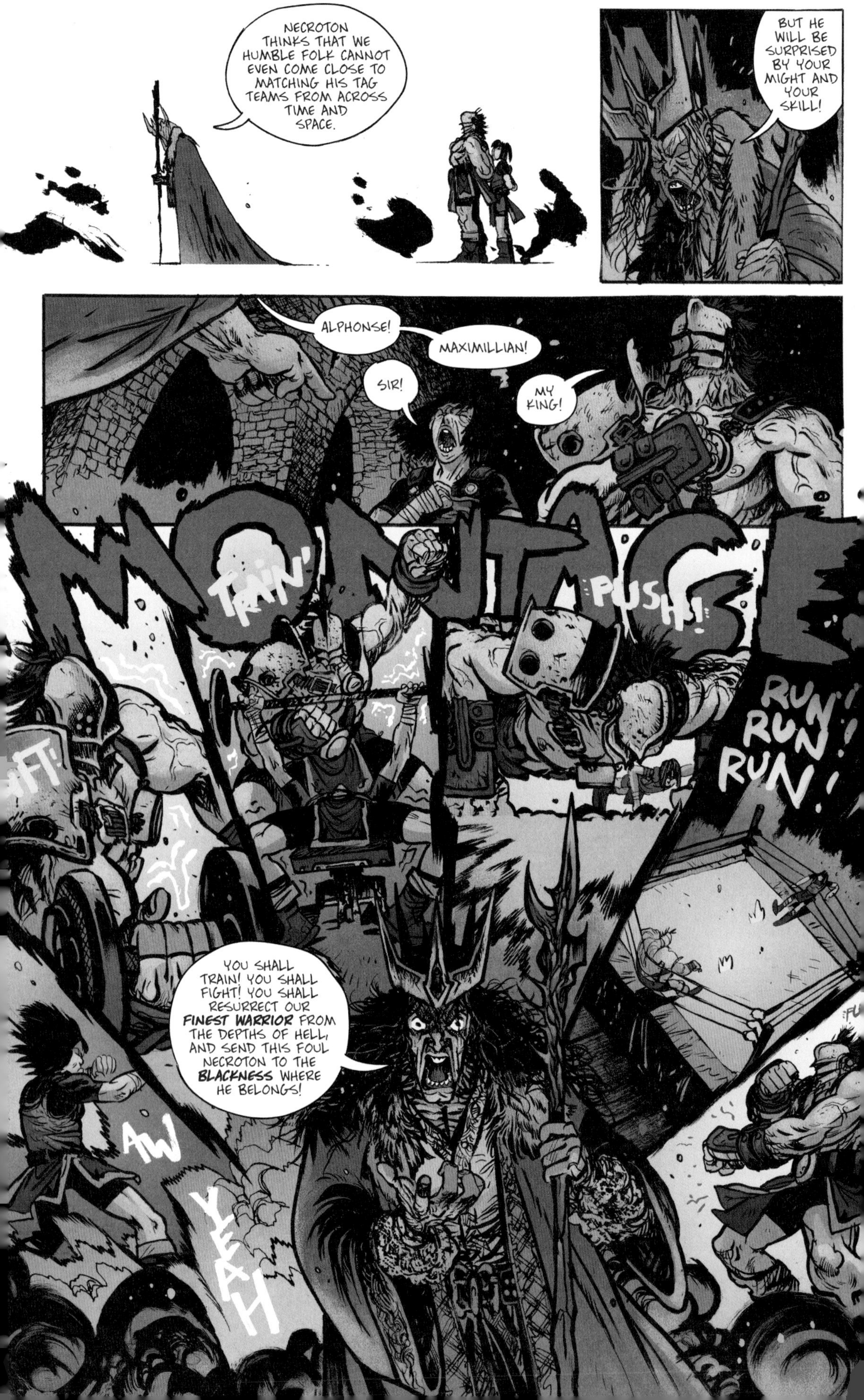
NECROTON THINKS THAT WE HUMBLE FOLK CANNOT EVEN COME CLOSE TO MATCHING HIS TAG TEAMS FROM ACROSS TIME AND SPACE.
BUT HE WILL BE SURPRISED BY YOUR MIGHT AND YOUR SKILL!
ALPHONSE!
MAXIMILLIAN!
SIR!
MY KING!
MONTAGE
TRAIN'
PUSH!
RUN RUN RUN!
YOU SHALL TRAIN! YOU SHALL FIGHT! YOU SHALL RESURRECT OUR **FINEST WARRIOR** FROM THE DEPTHS OF HELL, AND SEND THIS FOUL NECROTON TO THE **BLACKNESS** WHERE HE BELONGS!
AW YEAH

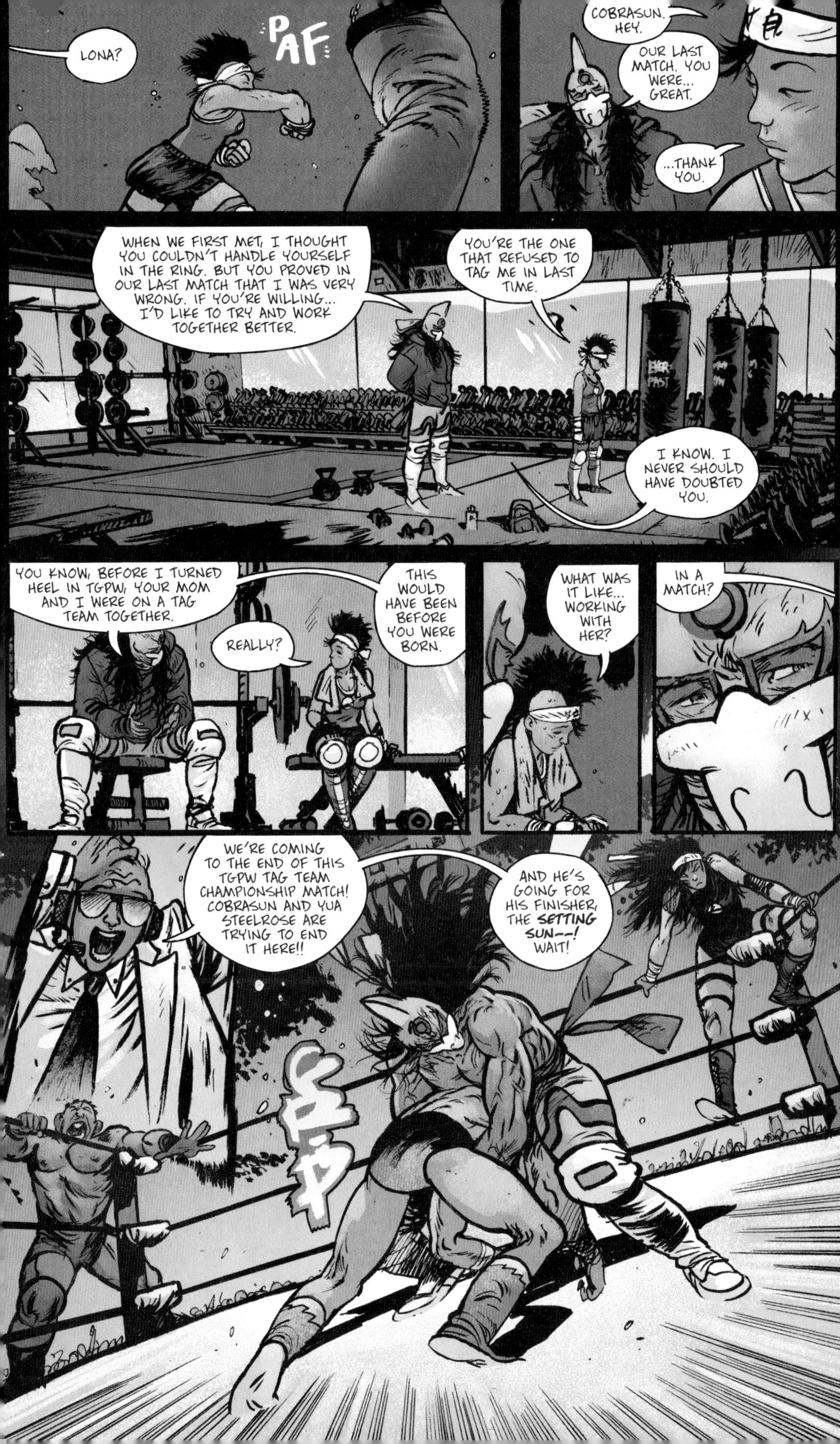
LONA?
PAF
COBRASUN. HEY.
OUR LAST MATCH. YOU WERE... GREAT.
...THANK YOU.
WHEN WE FIRST MET, I THOUGHT YOU COULDN'T HANDLE YOURSELF IN THE RING. BUT YOU PROVED IN OUR LAST MATCH THAT I WAS VERY WRONG. IF YOU'RE WILLING... I'D LIKE TO TRY AND WORK TOGETHER BETTER.
YOU'RE THE ONE THAT REFUSED TO TAG ME IN LAST TIME.
I KNOW. I NEVER SHOULD HAVE DOUBTED YOU.
YOU KNOW, BEFORE I TURNED HEEL IN TGPW, YOUR MOM AND I WERE ON A TAG TEAM TOGETHER.
THIS WOULD HAVE BEEN BEFORE YOU WERE BORN.
REALLY?
WHAT WAS IT LIKE... WORKING WITH HER?
IN A MATCH?
WE'RE COMING TO THE END OF THIS TGPW TAG TEAM CHAMPIONSHIP MATCH! COBRASUN AND YUA STEELROSE ARE TRYING TO END IT HERE!!
AND HE'S GOING FOR HIS FINISHER, THE **SETTING SUN--!** WAIT!

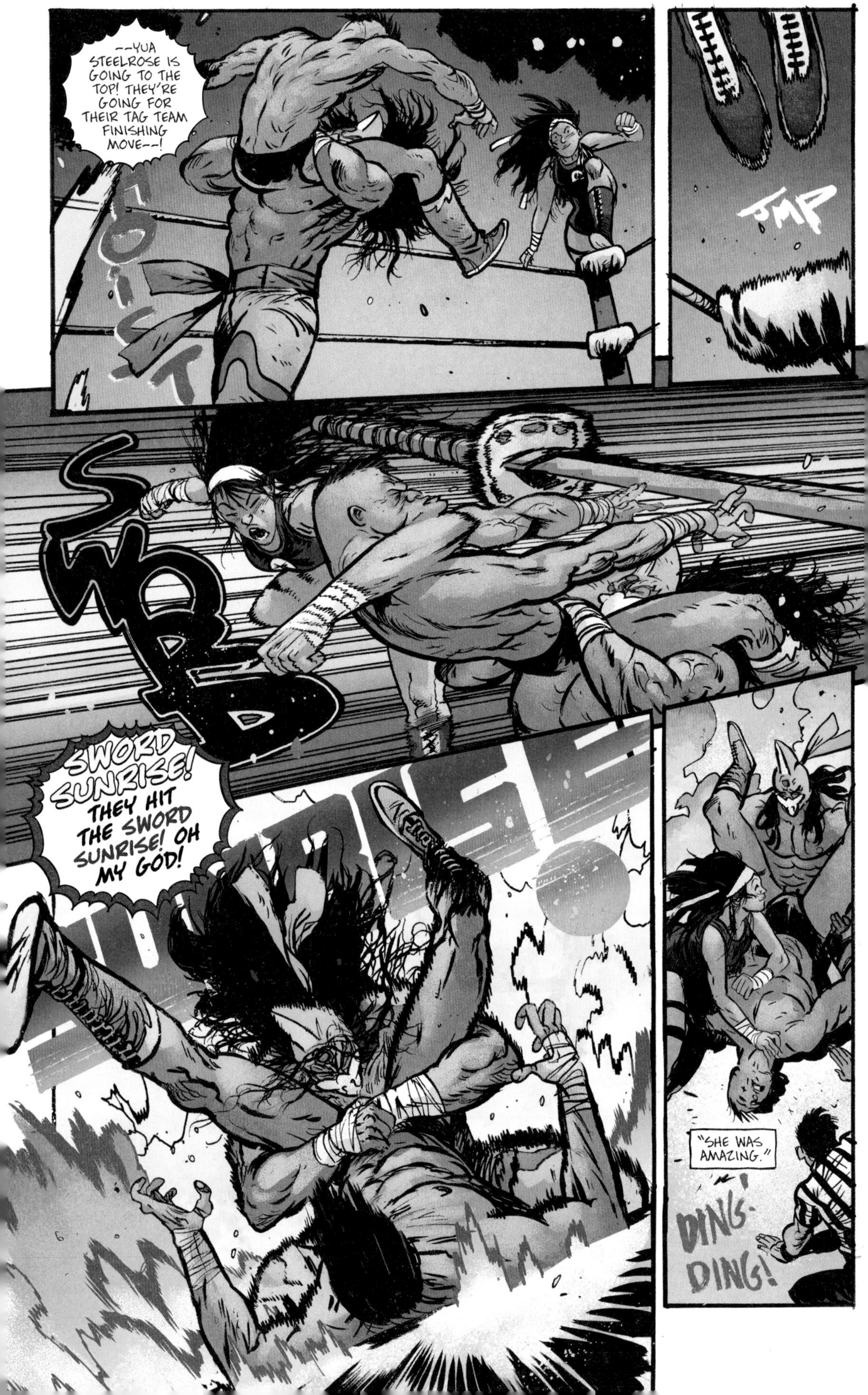
--YUA STEELROSE IS GOING TO THE TOP! THEY'RE GOING FOR THEIR TAG TEAM FINISHING MOVE--!
HOIST
JMP
SWORD
SWORD SUNRISE! THEY HIT THE SWORD SUNRISE! OH MY GOD!
"SHE WAS AMAZING."
DING-DING!

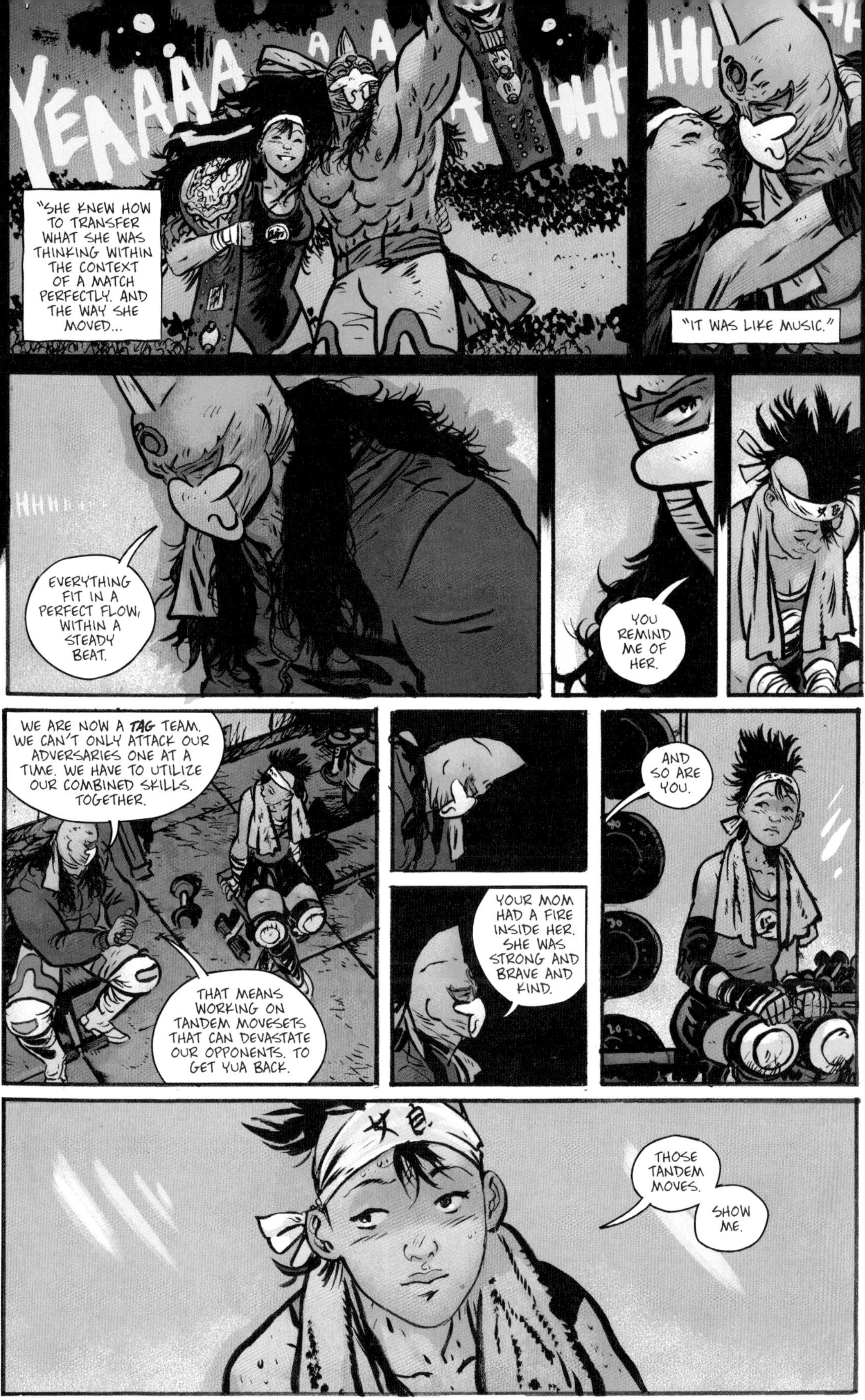
YEAAAAAAAAHHHHHH
"SHE KNEW HOW TO TRANSFER WHAT SHE WAS THINKING WITHIN THE CONTEXT OF A MATCH PERFECTLY. AND THE WAY SHE MOVED...
"IT WAS LIKE MUSIC."
EVERYTHING FIT IN A PERFECT FLOW, WITHIN A STEADY BEAT.
YOU REMIND ME OF HER.
WE ARE NOW A *TAG* TEAM. WE CAN'T ONLY ATTACK OUR ADVERSARIES ONE AT A TIME. WE HAVE TO UTILIZE OUR COMBINED SKILLS. TOGETHER.
THAT MEANS WORKING ON TANDEM MOVESETS THAT CAN DEVASTATE OUR OPPONENTS. TO GET YUA BACK.
YOUR MOM HAD A FIRE INSIDE HER. SHE WAS STRONG AND BRAVE AND KIND.
AND SO ARE YOU.
THOSE TANDEM MOVES.
SHOW ME.

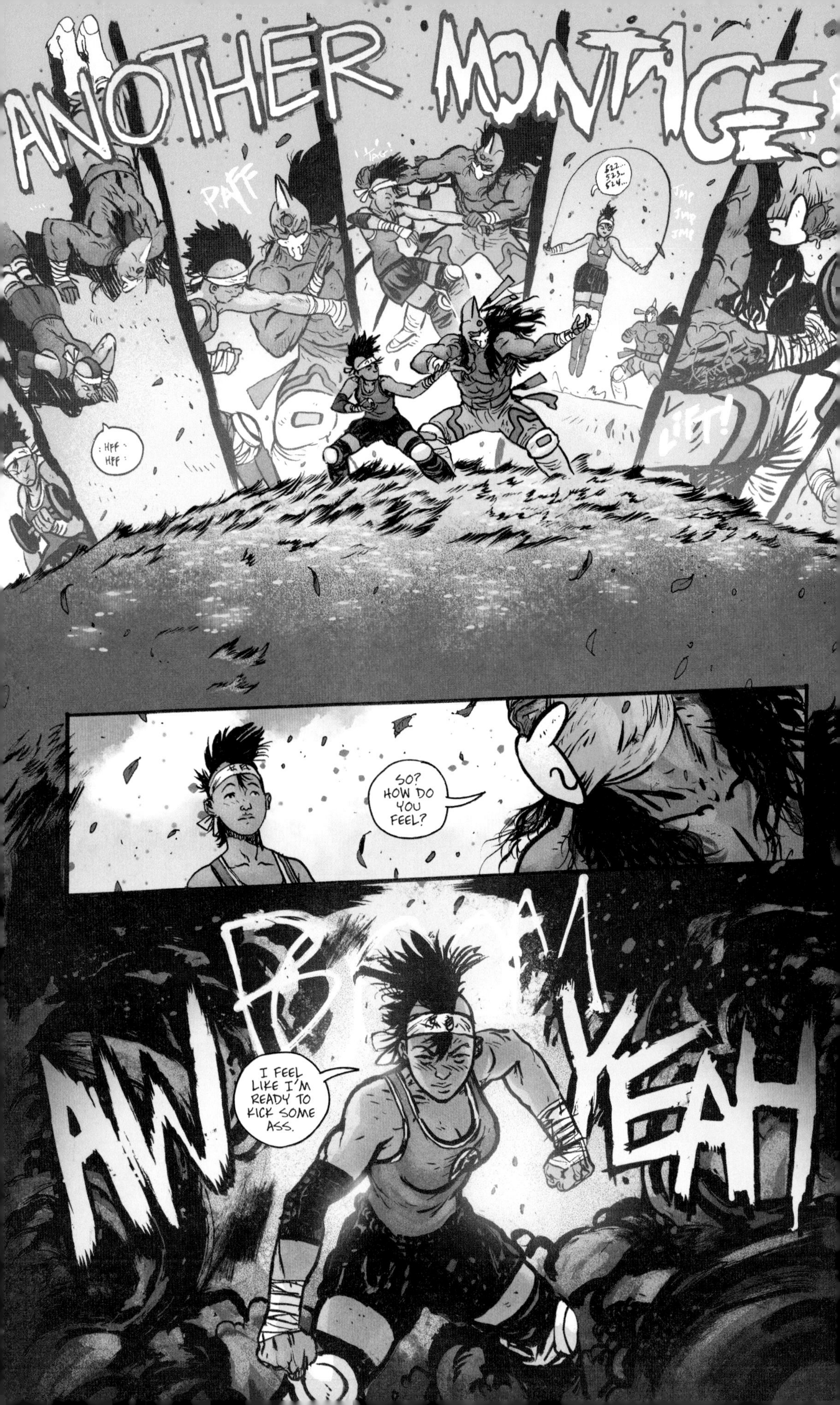
ANOTHER MONTAGE!
...
PAFF
TAG!
522... 523... 524...
JMP JMP JMP
HFF HFF
LIFT!
SO? HOW DO YOU FEEL?
I FEEL LIKE I'M READY TO KICK SOME ASS.
AW YEAH

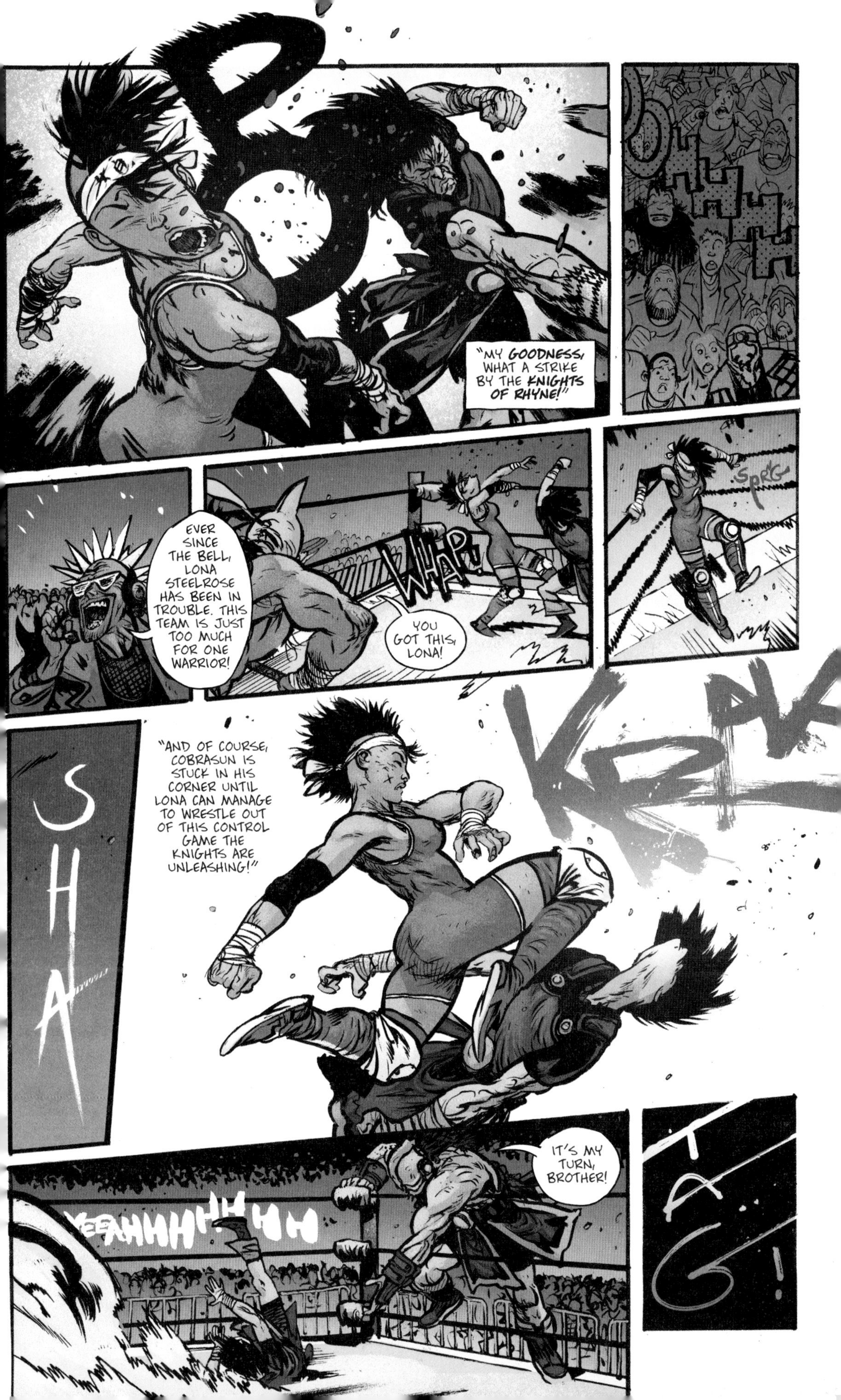
"MY GOODNESS, WHAT A STRIKE BY THE KNIGHTS OF RHYNE!"
EVER SINCE THE BELL, LONA STEELROSE HAS BEEN IN TROUBLE. THIS TEAM IS JUST TOO MUCH FOR ONE WARRIOR!
WHAP!
YOU GOT THIS, LONA!
SPRG
"AND OF COURSE, COBRASUN IS STUCK IN HIS CORNER UNTIL LONA CAN MANAGE TO WRESTLE OUT OF THIS CONTROL GAME THE KNIGHTS ARE UNLEASHING!"
SHA
IT'S MY TURN, BROTHER!
YEAHHHH!HHHH
TAG!

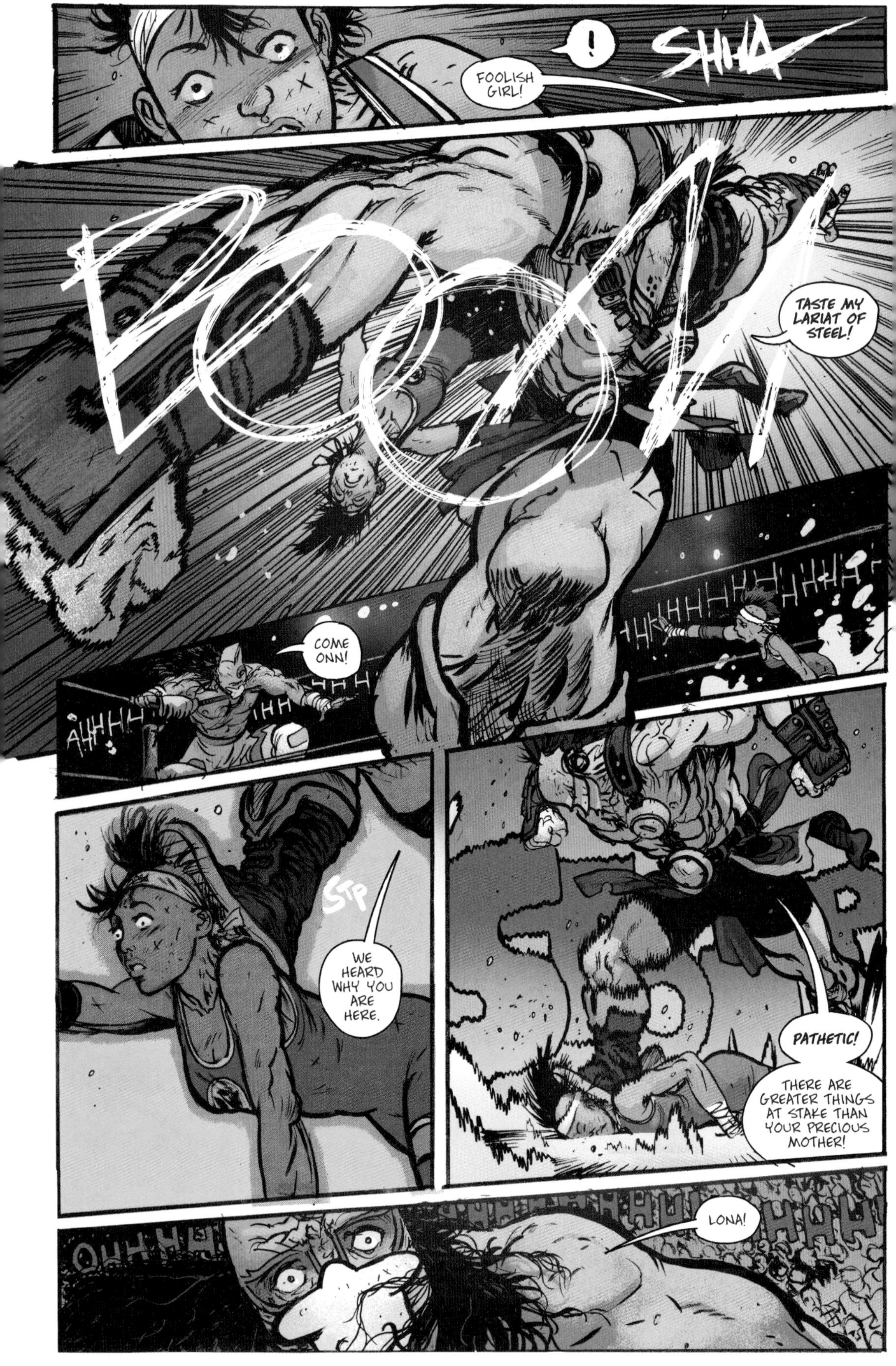

!
SHHA
FOOLISH GIRL!
BOOM
TASTE MY LARIAT OF STEEL!
COME ONN!
AHHHH
STP
WE HEARD WHY YOU ARE HERE.
PATHETIC!
THERE ARE GREATER THINGS AT STAKE THAN YOUR PRECIOUS MOTHER!
LONA!

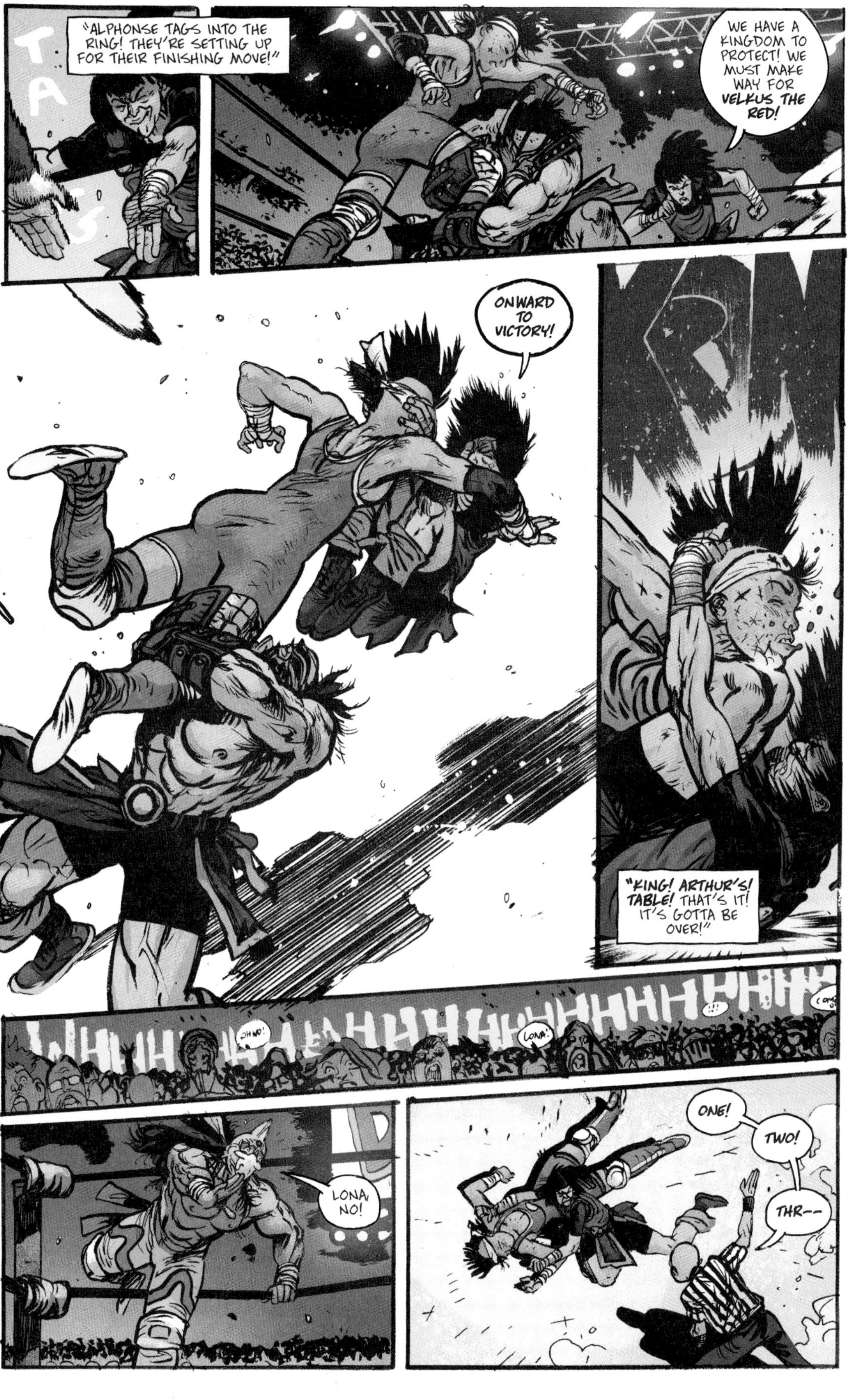
"ALPHONSE TAGS INTO THE RING! THEY'RE SETTING UP FOR THEIR FINISHING MOVE!"
TAG
WE HAVE A KINGDOM TO PROTECT! WE MUST MAKE WAY FOR VELKUS THE RED!
ONWARD TO VICTORY!
"KING! ARTHUR'S! TABLE! THAT'S IT! IT'S GOTTA BE OVER!"
OH NO!
LONA!
!!!
LONA, NO!
ONE!
TWO!
THR--

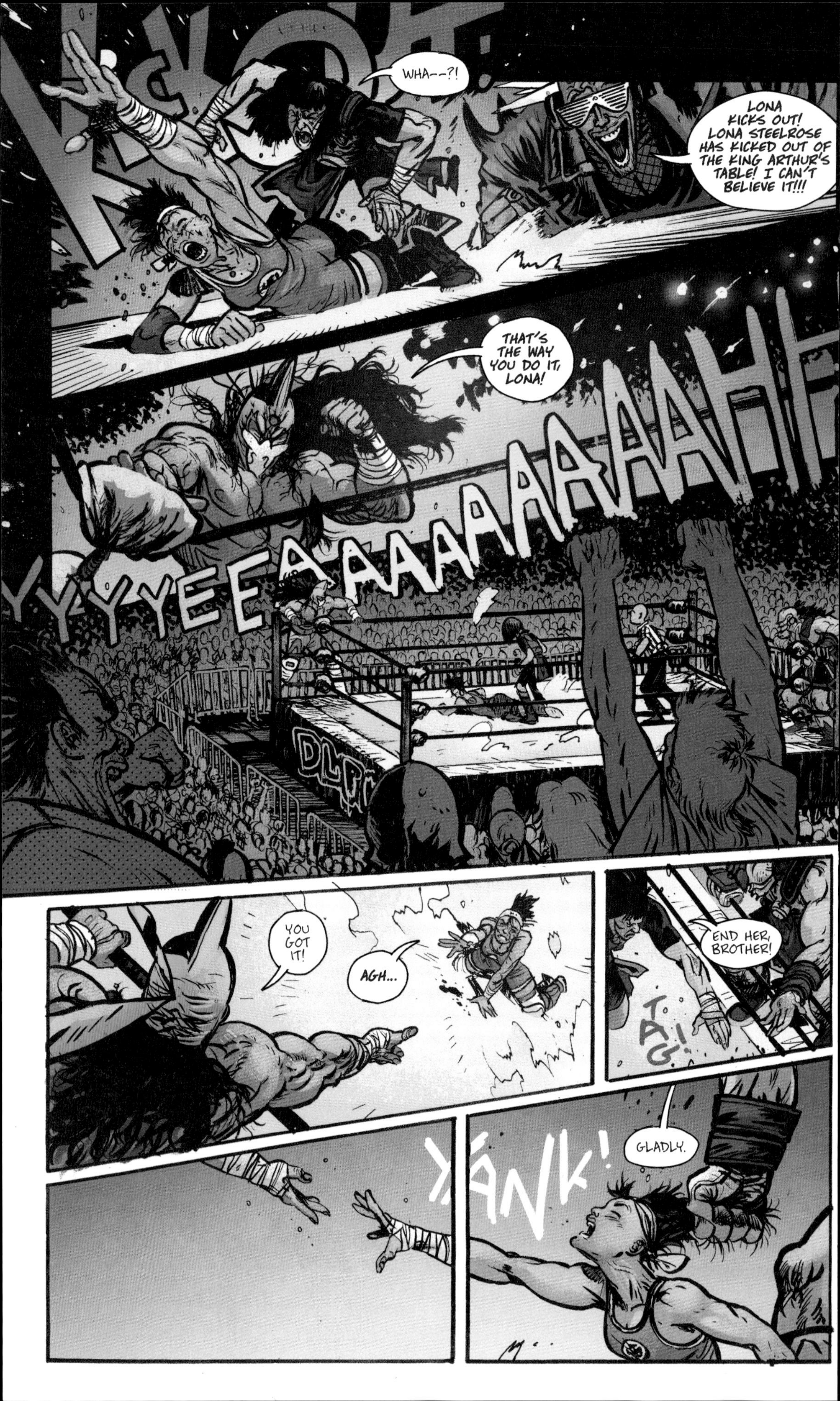
WHA--?!
LONA KICKS OUT! LONA STEELROSE HAS KICKED OUT OF THE KING ARTHUR'S TABLE! I CAN'T BELIEVE IT!!!
THAT'S THE WAY YOU DO IT, LONA!
YYYYEEAAAAAAAAAAAAAAHH
YOU GOT IT!
AGH...
END HER, BROTHER!
TAG!
GLADLY.
YANK!

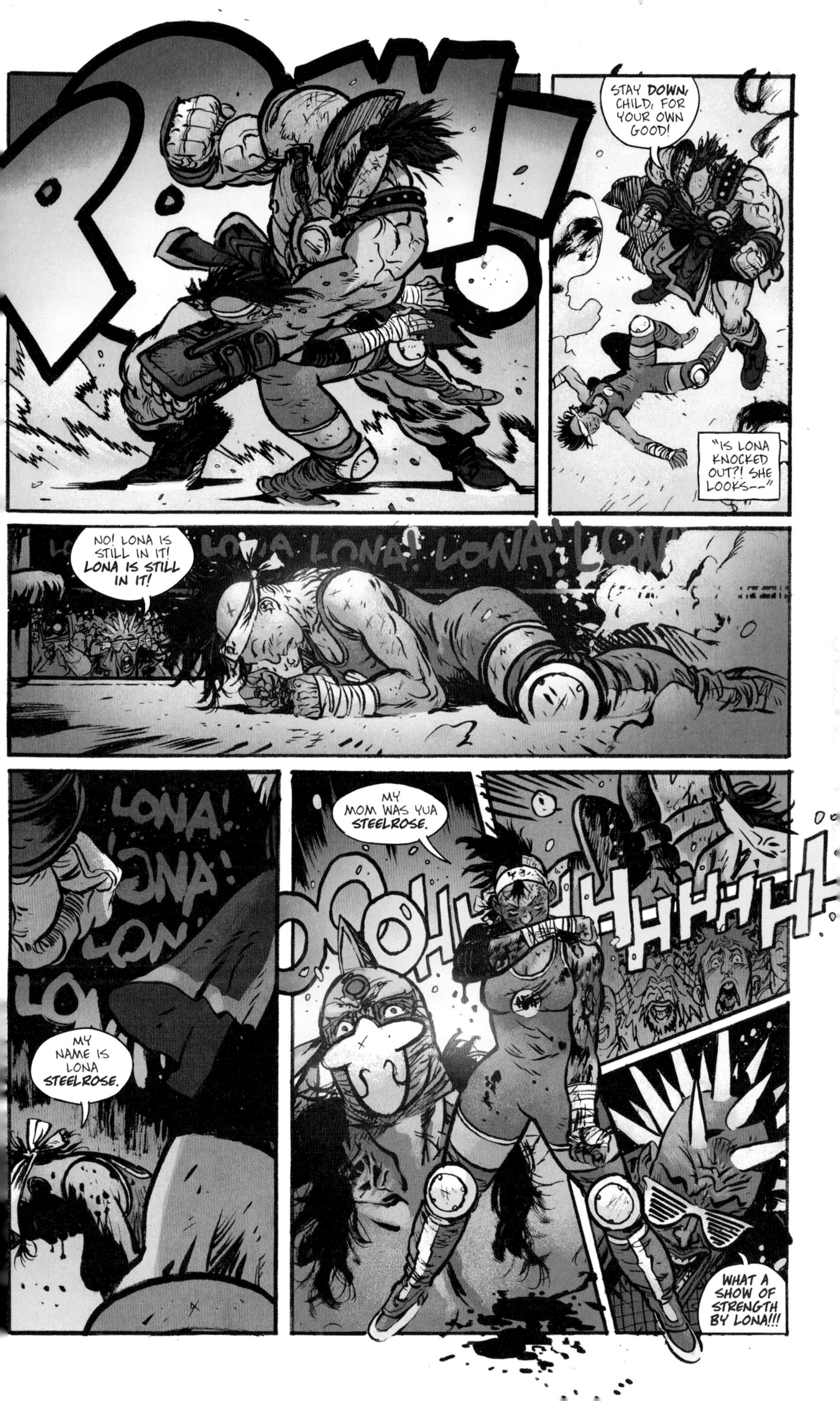
POW!
STAY DOWN, CHILD, FOR YOUR OWN GOOD!
"IS LONA KNOCKED OUT?! SHE LOOKS--"
LONA! LONA! LONA! LON
NO! LONA IS STILL IN IT! LONA IS STILL IN IT!
LONA! LONA! LON LO
MY NAME IS LONA STEELROSE.
MY MOM WAS YUA STEELROSE.
OOOHHHHHHHH
WHAT A SHOW OF STRENGTH BY LONA!!!

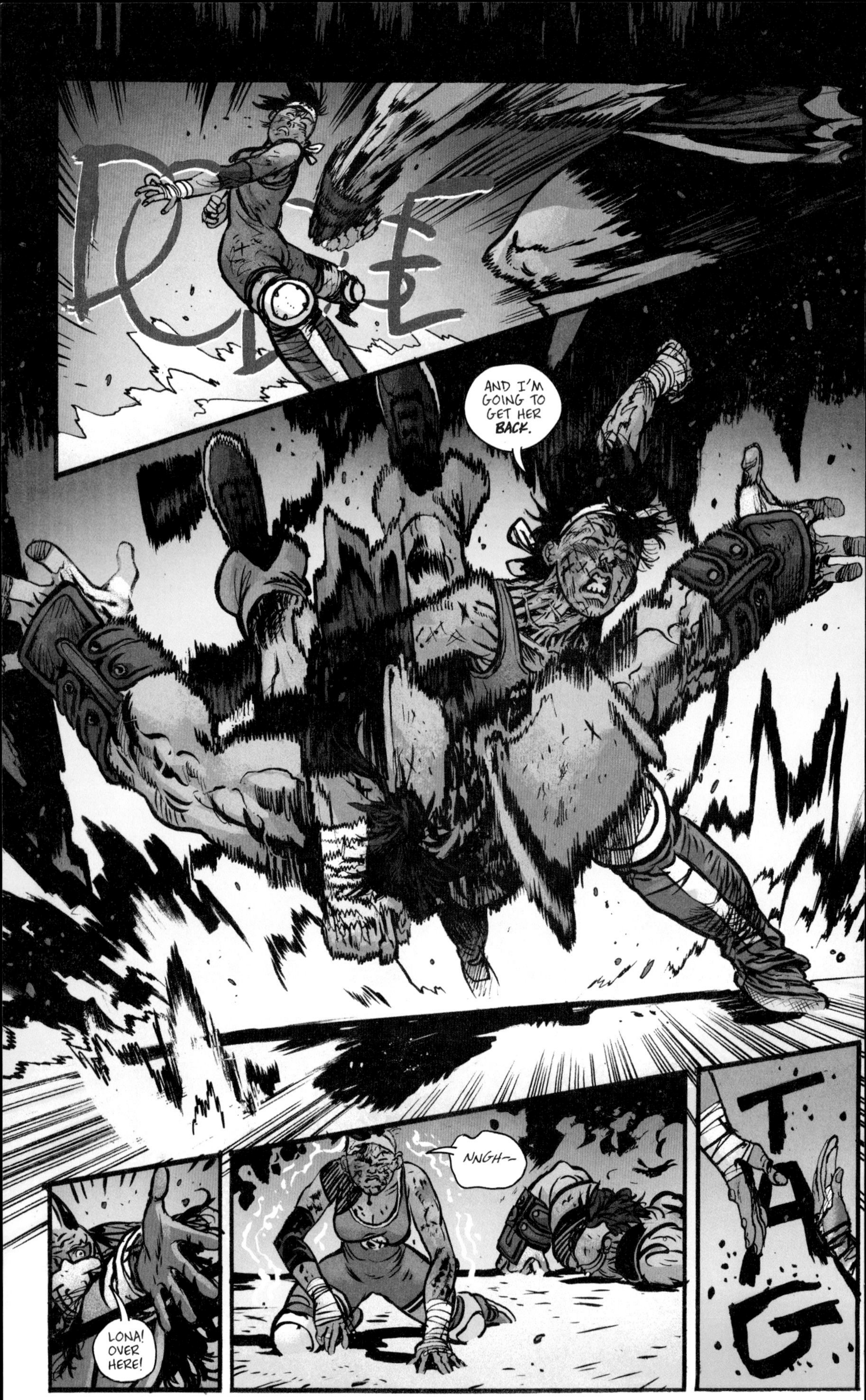
AND I'M GOING TO GET HER BACK.
NNGH--
LONA! OVER HERE!
THG

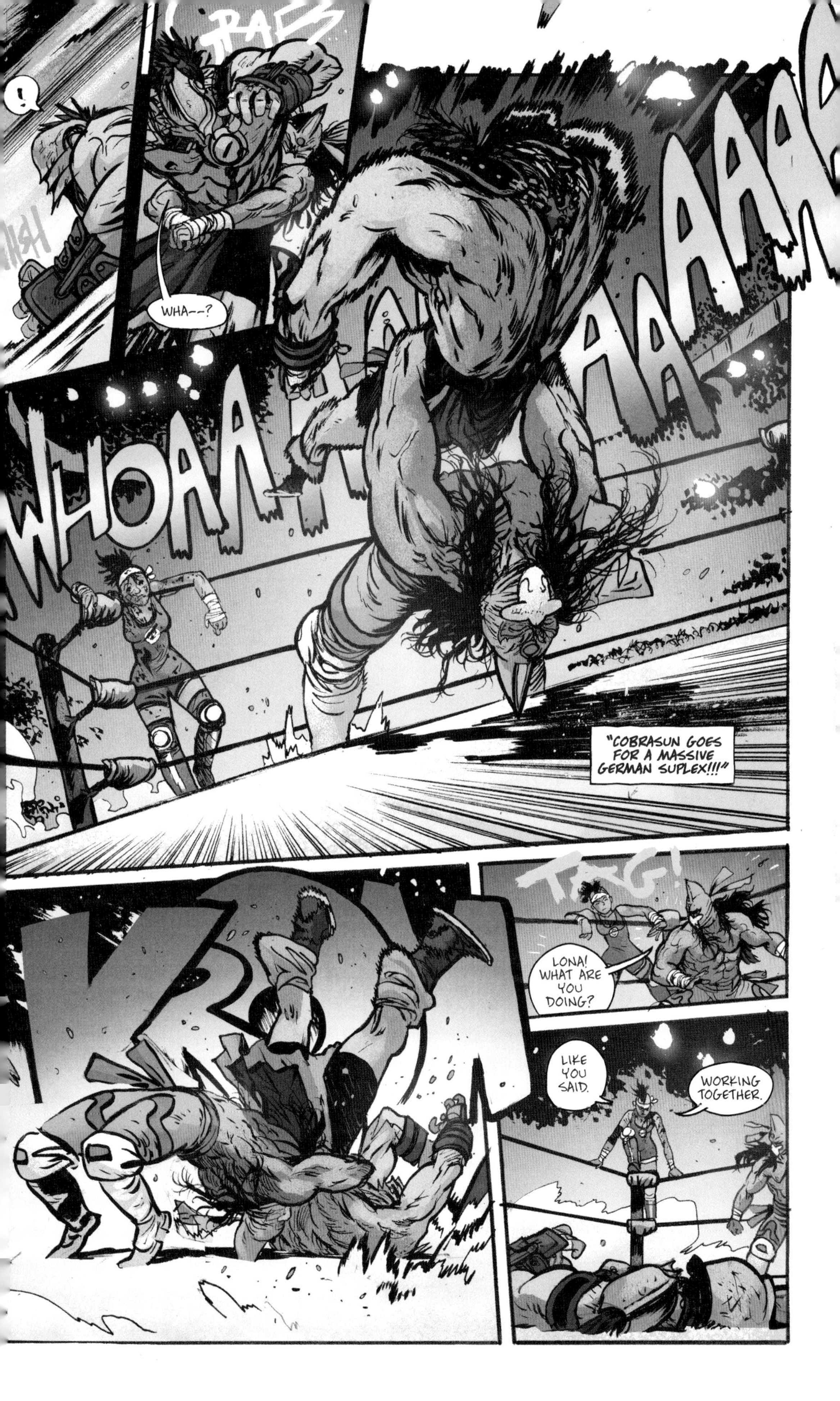

!
RAB
WHA--?
WHOAAAAAAA
"COBRASUN GOES FOR A MASSIVE GERMAN SUPLEX!!!"
TAG!
LONA! WHAT ARE YOU DOING?
LIKE YOU SAID.
WORKING TOGETHER.

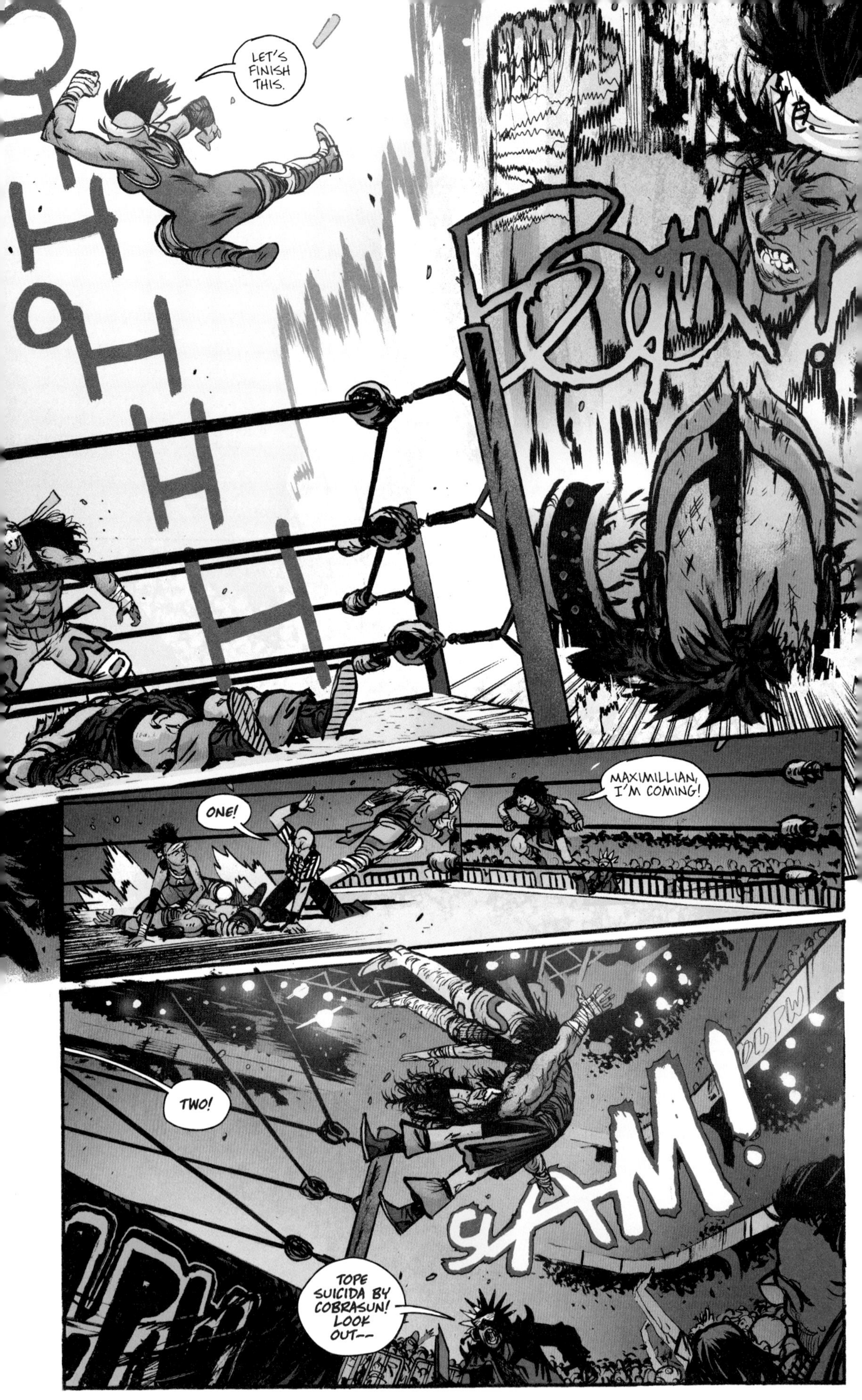
LET'S FINISH THIS.
BOOM!
MAXIMILLIAN, I'M COMING!
ONE!
TWO!
SLAM!
TOPE SUICIDA BY COBRASUN! LOOK OUT--

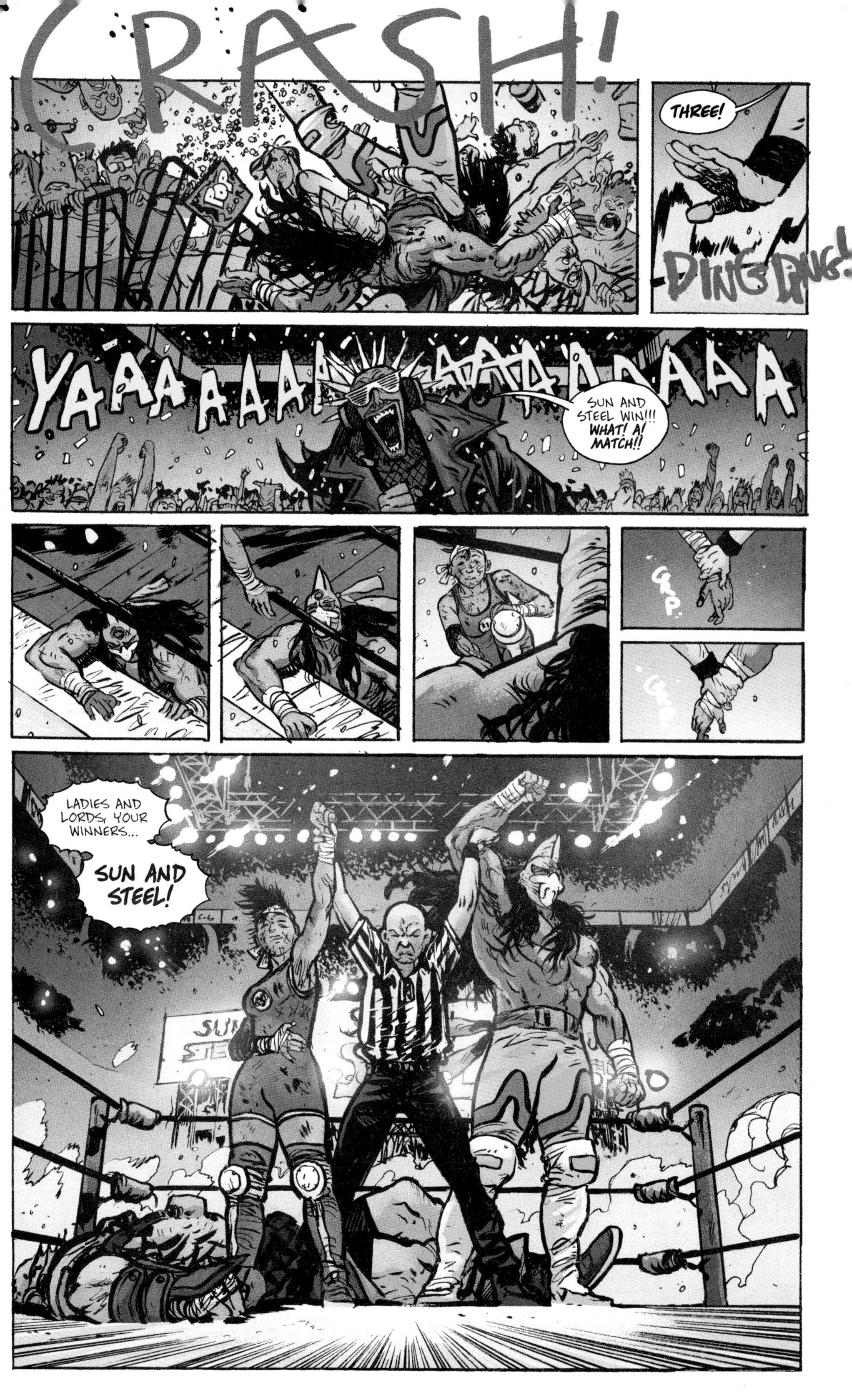
CRASH!
THREE!
DING DING!
YAAAAAAAAAAAAAAAAA
SUN AND STEEL WIN!!! WHAT! A! MATCH!!
GRP
GRP
LADIES AND LORDS, YOUR WINNERS...
SUN AND STEEL!

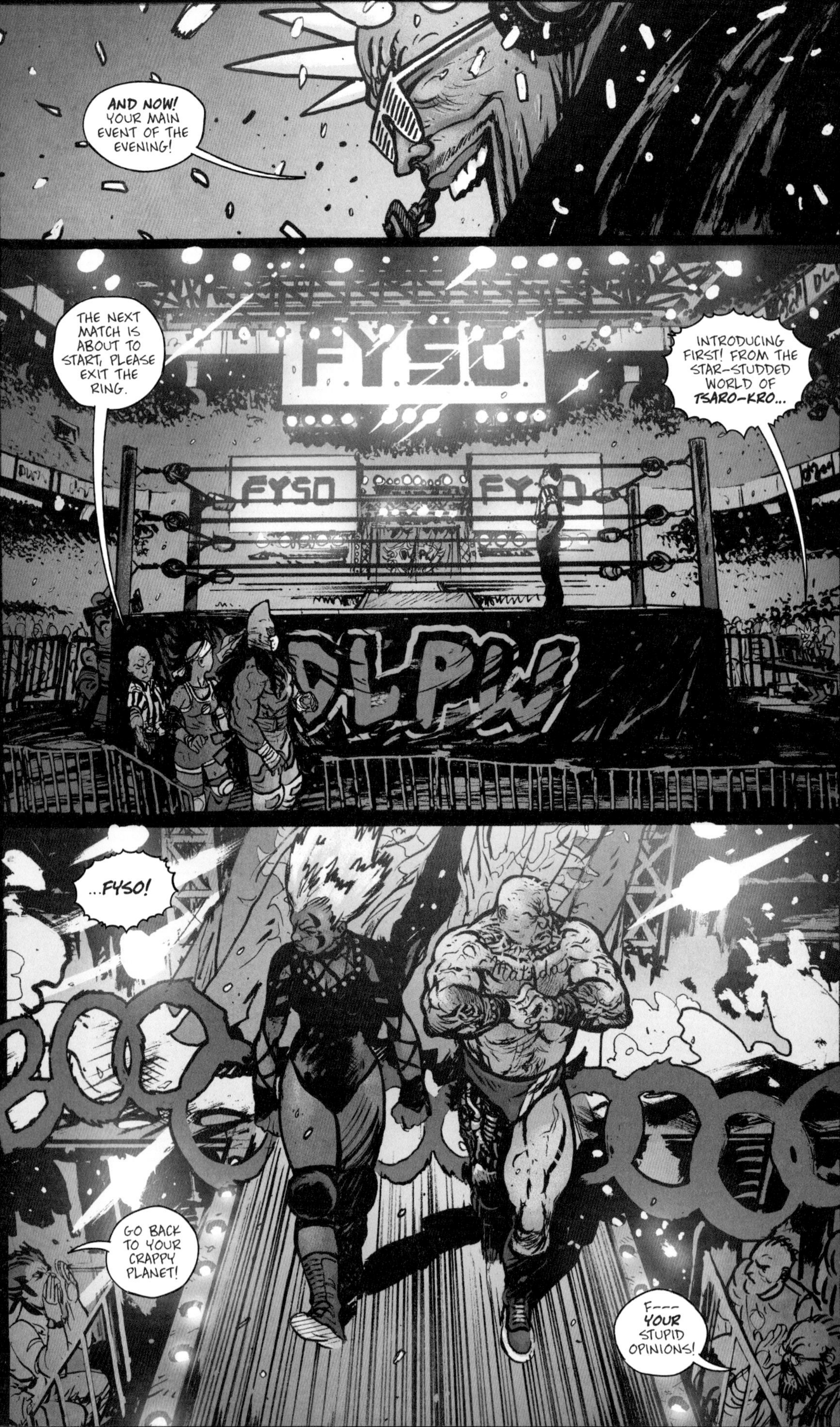
AND NOW! YOUR MAIN EVENT OF THE EVENING!
THE NEXT MATCH IS ABOUT TO START, PLEASE EXIT THE RING.
F.Y.S.O.
FYSO
DLPW
INTRODUCING FIRST! FROM THE STAR-STUDDED WORLD OF TSARO-KRO...
...FYSO!
BOOOOOOOO
GO BACK TO YOUR CRAPPY PLANET!
F--- YOUR STUPID OPINIONS!

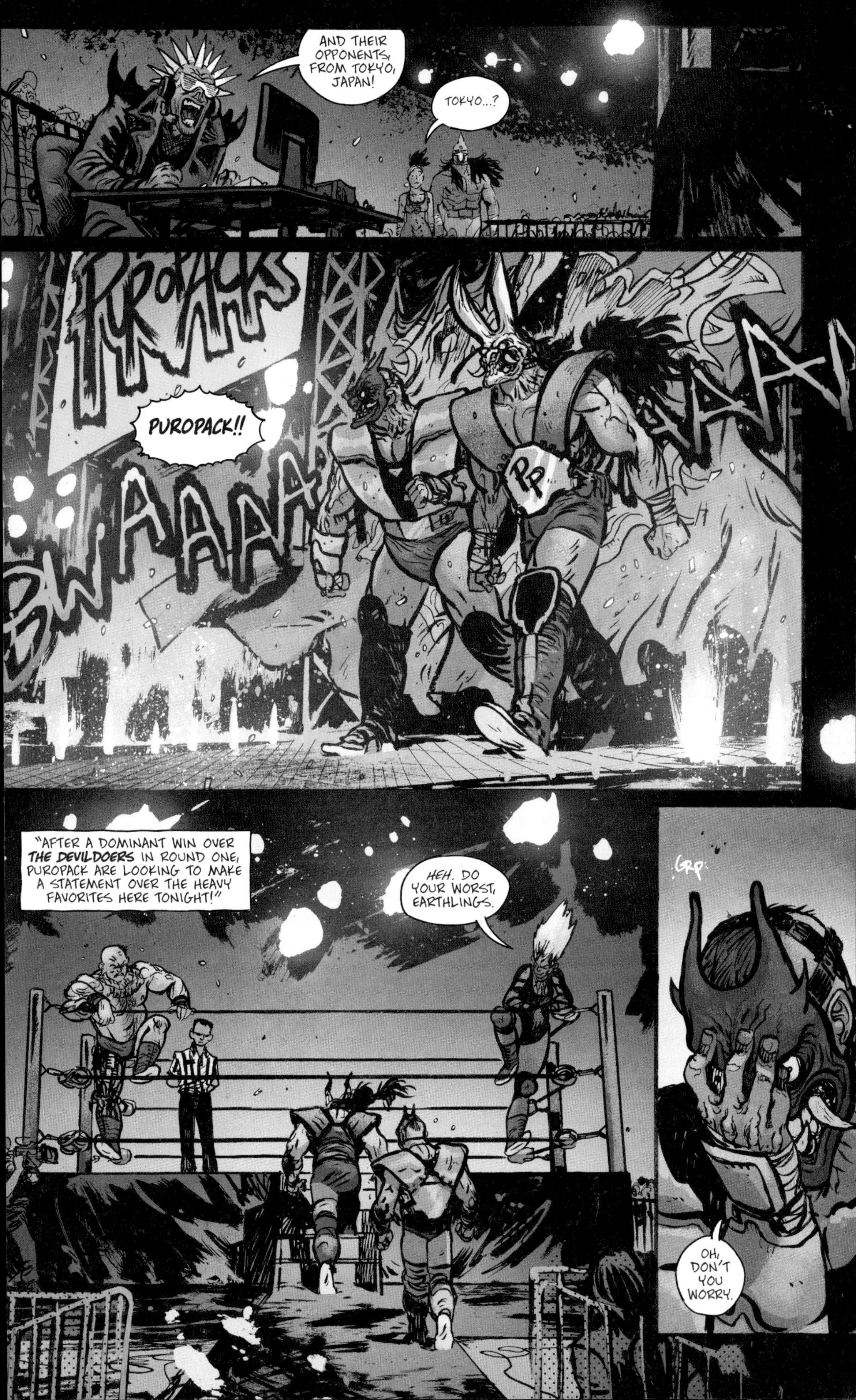
AND THEIR OPPONENTS, FROM TOKYO, JAPAN!
TOKYO...?
PUROPACK!!
PUROPACK!!
BWAAAAA
AAAA
PP
"AFTER A DOMINANT WIN OVER **THE DEVILDOERS** IN ROUND ONE, PUROPACK ARE LOOKING TO MAKE A STATEMENT OVER THE HEAVY FAVORITES HERE TONIGHT!"
HEH. DO YOUR WORST, EARTHLINGS.
GRP
OH, DON'T YOU WORRY.

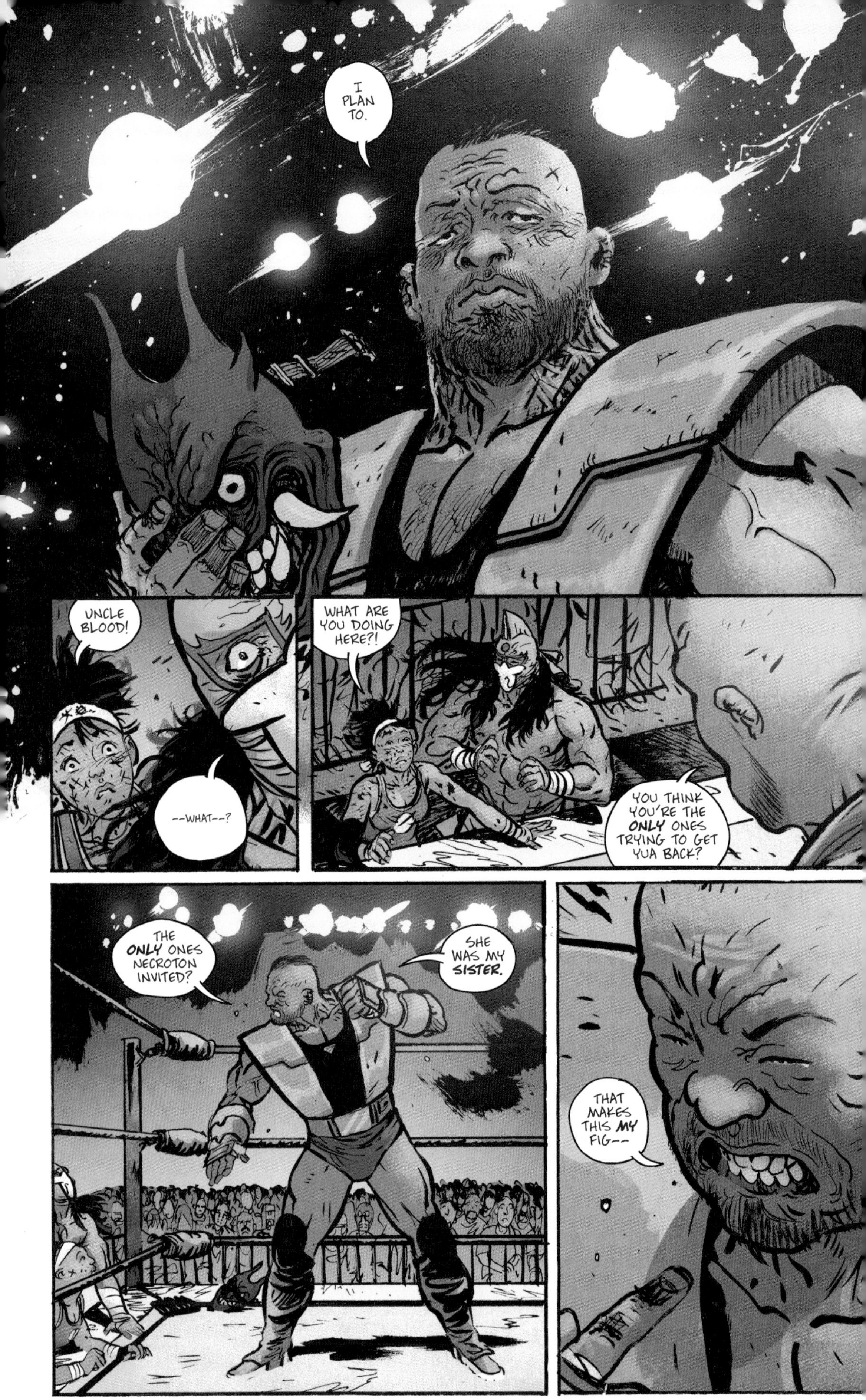
I PLAN TO.
UNCLE BLOOD!
--WHAT--?
WHAT ARE YOU DOING HERE?!
YOU THINK YOU'RE THE ONLY ONES TRYING TO GET YUA BACK?
THE ONLY ONES NECROTON INVITED?
SHE WAS MY SISTER.
THAT MAKES THIS MY FIG--

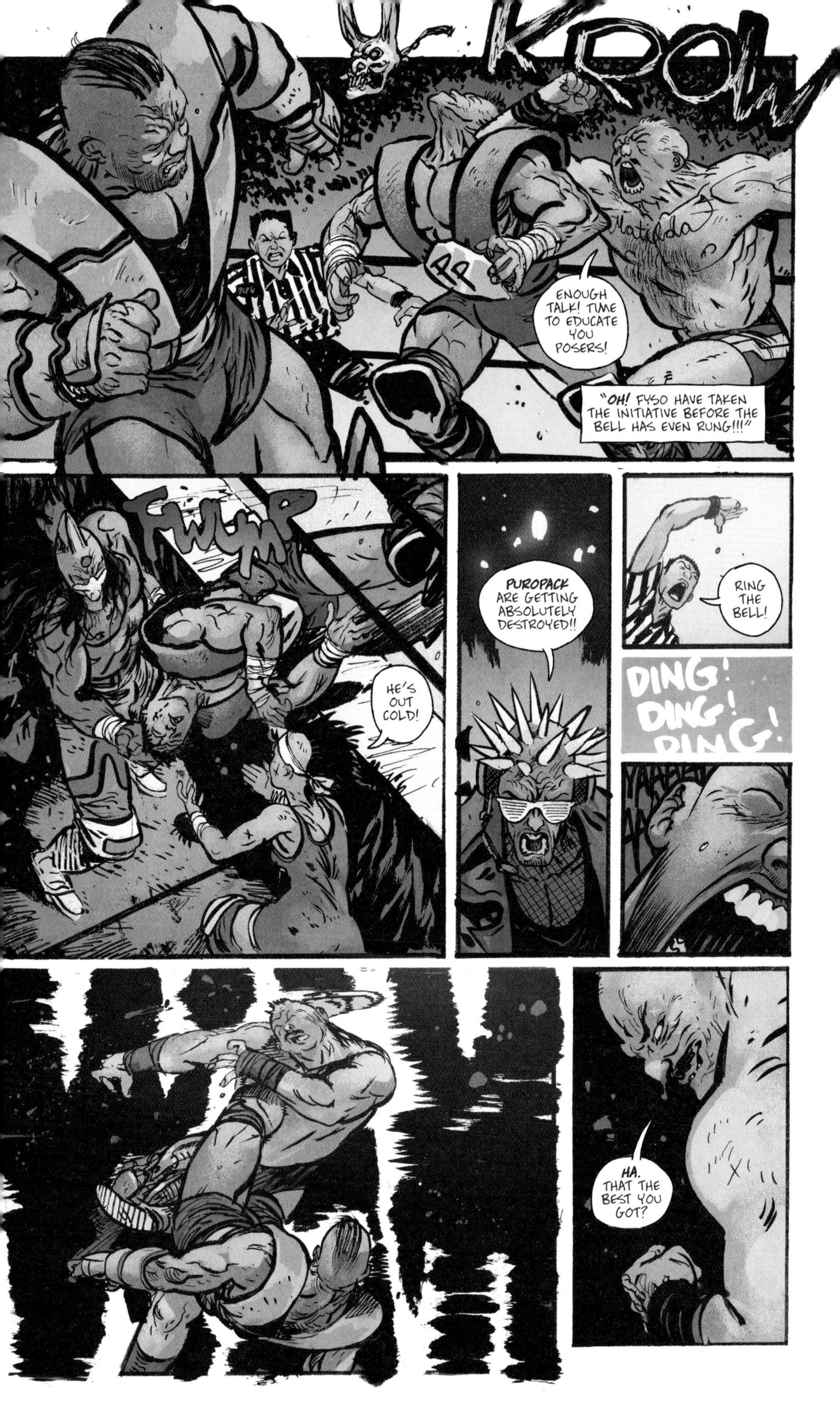

KROW
ENOUGH TALK! TIME TO EDUCATE YOU POSERS!
"OH! FYSO HAVE TAKEN THE INITIATIVE BEFORE THE BELL HAS EVEN RUNG!!!"
FWUMP
HE'S OUT COLD!
PUROPACK ARE GETTING ABSOLUTELY DESTROYED!!
RING THE BELL!
DING! DING! DING!
HA. THAT THE BEST YOU GOT?

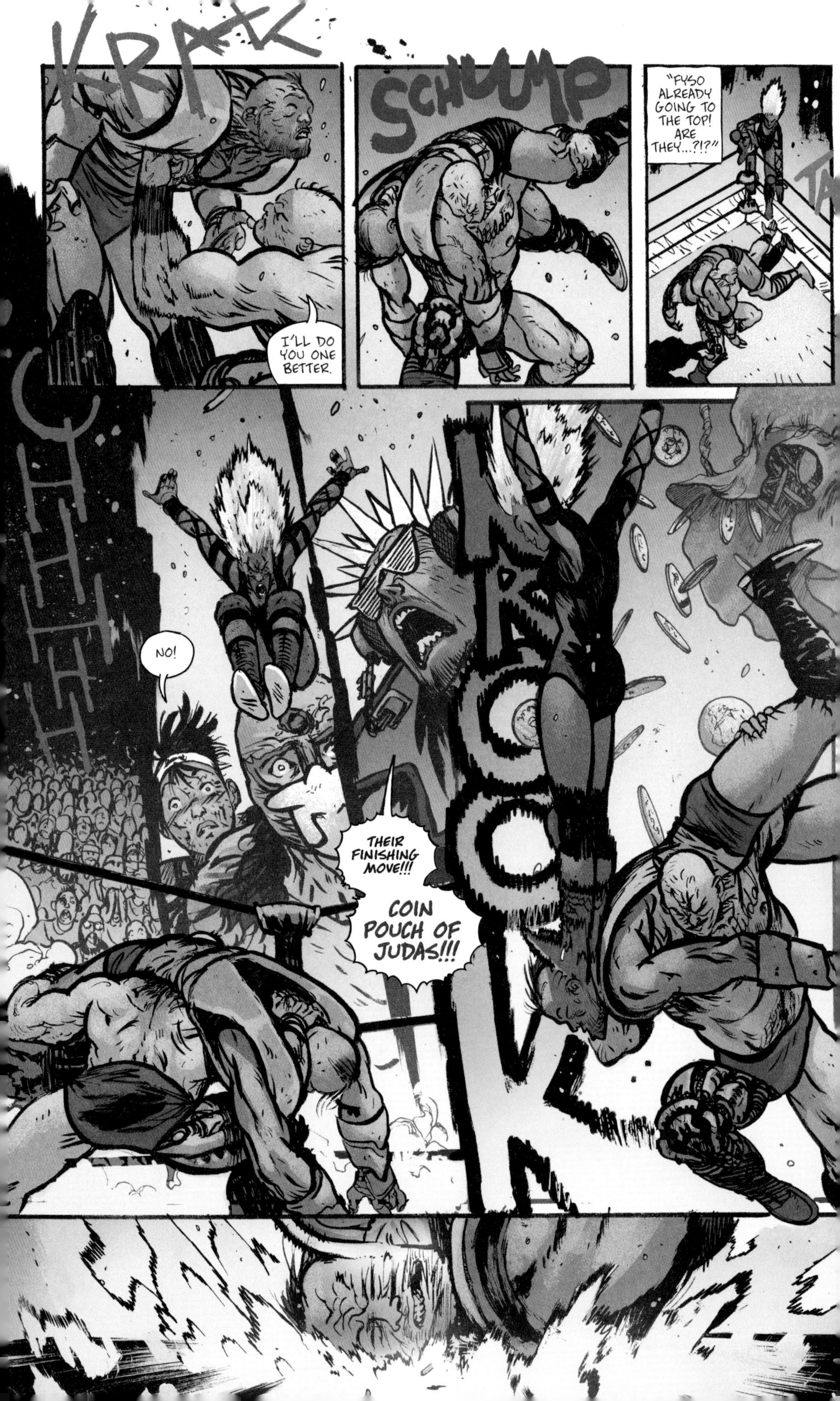
KRAK
I'LL DO YOU ONE BETTER.
SCHUMP
"FYSO ALREADY GOING TO THE TOP! ARE THEY...?!?"
NO!
THEIR FINISHING MOVE!!!
COIN POUCH OF JUDAS!!!

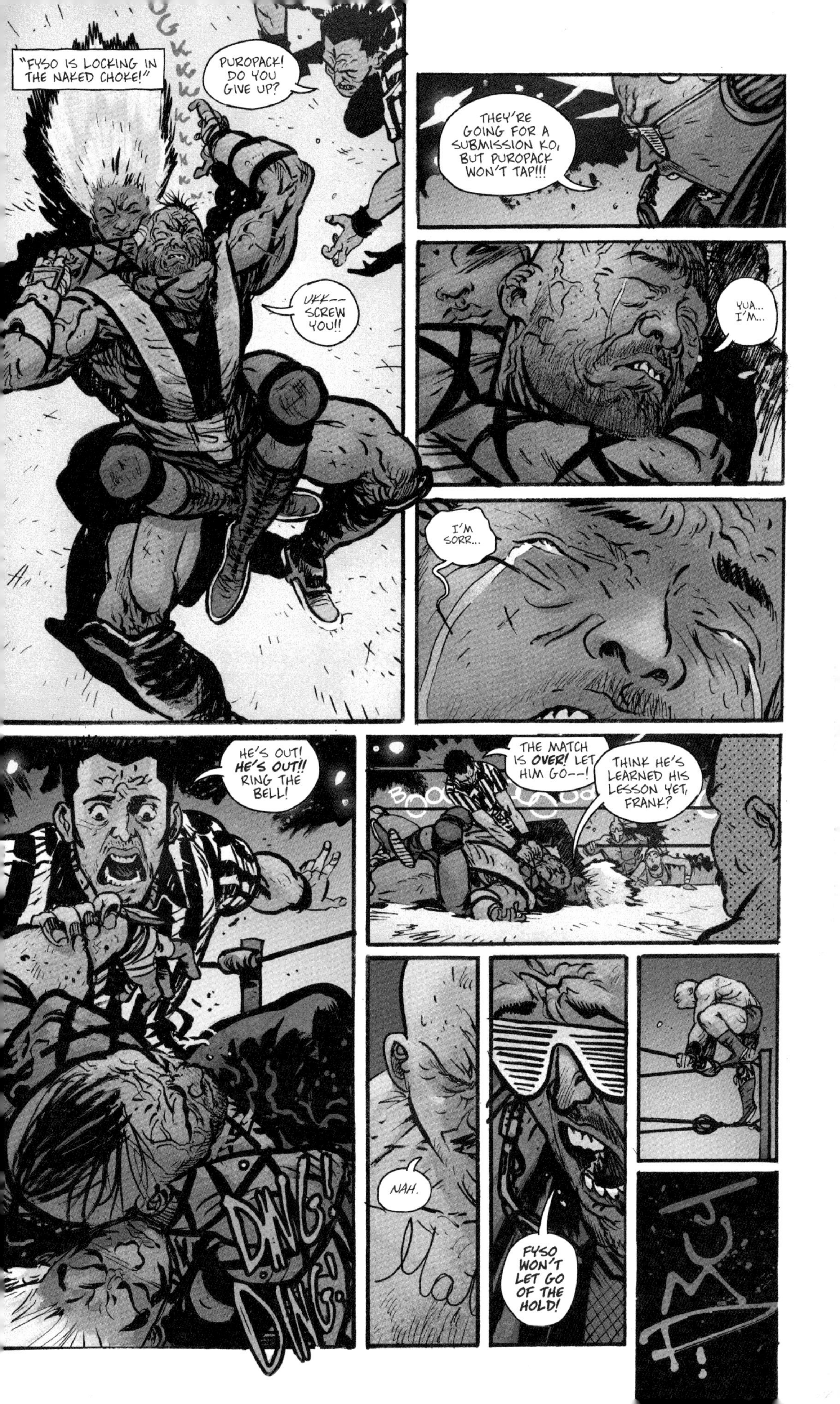
"FYSO IS LOCKING IN THE NAKED CHOKE!"
PUROPACK! DO YOU GIVE UP?
UKK-- SCREW YOU!!
THEY'RE GOING FOR A SUBMISSION KO, BUT PUROPACK WON'T TAP!!!
YUA... I'M...
I'M SORR...
HE'S OUT! HE'S OUT!! RING THE BELL!
DING!
DING!
THE MATCH IS OVER! LET HIM GO--!
THINK HE'S LEARNED HIS LESSON YET, FRANK?
NAH.
FYSO WON'T LET GO OF THE HOLD!

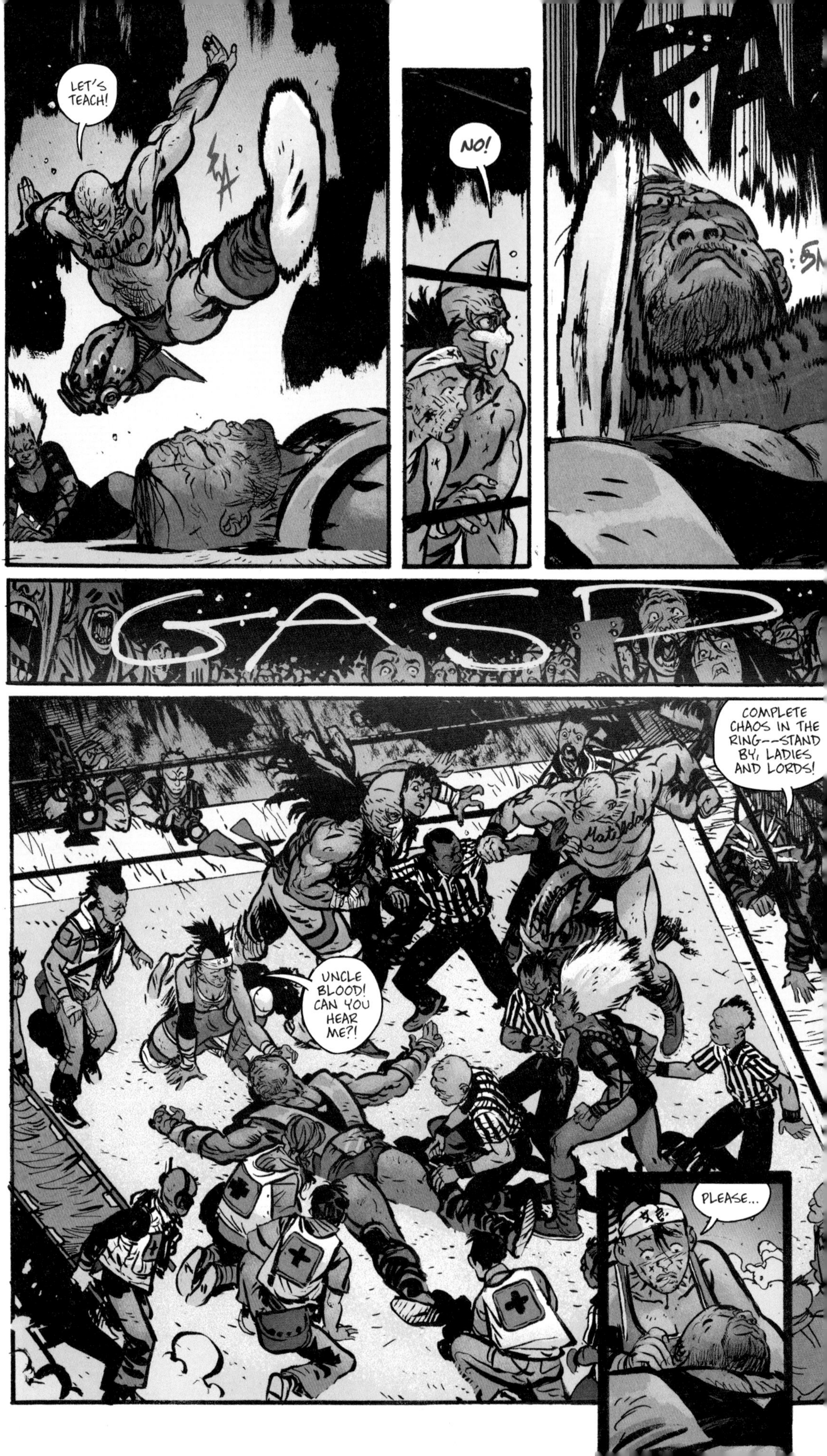
LET'S TEACH!
NO!
GASP
COMPLETE CHAOS IN THE RING--STAND BY, LADIES AND LORDS!
UNCLE BLOOD! CAN YOU HEAR ME?!
PLEASE...

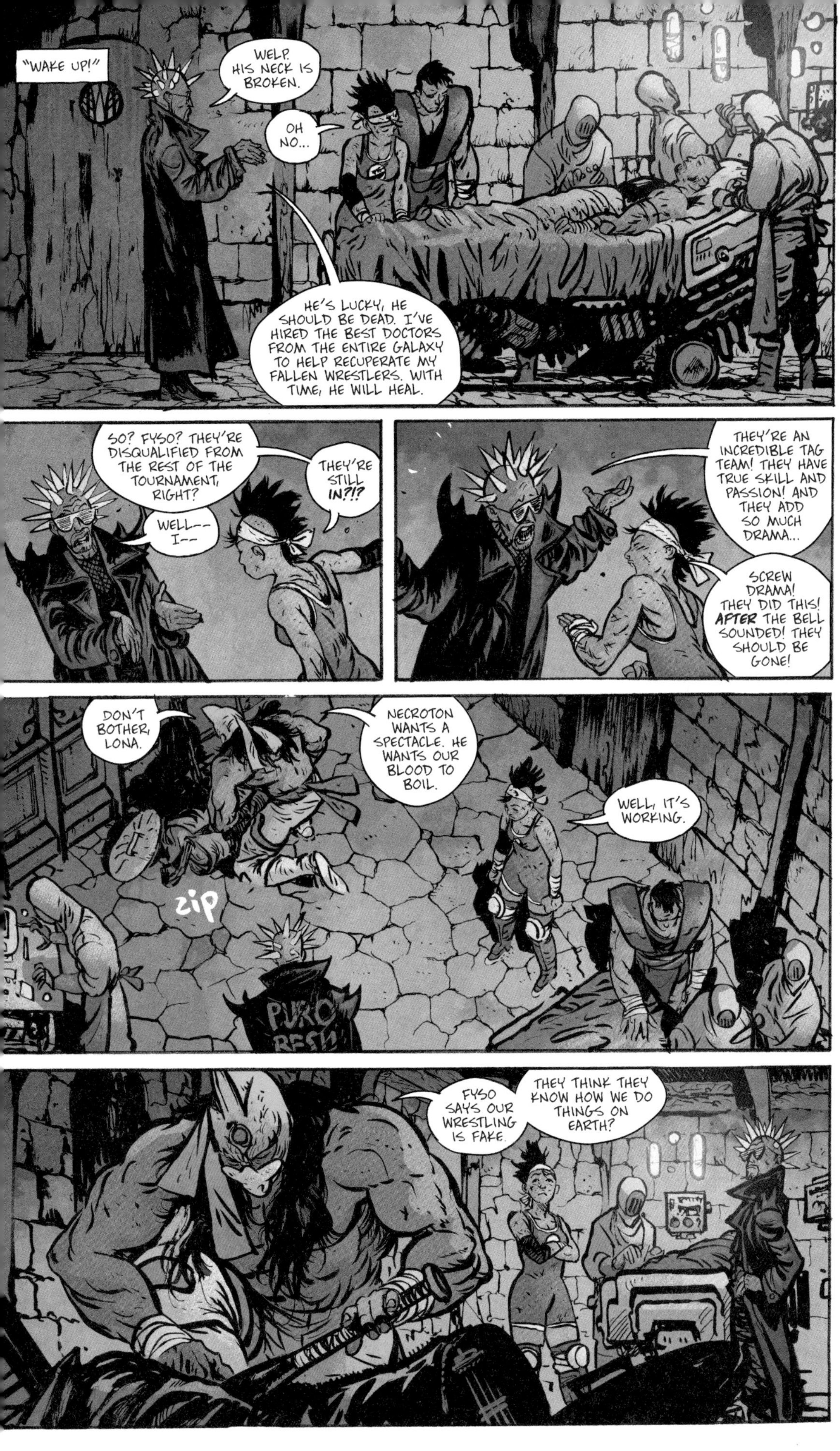
"WAKE UP!"
WELP. HIS NECK IS BROKEN.
OH NO...
HE'S LUCKY, HE SHOULD BE DEAD. I'VE HIRED THE BEST DOCTORS FROM THE ENTIRE GALAXY TO HELP RECUPERATE MY FALLEN WRESTLERS. WITH TIME, HE WILL HEAL.
SO? FYSO? THEY'RE DISQUALIFIED FROM THE REST OF THE TOURNAMENT, RIGHT?
WELL-- I--
THEY'RE STILL IN?!?
THEY'RE AN INCREDIBLE TAG TEAM! THEY HAVE TRUE SKILL AND PASSION! AND THEY ADD SO MUCH DRAMA...
SCREW DRAMA! THEY DID THIS! AFTER THE BELL SOUNDED! THEY SHOULD BE GONE!
DON'T BOTHER, LONA.
NECROTON WANTS A SPECTACLE. HE WANTS OUR BLOOD TO BOIL.
WELL, IT'S WORKING.
zip
FYSO SAYS OUR WRESTLING IS FAKE.
THEY THINK THEY KNOW HOW WE DO THINGS ON EARTH?

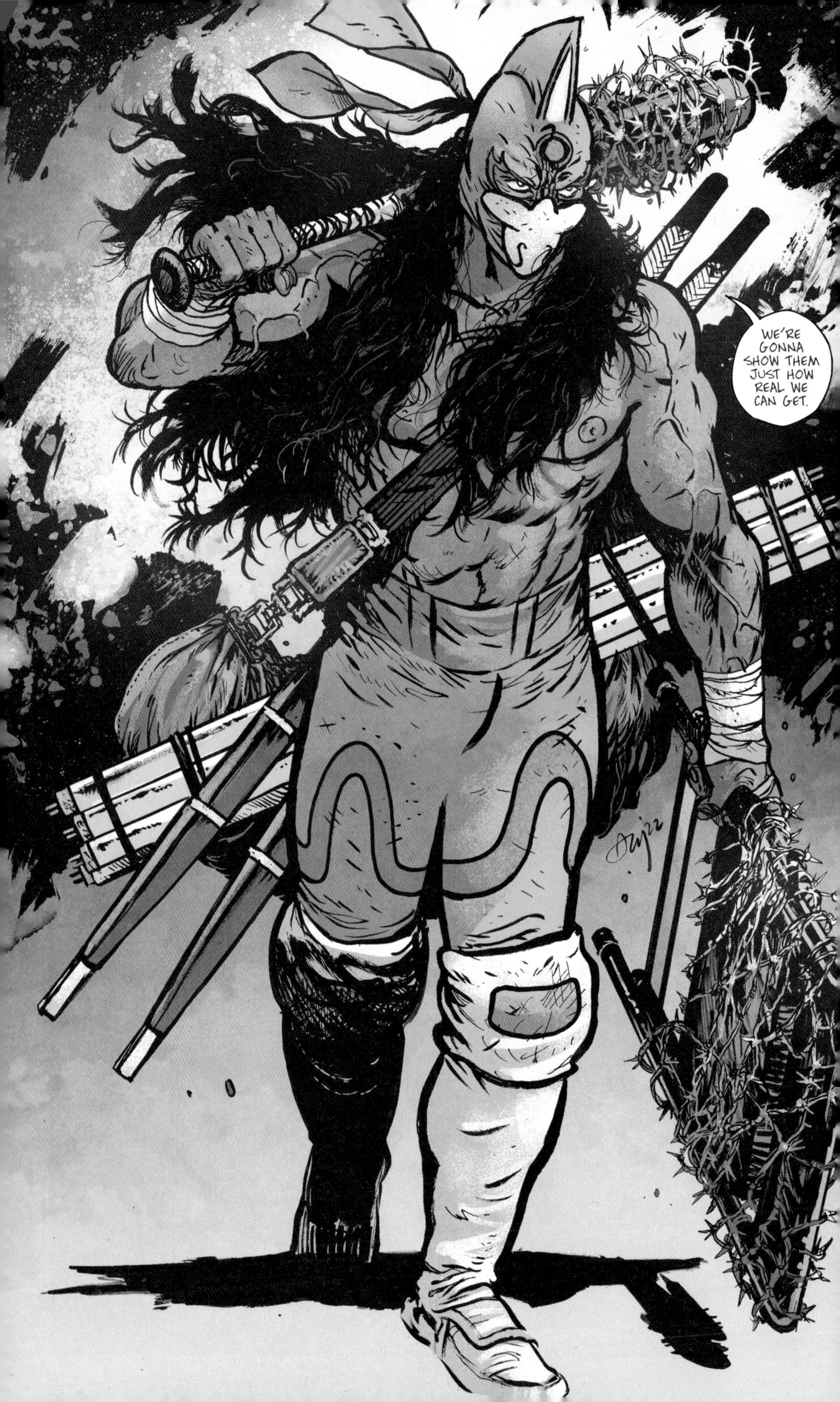
WE'RE GONNA SHOW THEM JUST HOW REAL WE CAN GET.

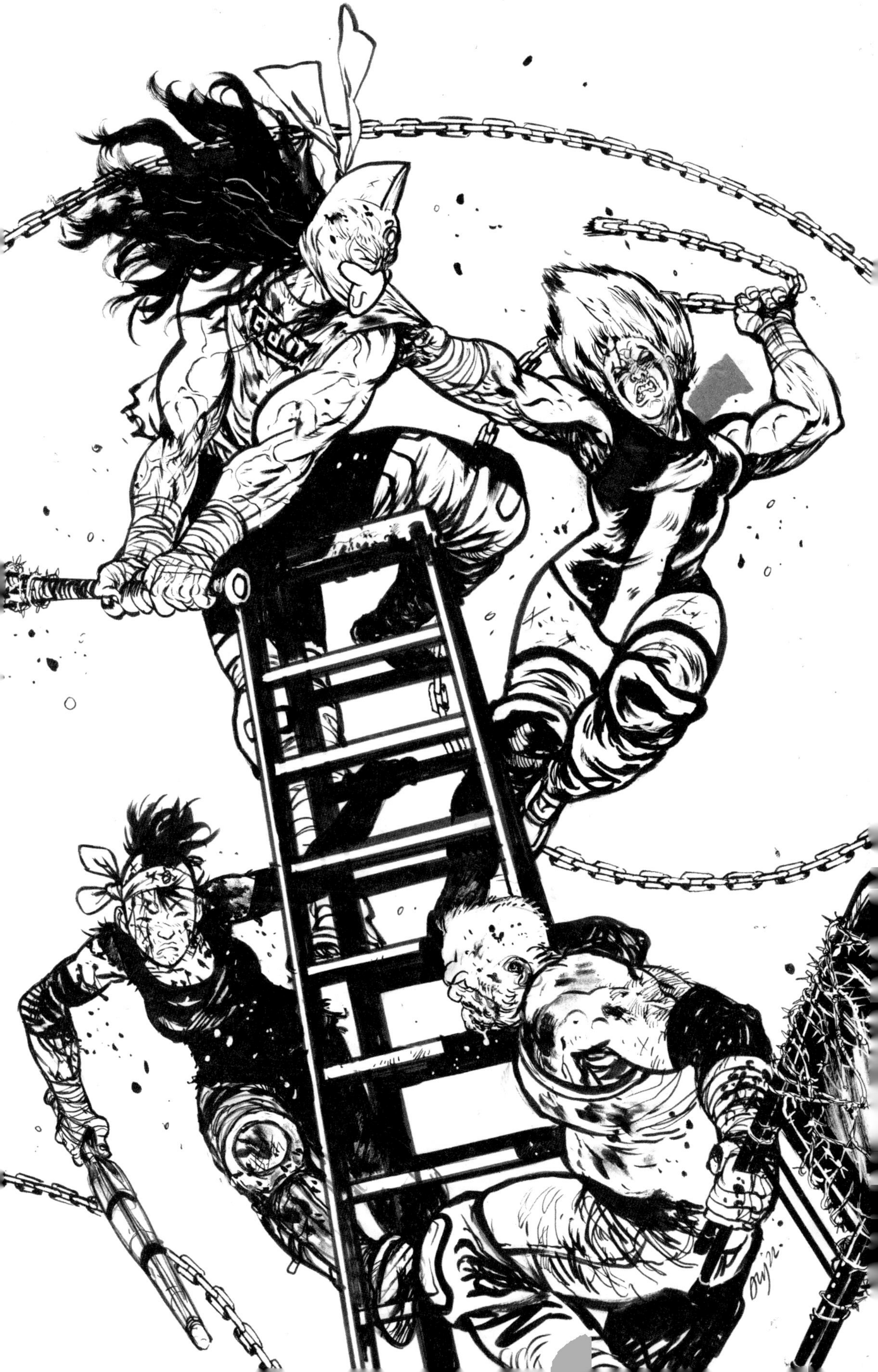

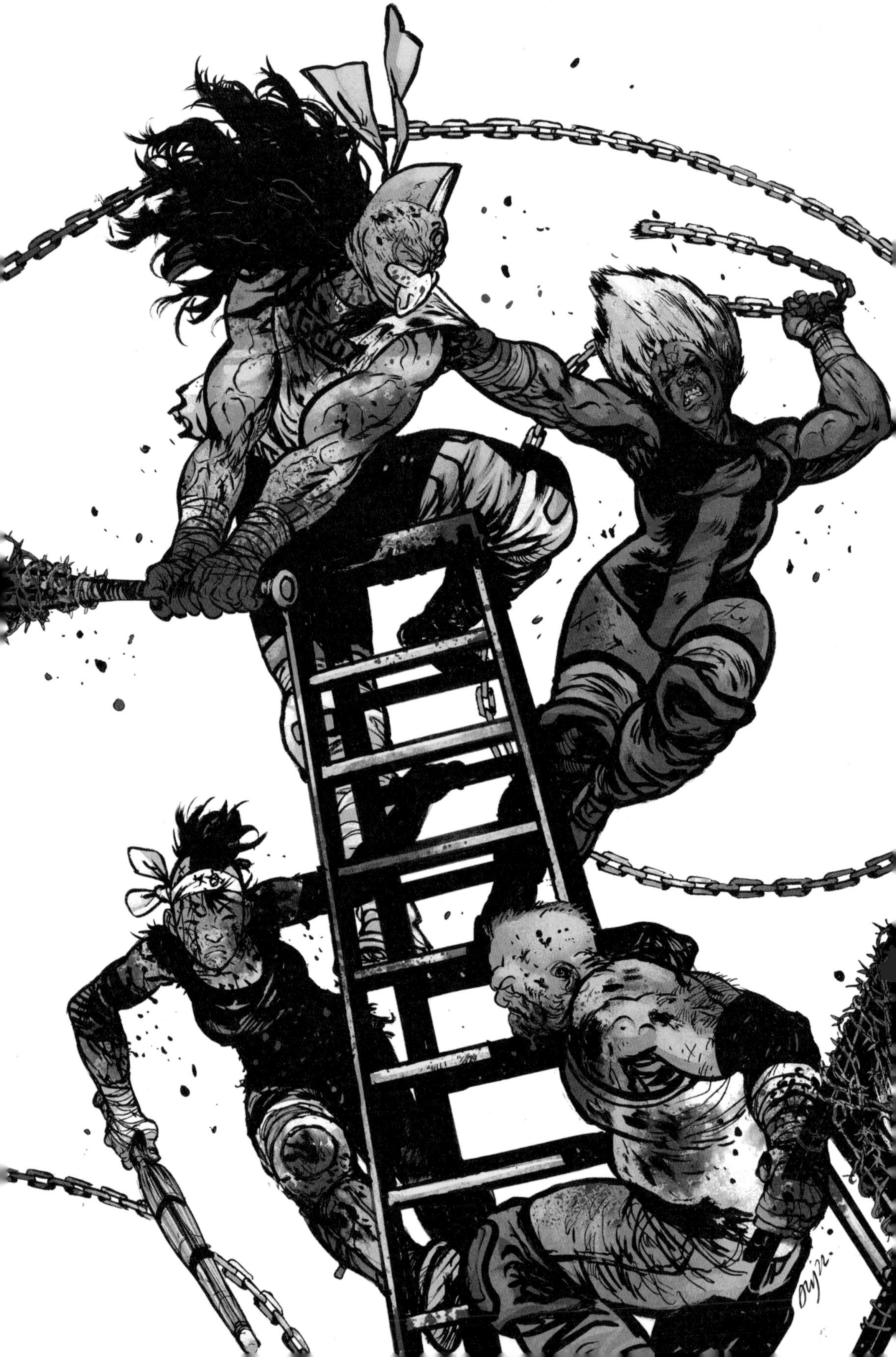

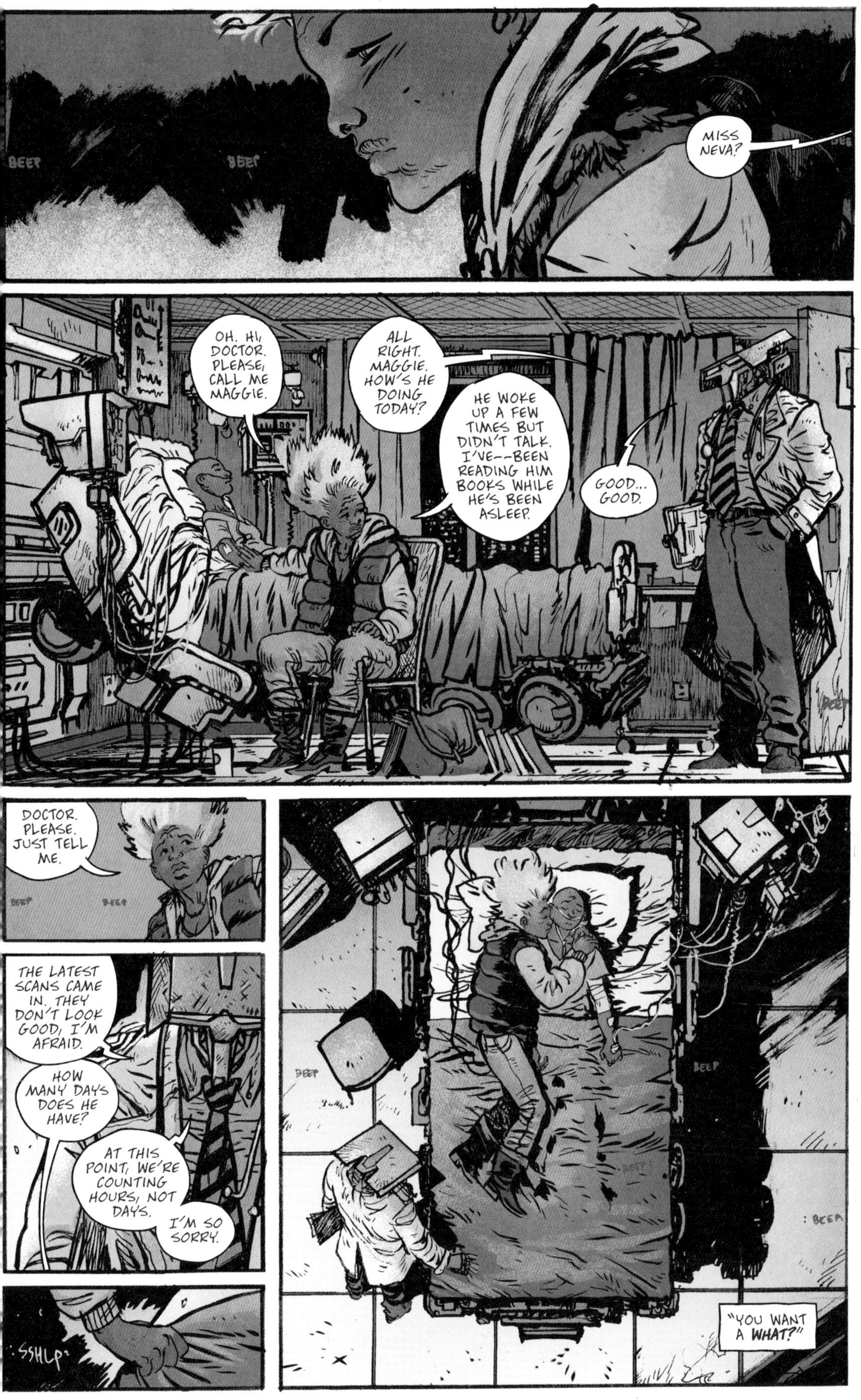
BEEP BEEP
MISS NEVA?
BEEP
OH. HI, DOCTOR. PLEASE, CALL ME MAGGIE.
ALL RIGHT. MAGGIE. HOW'S HE DOING TODAY?
HE WOKE UP A FEW TIMES BUT DIDN'T TALK. I'VE--BEEN READING HIM BOOKS WHILE HE'S BEEN ASLEEP.
GOOD... GOOD.
BEEP
DOCTOR. PLEASE. JUST TELL ME.
BEEP BEEP
THE LATEST SCANS CAME IN. THEY DON'T LOOK GOOD, I'M AFRAID.
HOW MANY DAYS DOES HE HAVE?
AT THIS POINT, WE'RE COUNTING HOURS, NOT DAYS.
I'M SO SORRY.
SSHLP
BEEP
BEEP
BEEP
"YOU WANT A WHAT?"

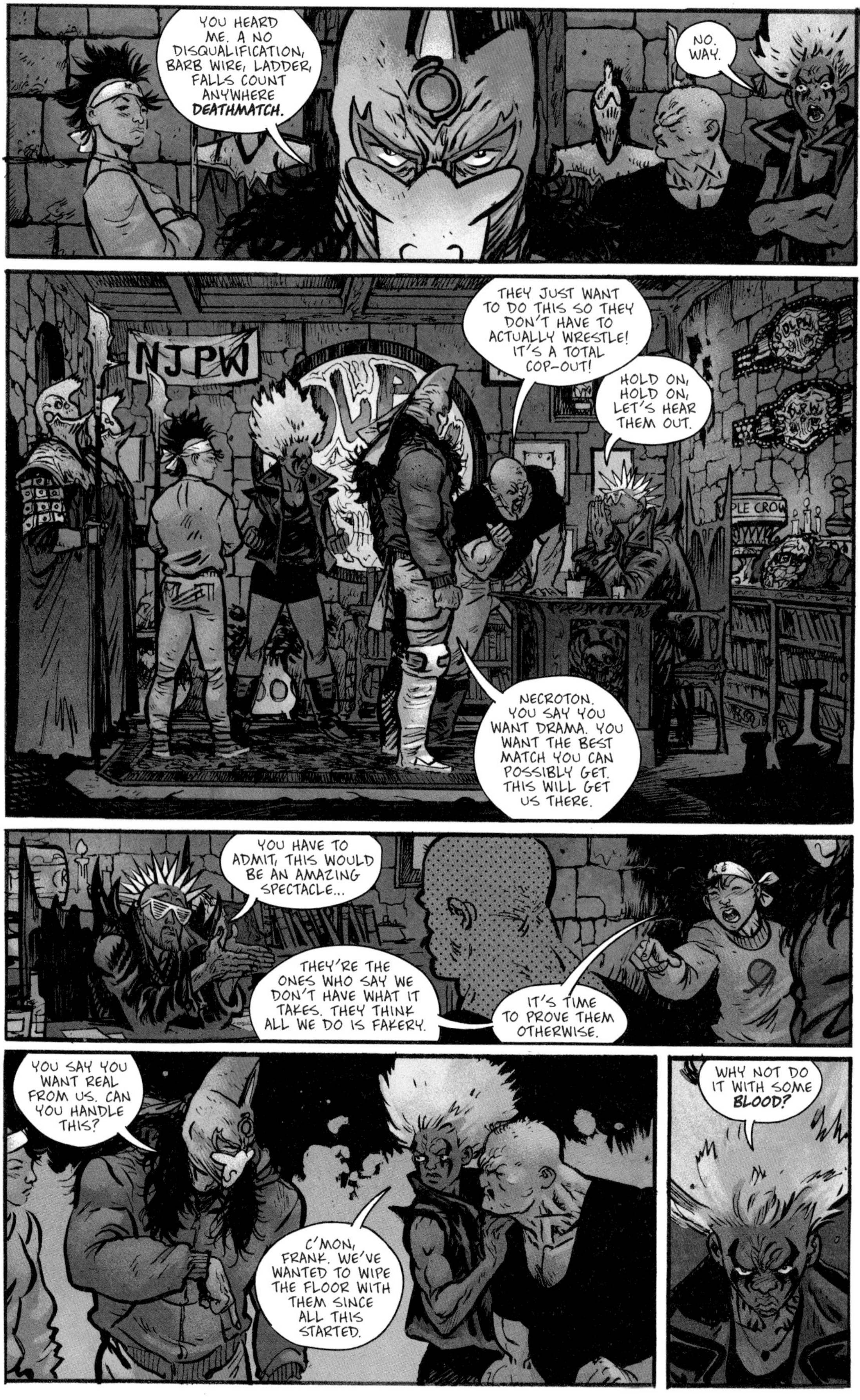

YOU HEARD ME. A NO DISQUALIFICATION, BARB WIRE, LADDER, FALLS COUNT ANYWHERE **DEATHMATCH.**
NO. WAY.
NJPW
THEY JUST WANT TO DO THIS SO THEY DON'T HAVE TO ACTUALLY WRESTLE! IT'S A TOTAL COP-OUT!
HOLD ON, HOLD ON, LET'S HEAR THEM OUT.
NECROTON. YOU SAY YOU WANT DRAMA. YOU WANT THE BEST MATCH YOU CAN POSSIBLY GET. THIS WILL GET US THERE.
YOU HAVE TO ADMIT, THIS WOULD BE AN AMAZING SPECTACLE...
THEY'RE THE ONES WHO SAY WE DON'T HAVE WHAT IT TAKES. THEY THINK ALL WE DO IS FAKERY.
IT'S TIME TO PROVE THEM OTHERWISE.
YOU SAY YOU WANT REAL FROM US. CAN YOU HANDLE THIS?
C'MON, FRANK. WE'VE WANTED TO WIPE THE FLOOR WITH THEM SINCE ALL THIS STARTED.
WHY NOT DO IT WITH SOME **BLOOD?**

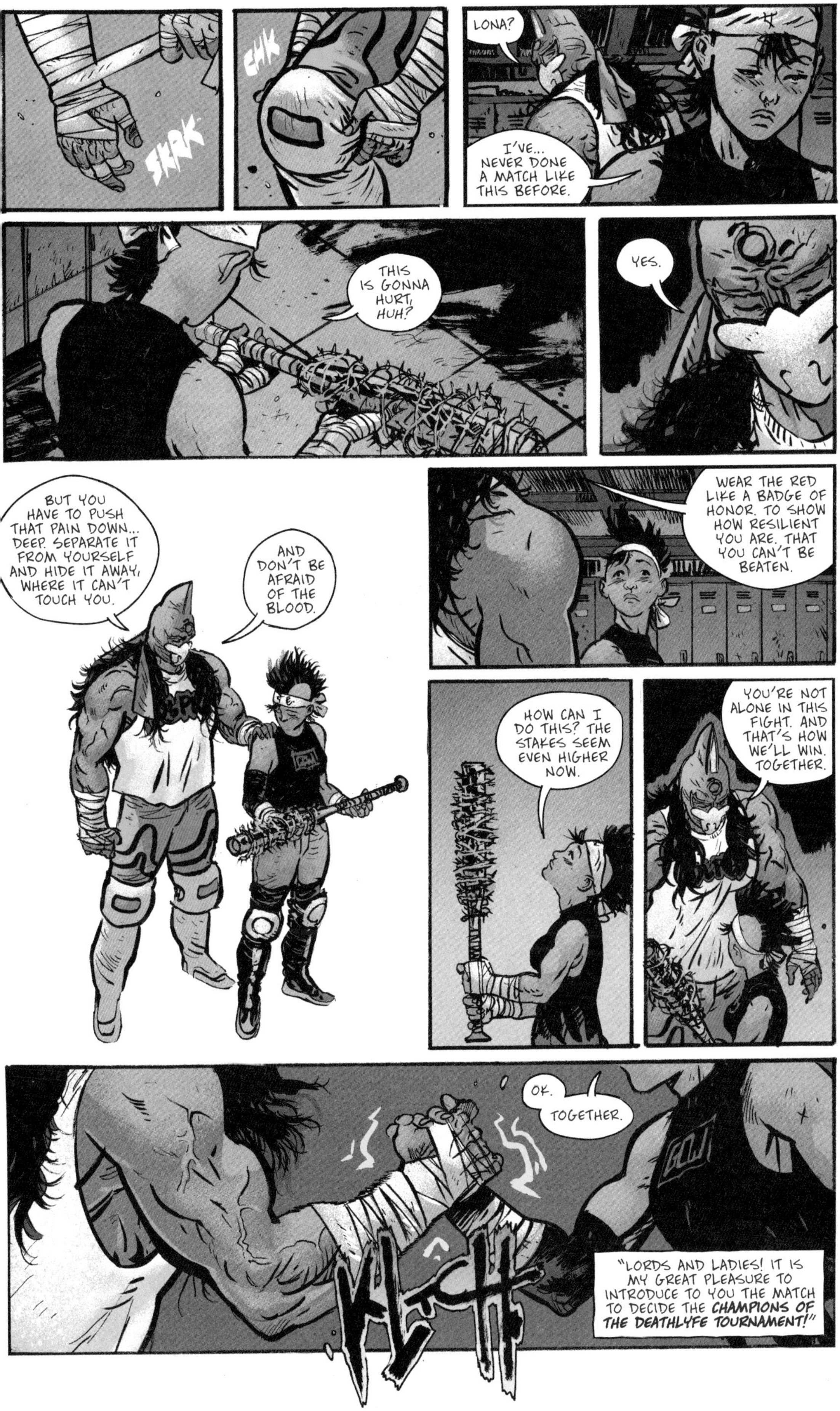
SKRK
CHK
LONA?
I'VE... NEVER DONE A MATCH LIKE THIS BEFORE.
THIS IS GONNA HURT, HUH?
YES.
BUT YOU HAVE TO PUSH THAT PAIN DOWN... DEEP. SEPARATE IT FROM YOURSELF AND HIDE IT AWAY, WHERE IT CAN'T TOUCH YOU.
AND DON'T BE AFRAID OF THE BLOOD.
WEAR THE RED LIKE A BADGE OF HONOR. TO SHOW HOW RESILIENT YOU ARE. THAT YOU CAN'T BE BEATEN.
HOW CAN I DO THIS? THE STAKES SEEM EVEN HIGHER NOW.
YOU'RE NOT ALONE IN THIS FIGHT. AND THAT'S HOW WE'LL WIN. TOGETHER.
OK.
TOGETHER.
"LORDS AND LADIES! IT IS MY GREAT PLEASURE TO INTRODUCE TO YOU THE MATCH TO DECIDE THE **CHAMPIONS OF THE DEATHLYFE TOURNAMENT!**"

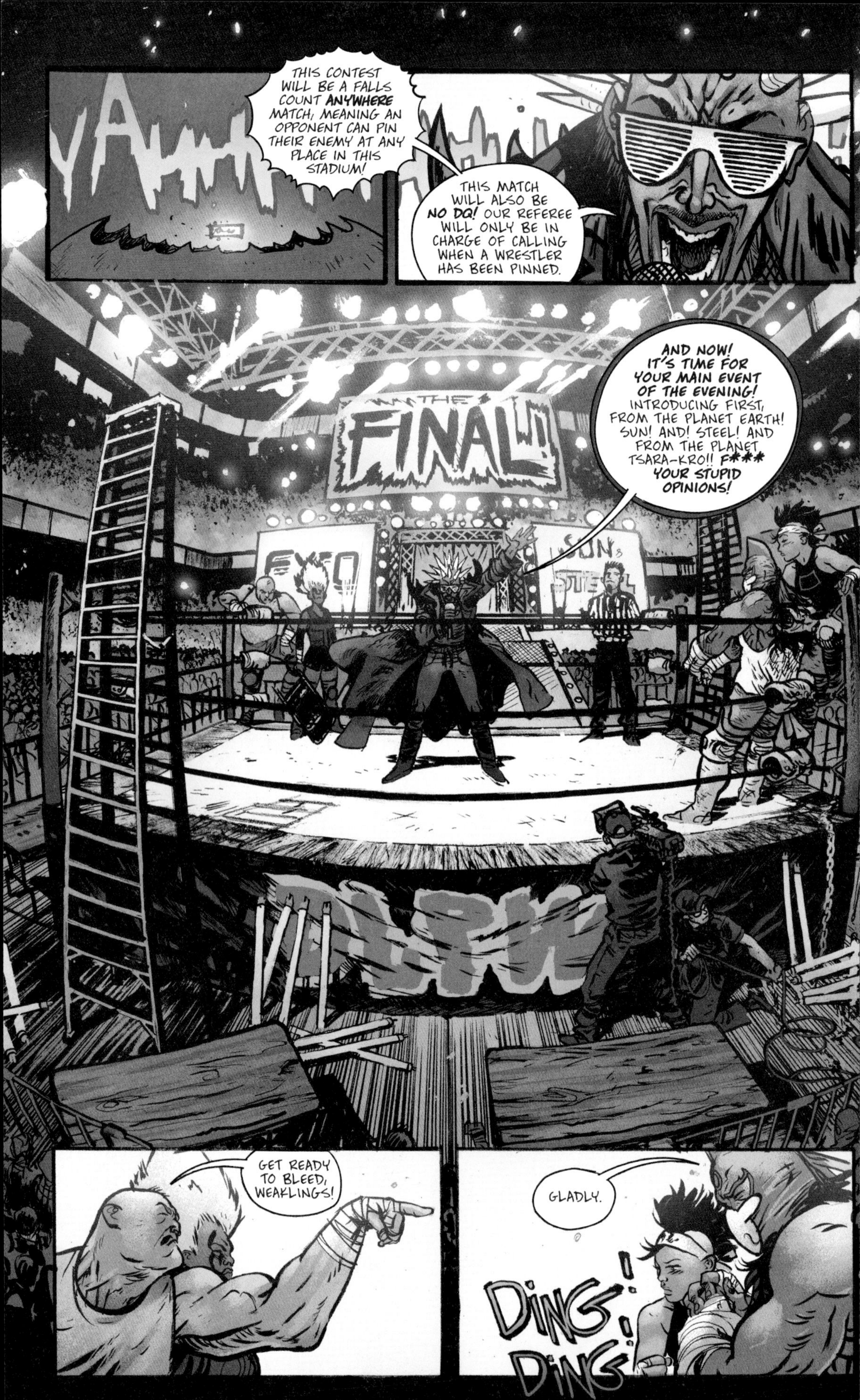

THIS CONTEST WILL BE A FALLS COUNT **ANYWHERE** MATCH, MEANING AN OPPONENT CAN PIN THEIR ENEMY AT ANY PLACE IN THIS STADIUM!
THIS MATCH WILL ALSO BE **NO DQ!** OUR REFEREE WILL ONLY BE IN CHARGE OF CALLING WHEN A WRESTLER HAS BEEN PINNED.
THE FINAL!
AND NOW! IT'S TIME FOR YOUR MAIN EVENT OF THE EVENING! INTRODUCING FIRST, FROM THE PLANET EARTH! SUN! AND! STEEL! AND FROM THE PLANET TSARA-KRO!! **F*** YOUR STUPID OPINIONS!**
GET READY TO BLEED, WEAKLINGS!
GLADLY.
DING! DING!

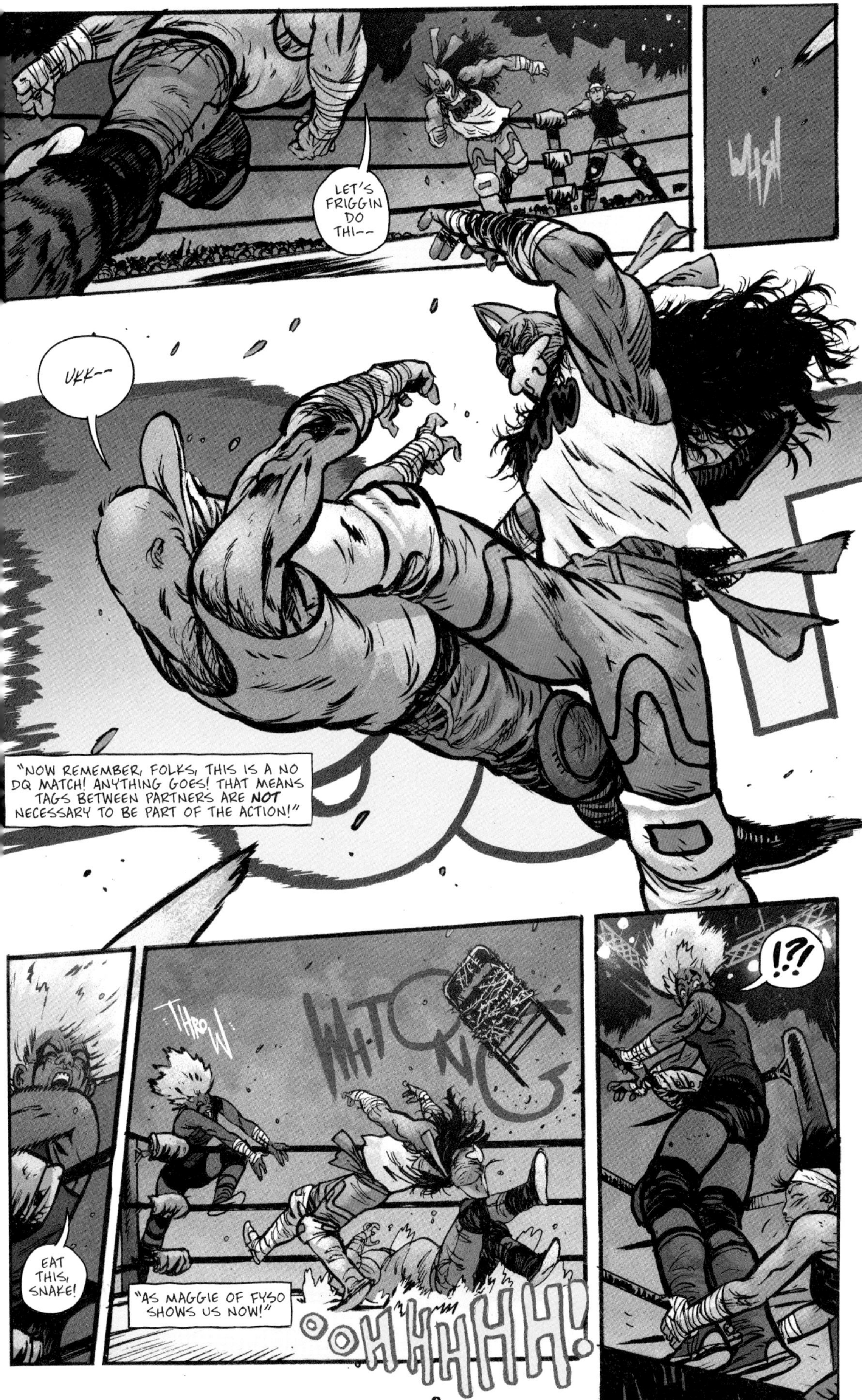
LET'S FRIGGIN DO THI--
WASH
UKK--
"NOW REMEMBER, FOLKS, THIS IS A NO DQ MATCH! ANYTHING GOES! THAT MEANS TAGS BETWEEN PARTNERS ARE **NOT** NECESSARY TO BE PART OF THE ACTION!"
EAT THIS, SNAKE!
THROW
WHTONG
"AS MAGGIE OF FYSO SHOWS US NOW!"
OOHHHHHH!
!?!

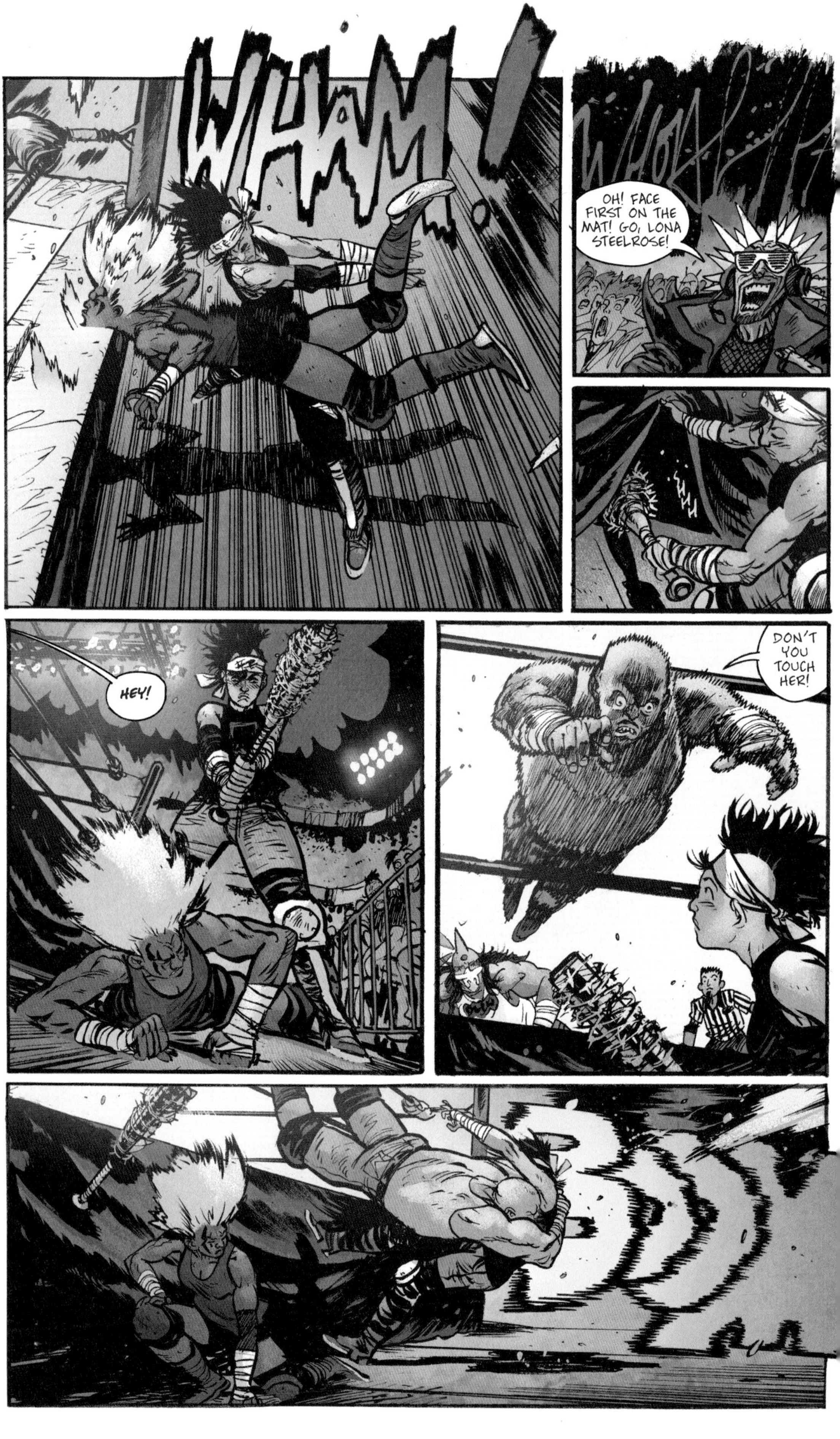
WHAM!
OH! FACE FIRST ON THE MAT! GO, LONA STEELROSE!
HEY!
DON'T YOU TOUCH HER!

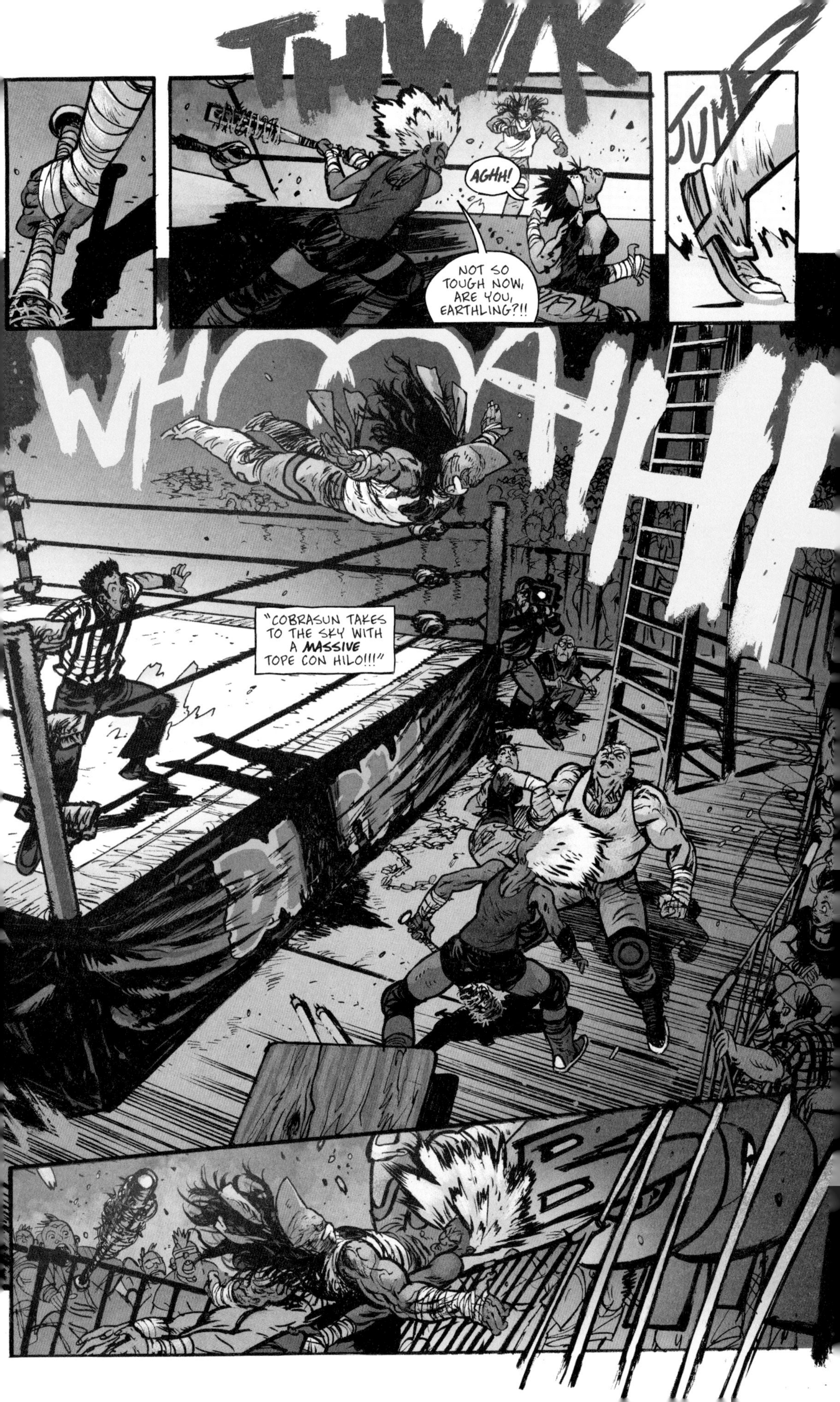
THWAK
AGHH!
NOT SO TOUGH NOW, ARE YOU, EARTHLING?!!
JUMP
WHOOAHH
"COBRASUN TAKES TO THE SKY WITH A **MASSIVE** TOPE CON HILO!!!"

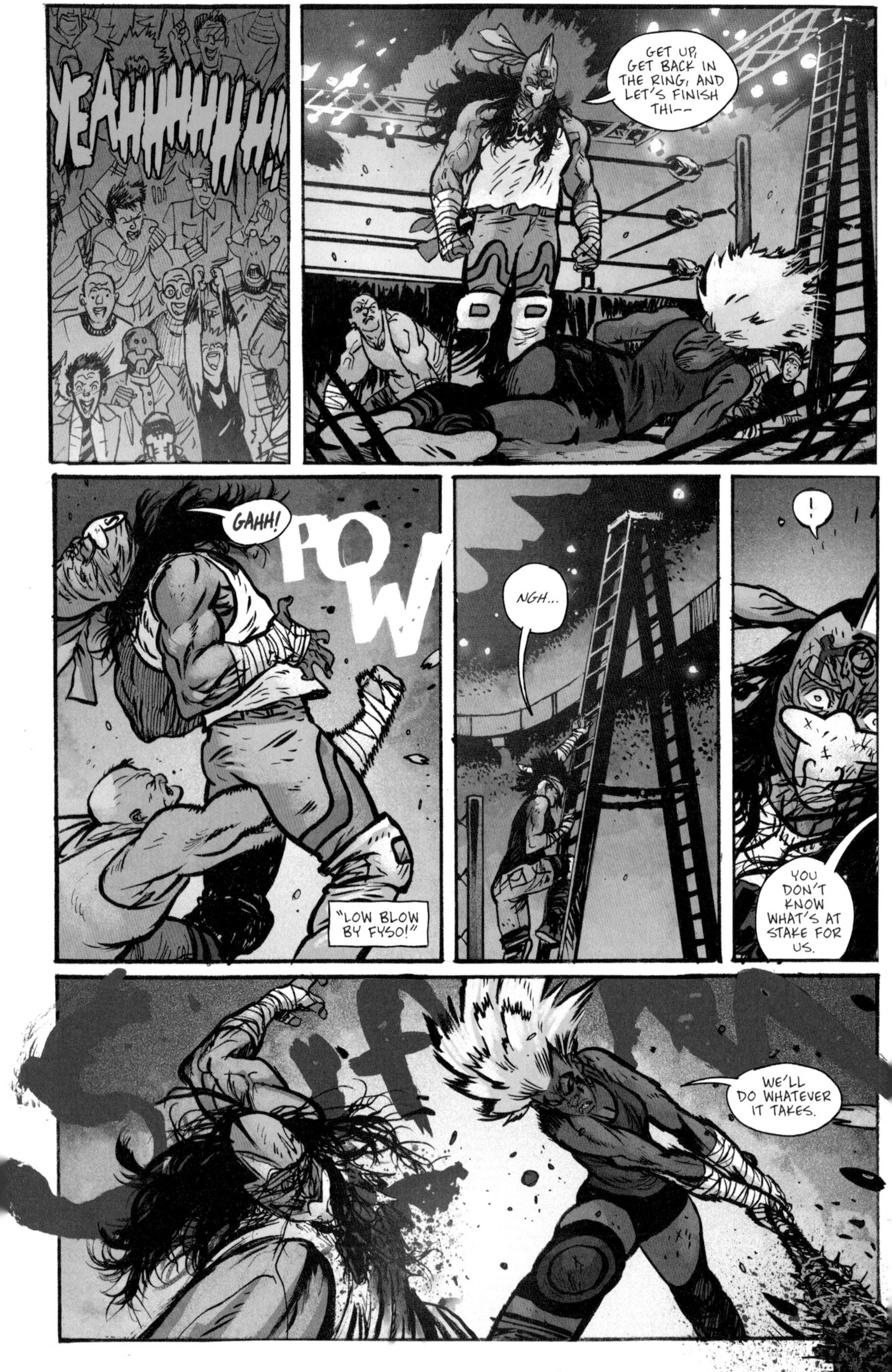
YEAHHHHHH!!
GET UP, GET BACK IN THE RING, AND LET'S FINISH THI--
GAHH!
POW
"LOW BLOW BY FYSO!"
NGH...
!
YOU DON'T KNOW WHAT'S AT STAKE FOR US.
WE'LL DO WHATEVER IT TAKES.

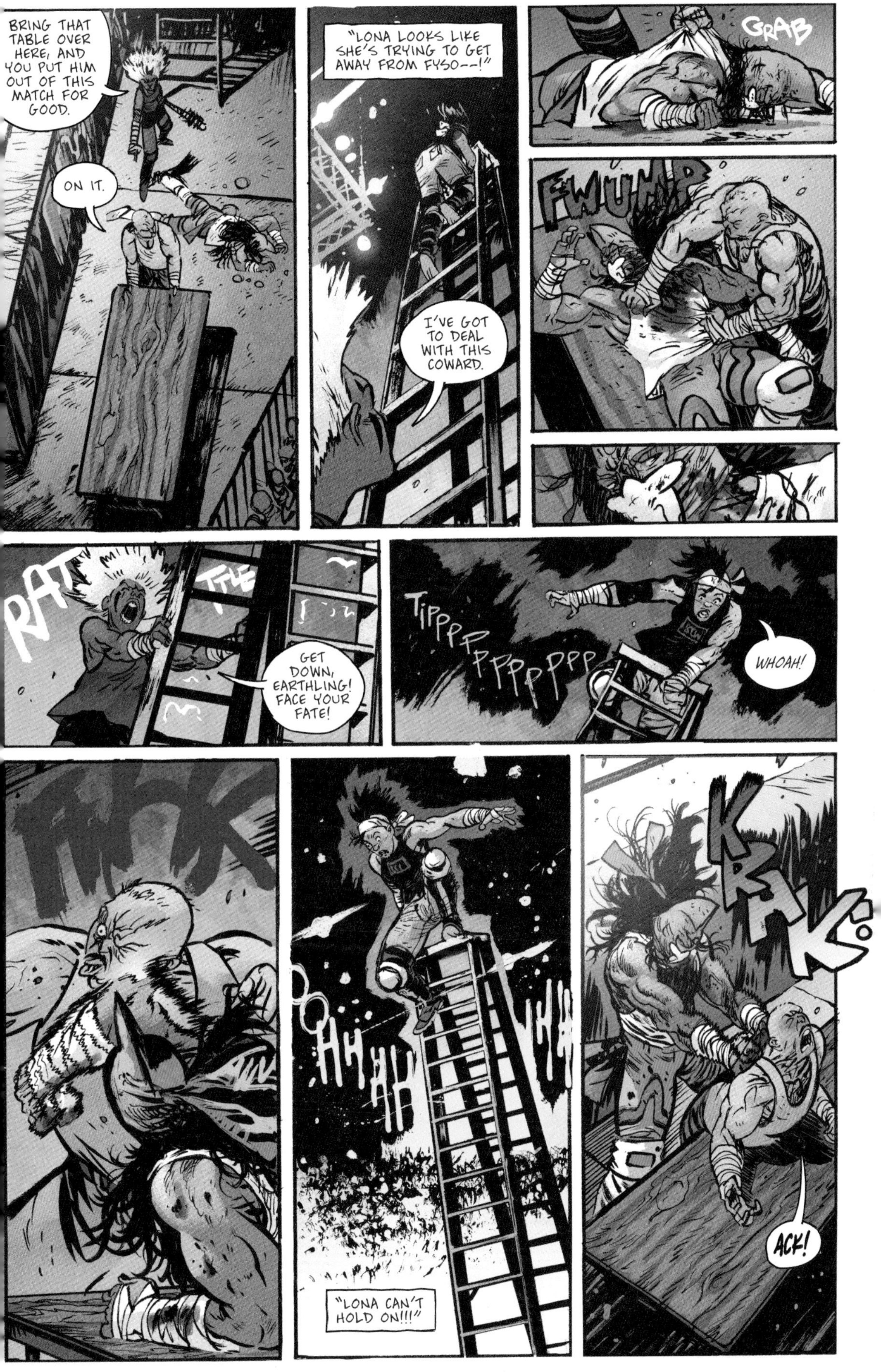
BRING THAT TABLE OVER HERE, AND YOU PUT HIM OUT OF THIS MATCH FOR GOOD.
ON IT.
"LONA LOOKS LIKE SHE'S TRYING TO GET AWAY FROM FYSO--!"
I'VE GOT TO DEAL WITH THIS COWARD.
GRAB
FWUMP
RATTLE
GET DOWN, EARTHLING! FACE YOUR FATE!
TIPPPPPPPPPPP
WHOAH!
THAK
OHHHHHHHH
"LONA CAN'T HOLD ON!!!"
KRAK!
ACK!

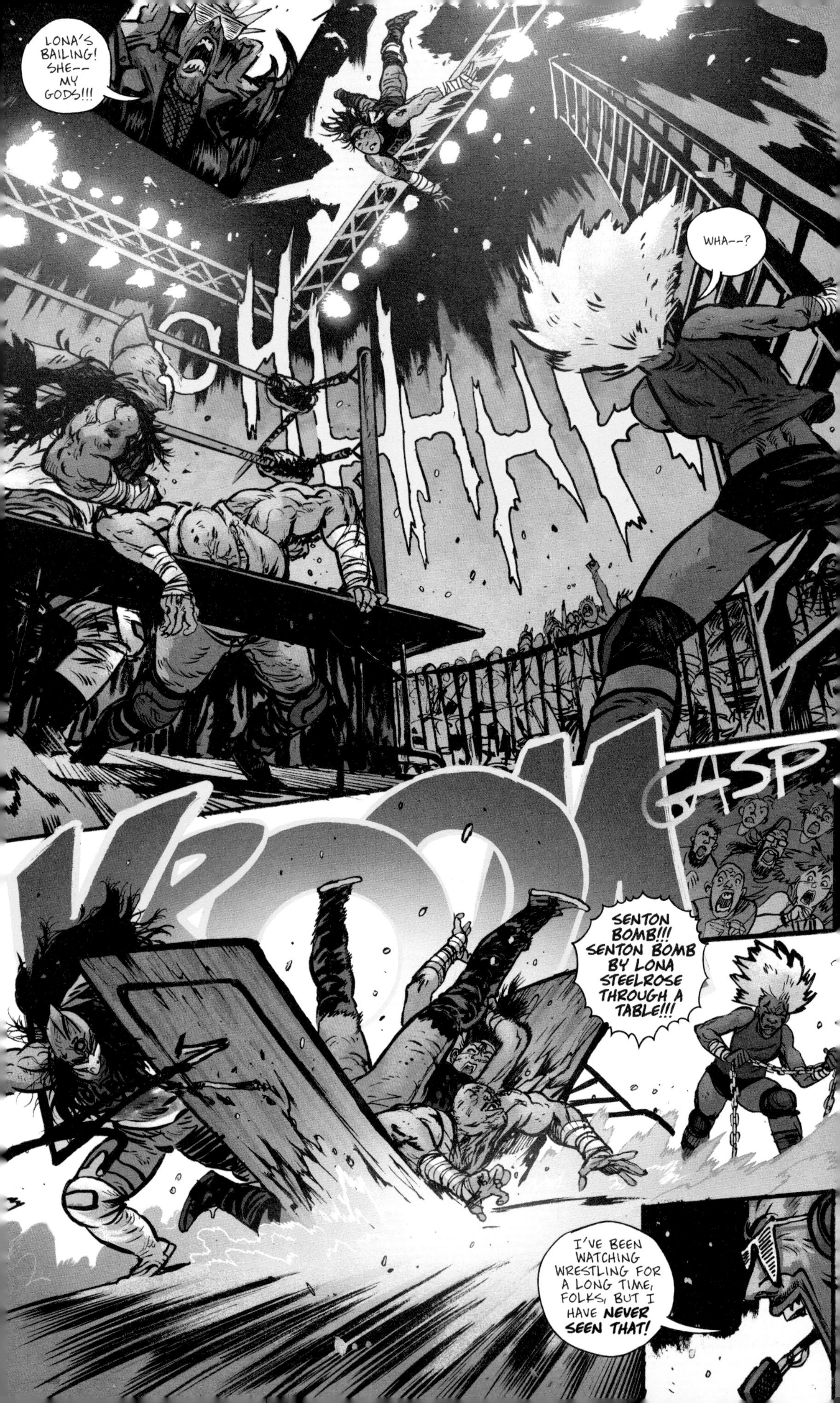
LONA'S BAILING! SHE-- MY GODS!!!
WHOOSH
WHA--?
GASP
KRAKOOM
SENTON BOMB!!! SENTON BOMB BY LONA STEELROSE THROUGH A TABLE!!!
I'VE BEEN WATCHING WRESTLING FOR A LONG TIME, FOLKS, BUT I HAVE **NEVER** SEEN THAT!

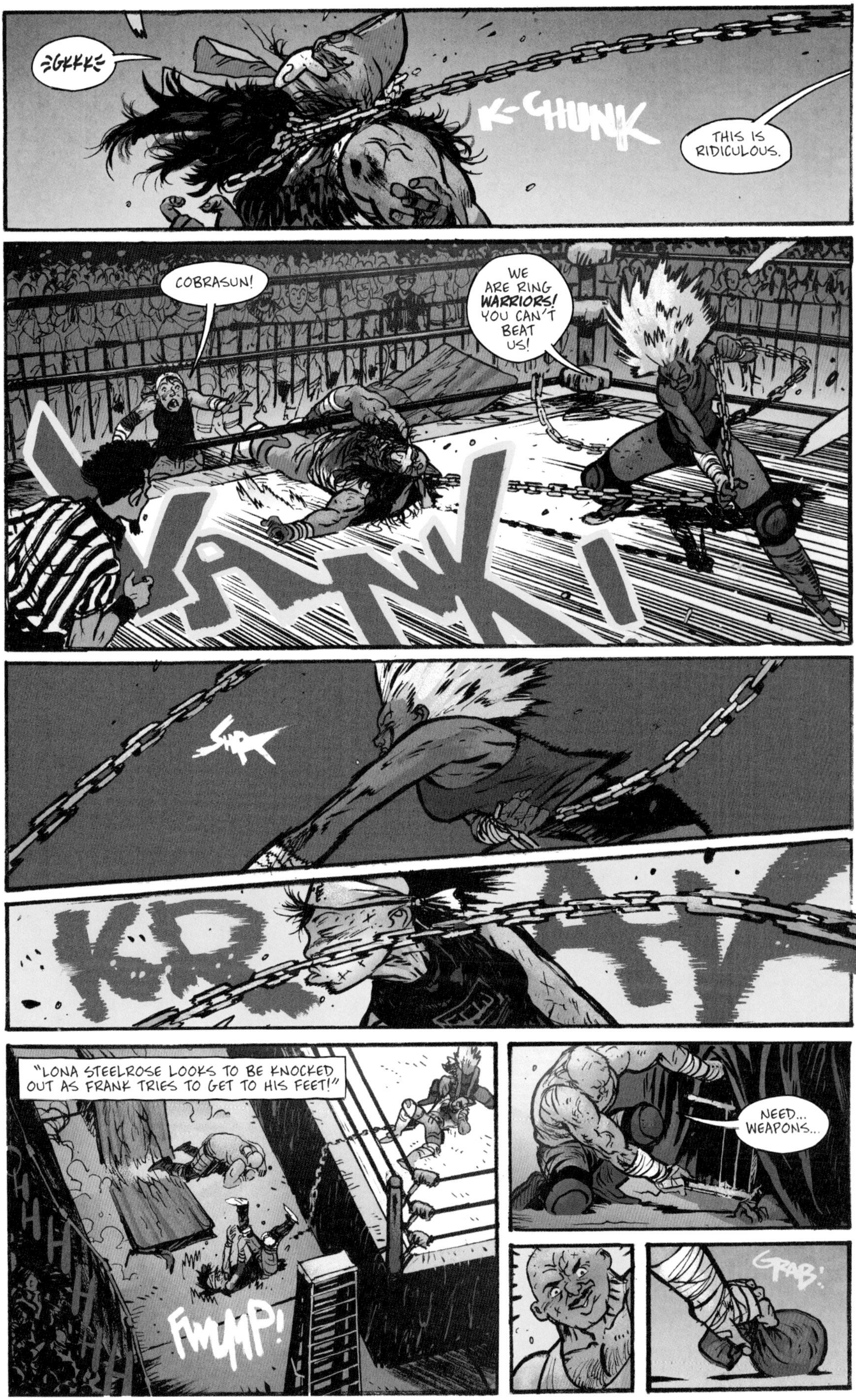

GKKK
K-CHUNK
THIS IS RIDICULOUS.
COBRASUN!
WE ARE RING **WARRIORS!** YOU CAN'T BEAT US!
SHRAK
"LONA STEELROSE LOOKS TO BE KNOCKED OUT AS FRANK TRIES TO GET TO HIS FEET!"
FWUMP!
NEED... WEAPONS...
GRAB!

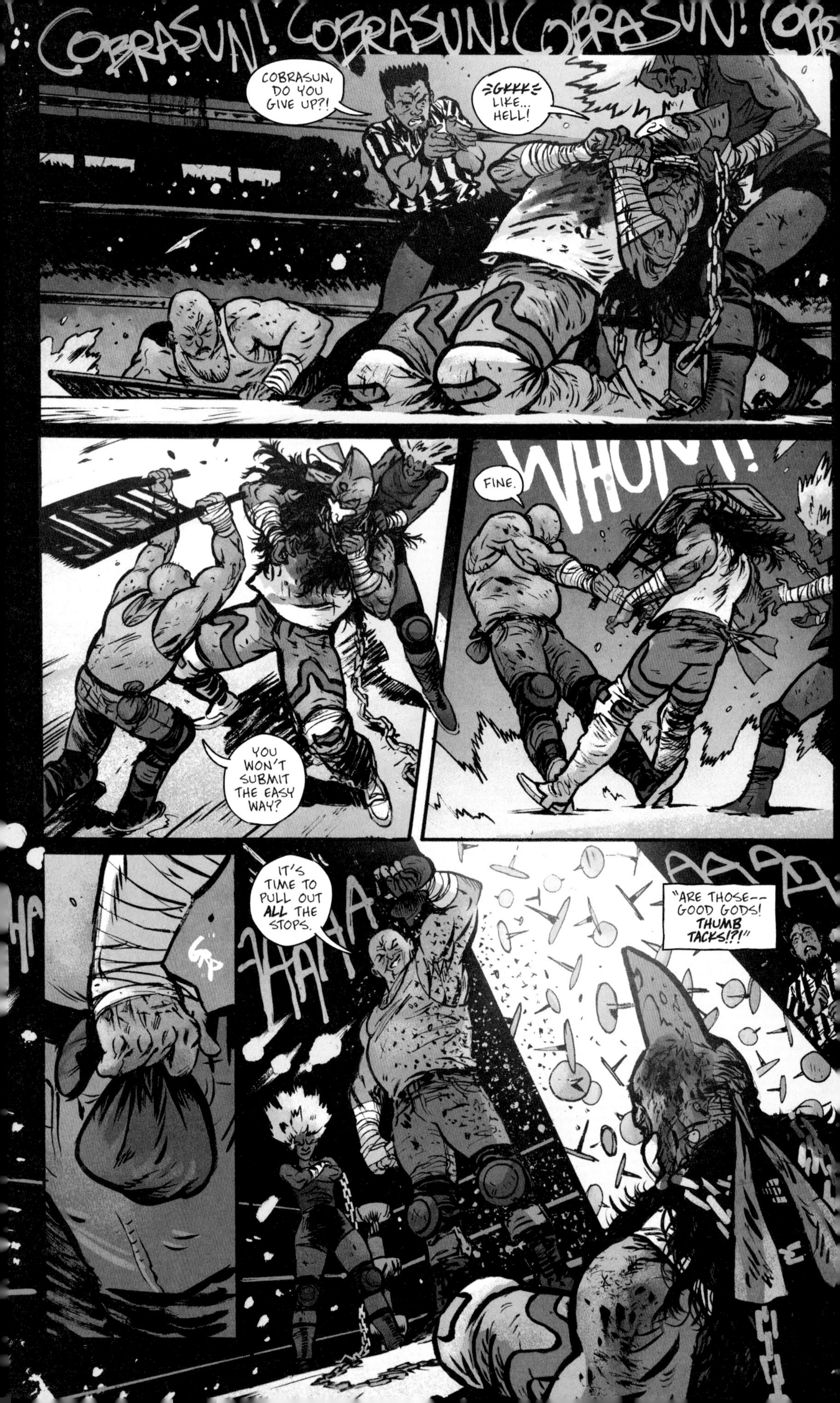
COBRASUN! COBRASUN! COBRASUN!
COBRASUN, DO YOU GIVE UP?!
GKKK LIKE... HELL!
YOU WON'T SUBMIT THE EASY WAY?
WHOM!
FINE.
IT'S TIME TO PULL OUT ALL THE STOPS.
"ARE THOSE--GOOD GODS! THUMB TACKS!?!"

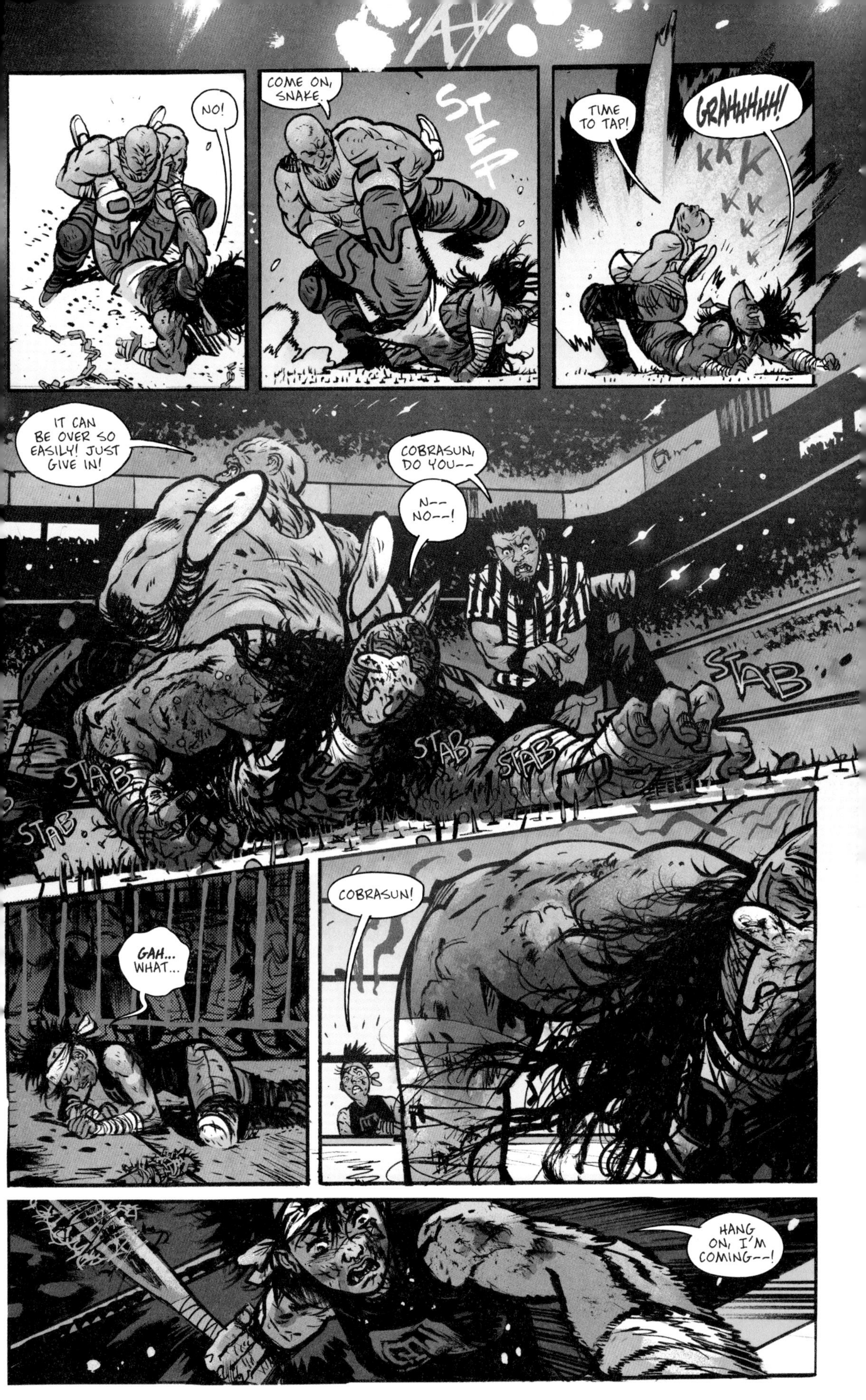

AAY
NO!
COME ON, SNAKE.
STEP
TIME TO TAP!
GRAHHHHH!
KKKKKKKKK
IT CAN BE OVER SO EASILY! JUST GIVE IN!
COBRASUN, DO YOU--
N-- NO--!
STAB
STAB
STAB
STAB
STAB
GAH... WHAT...
COBRASUN!
HANG ON, I'M COMING--!

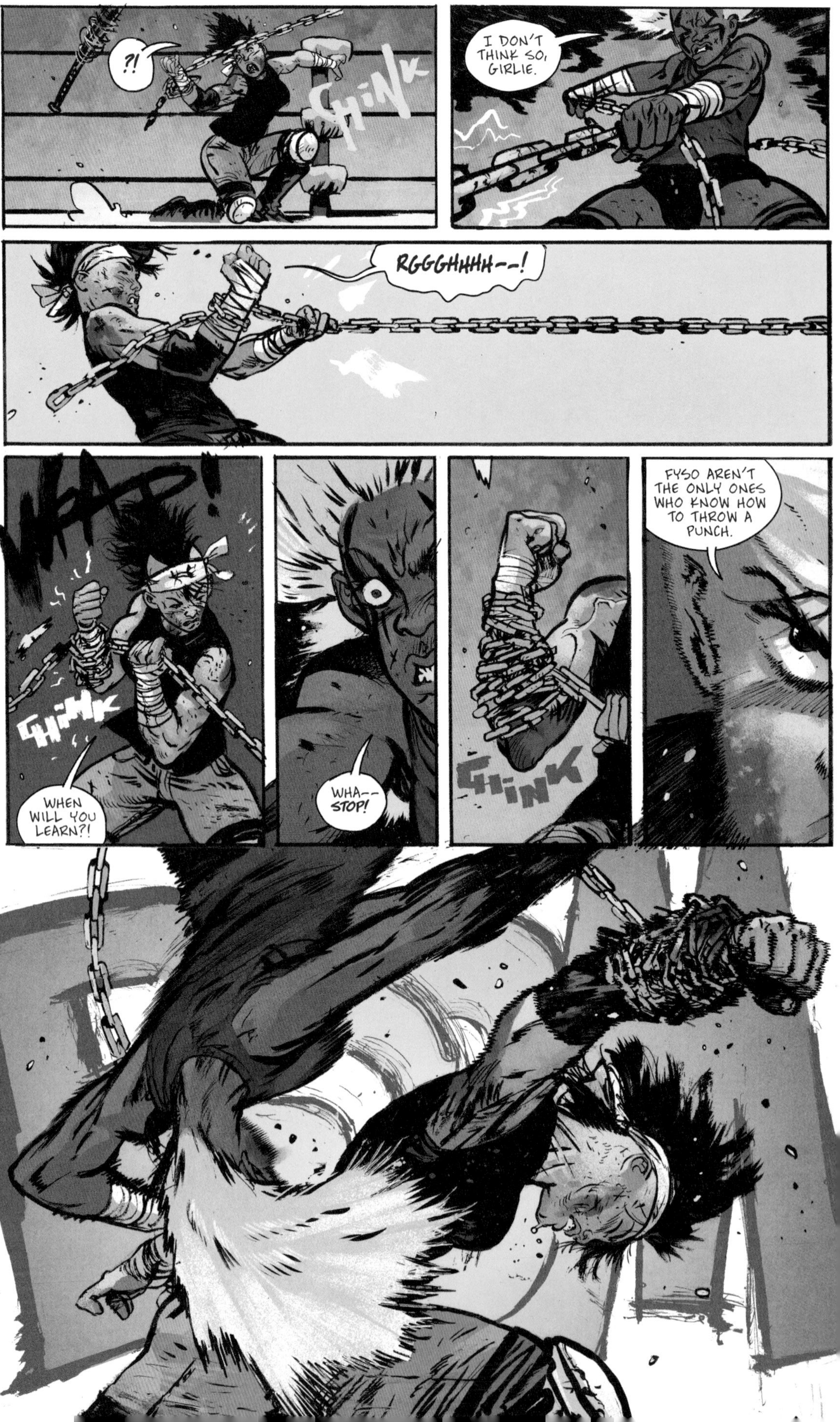
?!
CHINK
I DON'T THINK SO, GIRLIE.
RGGGHHHH--!
WHAP!
CHINK
WHEN WILL YOU LEARN?!
WHA--STOP!
CHINK
FYSO AREN'T THE ONLY ONES WHO KNOW HOW TO THROW A PUNCH.

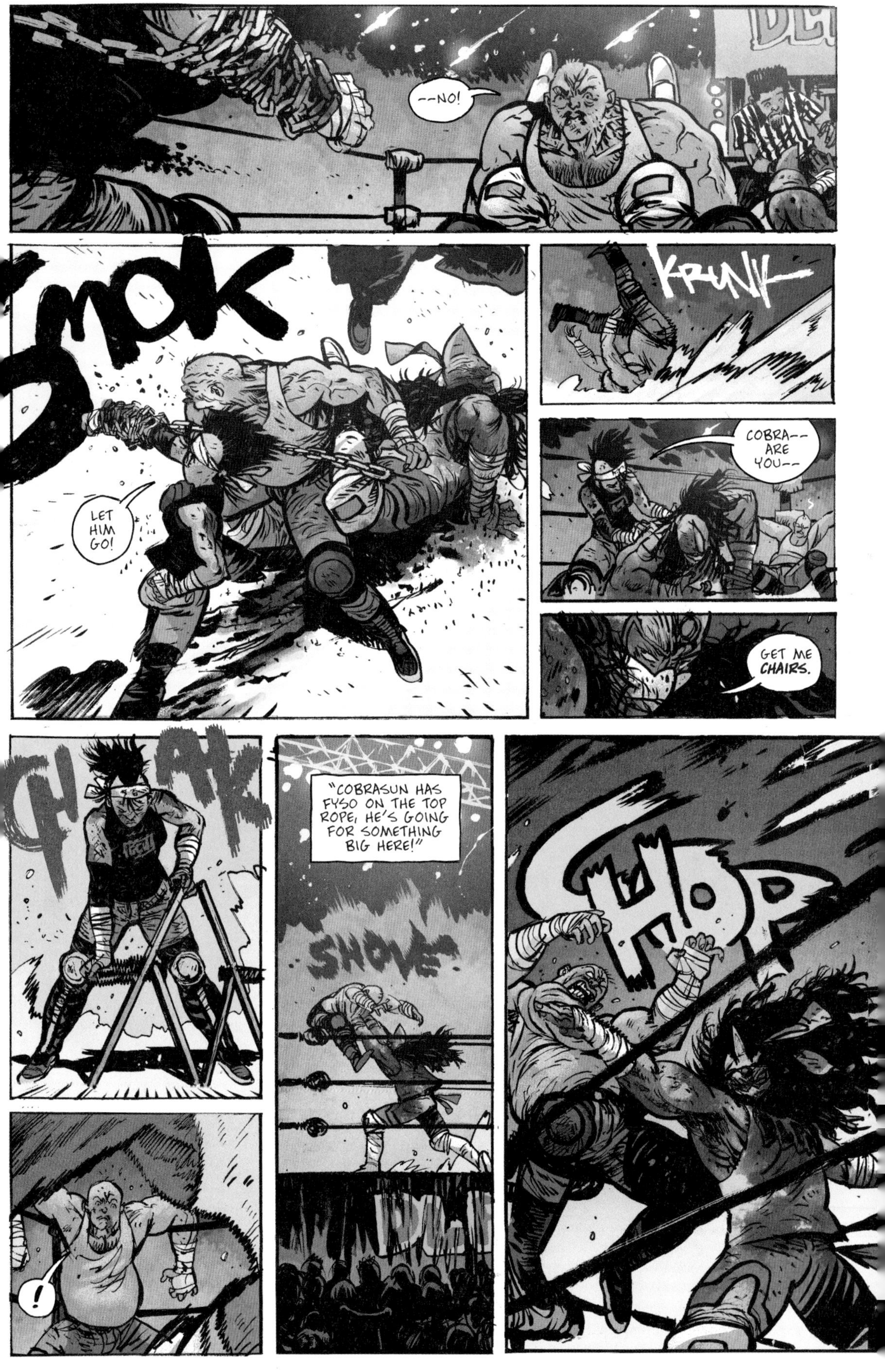
--NO!
SMOK
LET HIM GO!
KRUNK
COBRA-- ARE YOU--
GET ME CHAIRS.
CHAK
"COBRASUN HAS FYSO ON THE TOP ROPE, HE'S GOING FOR SOMETHING BIG HERE!"
SHOVE
!
HOP

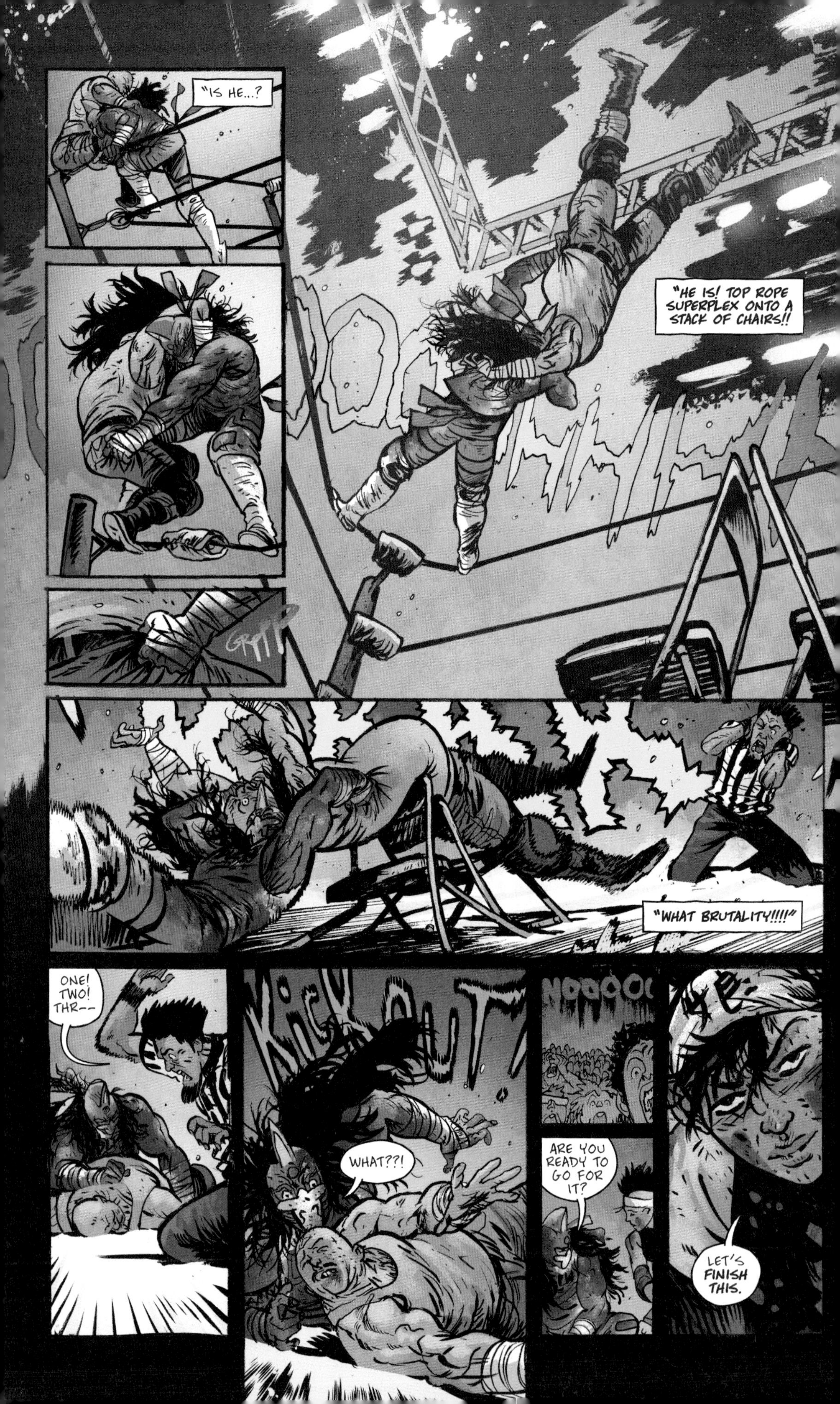
"IS HE...?
GRIP
"HE IS! TOP ROPE SUPERPLEX ONTO A STACK OF CHAIRS!!
"WHAT BRUTALITY!!!!"
ONE! TWO! THR--
KICK OUT
WHAT??!
NOOOOO
ARE YOU READY TO GO FOR IT?
LET'S FINISH THIS.

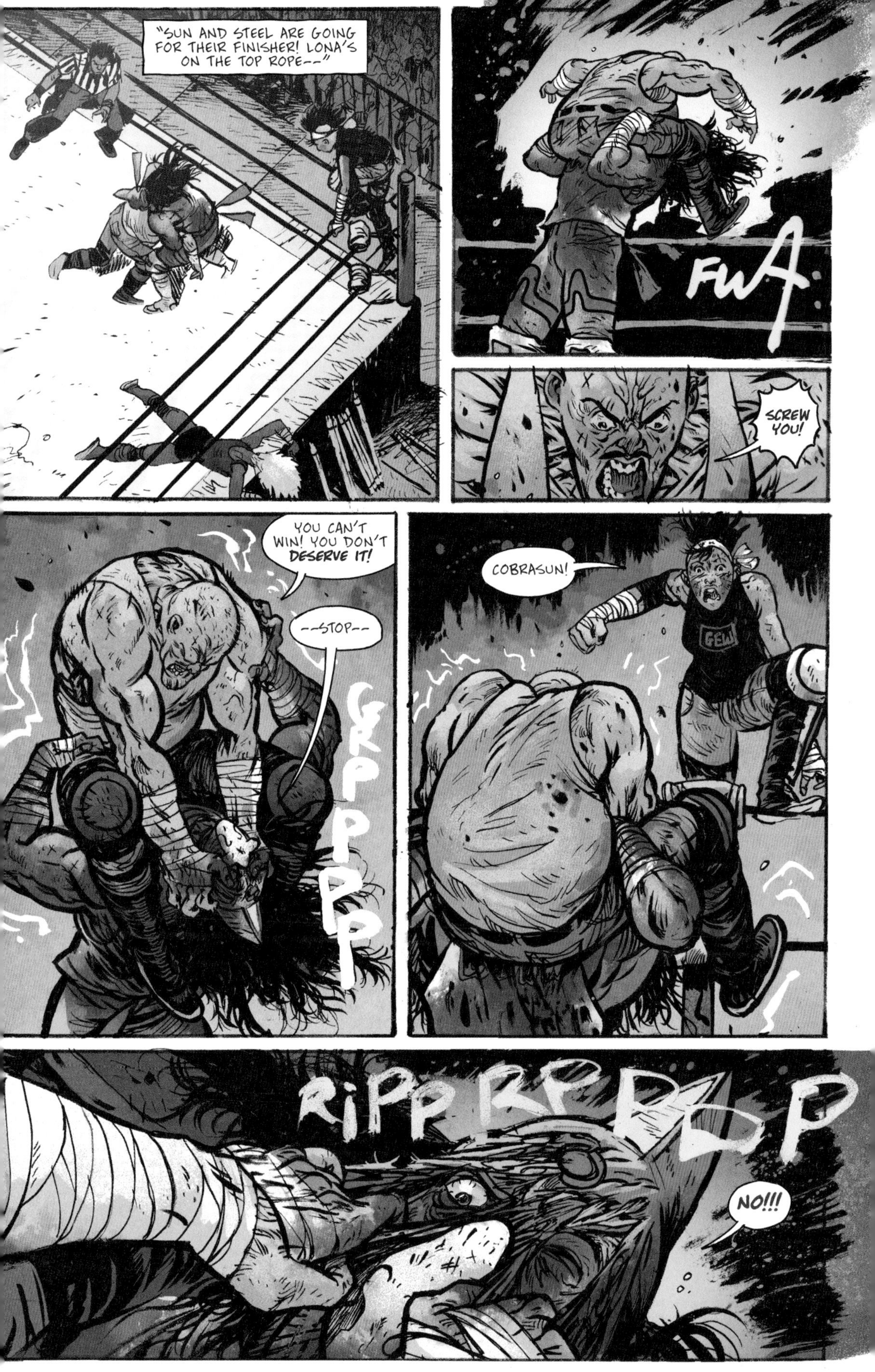
"SUN AND STEEL ARE GOING FOR THEIR FINISHER! LONA'S ON THE TOP ROPE--"
FWA
SCREW YOU!
YOU CAN'T WIN! YOU DON'T DESERVE IT!
--STOP--
GRPPPP
COBRASUN!
GFW
RIPP RPPPP
NO!!!

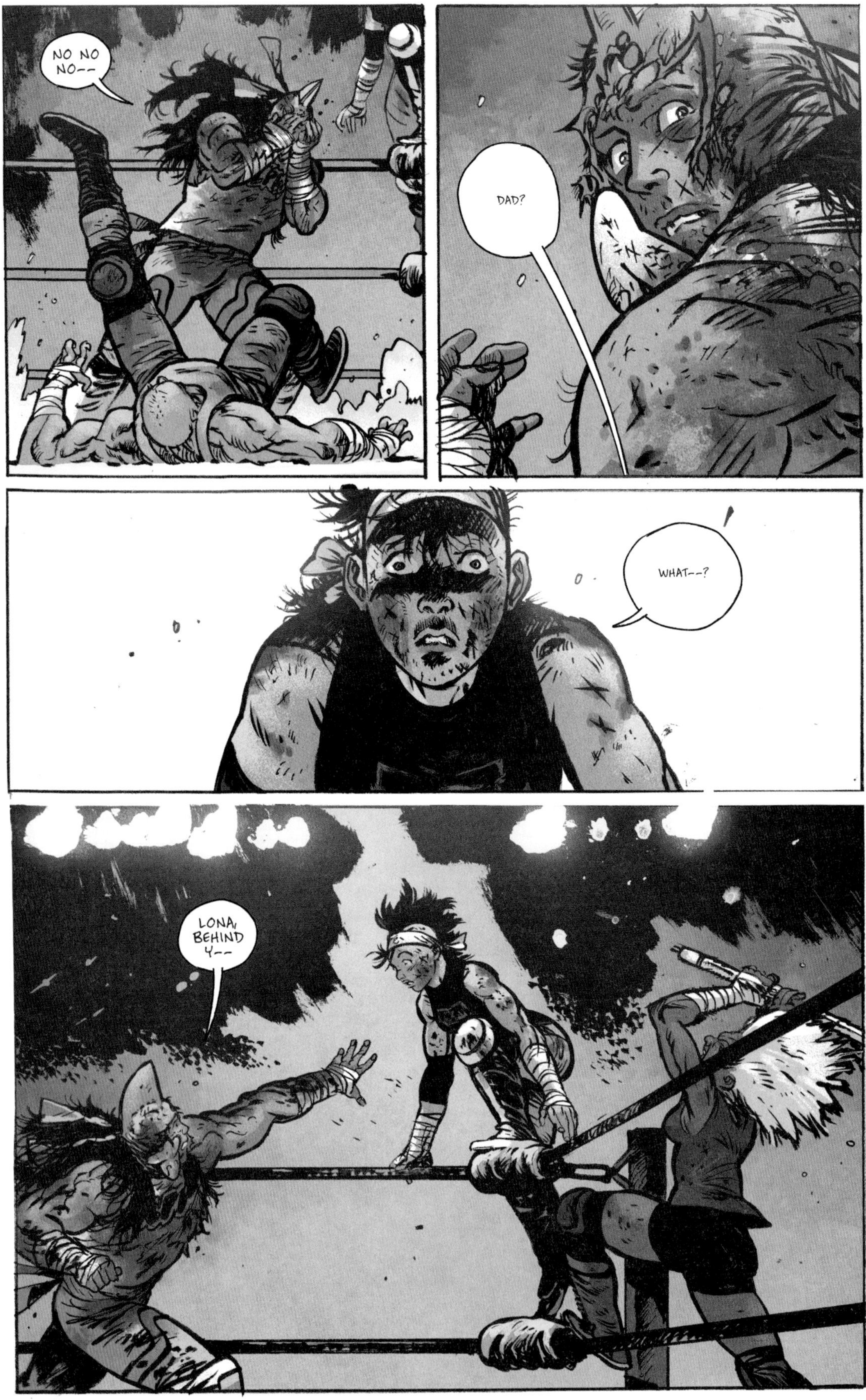
NO NO NO--
DAD?
WHAT--?
LONA, BEHIND Y--

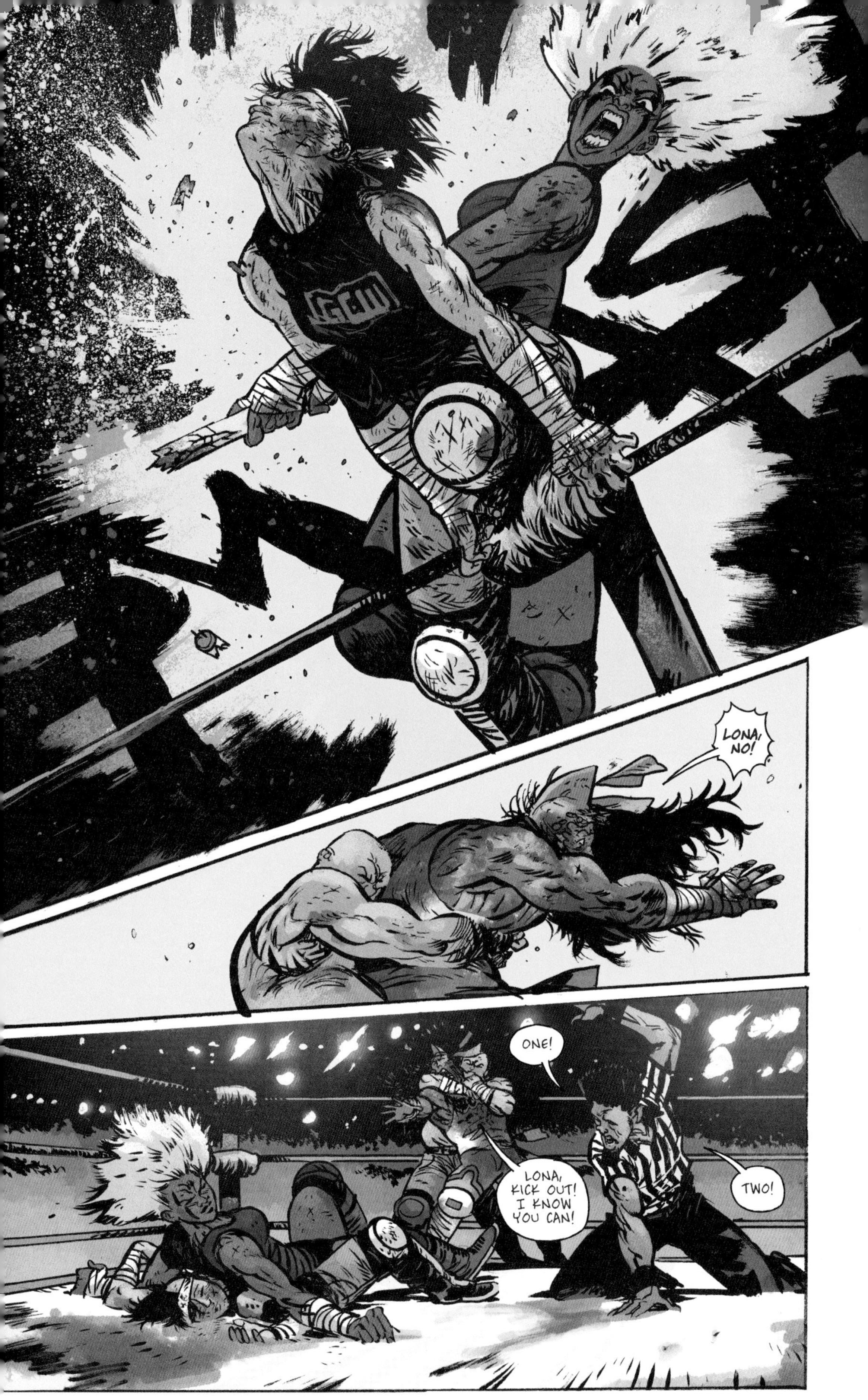
LONA, NO!
ONE!
LONA, KICK OUT! I KNOW YOU CAN!
TWO!

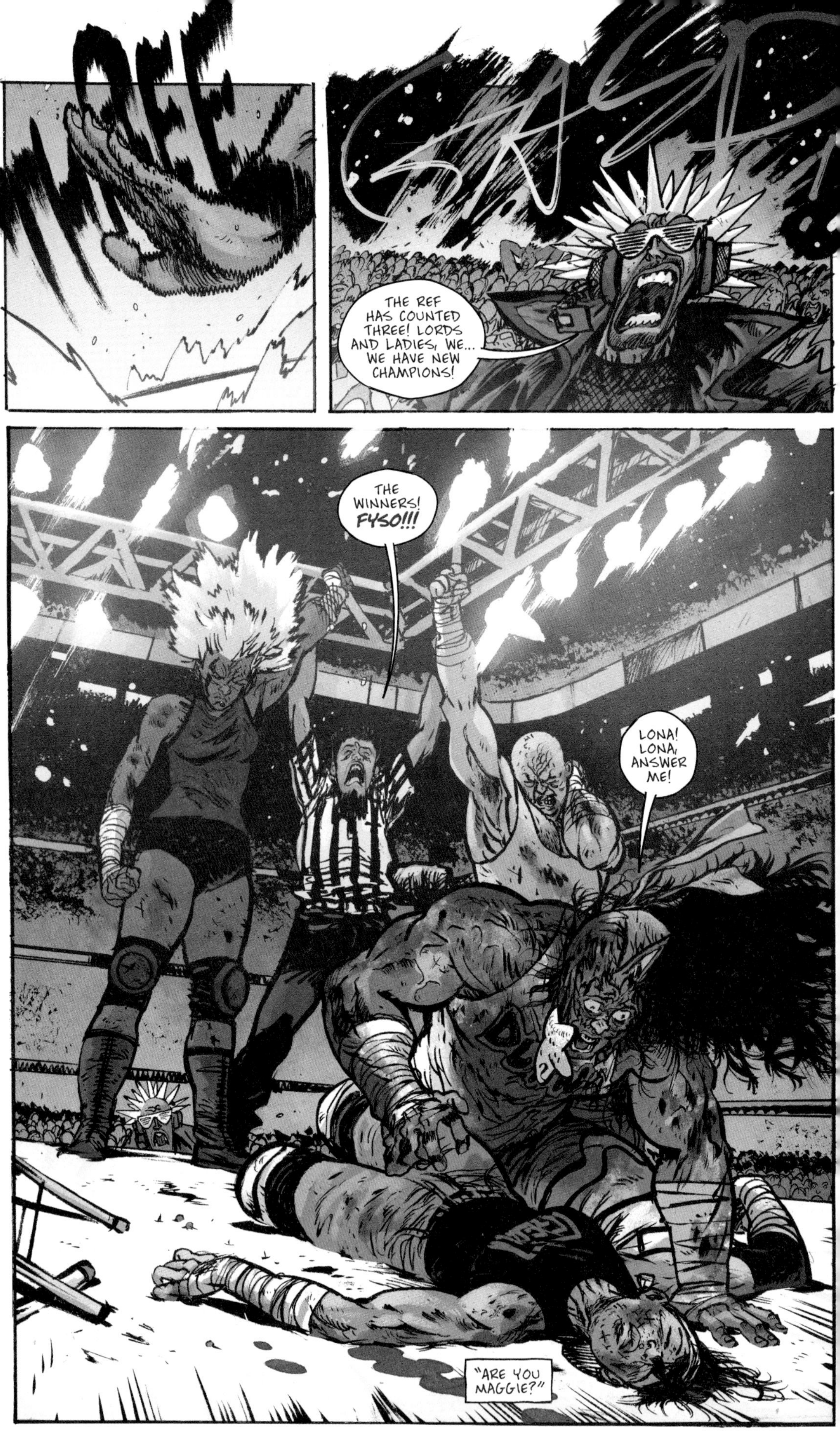
THE REF HAS COUNTED THREE! LORDS AND LADIES, WE... WE HAVE NEW CHAMPIONS!
THE WINNERS! **FYSO!!!**
LONA! LONA, ANSWER ME!
"ARE YOU MAGGIE?"

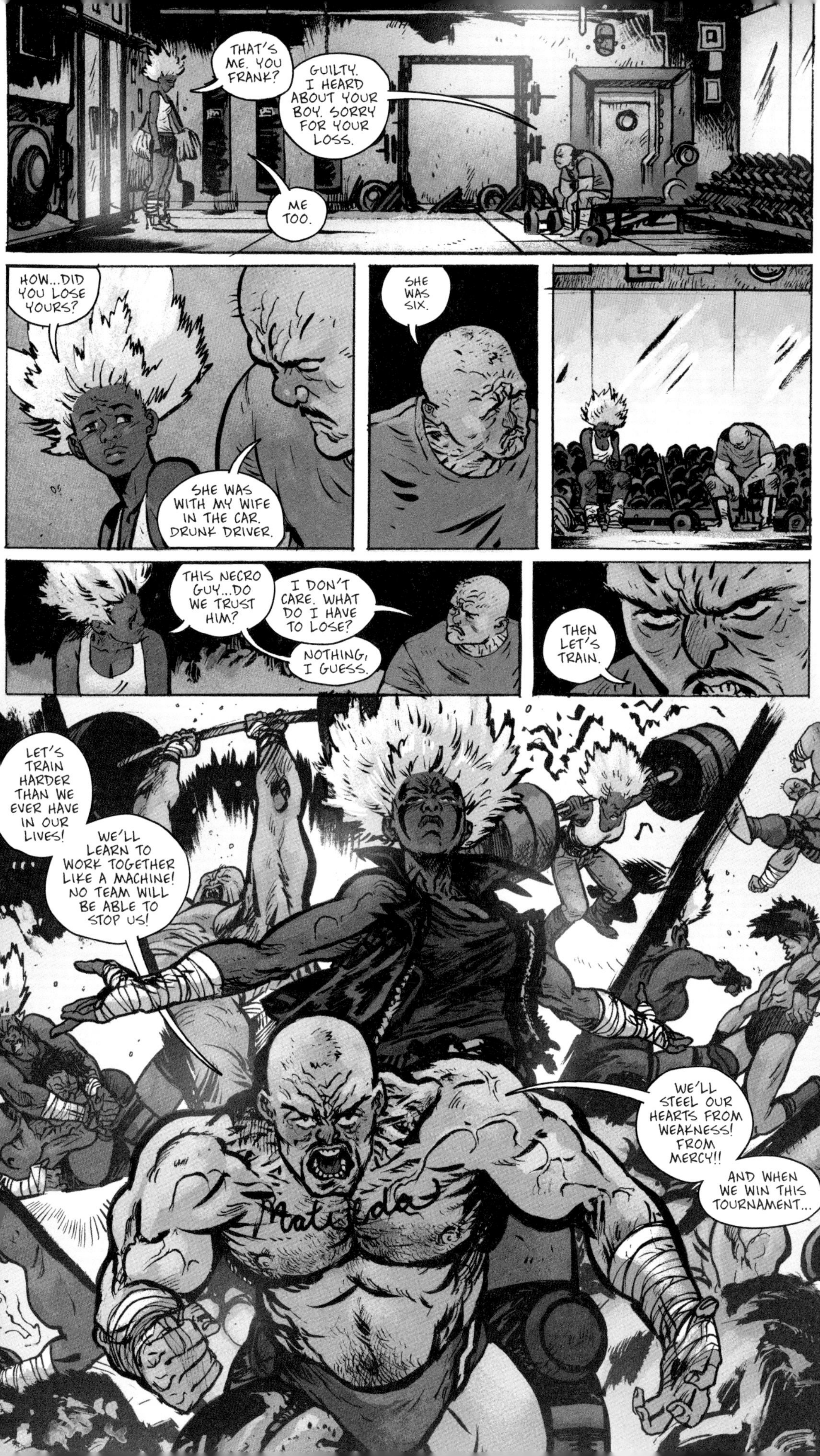

THAT'S ME. YOU FRANK?
GUILTY. I HEARD ABOUT YOUR BOY. SORRY FOR YOUR LOSS.
ME TOO.
HOW...DID YOU LOSE YOURS?
SHE WAS WITH MY WIFE IN THE CAR. DRUNK DRIVER.
SHE WAS SIX.
THIS NECRO GUY...DO WE TRUST HIM?
I DON'T CARE. WHAT DO I HAVE TO LOSE?
NOTHING, I GUESS.
THEN LET'S TRAIN.
LET'S TRAIN HARDER THAN WE EVER HAVE IN OUR LIVES!
WE'LL LEARN TO WORK TOGETHER LIKE A MACHINE! NO TEAM WILL BE ABLE TO STOP US!
Matilda
WE'LL STEEL OUR HEARTS FROM WEAKNESS! FROM MERCY!!
AND WHEN WE WIN THIS TOURNAMENT...

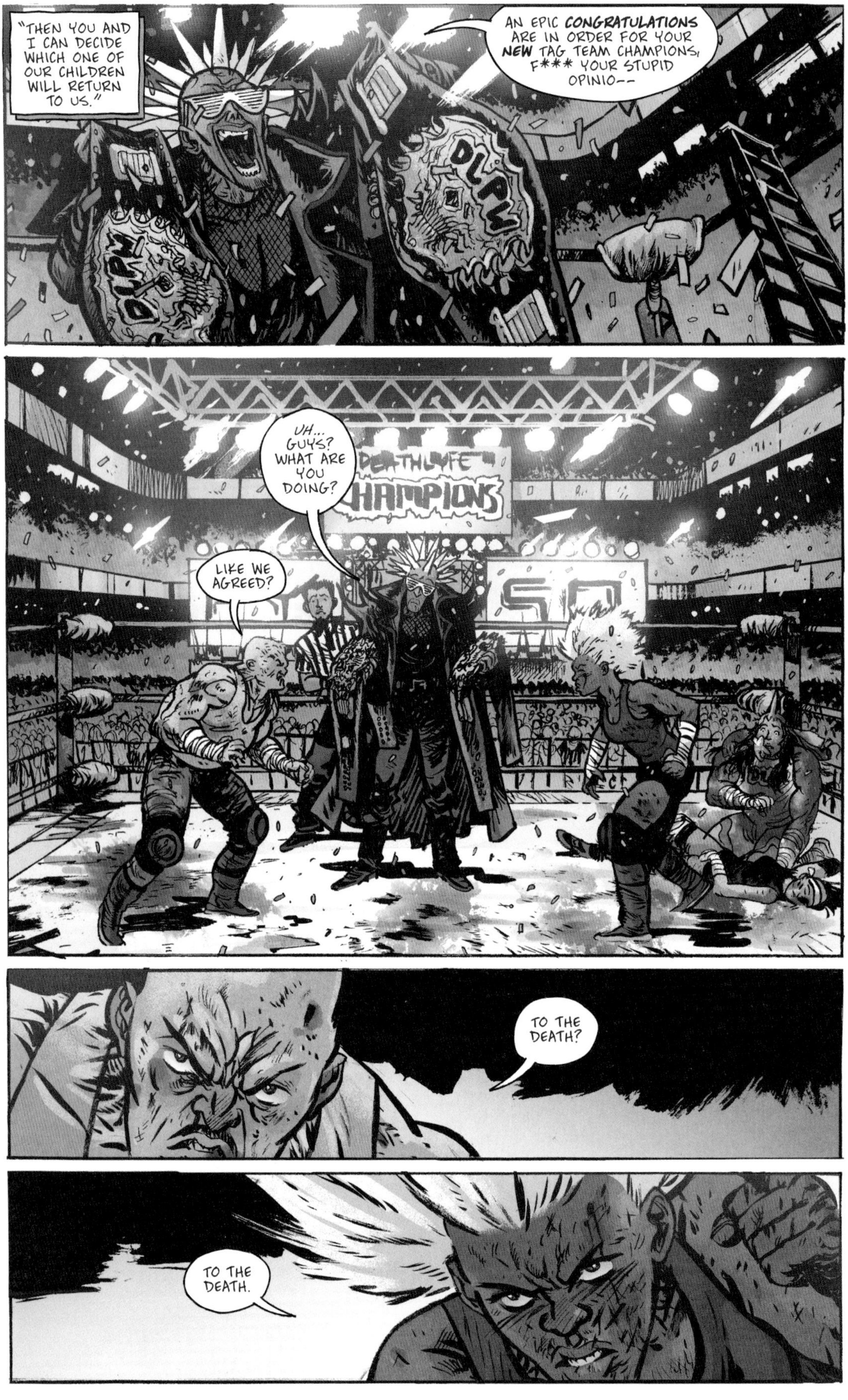
"THEN YOU AND I CAN DECIDE WHICH ONE OF OUR CHILDREN WILL RETURN TO US."
AN EPIC **CONGRATULATIONS** ARE IN ORDER FOR YOUR **NEW** TAG TEAM CHAMPIONS, F*** YOUR STUPID OPINIO--
DLPW
CHAMPIONS
UH... GUYS? WHAT ARE YOU DOING?
LIKE WE AGREED?
TO THE DEATH?
TO THE DEATH.

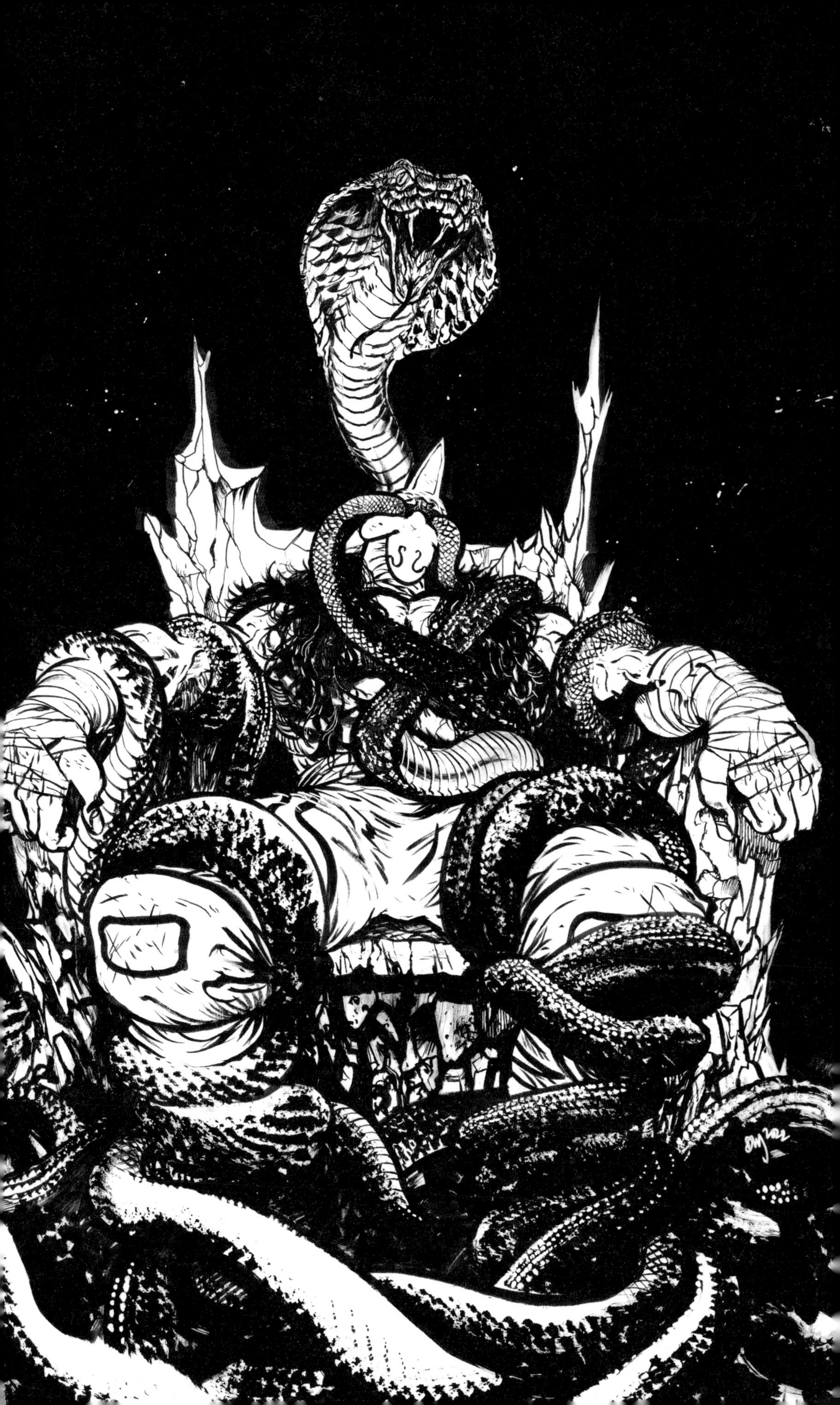

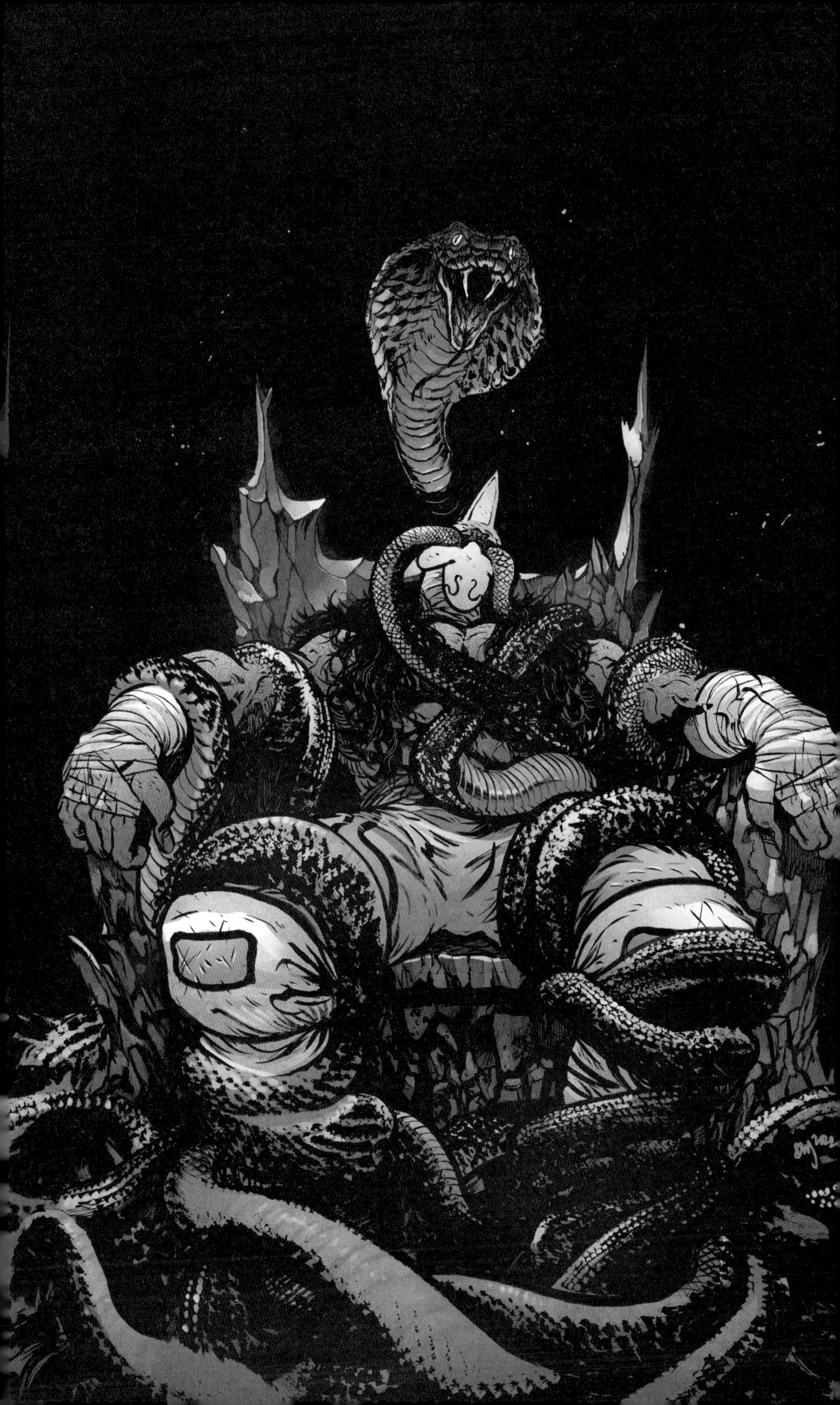

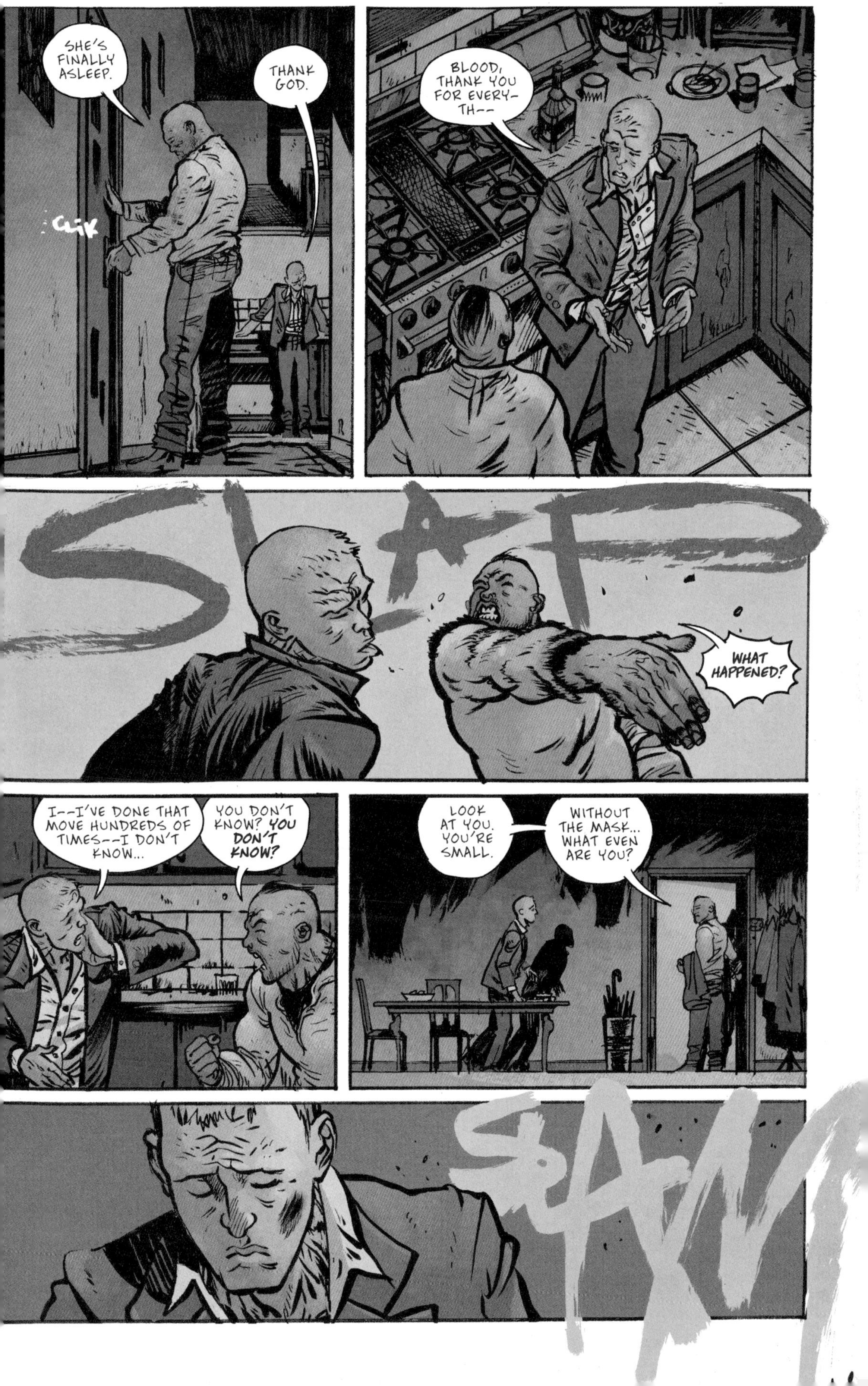
SHE'S FINALLY ASLEEP.
CLIK
THANK GOD.
BLOOD, THANK YOU FOR EVERY-TH--
SLAP
WHAT HAPPENED?
I--I'VE DONE THAT MOVE HUNDREDS OF TIMES--I DON'T KNOW...
YOU DON'T KNOW? **YOU DON'T KNOW?**
LOOK AT YOU. YOU'RE SMALL.
WITHOUT THE MASK... WHAT EVEN ARE YOU?

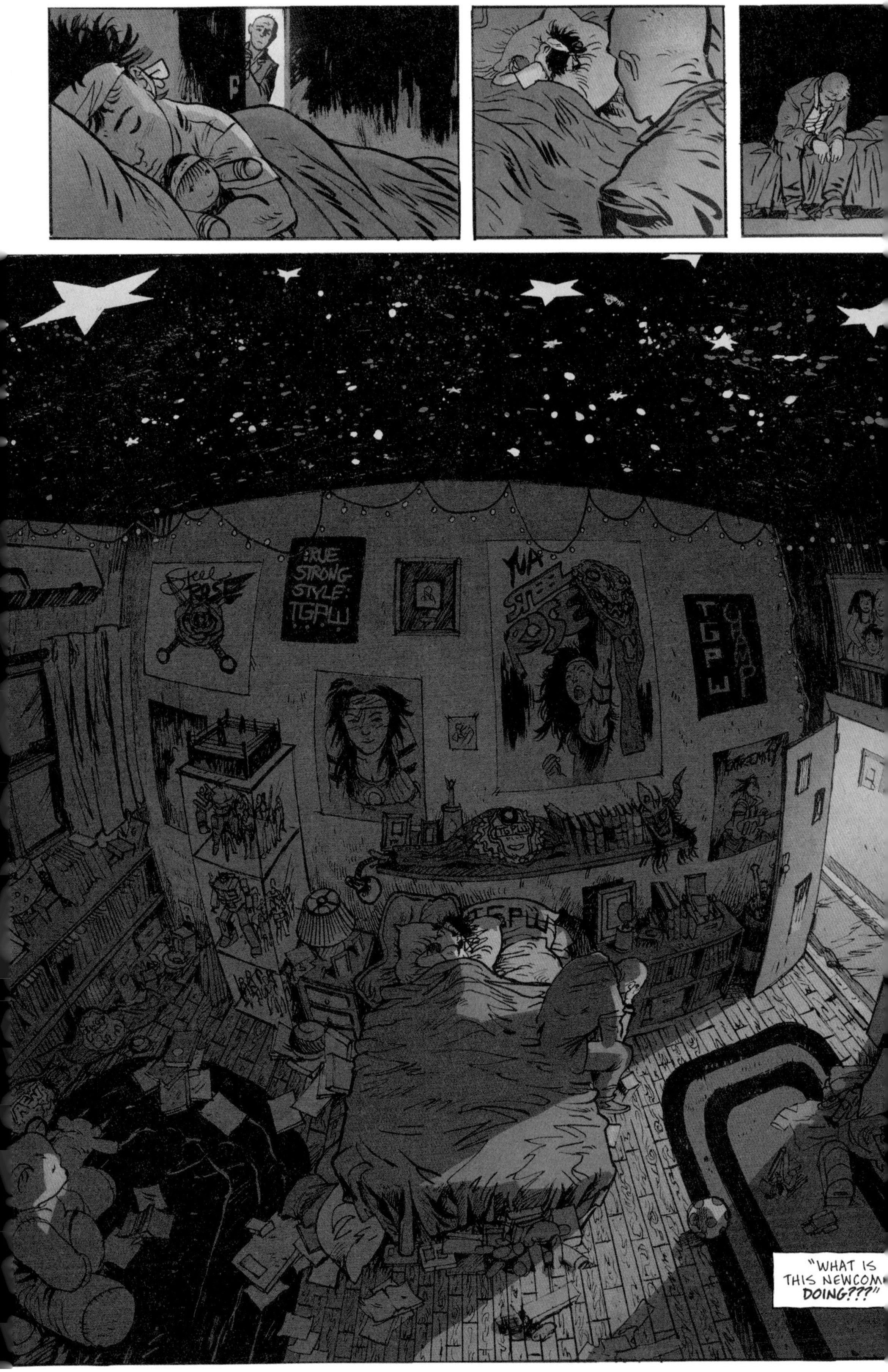
TRUE STRONG STYLE TGPW
TGPW CHAMP
"WHAT IS THIS NEWCOM DOING???"

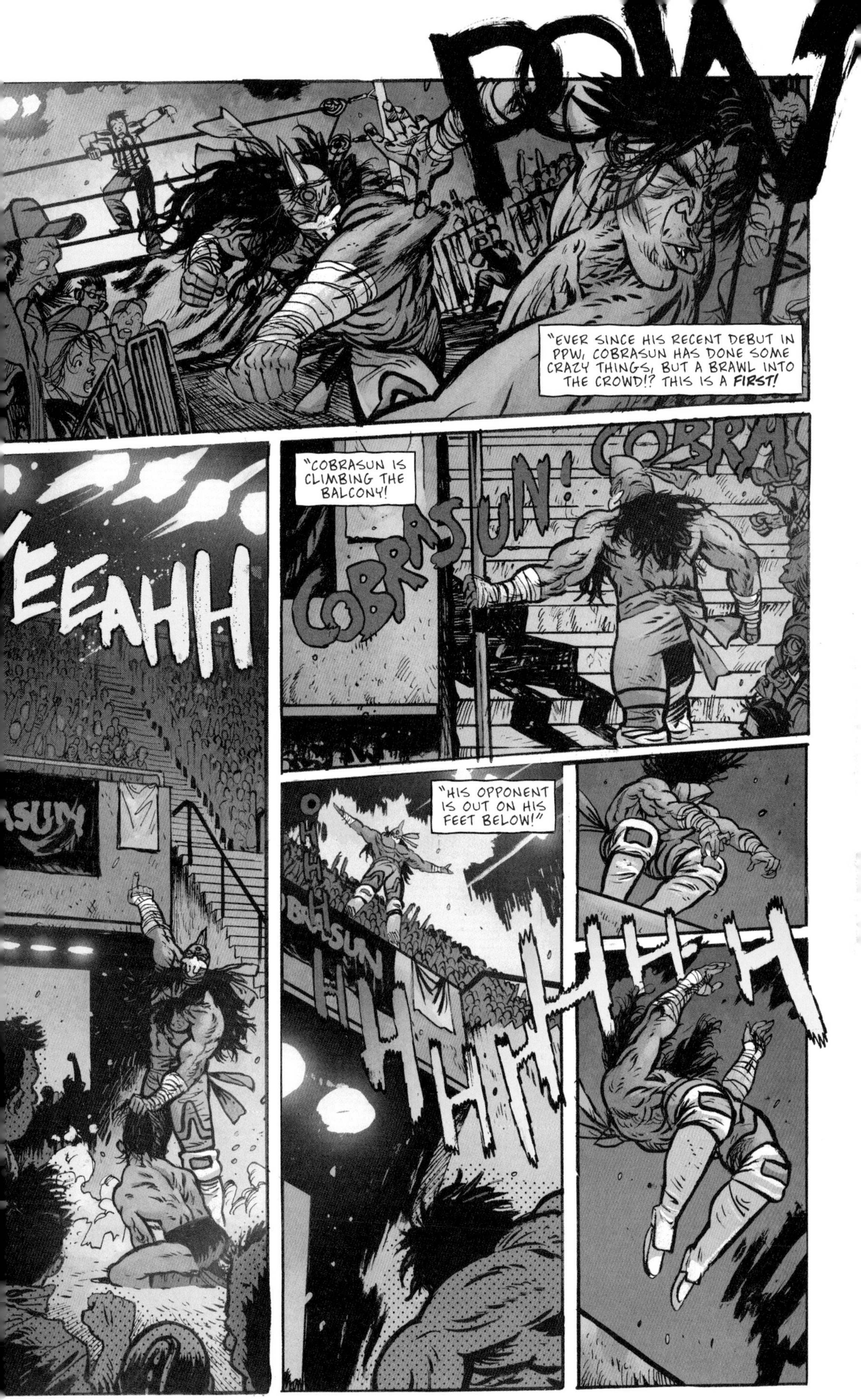

POW
"EVER SINCE HIS RECENT DEBUT IN PPW, COBRASUN HAS DONE SOME CRAZY THINGS, BUT A BRAWL INTO THE CROWD!? THIS IS A FIRST!
YEEAHH
"COBRASUN IS CLIMBING THE BALCONY!
COBRASUN! COBRA
"HIS OPPONENT IS OUT ON HIS FEET BELOW!"
OHHHHHHHHH

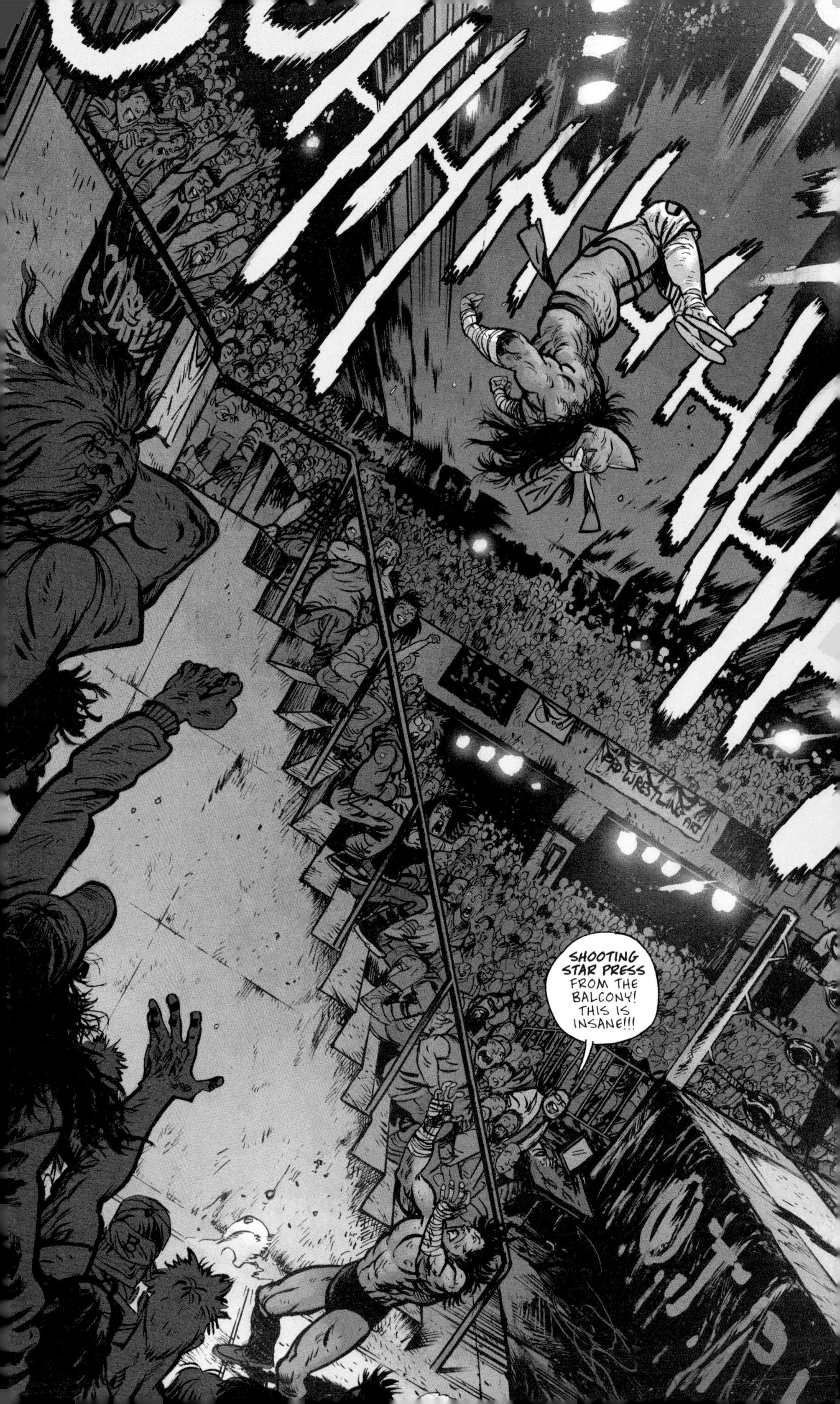
SHOOTING STAR PRESS FROM THE BALCONY! THIS IS INSANE!!!
PRO WRESTLING

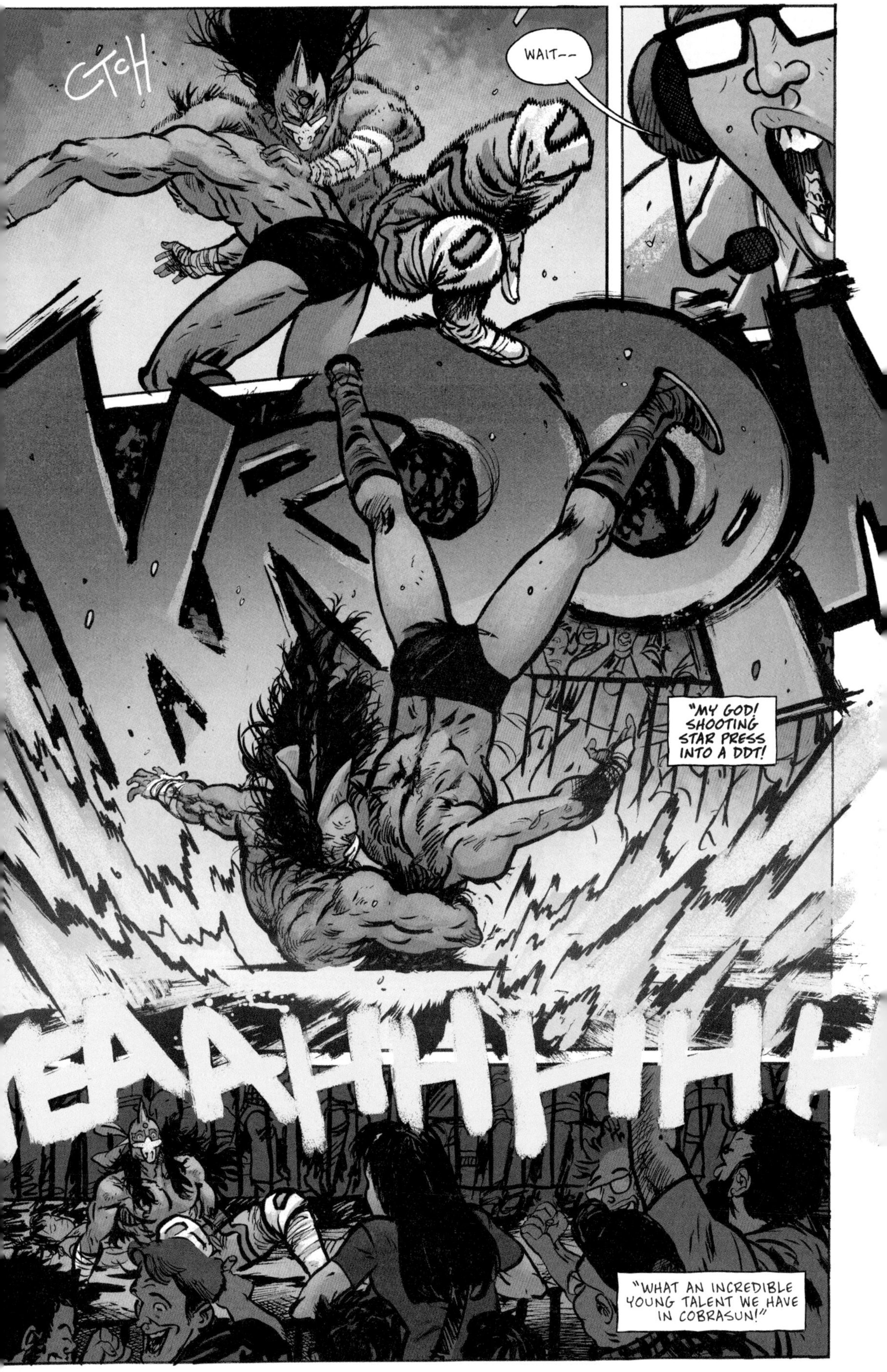
CTCH
WAIT--
"MY GOD! SHOOTING STAR PRESS INTO A DDT!
"WHAT AN INCREDIBLE YOUNG TALENT WE HAVE IN COBRASUN!"

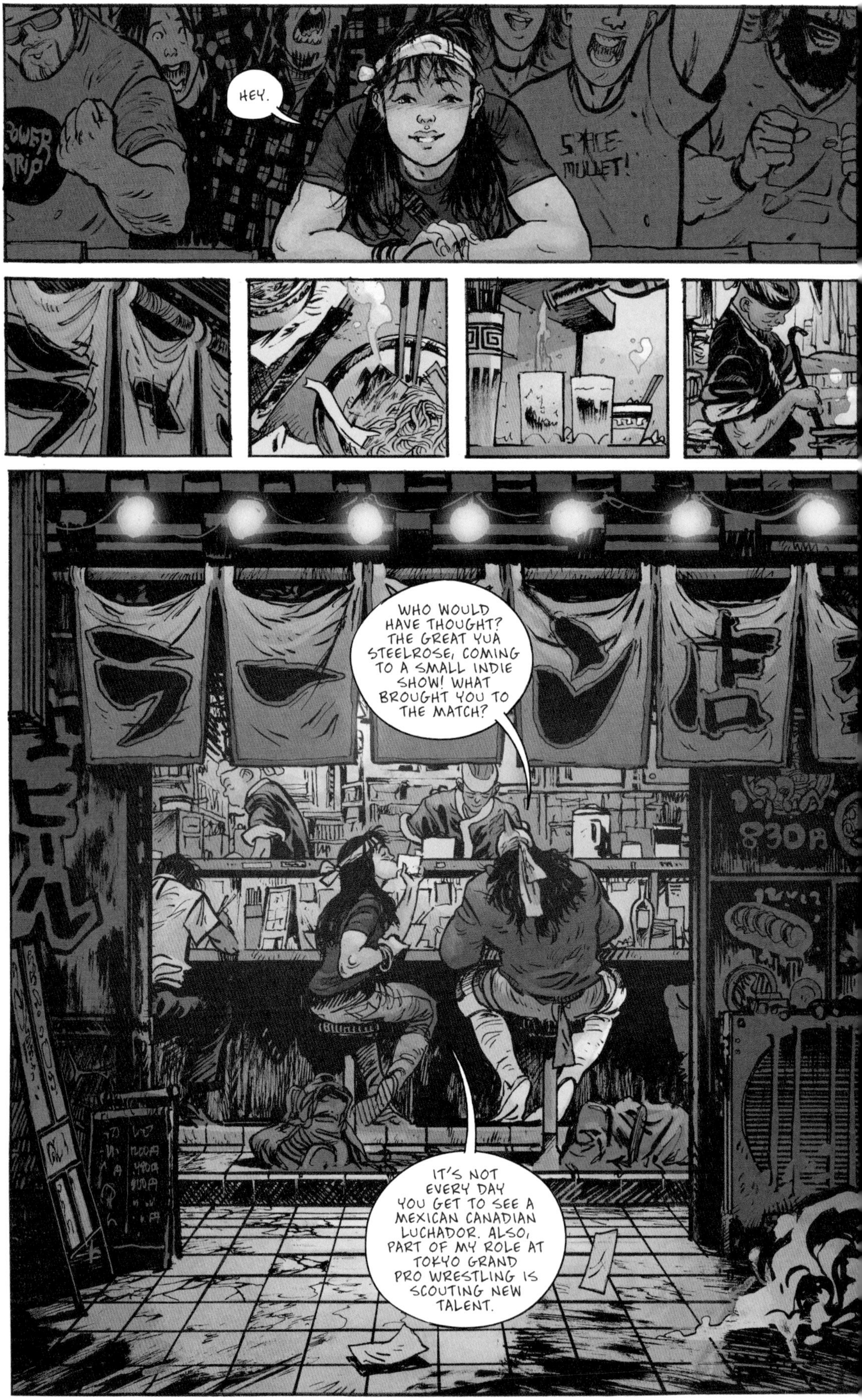
HEY.
POWER TRIP
SPACE MULLET!
WHO WOULD HAVE THOUGHT? THE GREAT YUA STEELROSE, COMING TO A SMALL INDIE SHOW! WHAT BROUGHT YOU TO THE MATCH?
IT'S NOT EVERY DAY YOU GET TO SEE A MEXICAN CANADIAN LUCHADOR. ALSO, PART OF MY ROLE AT TOKYO GRAND PRO WRESTLING IS SCOUTING NEW TALENT.

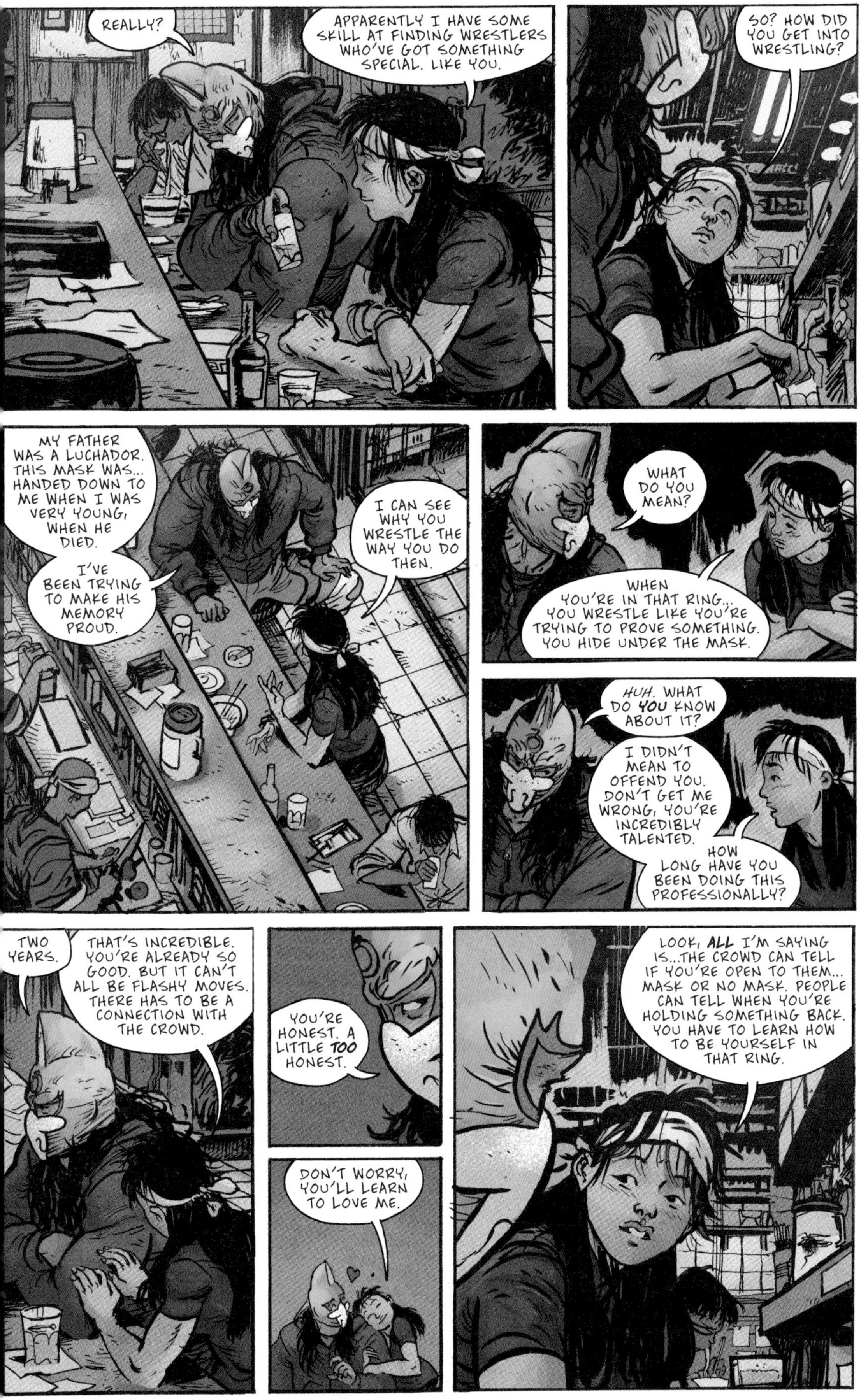

REALLY?
APPARENTLY I HAVE SOME SKILL AT FINDING WRESTLERS WHO'VE GOT SOMETHING SPECIAL. LIKE YOU.
SO? HOW DID YOU GET INTO WRESTLING?
MY FATHER WAS A LUCHADOR. THIS MASK WAS... HANDED DOWN TO ME WHEN I WAS VERY YOUNG, WHEN HE DIED.
I'VE BEEN TRYING TO MAKE HIS MEMORY PROUD.
I CAN SEE WHY YOU WRESTLE THE WAY YOU DO THEN.
WHAT DO YOU MEAN?
WHEN YOU'RE IN THAT RING... YOU WRESTLE LIKE YOU'RE TRYING TO PROVE SOMETHING. YOU HIDE UNDER THE MASK.
HUH. WHAT DO YOU KNOW ABOUT IT?
I DIDN'T MEAN TO OFFEND YOU. DON'T GET ME WRONG, YOU'RE INCREDIBLY TALENTED.
HOW LONG HAVE YOU BEEN DOING THIS PROFESSIONALLY?
TWO YEARS.
THAT'S INCREDIBLE. YOU'RE ALREADY SO GOOD. BUT IT CAN'T ALL BE FLASHY MOVES. THERE HAS TO BE A CONNECTION WITH THE CROWD.
YOU'RE HONEST. A LITTLE TOO HONEST.
DON'T WORRY, YOU'LL LEARN TO LOVE ME.
LOOK, ALL I'M SAYING IS...THE CROWD CAN TELL IF YOU'RE OPEN TO THEM... MASK OR NO MASK. PEOPLE CAN TELL WHEN YOU'RE HOLDING SOMETHING BACK. YOU HAVE TO LEARN HOW TO BE YOURSELF IN THAT RING.

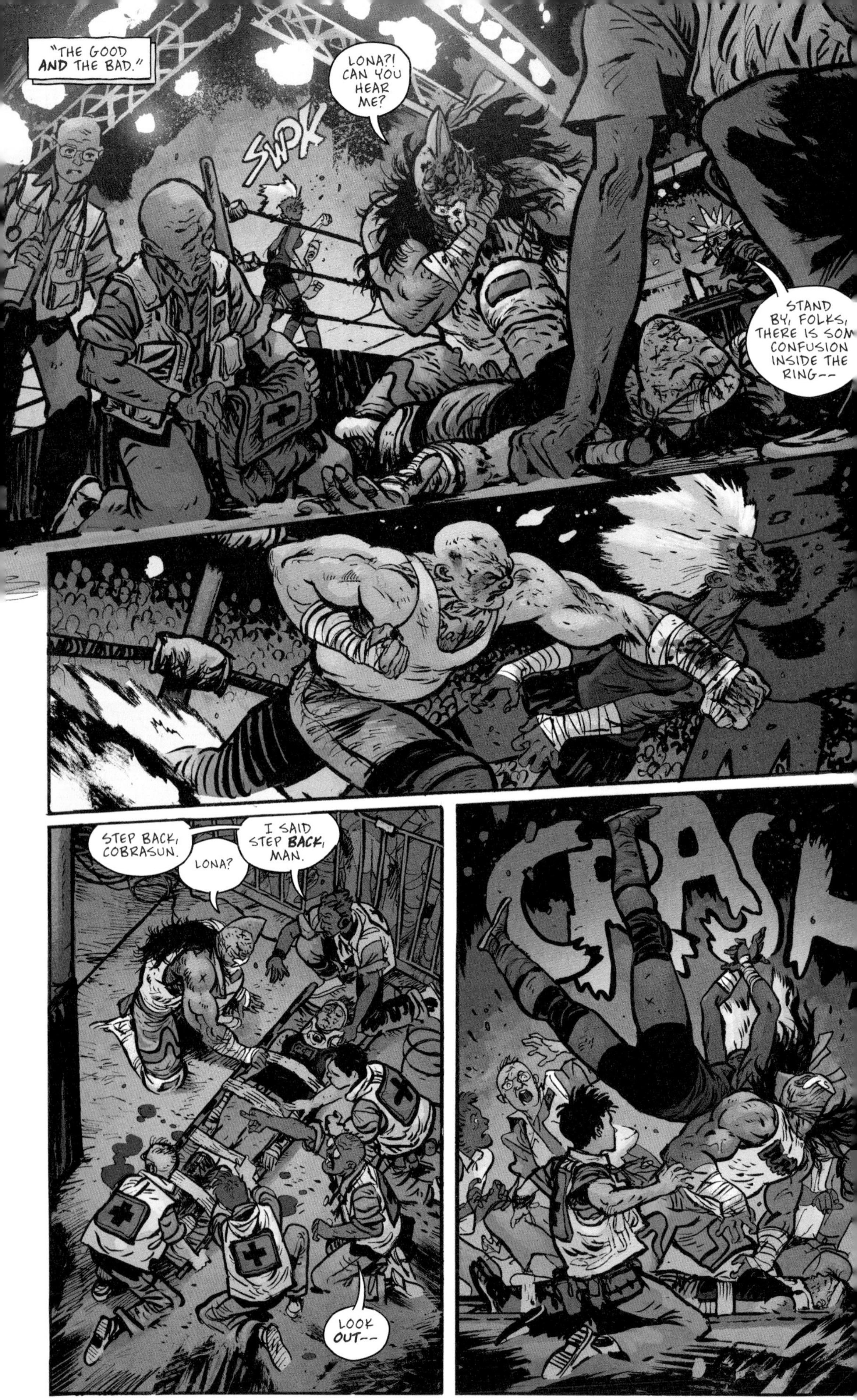
"THE GOOD AND THE BAD."
LONA?! CAN YOU HEAR ME?
SWPK
STAND BY, FOLKS, THERE IS SOM CONFUSION INSIDE THE RING--
STEP BACK, COBRASUN.
LONA?
I SAID STEP BACK, MAN.
LOOK OUT--

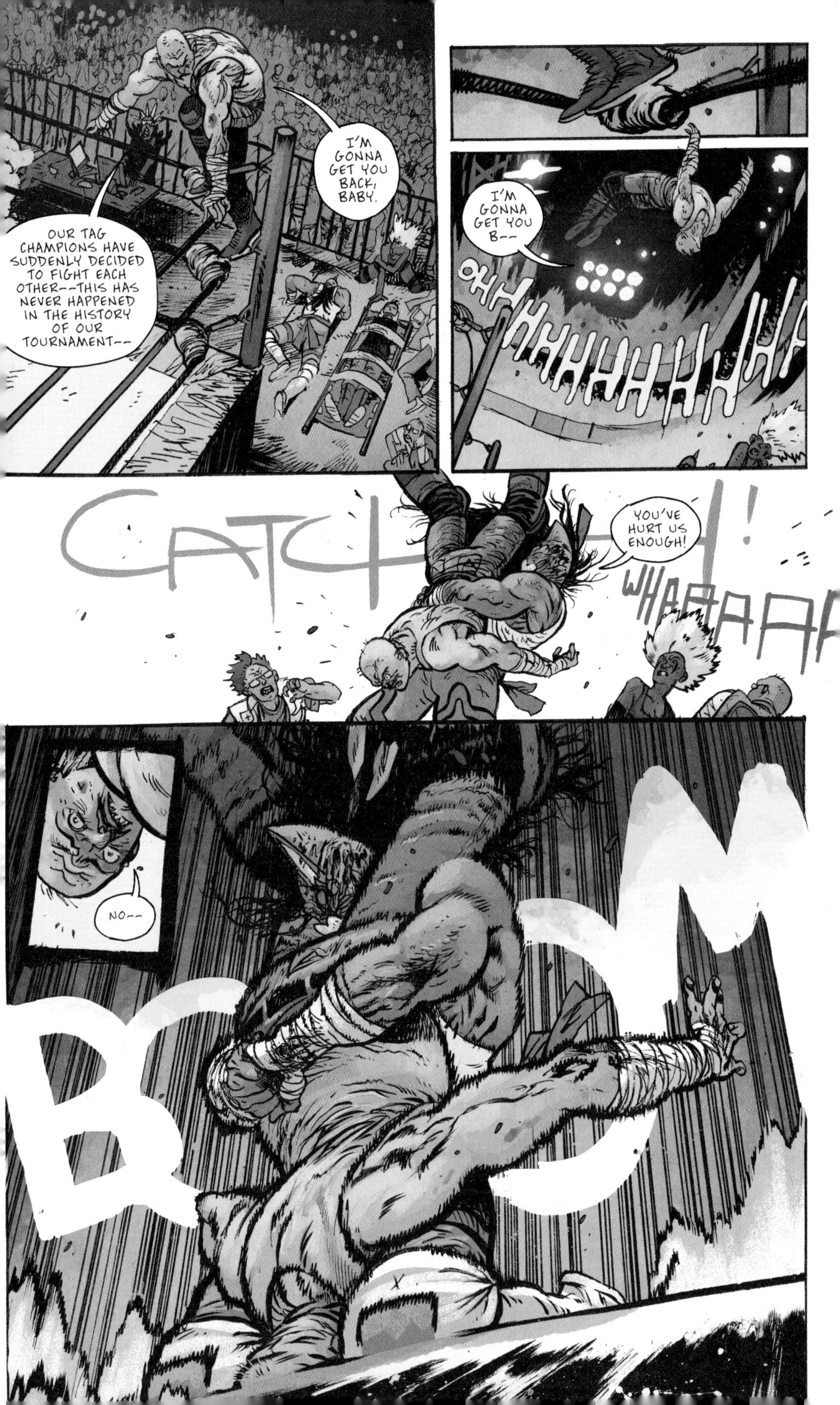

OUR TAG CHAMPIONS HAVE SUDDENLY DECIDED TO FIGHT EACH OTHER--THIS HAS NEVER HAPPENED IN THE HISTORY OF OUR TOURNAMENT--
I'M GONNA GET YOU BACK, BABY.
I'M GONNA GET YOU B--
OHHHHHHHHHHHHHHHHHA
CATCH!
YOU'VE HURT US ENOUGH!
WHAAAAA
NO--
BOOM

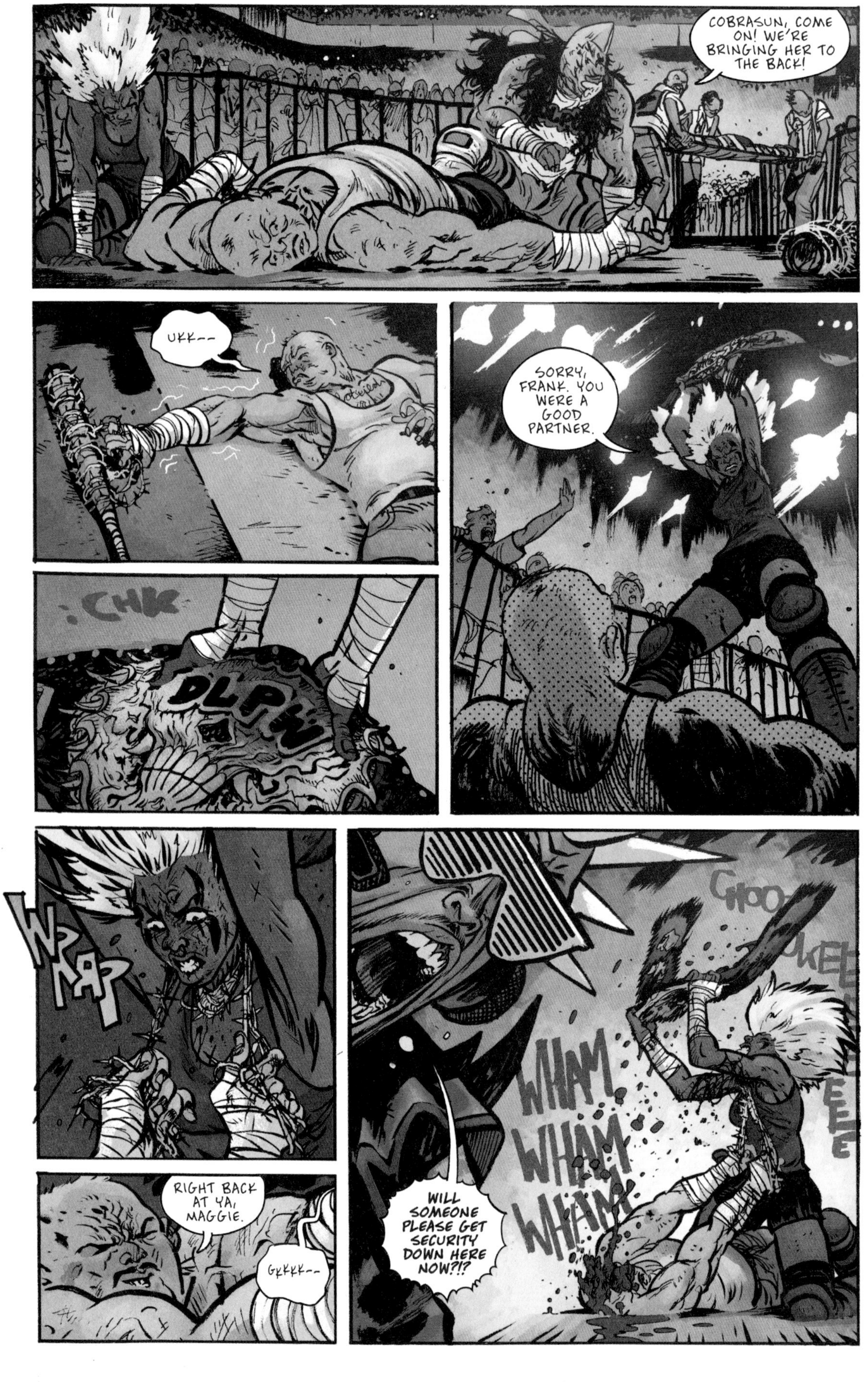

COBRASUN, COME ON! WE'RE BRINGING HER TO THE BACK!
UKK--
SORRY, FRANK. YOU WERE A GOOD PARTNER.
CHK
DLPW
RIGHT BACK AT YA, MAGGIE.
GKKKK--
WILL SOMEONE PLEASE GET SECURITY DOWN HERE NOW?!?
WHAM
WHAM
WHAM

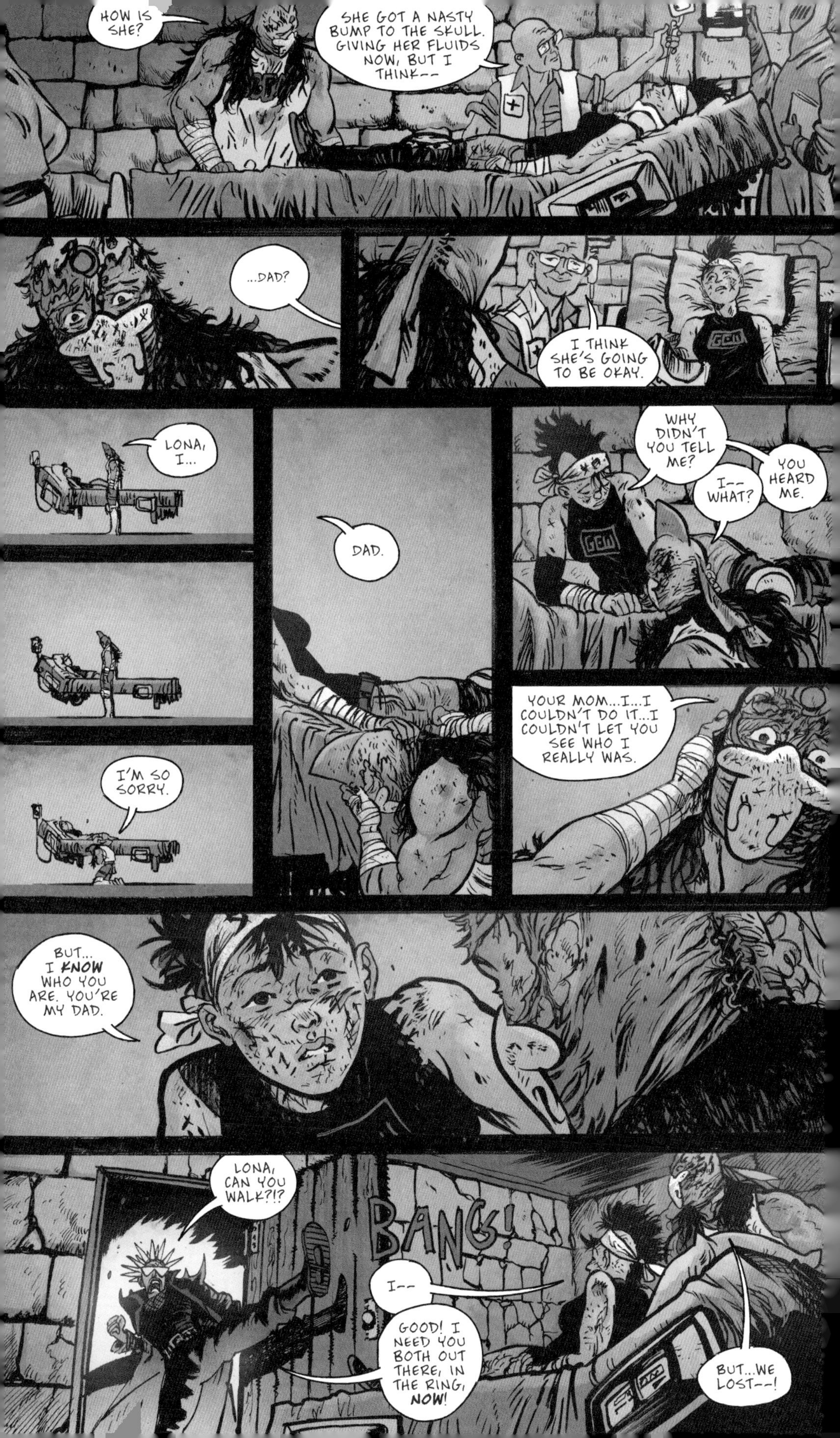
HOW IS SHE?
SHE GOT A NASTY BUMP TO THE SKULL. GIVING HER FLUIDS NOW, BUT I THINK--
...DAD?
I THINK SHE'S GOING TO BE OKAY.
LONA, I...
I'M SO SORRY.
DAD.
WHY DIDN'T YOU TELL ME?
I-- WHAT?
YOU HEARD ME.
YOUR MOM...I...I COULDN'T DO IT...I COULDN'T LET YOU SEE WHO I REALLY WAS.
BUT... I **KNOW** WHO YOU ARE. YOU'RE MY DAD.
LONA, CAN YOU WALK?!?
BANG!
I--
GOOD! I NEED YOU BOTH OUT THERE, IN THE RING, **NOW**!
BUT...WE LOST--!

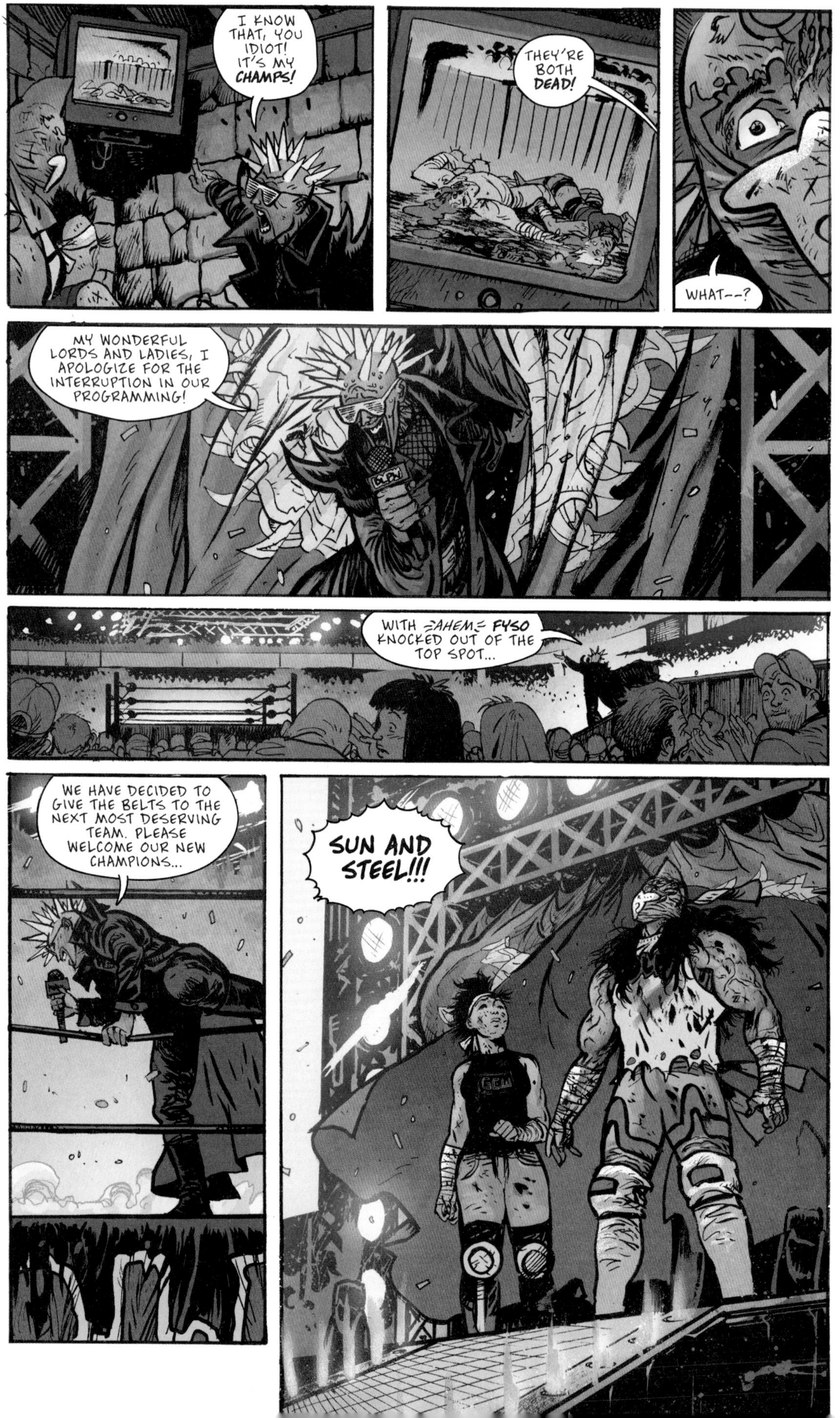
I KNOW THAT, YOU IDIOT! IT'S MY CHAMPS!
THEY'RE BOTH DEAD!
WHAT--?
MY WONDERFUL LORDS AND LADIES, I APOLOGIZE FOR THE INTERRUPTION IN OUR PROGRAMMING!
WITH =AHEM= FYSO KNOCKED OUT OF THE TOP SPOT...
WE HAVE DECIDED TO GIVE THE BELTS TO THE NEXT MOST DESERVING TEAM. PLEASE WELCOME OUR NEW CHAMPIONS...
SUN AND STEEL!!!

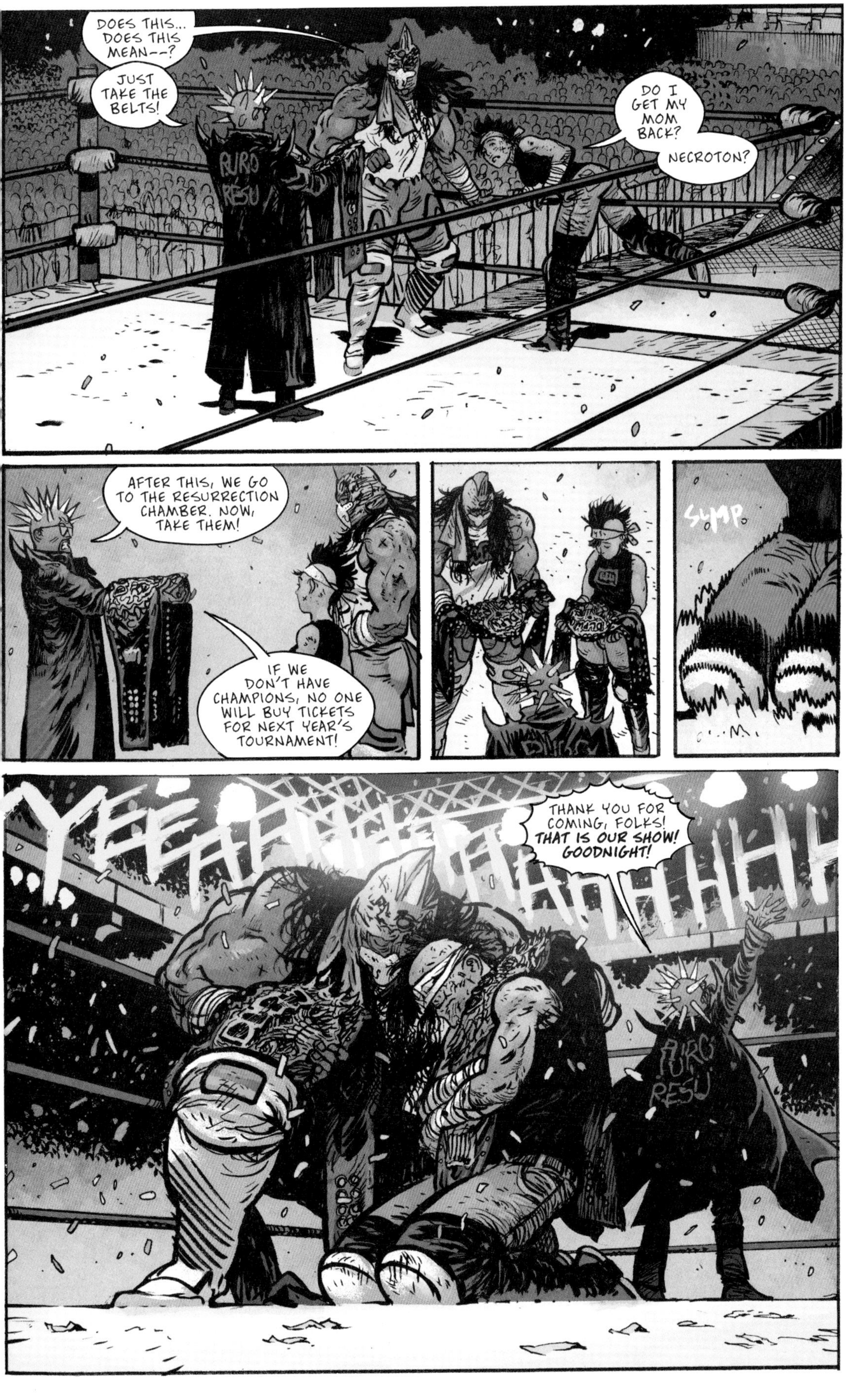
DOES THIS... DOES THIS MEAN--?
JUST TAKE THE BELTS!
DO I GET MY MOM BACK?
NECROTON?
RURO RESU
AFTER THIS, WE GO TO THE RESURRECTION CHAMBER. NOW, TAKE THEM!
IF WE DON'T HAVE CHAMPIONS, NO ONE WILL BUY TICKETS FOR NEXT YEAR'S TOURNAMENT!
SLUMP
YEEAAHHHHHAAHHHH
THANK YOU FOR COMING, FOLKS! **THAT IS OUR SHOW! GOODNIGHT!**
RURO RESU

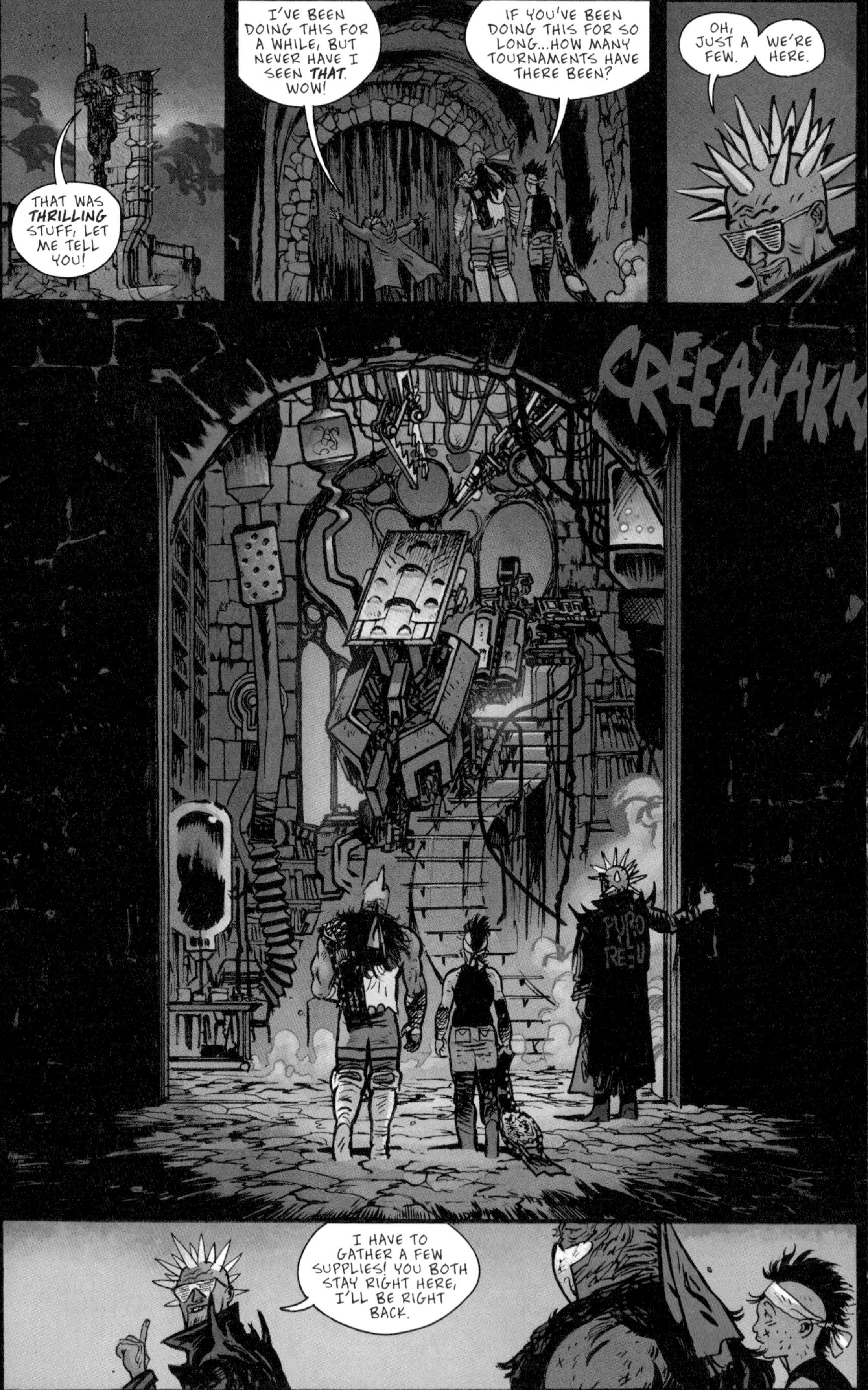
THAT WAS THRILLING STUFF, LET ME TELL YOU!
I'VE BEEN DOING THIS FOR A WHILE, BUT NEVER HAVE I SEEN THAT. WOW!
IF YOU'VE BEEN DOING THIS FOR SO LONG...HOW MANY TOURNAMENTS HAVE THERE BEEN?
OH, JUST A FEW.
WE'RE HERE.
CREEAAAKK
I HAVE TO GATHER A FEW SUPPLIES! YOU BOTH STAY RIGHT HERE, I'LL BE RIGHT BACK.

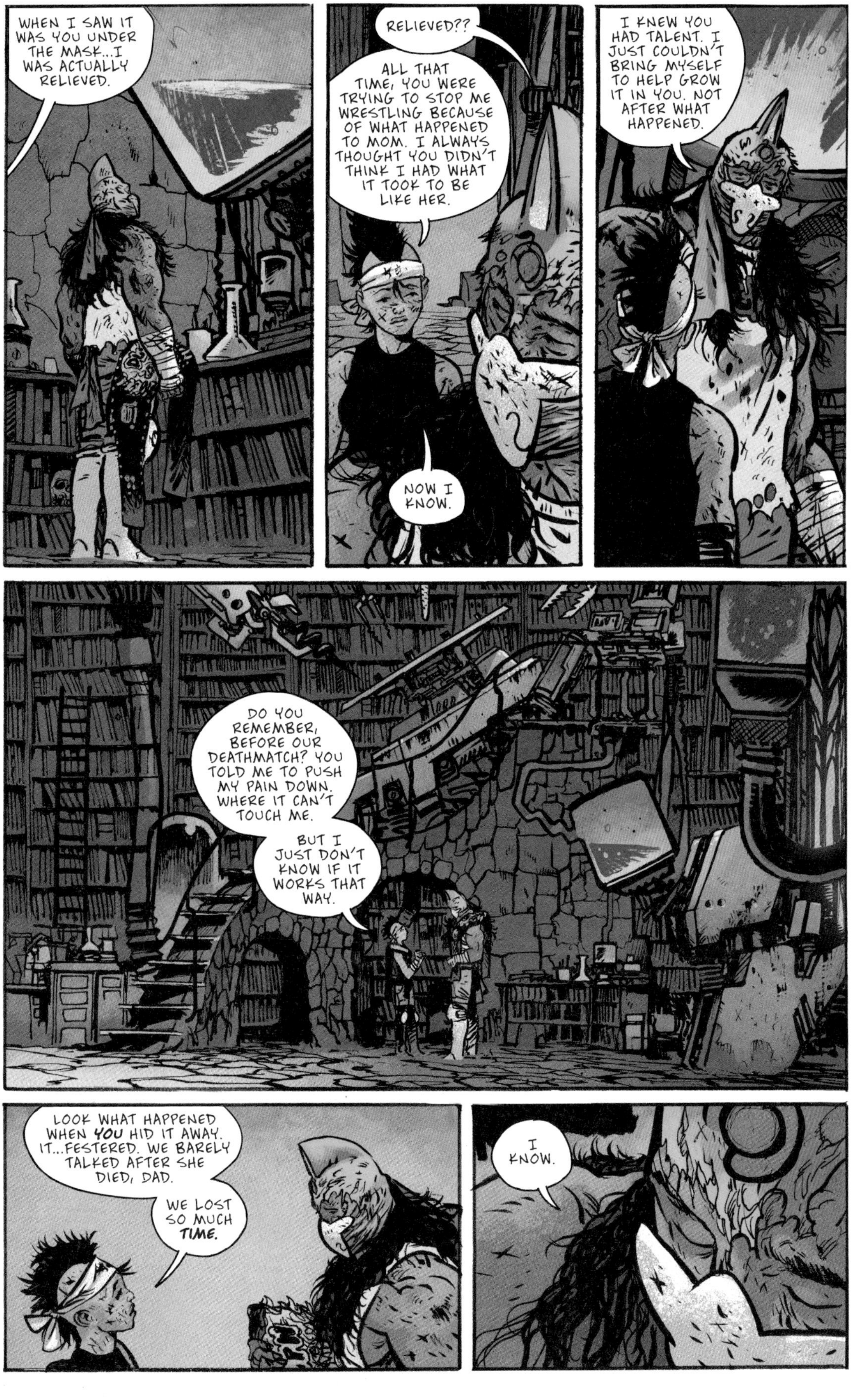
WHEN I SAW IT WAS YOU UNDER THE MASK...I WAS ACTUALLY RELIEVED.
RELIEVED??
ALL THAT TIME, YOU WERE TRYING TO STOP ME WRESTLING BECAUSE OF WHAT HAPPENED TO MOM. I ALWAYS THOUGHT YOU DIDN'T THINK I HAD WHAT IT TOOK TO BE LIKE HER.
NOW I KNOW.
I KNEW YOU HAD TALENT. I JUST COULDN'T BRING MYSELF TO HELP GROW IT IN YOU. NOT AFTER WHAT HAPPENED.
DO YOU REMEMBER, BEFORE OUR DEATHMATCH? YOU TOLD ME TO PUSH MY PAIN DOWN. WHERE IT CAN'T TOUCH ME.
BUT I JUST DON'T KNOW IF IT WORKS THAT WAY.
LOOK WHAT HAPPENED WHEN **YOU** HID IT AWAY. IT...FESTERED. WE BARELY TALKED AFTER SHE DIED, DAD.
WE LOST SO MUCH **TIME.**
I KNOW.

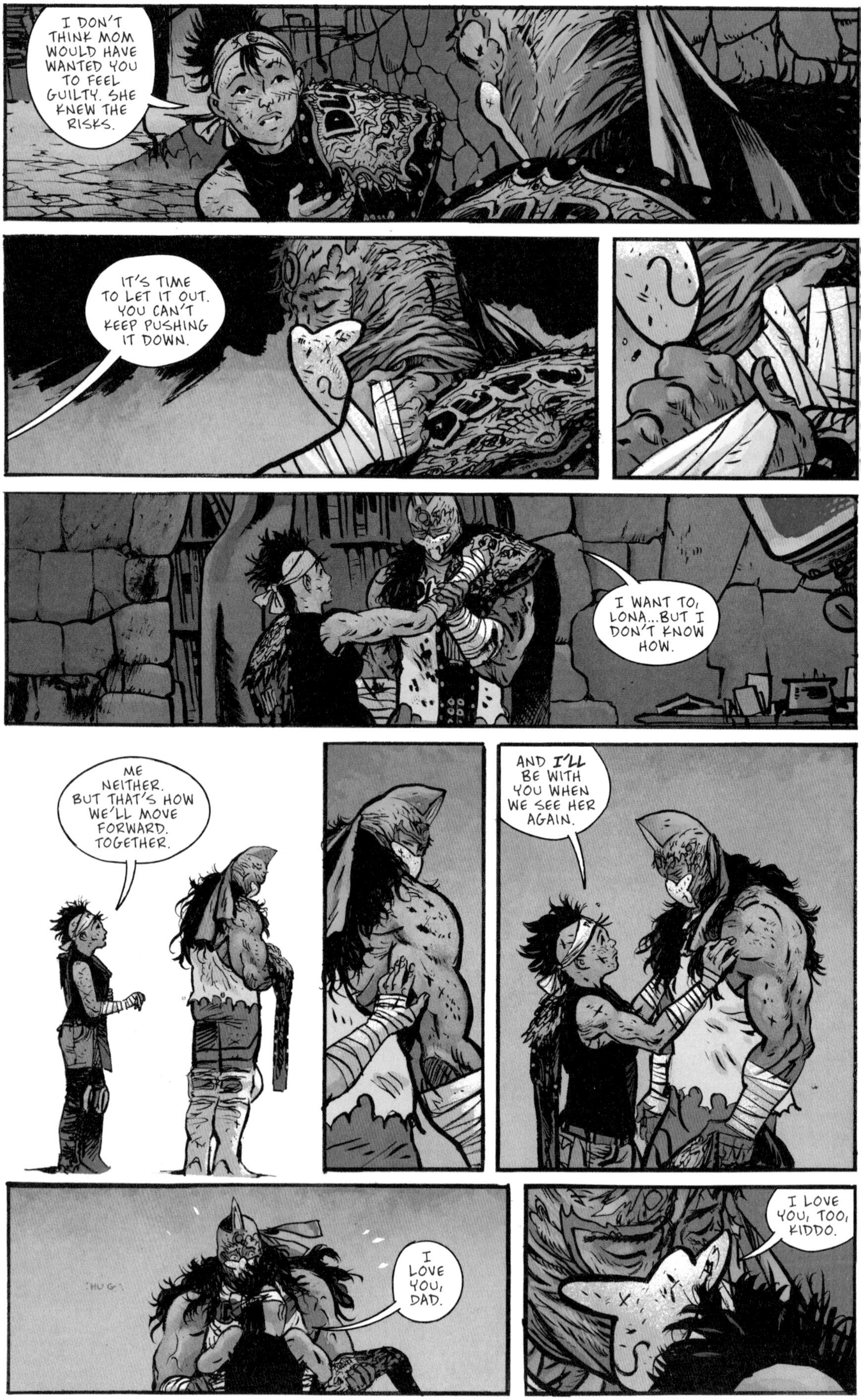
I DON'T THINK MOM WOULD HAVE WANTED YOU TO FEEL GUILTY. SHE KNEW THE RISKS.
IT'S TIME TO LET IT OUT. YOU CAN'T KEEP PUSHING IT DOWN.
I WANT TO, LONA...BUT I DON'T KNOW HOW.
ME NEITHER. BUT THAT'S HOW WE'LL MOVE FORWARD. TOGETHER.
AND I'LL BE WITH YOU WHEN WE SEE HER AGAIN.
I LOVE YOU, DAD.
I LOVE YOU, TOO, KIDDO.

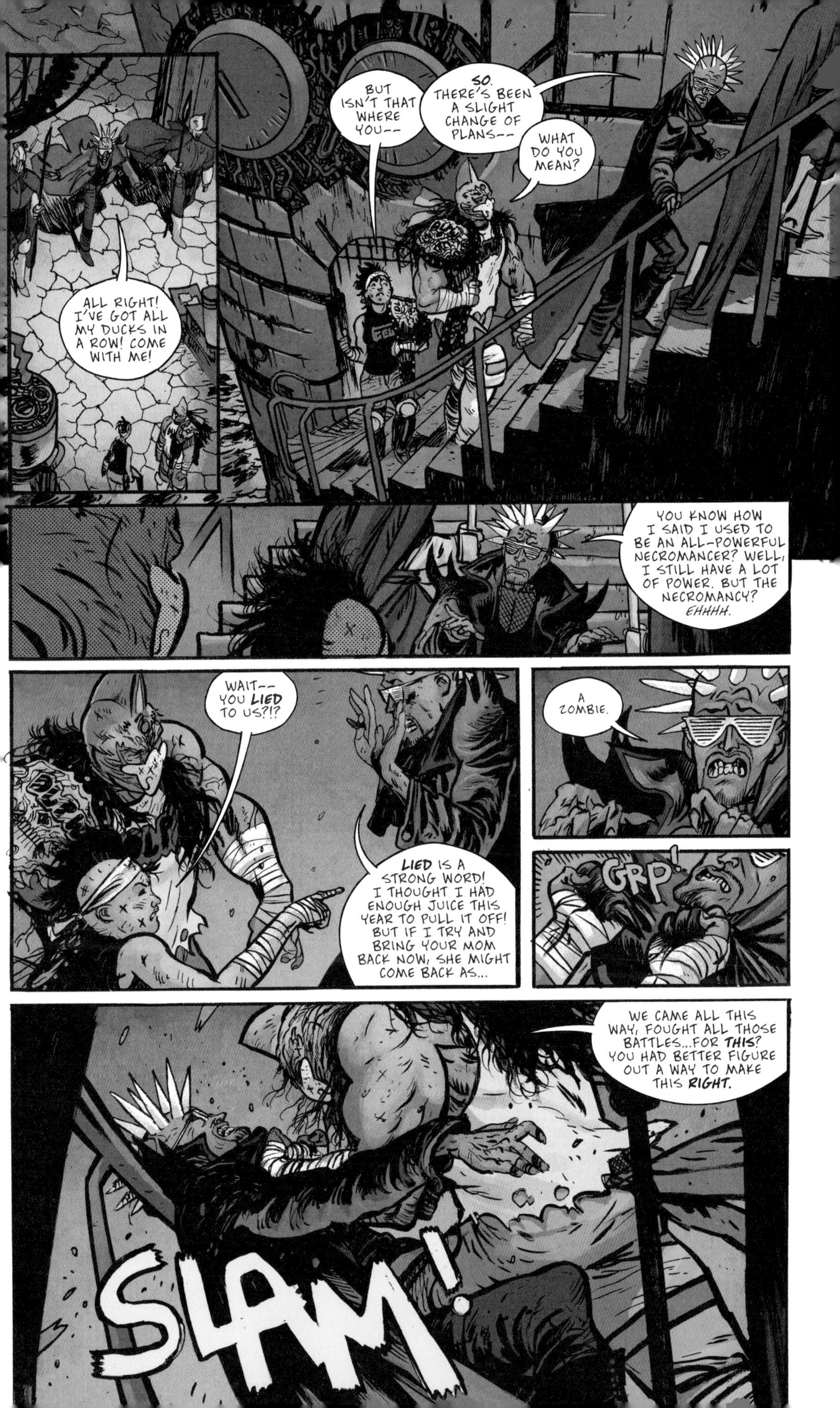
ALL RIGHT! I'VE GOT ALL MY DUCKS IN A ROW! COME WITH ME!
SO. THERE'S BEEN A SLIGHT CHANGE OF PLANS--
BUT ISN'T THAT WHERE YOU--
WHAT DO YOU MEAN?
YOU KNOW HOW I SAID I USED TO BE AN ALL-POWERFUL NECROMANCER? WELL, I STILL HAVE A LOT OF POWER. BUT THE NECROMANCY? EHHHH.
WAIT-- YOU LIED TO US?!?
LIED IS A STRONG WORD! I THOUGHT I HAD ENOUGH JUICE THIS YEAR TO PULL IT OFF! BUT IF I TRY AND BRING YOUR MOM BACK NOW, SHE MIGHT COME BACK AS...
A ZOMBIE.
GRP!
WE CAME ALL THIS WAY, FOUGHT ALL THOSE BATTLES...FOR THIS? YOU HAD BETTER FIGURE OUT A WAY TO MAKE THIS RIGHT.
SLAM!

YOU FORGET WHO I **AM**.

I MAY BE AN ENTERTAINER NOW, BUT BEFORE I WAS DOING THIS, I WAS A CONQUEROR OF **WORLDS**. DO YOU KNOW HOW MANY **MILLIONS OF SOULS** I HAVE **CRUSHED** TO **DUST**? DO YOU THINK I'VE FORGOTTEN HOW TO PROTECT MYSELF AND MY INTERESTS?

I MAY NOT BE ABLE TO **RAISE** A LIFE, BUT I CAN STILL **TAKE YOURS**.

WHEW. NOW, I WANT TO HELP YOU, **I DO**. AND I WANT TO SEE YOU GET YOUR MOTHER BACK. SO I HAVE MADE...

ALTERNATE ARRANGEMENTS.

WHAT DOES THAT MEAN?

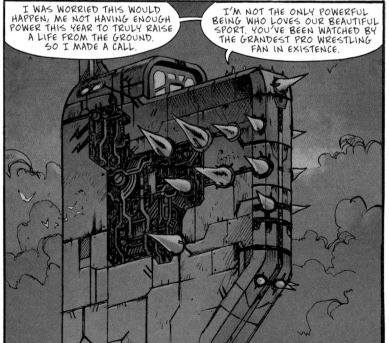

I WAS WORRIED THIS WOULD HAPPEN, ME NOT HAVING ENOUGH POWER THIS YEAR TO TRULY RAISE A LIFE FROM THE GROUND. SO I MADE A CALL.

I'M NOT THE ONLY POWERFUL BEING WHO LOVES OUR BEAUTIFUL SPORT. YOU'VE BEEN WATCHED BY THE GRANDEST PRO WRESTLING FAN IN EXISTENCE.

THEY SAID THEY'RE WILLING TO FIGHT YOU IN A 2-ON-1 HANDICAP MATCH. AND **THEY** CAN RAISE THE DEAD WITH A SNAP OF THEIR FINGERS.

ANOTHER NECROMANCER?

NOT... EXACTLY. THINK HIGHER.

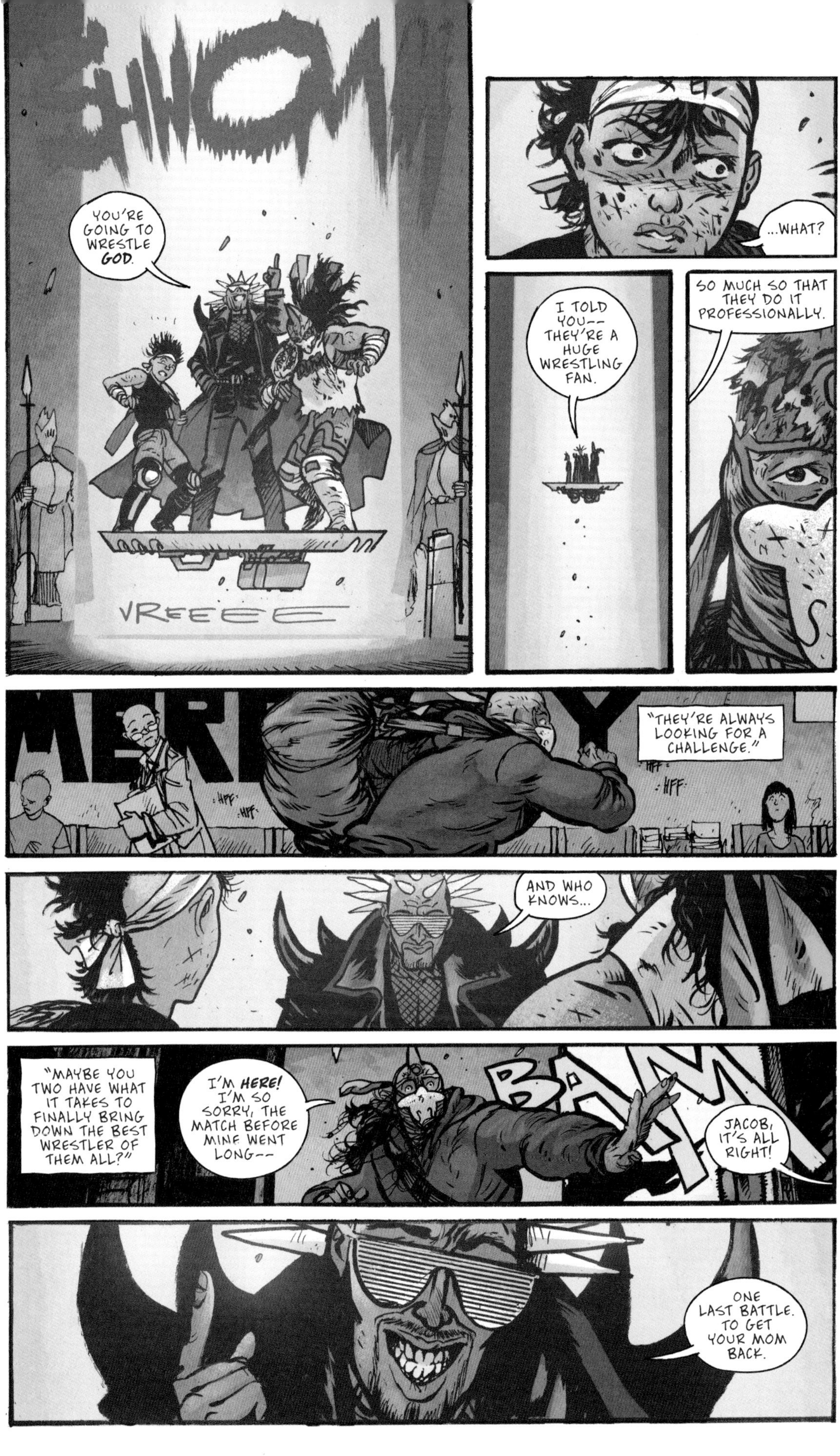
SHWOM
YOU'RE GOING TO WRESTLE GOD.
VREEEE
...WHAT?
I TOLD YOU-- THEY'RE A HUGE WRESTLING FAN.
SO MUCH SO THAT THEY DO IT PROFESSIONALLY.
"THEY'RE ALWAYS LOOKING FOR A CHALLENGE."
HFF
HFF
HFF
HFF
AND WHO KNOWS...
"MAYBE YOU TWO HAVE WHAT IT TAKES TO FINALLY BRING DOWN THE BEST WRESTLER OF THEM ALL?"
I'M HERE! I'M SO SORRY, THE MATCH BEFORE MINE WENT LONG--
BAM
JACOB, IT'S ALL RIGHT!
ONE LAST BATTLE. TO GET YOUR MOM BACK.

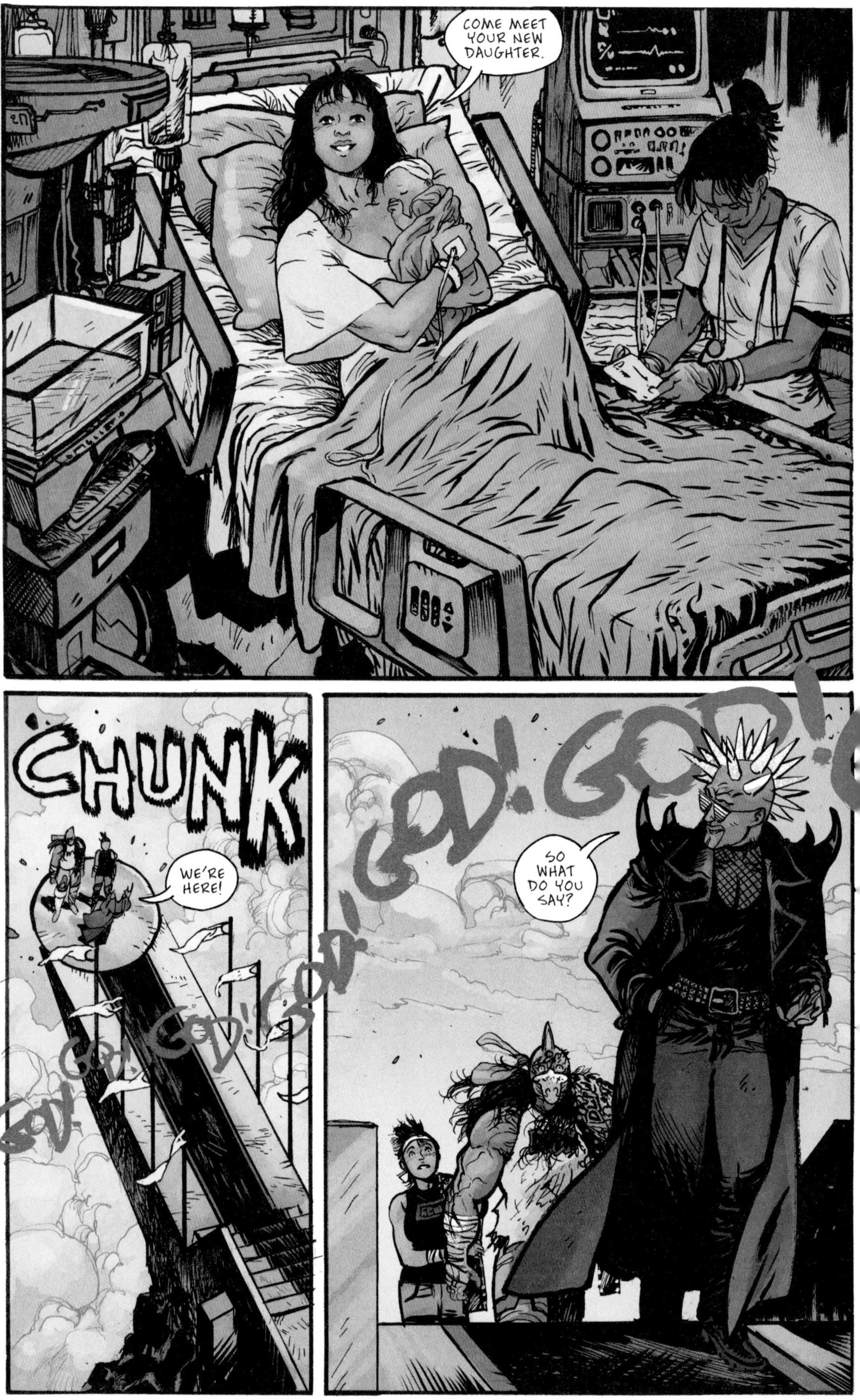
COME MEET YOUR NEW DAUGHTER.
CHUNK
WE'RE HERE!
GOD! GOD! GOD! GOD!
SO WHAT DO YOU SAY?
GOD! GOD!

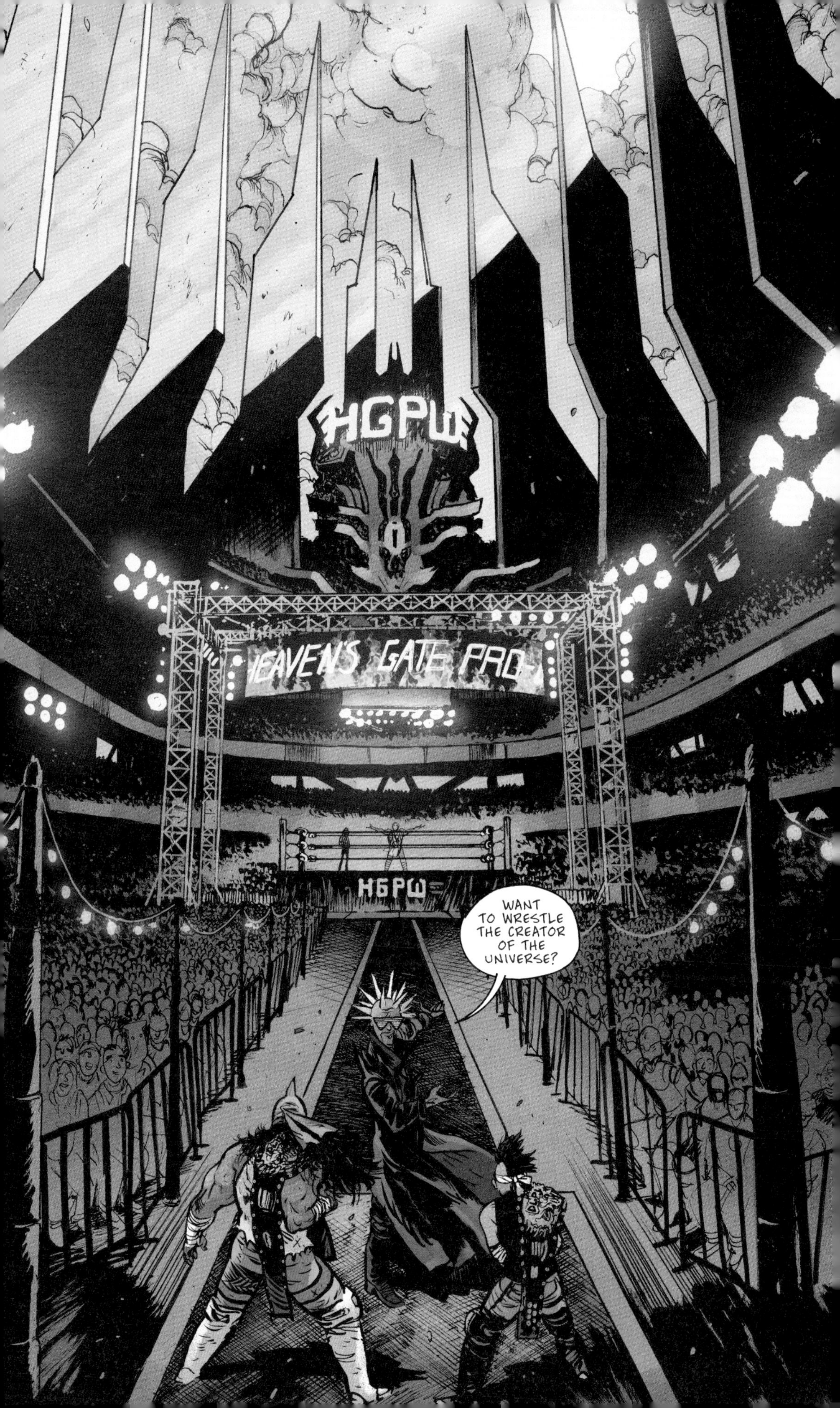
HGPW
HEAVEN'S GATE PRO
HGPW
WANT TO WRESTLE THE CREATOR OF THE UNIVERSE?

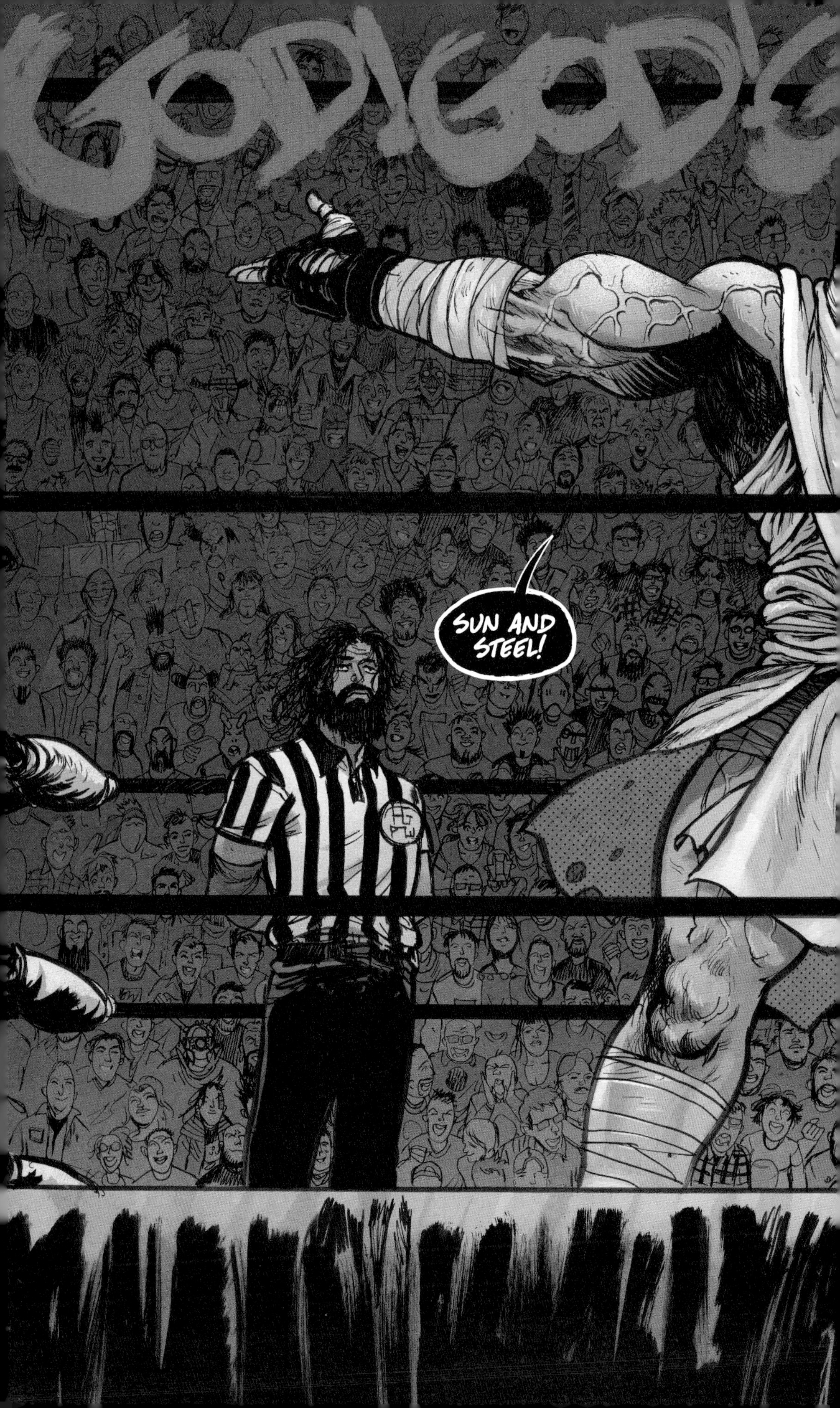
GOD! GOD!
SUN AND STEEL!

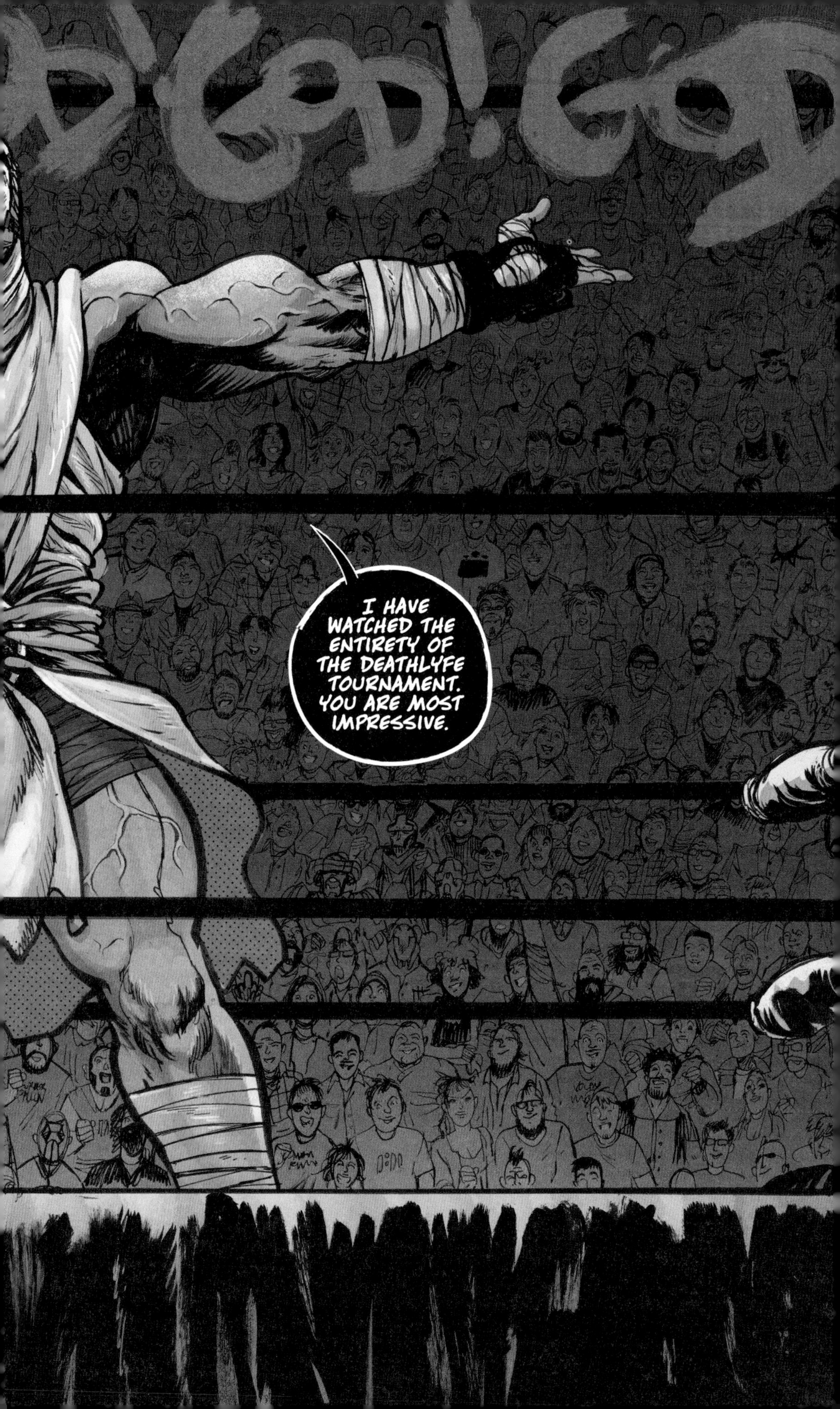
I HAVE WATCHED THE ENTIRETY OF THE DEATHLYFE TOURNAMENT. YOU ARE MOST IMPRESSIVE.

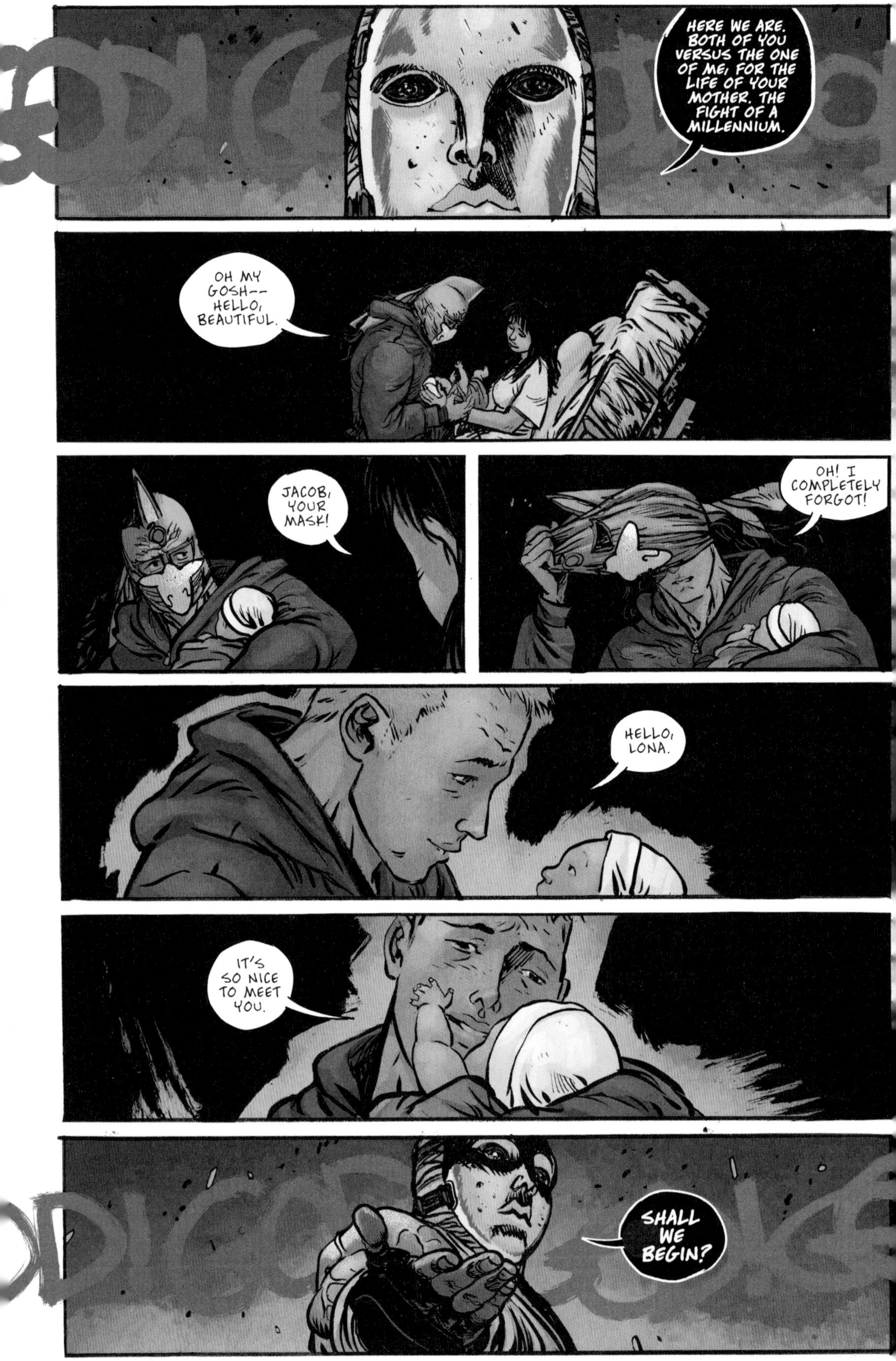
HERE WE ARE. BOTH OF YOU VERSUS THE ONE OF ME, FOR THE LIFE OF YOUR MOTHER. THE FIGHT OF A MILLENNIUM.
OH MY GOSH-- HELLO, BEAUTIFUL.
JACOB, YOUR MASK!
OH! I COMPLETELY FORGOT!
HELLO, LONA.
IT'S SO NICE TO MEET YOU.
SHALL WE BEGIN?

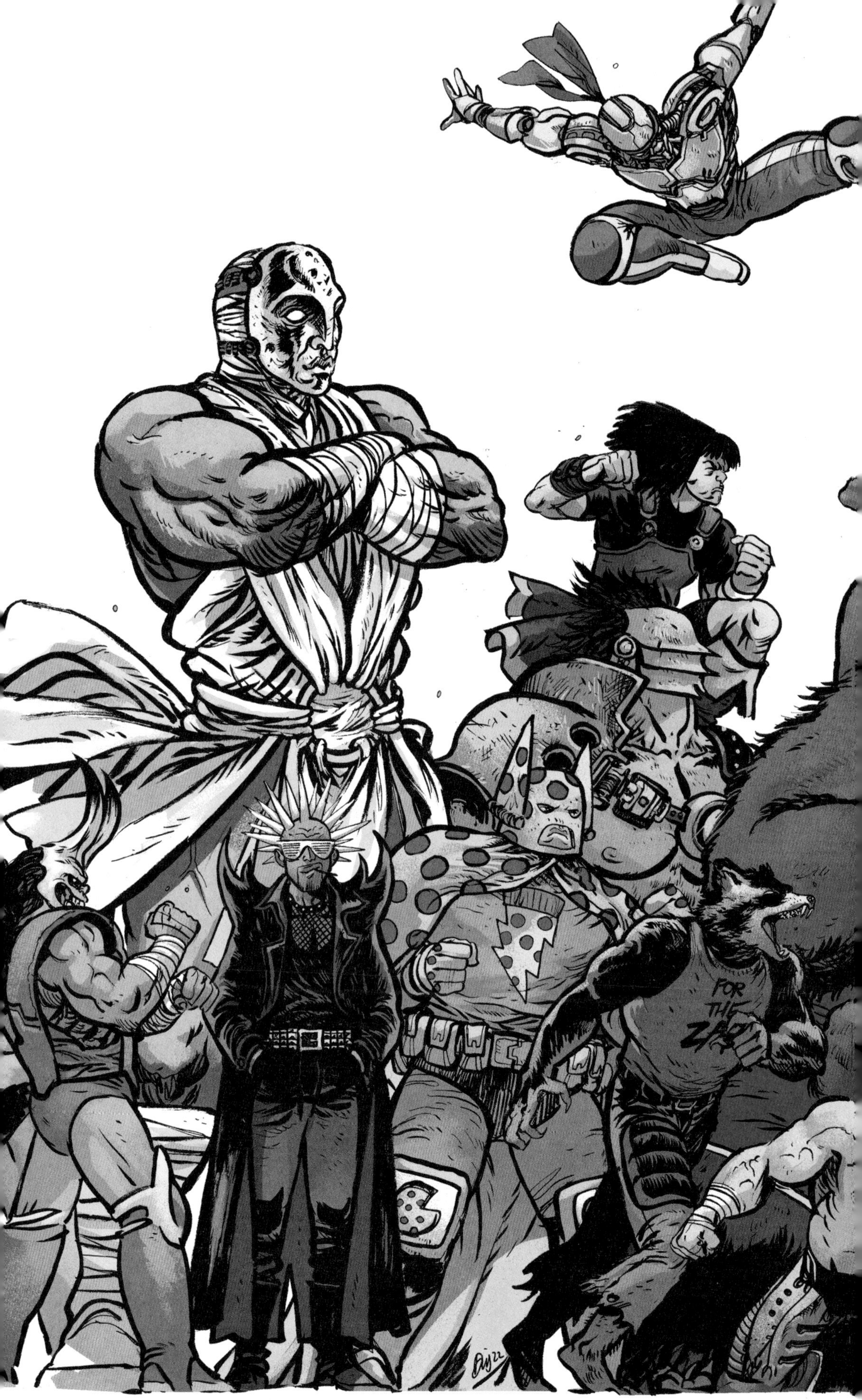
FOR THE

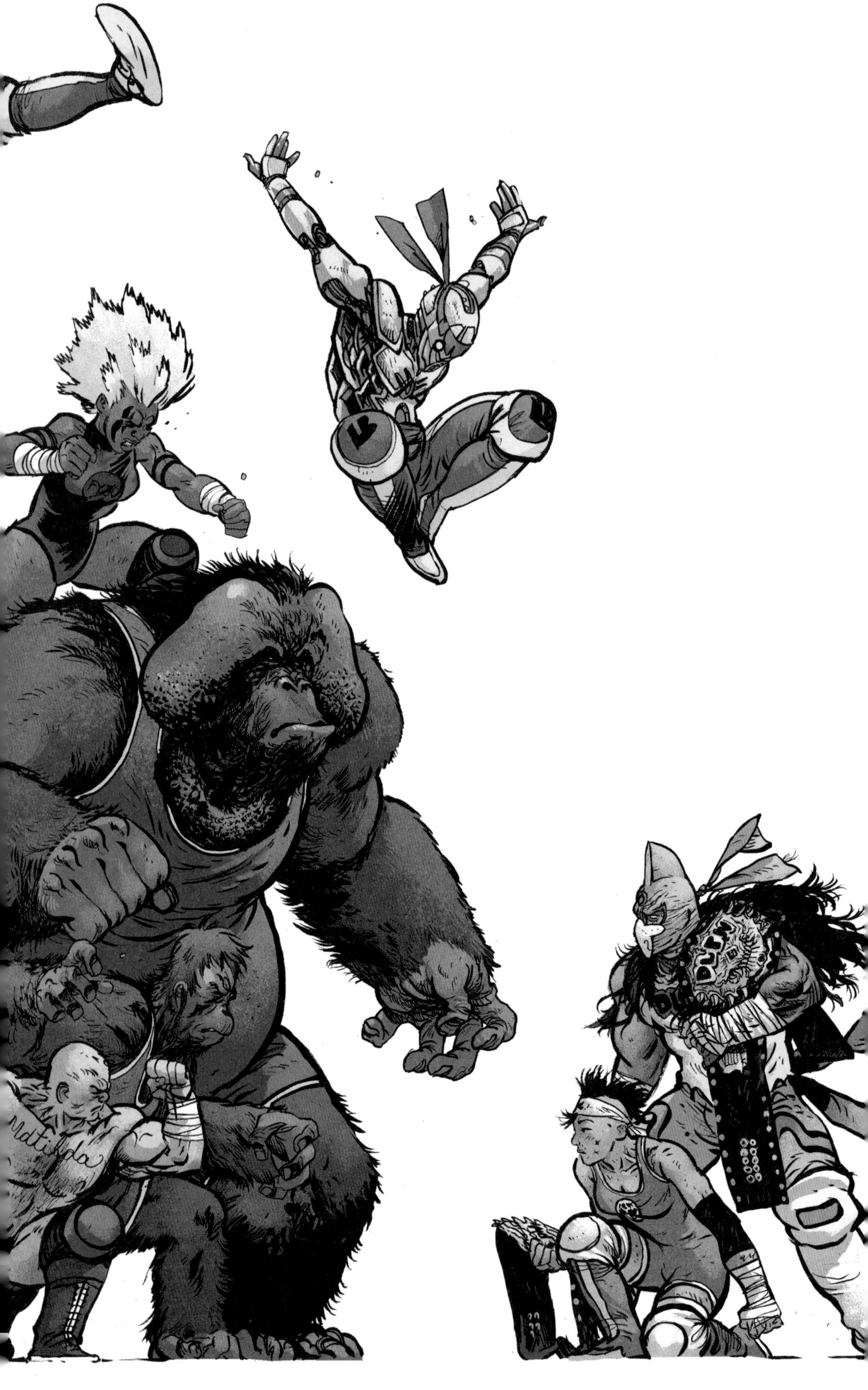
Matilda

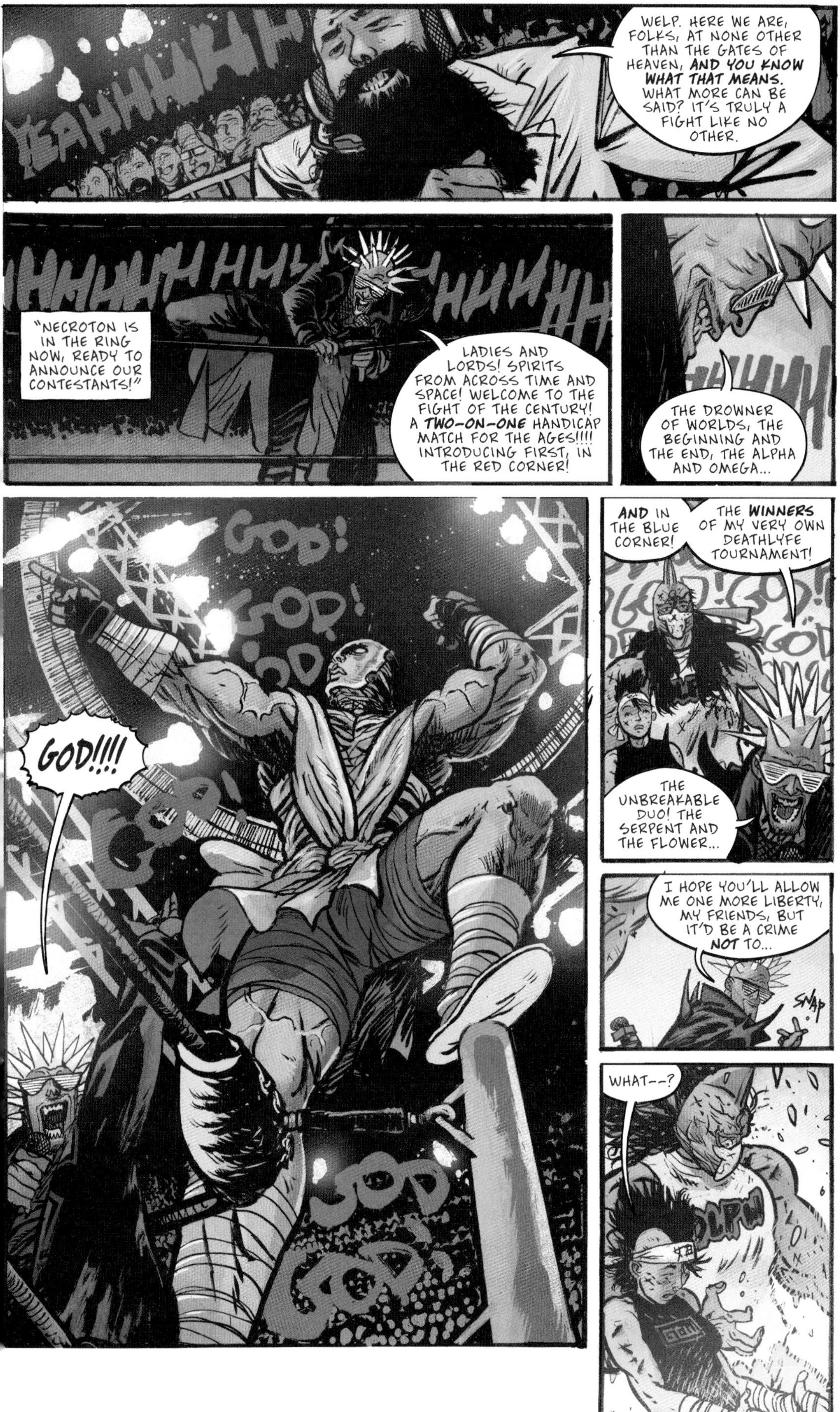
WELP. HERE WE ARE, FOLKS, AT NONE OTHER THAN THE GATES OF HEAVEN, **AND YOU KNOW WHAT THAT MEANS.** WHAT MORE CAN BE SAID? IT'S TRULY A FIGHT LIKE NO OTHER.
"NECROTON IS IN THE RING NOW, READY TO ANNOUNCE OUR CONTESTANTS!"
LADIES AND LORDS! SPIRITS FROM ACROSS TIME AND SPACE! WELCOME TO THE FIGHT OF THE CENTURY! A **TWO-ON-ONE** HANDICAP MATCH FOR THE AGES!!!! INTRODUCING FIRST, IN THE RED CORNER!
THE DROWNER OF WORLDS, THE BEGINNING AND THE END, THE ALPHA AND OMEGA...
GOD!
GOD!
GOD!!!!
AND IN THE BLUE CORNER!
THE **WINNERS** OF MY VERY OWN DEATHLYFE TOURNAMENT!
THE UNBREAKABLE DUO! THE SERPENT AND THE FLOWER...
I HOPE YOU'LL ALLOW ME ONE MORE LIBERTY, MY FRIENDS, BUT IT'D BE A CRIME **NOT** TO...
SNAP
WHAT--?

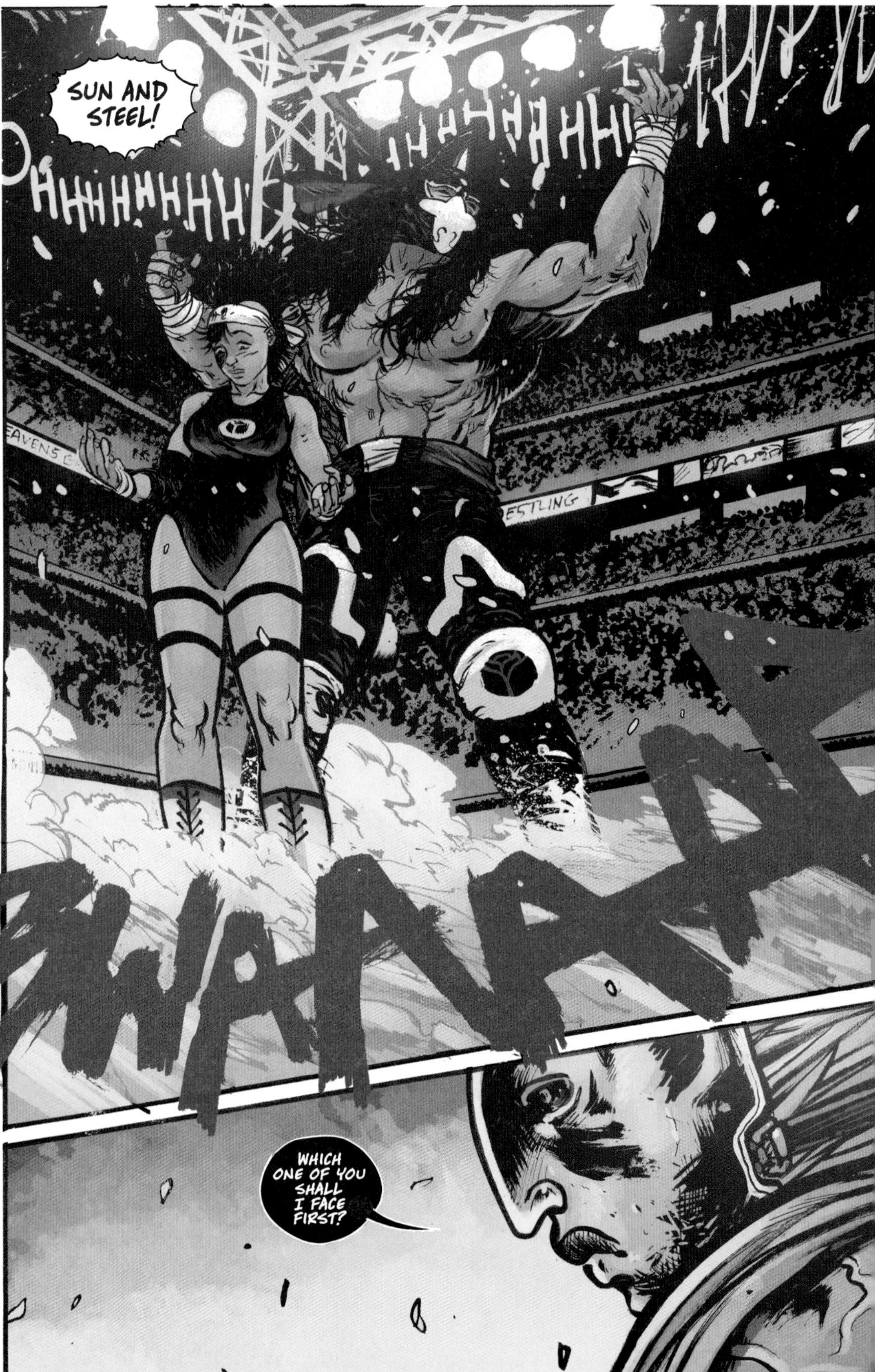
SUN AND STEEL!
WHICH ONE OF YOU SHALL I FACE FIRST?

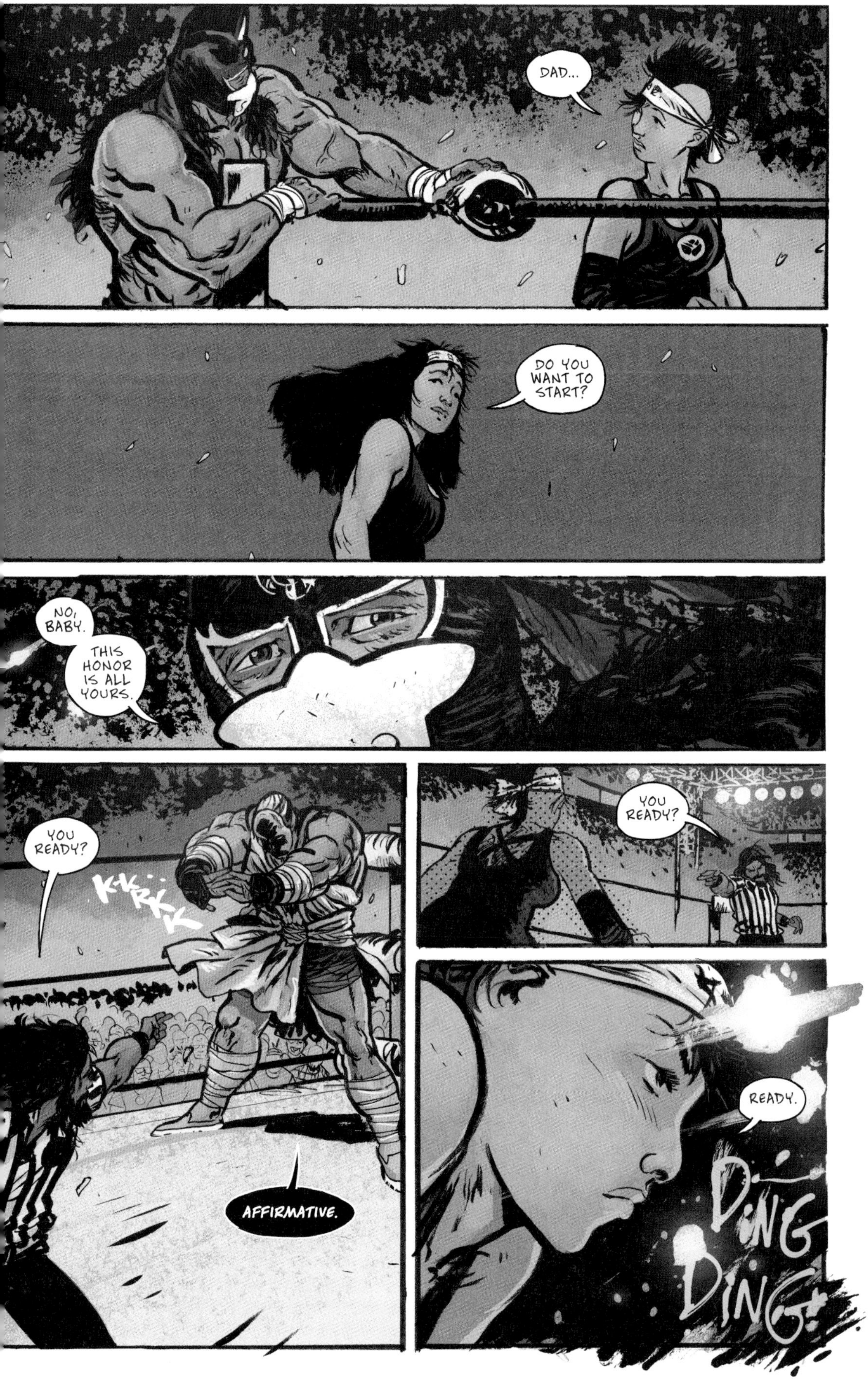
DAD...
DO YOU WANT TO START?
NO, BABY.
THIS HONOR IS ALL YOURS.
YOU READY?
K-K-K-K
AFFIRMATIVE.
YOU READY?
READY.
DING DING!

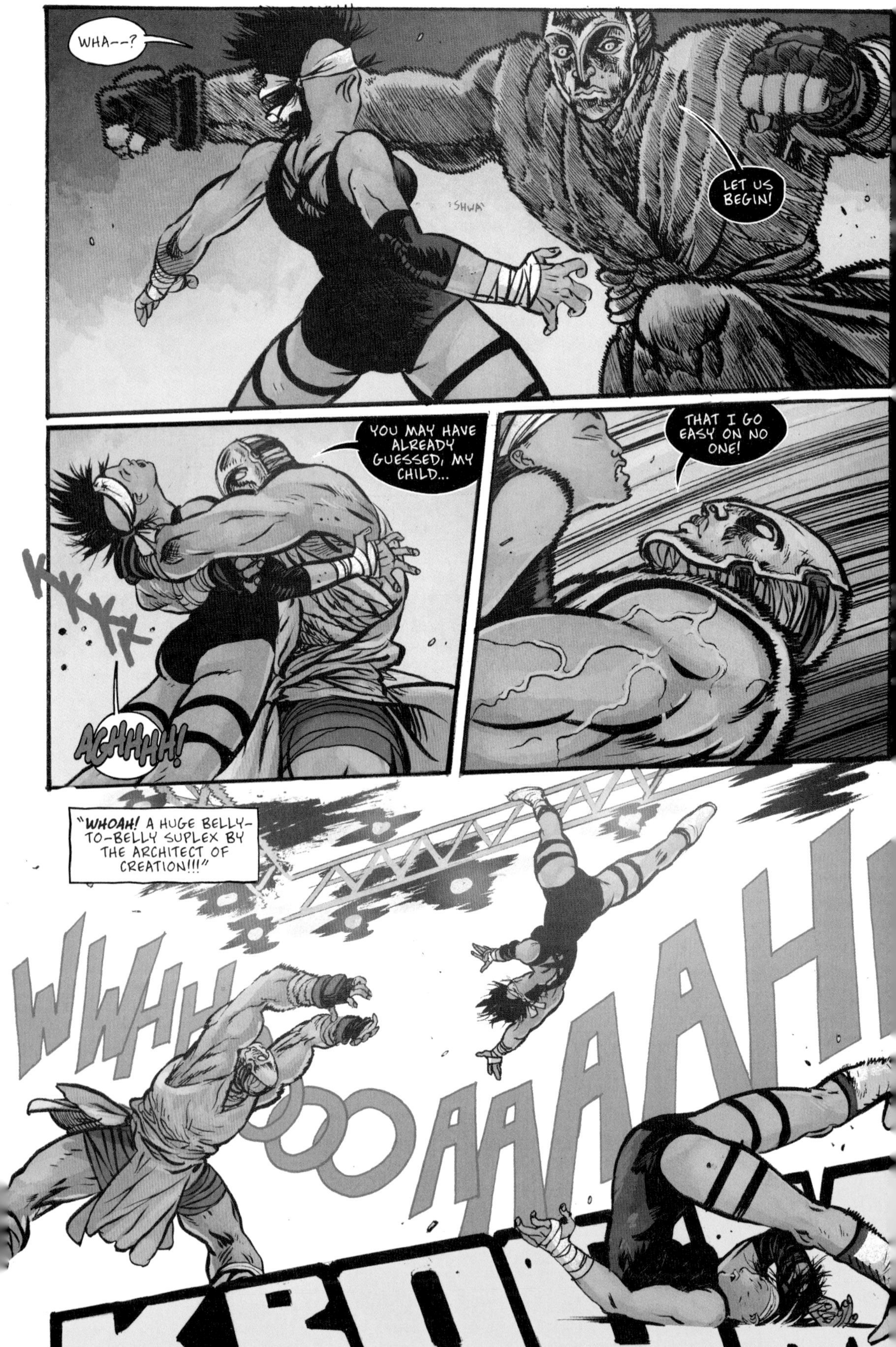
WHA--?
SHWA
LET US BEGIN!
YOU MAY HAVE ALREADY GUESSED, MY CHILD...
KKKKK
AGHHHH!
THAT I GO EASY ON NO ONE!
"WHOAH! A HUGE BELLY-TO-BELLY SUPLEX BY THE ARCHITECT OF CREATION!!!"
WWHHOOOAAAAAH
KROOM

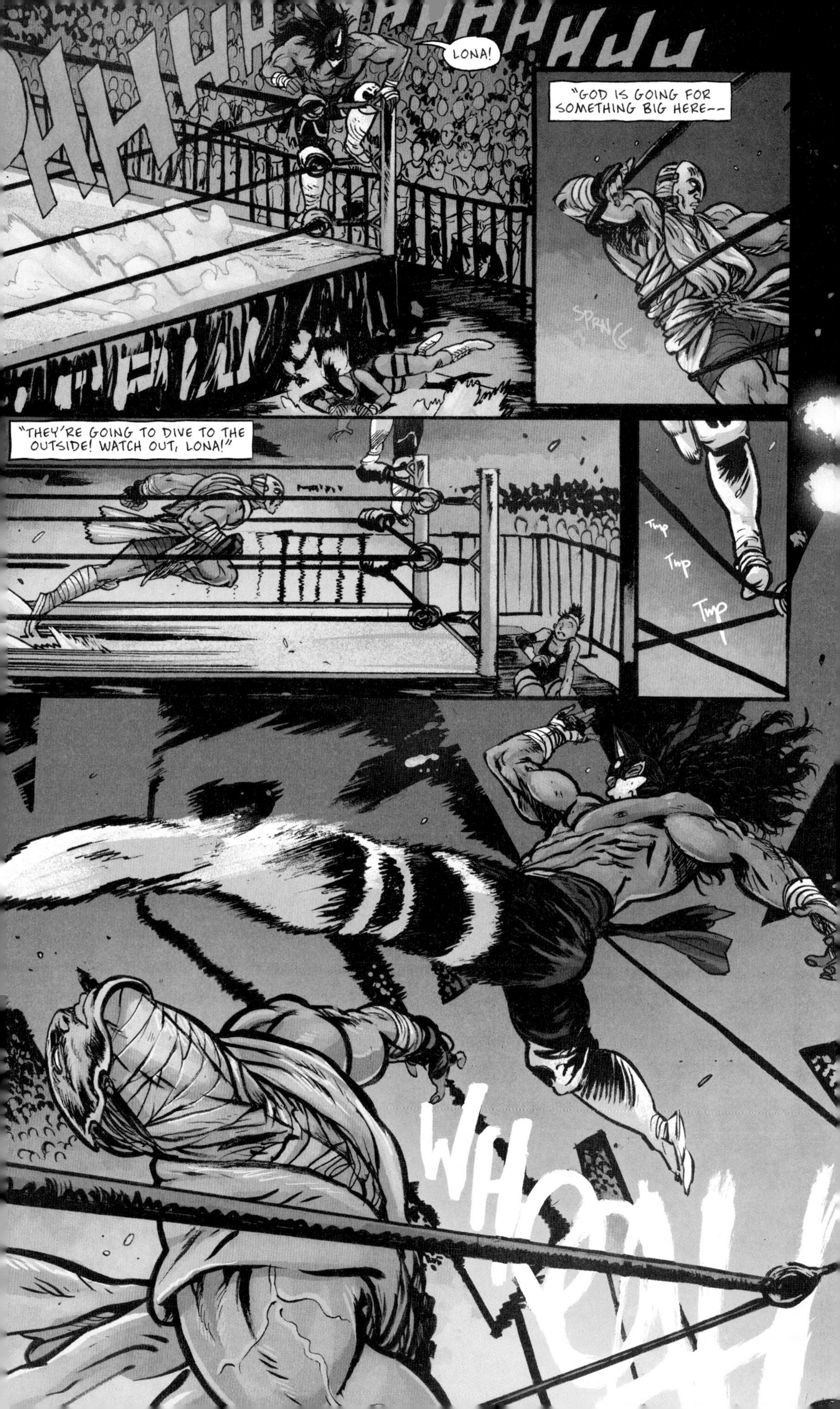
LONA!
"GOD IS GOING FOR SOMETHING BIG HERE--
SPRANG
"THEY'RE GOING TO DIVE TO THE OUTSIDE! WATCH OUT, LONA!"
Tmp
Tmp
Tmp

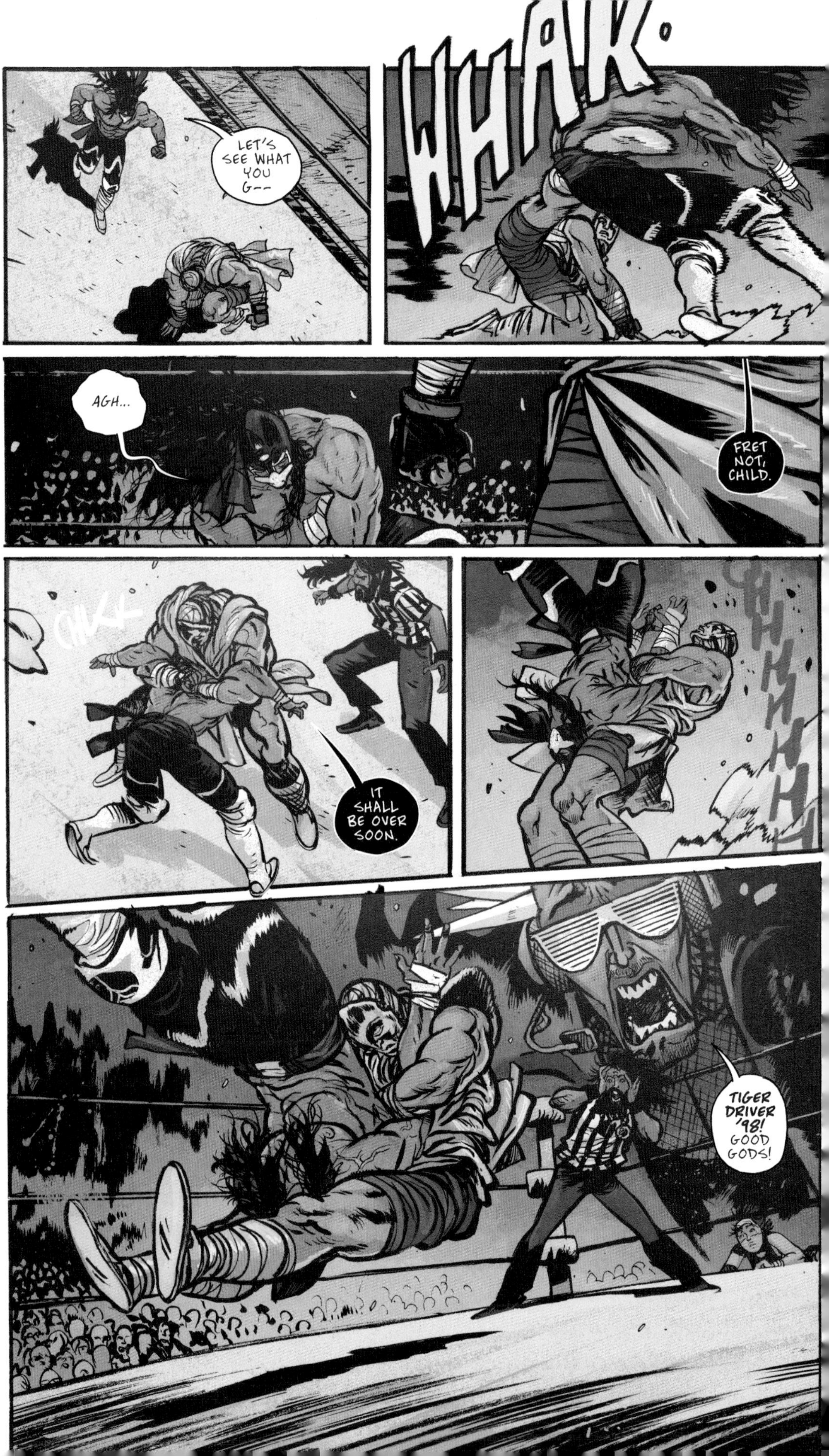

LET'S SEE WHAT YOU G--
WHAK
AGH...
FRET NOT, CHILD.
CHUK
IT SHALL BE OVER SOON.
TIGER DRIVER '98! GOOD GODS!

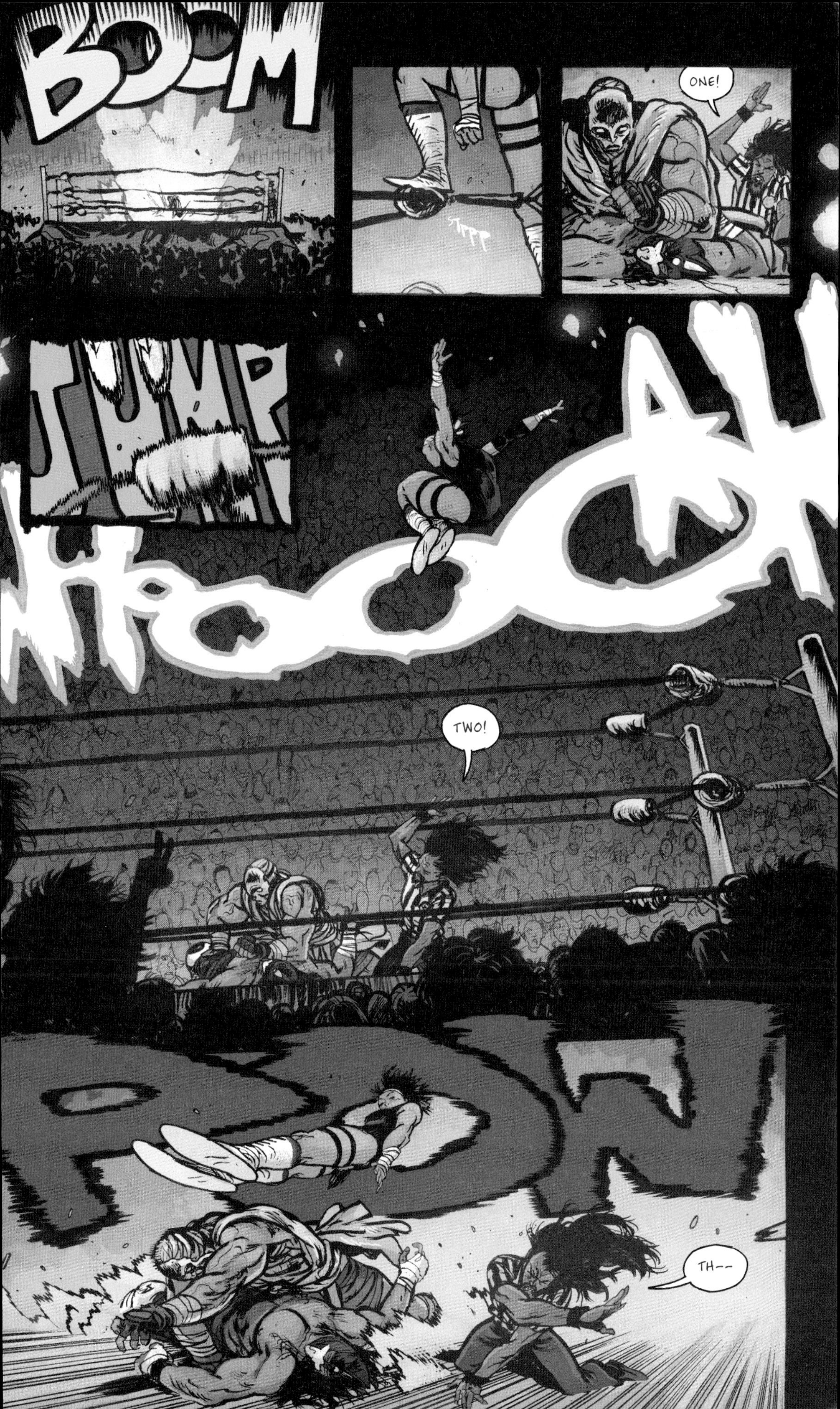
BOOM
ONE!
TWO!
TH--

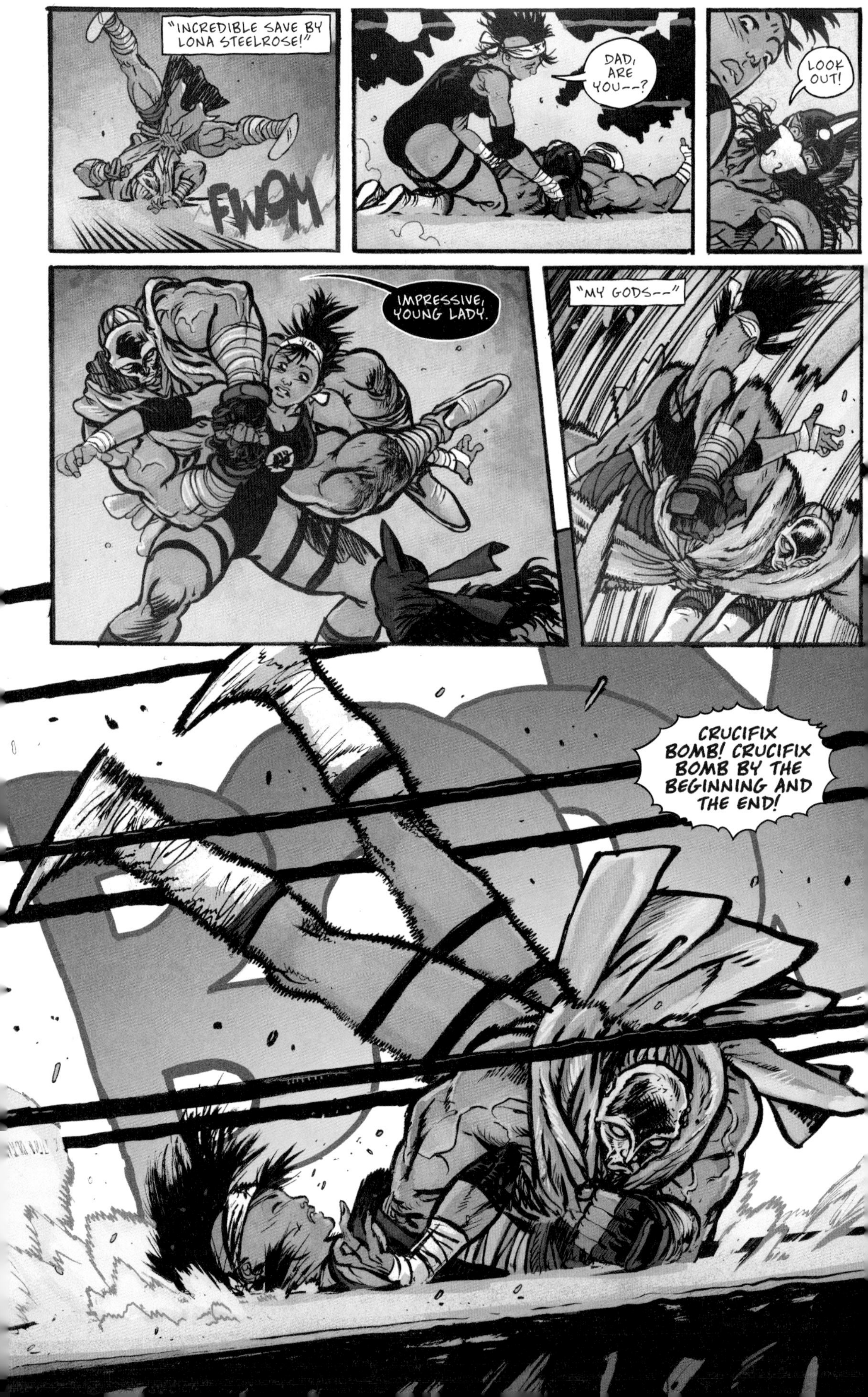
"INCREDIBLE SAVE BY LONA STEELROSE!"
FWOM
DAD, ARE YOU--?
LOOK OUT!
IMPRESSIVE, YOUNG LADY.
"MY GODS--"
CRUCIFIX BOMB! CRUCIFIX BOMB BY THE BEGINNING AND THE END!

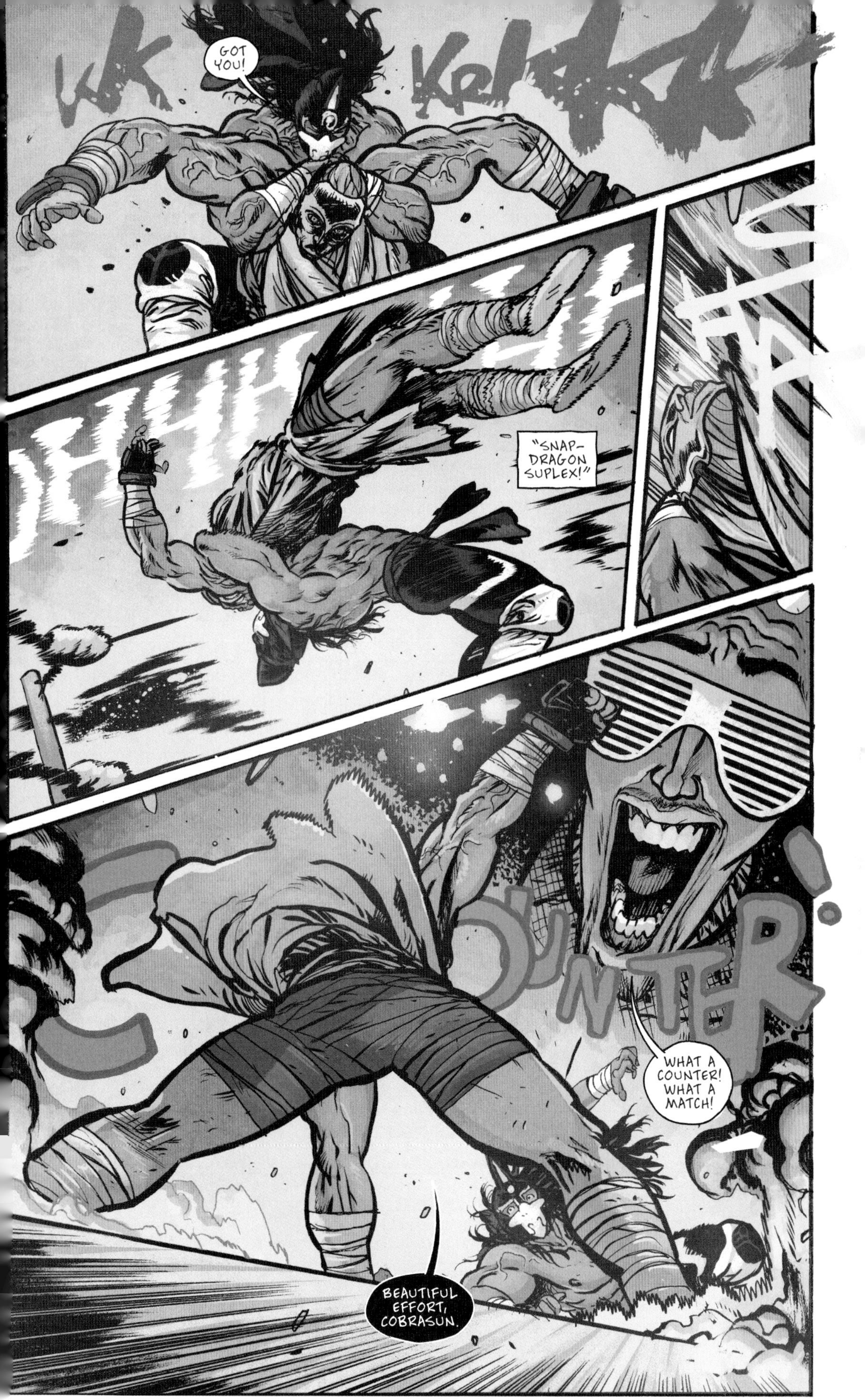

GOT YOU!
"SNAP-DRAGON SUPLEX!"
WHAT A COUNTER! WHAT A MATCH!
BEAUTIFUL EFFORT, COBRASUN.

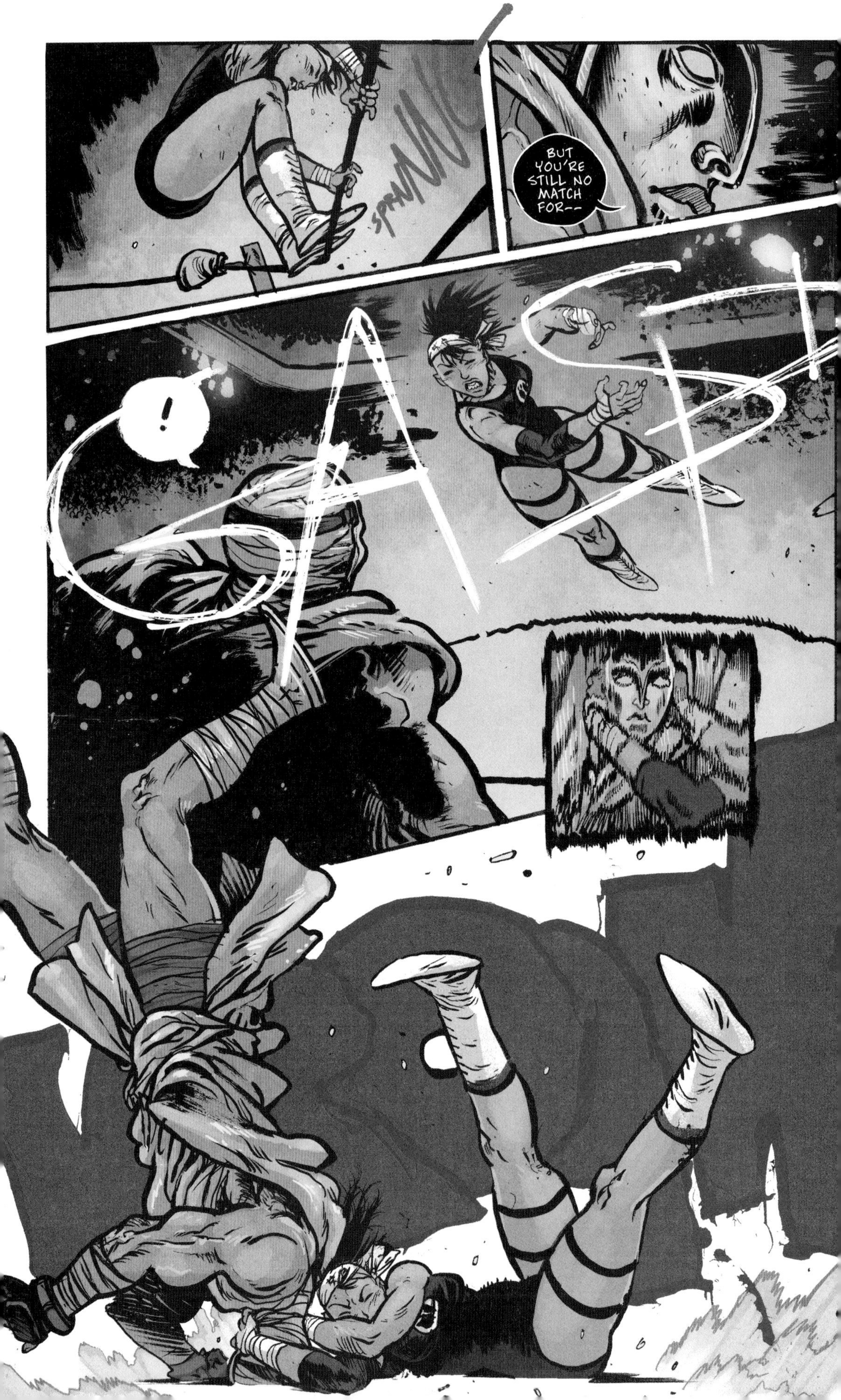
SPANNG
BUT YOU'RE STILL NO MATCH FOR--
!
GASP

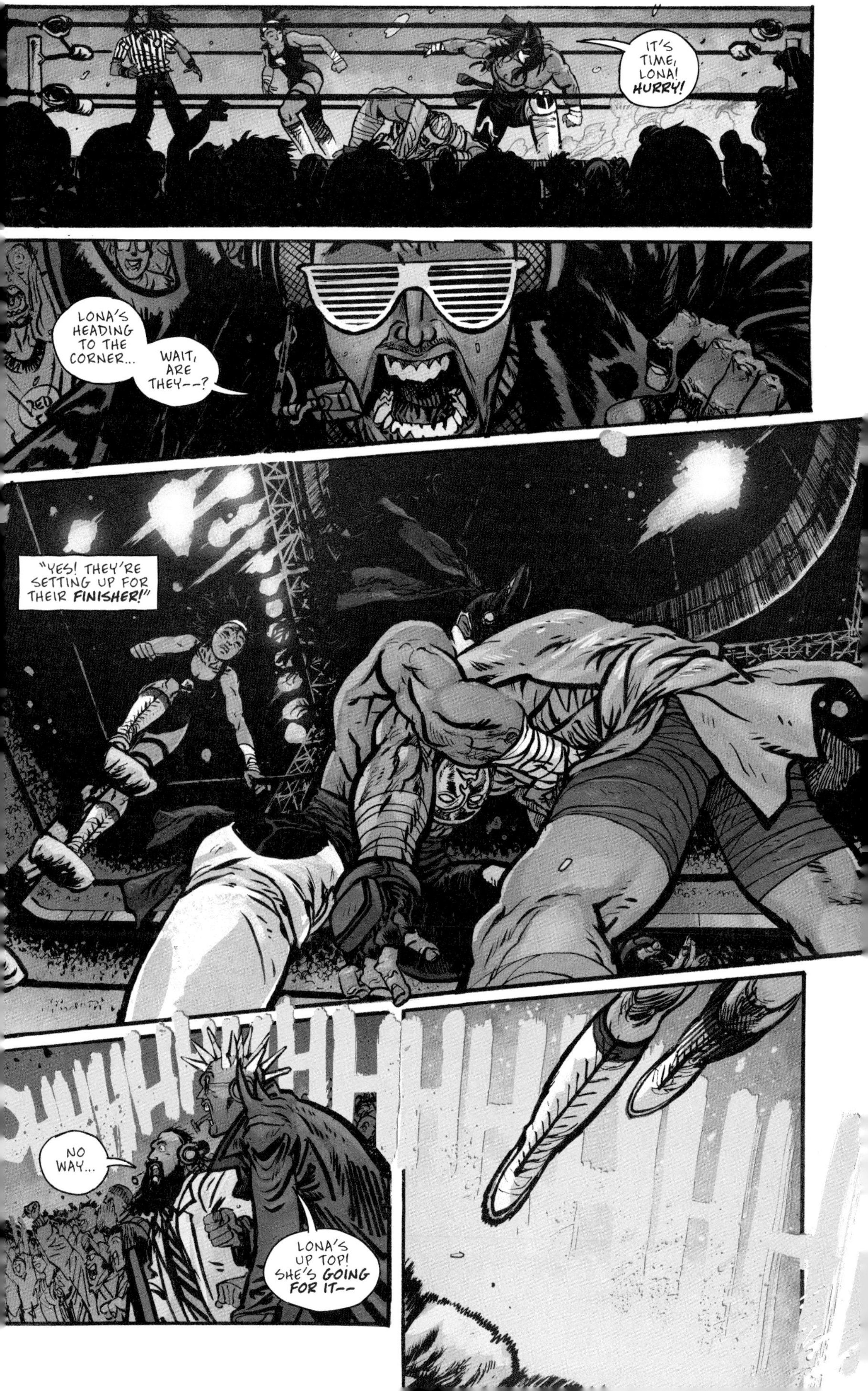
IT'S TIME, LONA! HURRY!
LONA'S HEADING TO THE CORNER...
WAIT, ARE THEY--?
"YES! THEY'RE SETTING UP FOR THEIR FINISHER!"
NO WAY...
LONA'S UP TOP! SHE'S GOING FOR IT--

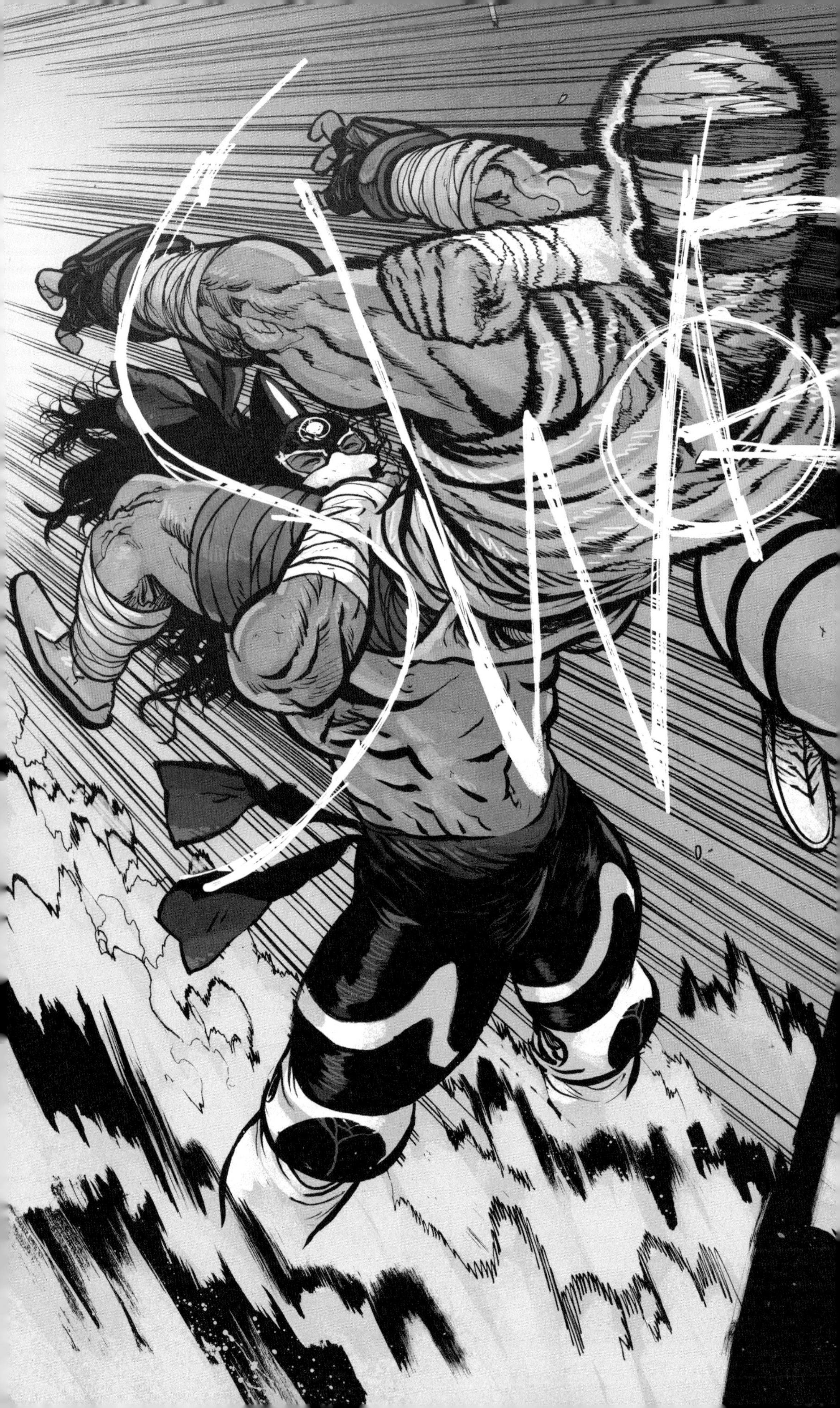

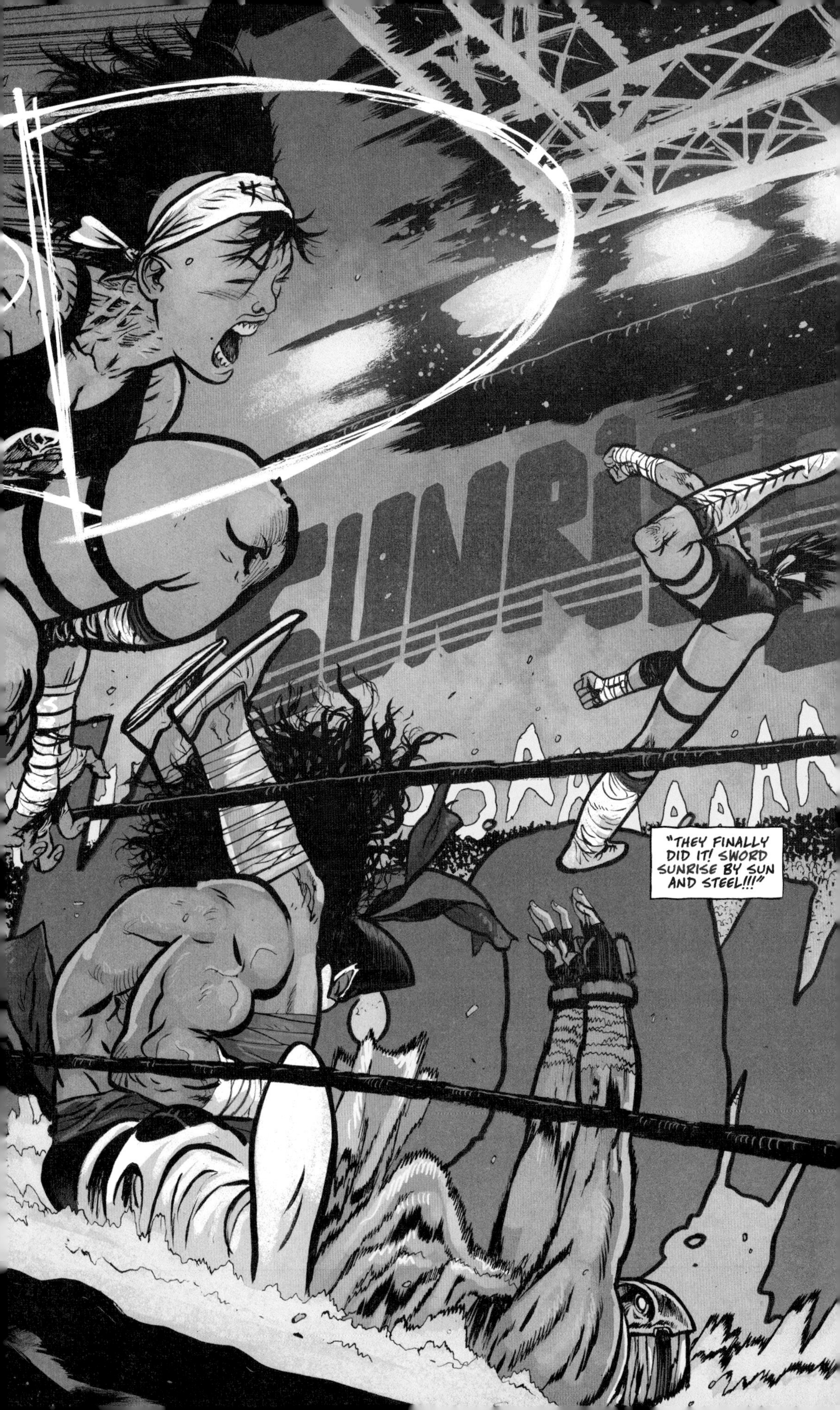
"THEY FINALLY DID IT! SWORD SUNRISE BY SUN AND STEEL!!!"

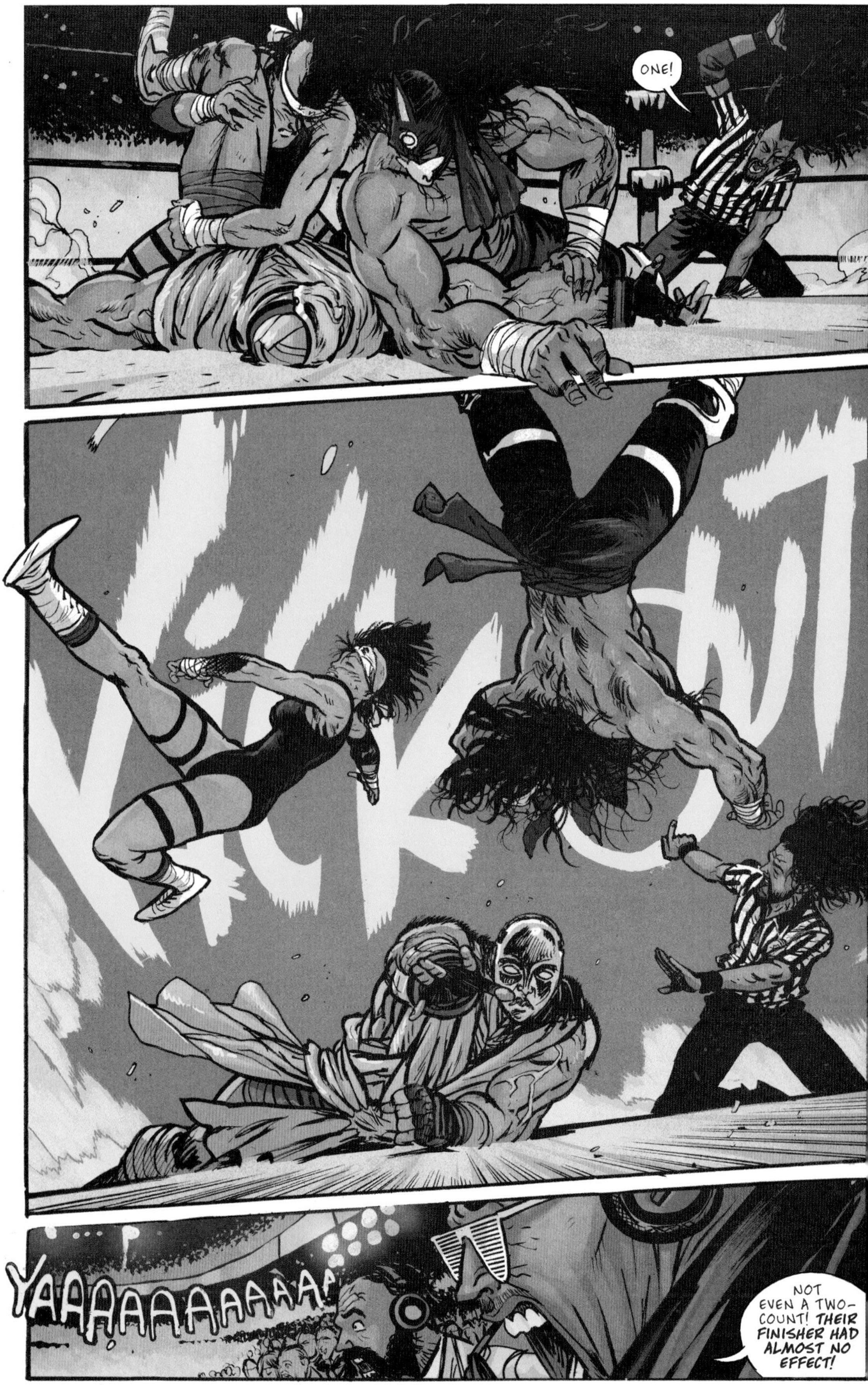
ONE!
YAAAAAAAAAA
NOT EVEN A TWO-COUNT! THEIR FINISHER HAD ALMOST NO EFFECT!

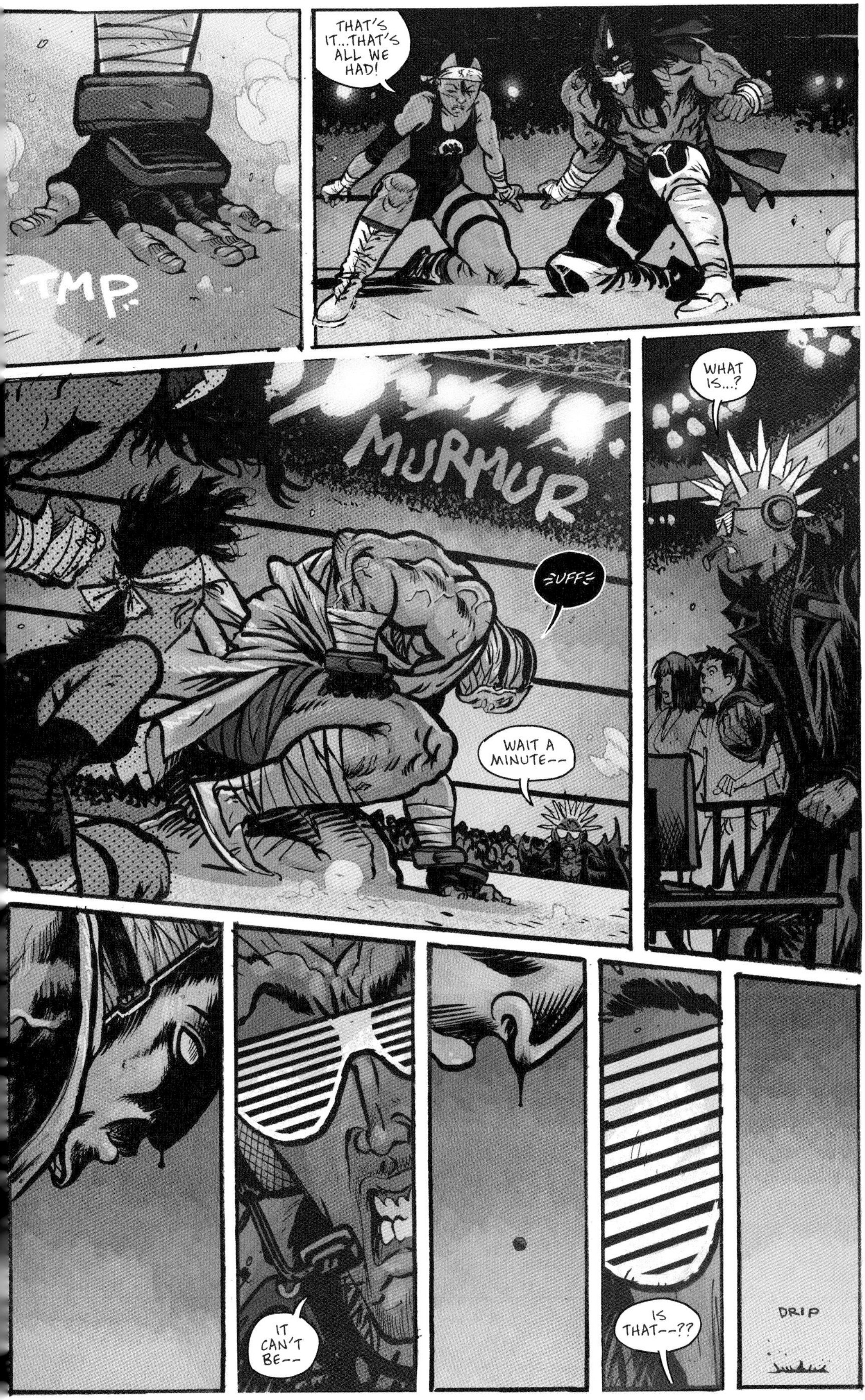
TMP
THAT'S IT...THAT'S ALL WE HAD!
MURMUR
UFF
WAIT A MINUTE--
WHAT IS...?
IT CAN'T BE--
IS THAT--??
DRIP

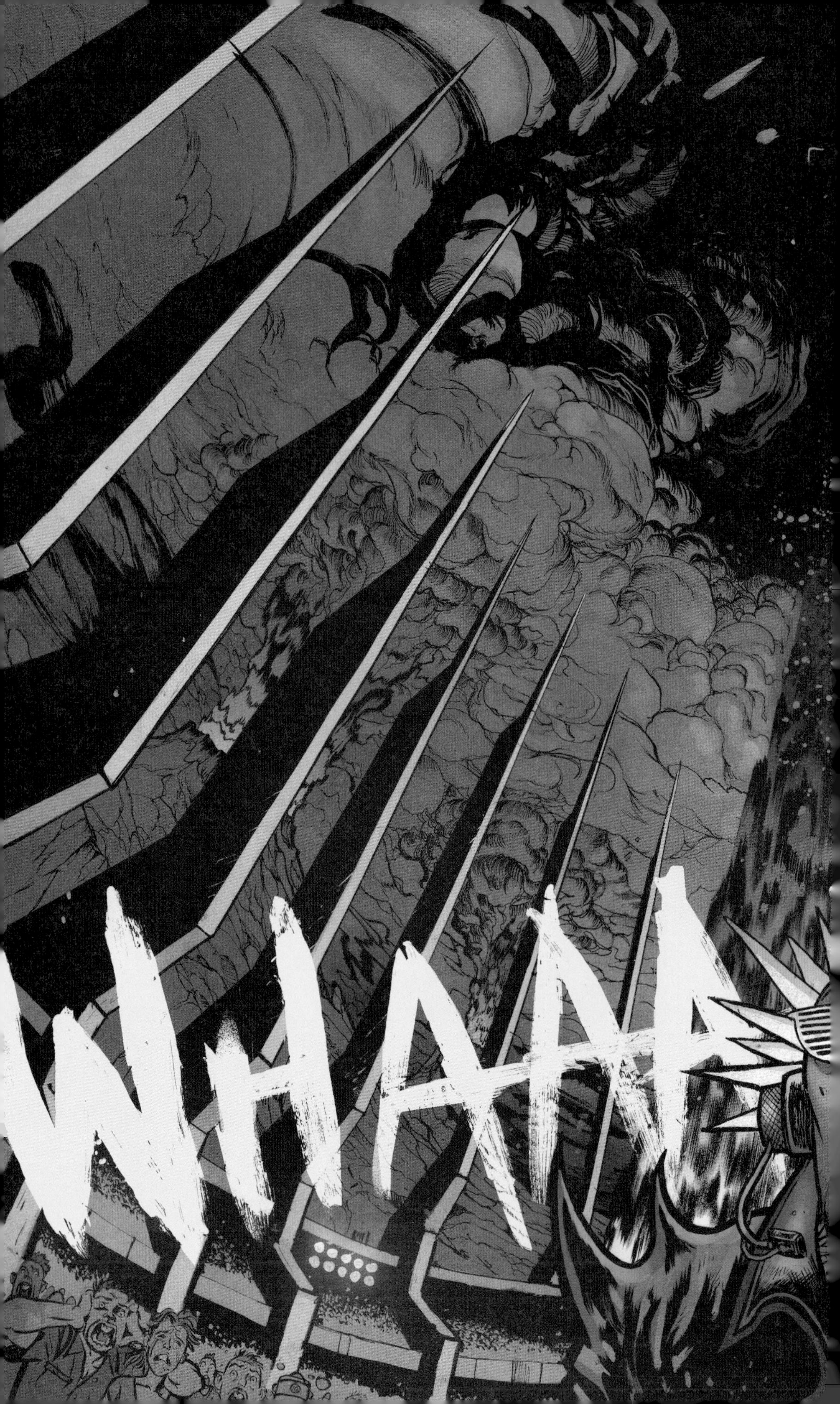
WHAAA

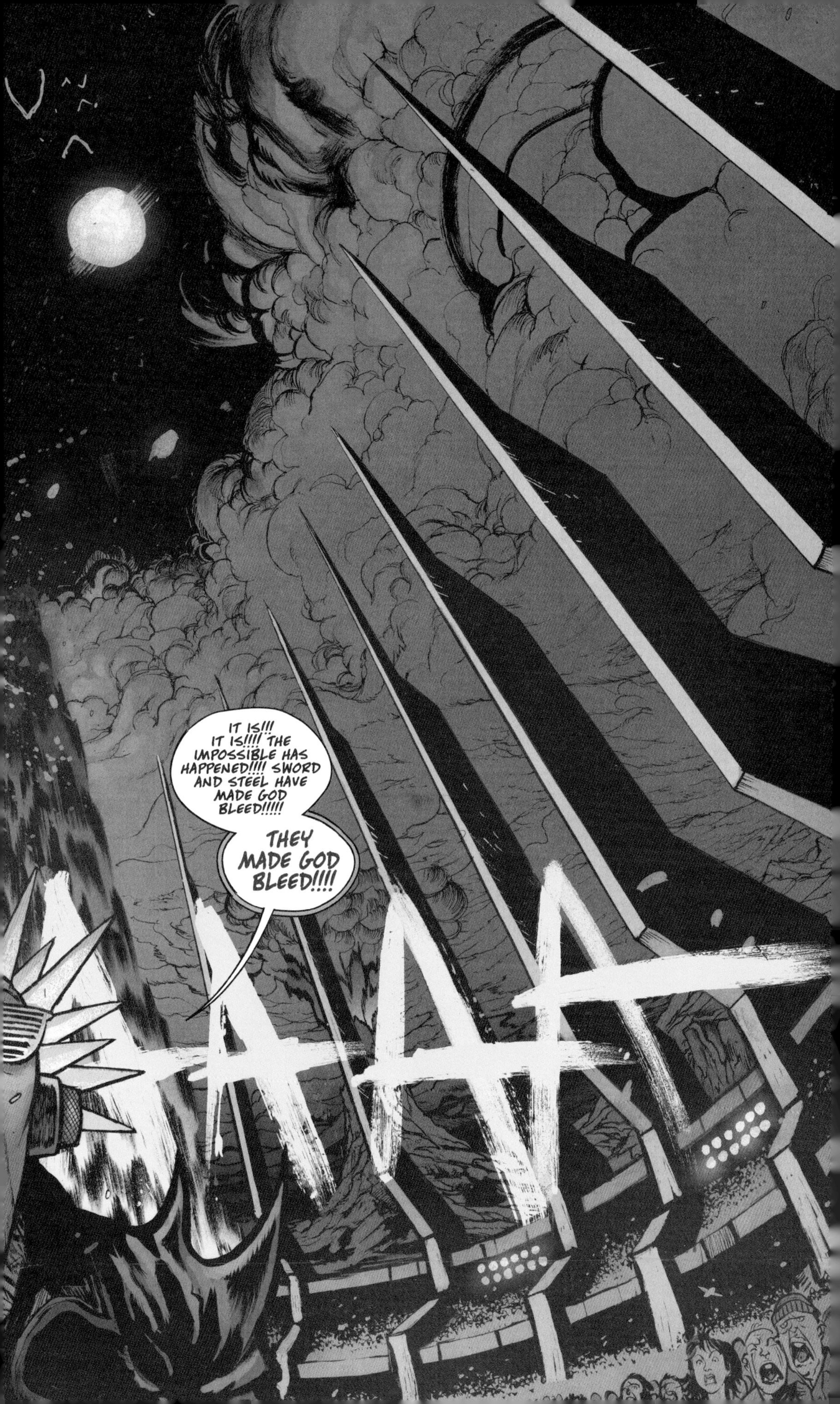
IT IS!!! IT IS!!!! THE IMPOSSIBLE HAS HAPPENED!!!! SWORD AND STEEL HAVE MADE GOD BLEED!!!!!
THEY MADE GOD BLEED!!!!

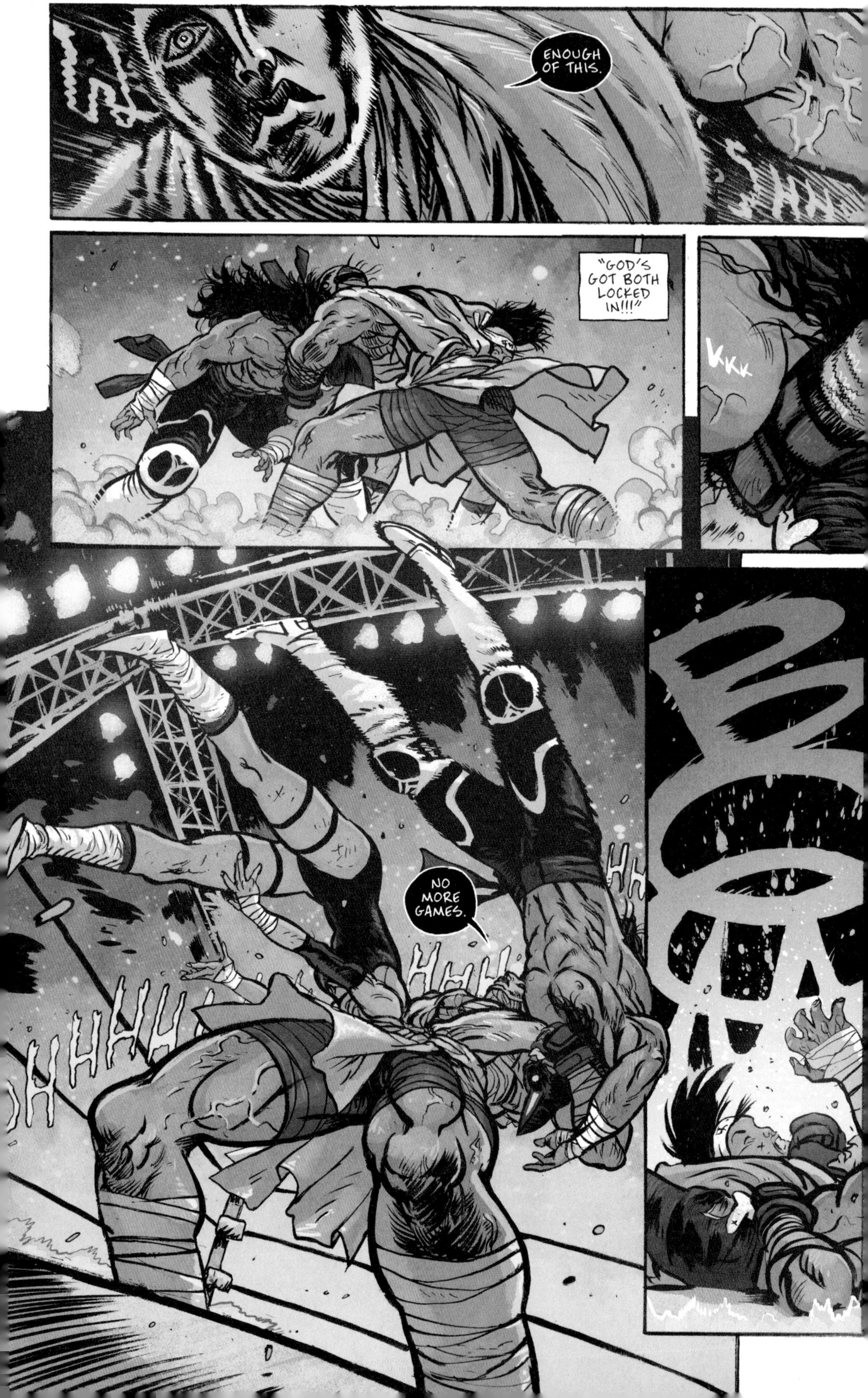
ENOUGH OF THIS.
"GOD'S GOT BOTH LOCKED IN!!!"
NO MORE GAMES.

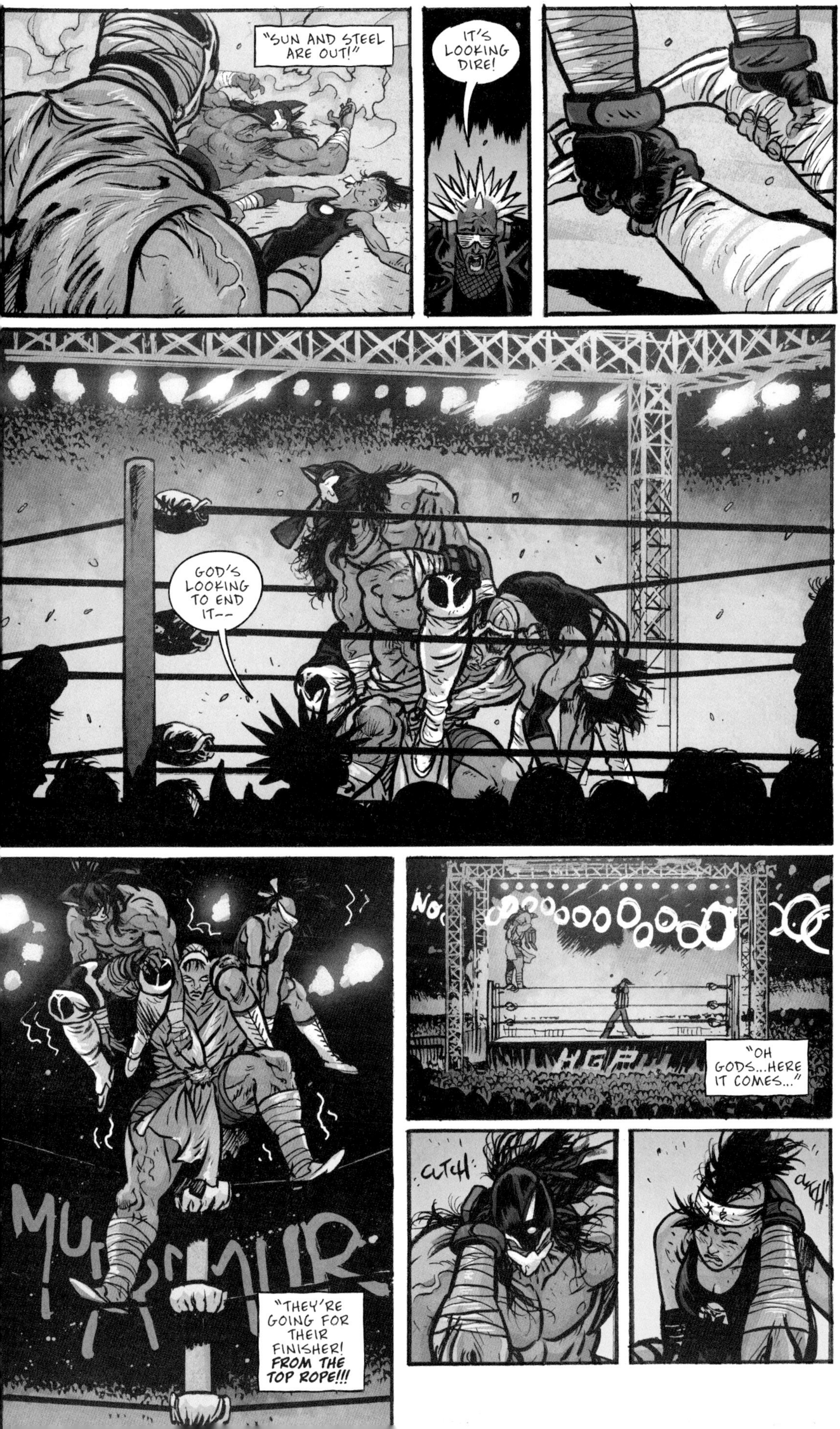
"SUN AND STEEL ARE OUT!"
IT'S LOOKING DIRE!
GOD'S LOOKING TO END IT--
"THEY'RE GOING FOR THEIR FINISHER! **FROM THE TOP ROPE!!!**
NOOOOOOOOOOOOOOO
"OH GODS...HERE IT COMES..."
CLTCH

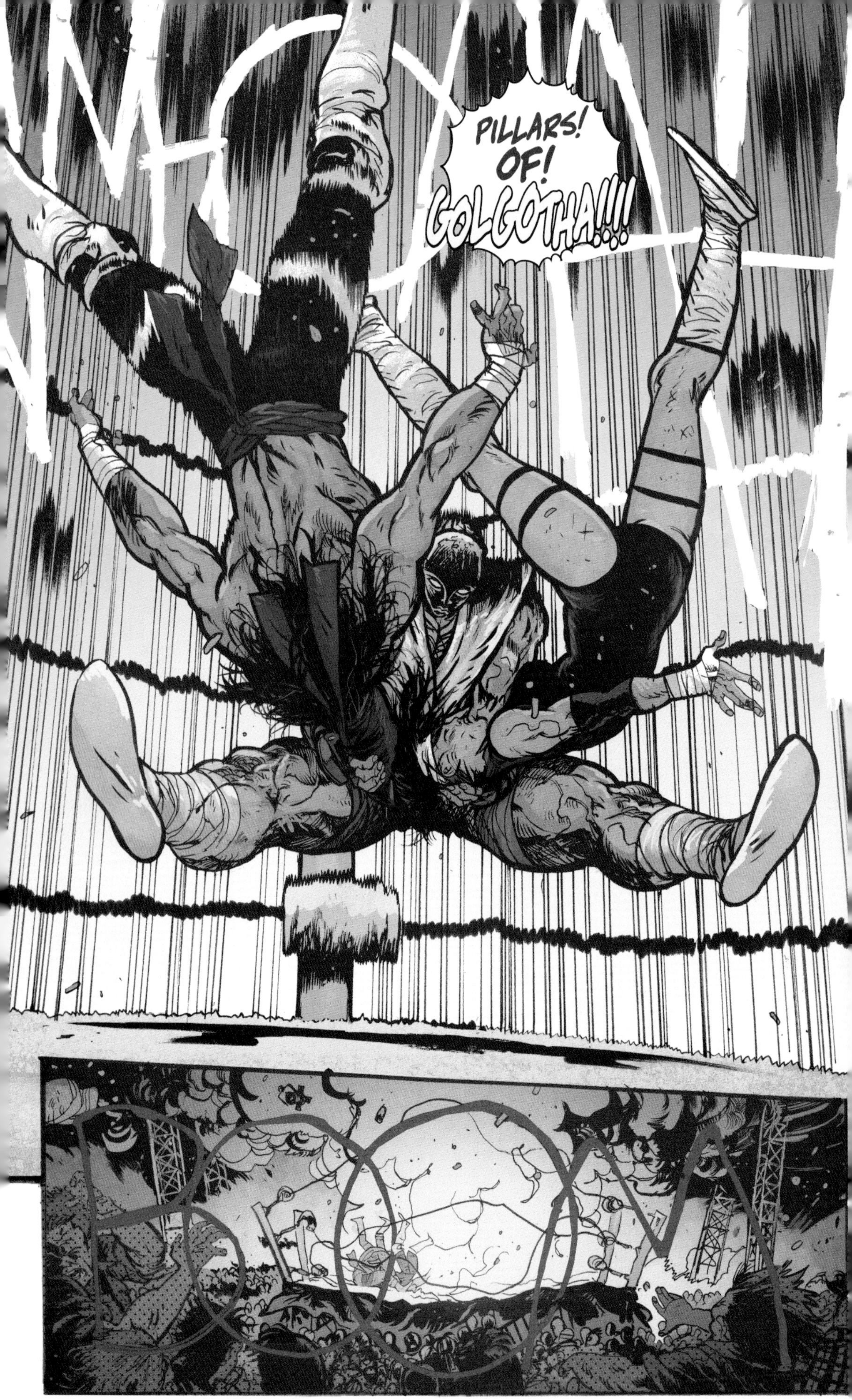
PILLARS! OF! GOLGOTHA!!!!
BOOM

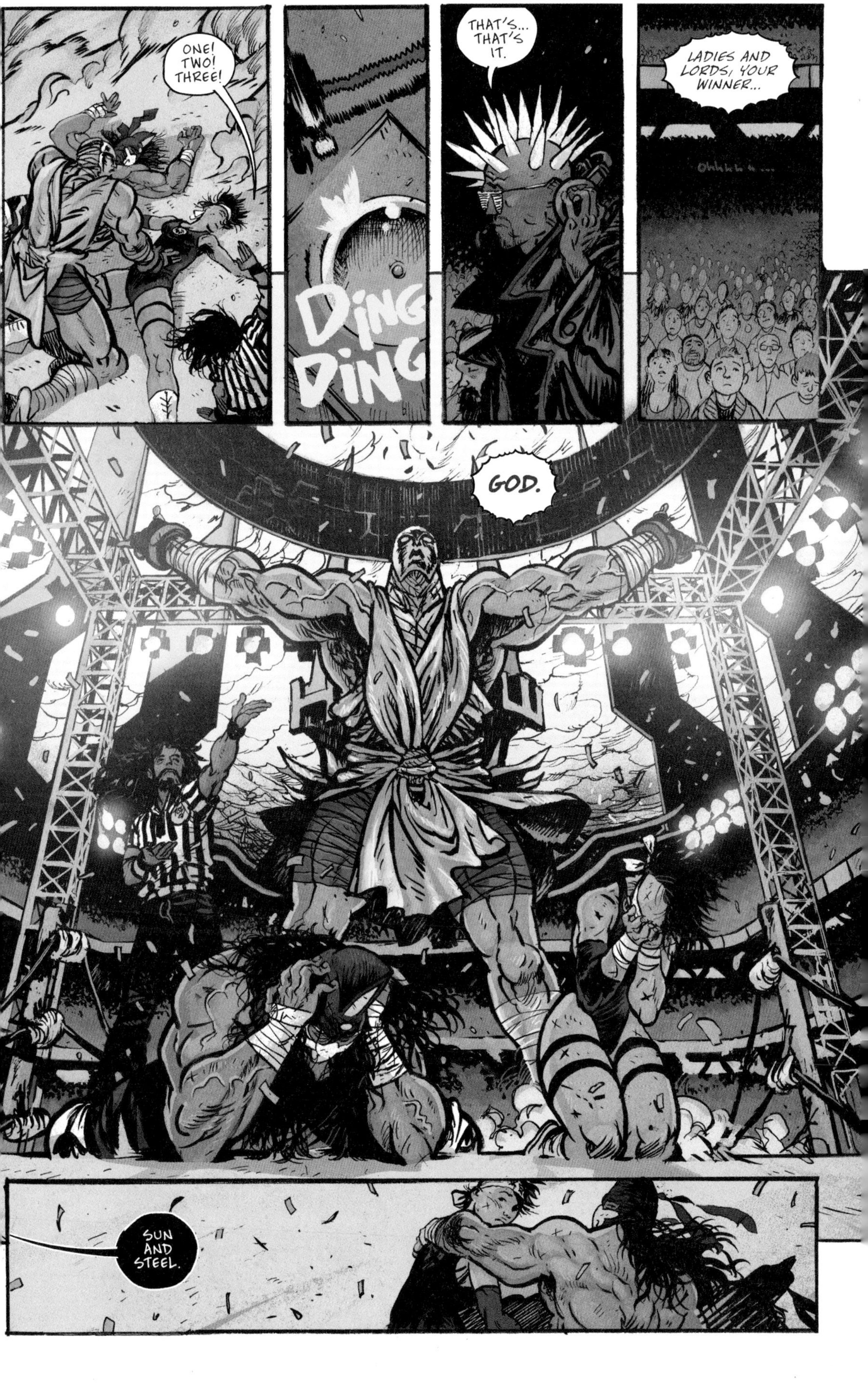
ONE! TWO! THREE!
DING DING
THAT'S... THAT'S IT.
LADIES AND LORDS, YOUR WINNER...
GOD.
SUN AND STEEL.

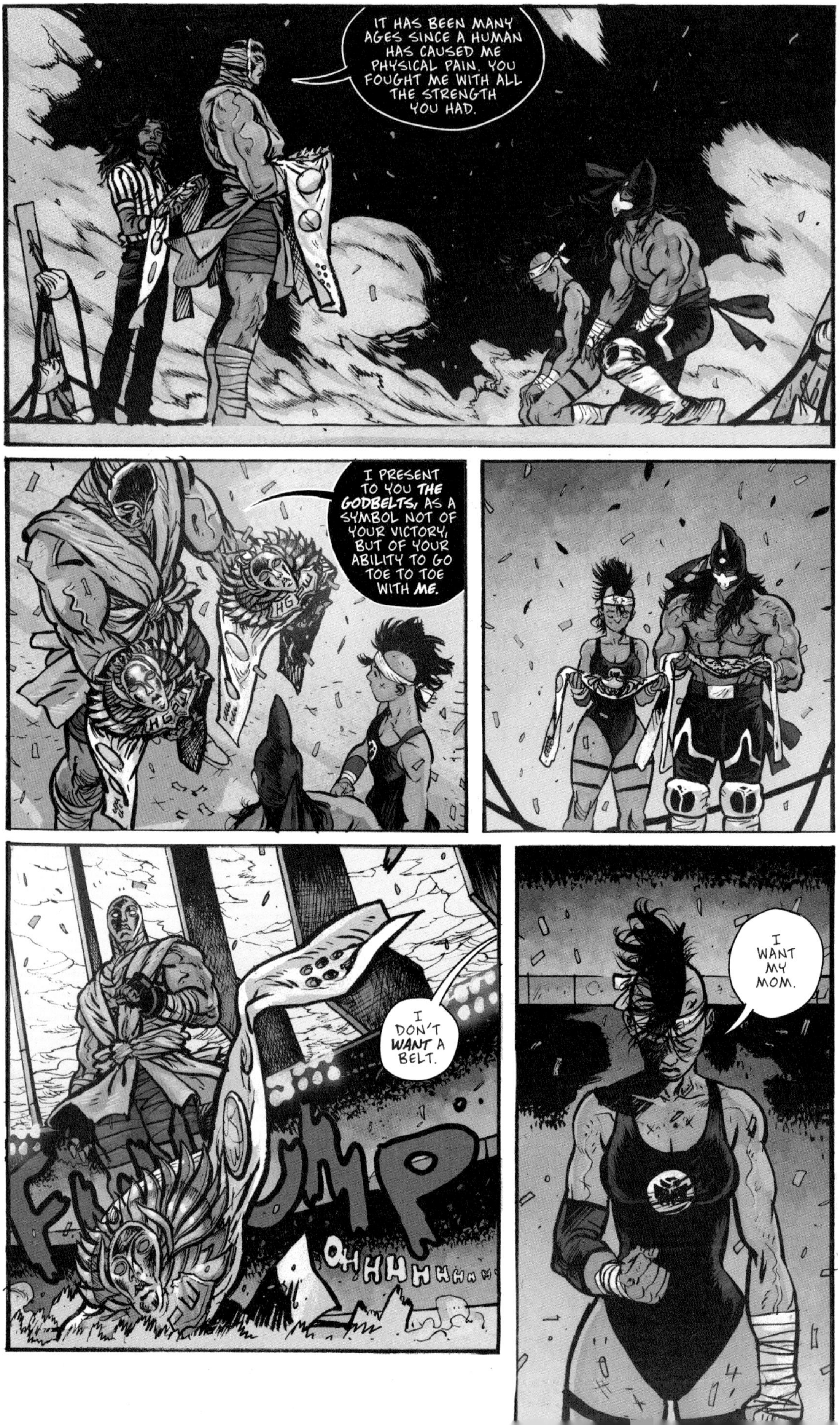
IT HAS BEEN MANY AGES SINCE A HUMAN HAS CAUSED ME PHYSICAL PAIN. YOU FOUGHT ME WITH ALL THE STRENGTH YOU HAD.
I PRESENT TO YOU **THE GODBELTS,** AS A SYMBOL NOT OF YOUR VICTORY, BUT OF YOUR ABILITY TO GO TOE TO TOE WITH **ME.**
I DON'T **WANT** A BELT.
OHHHHHHHHH
I WANT MY MOM.

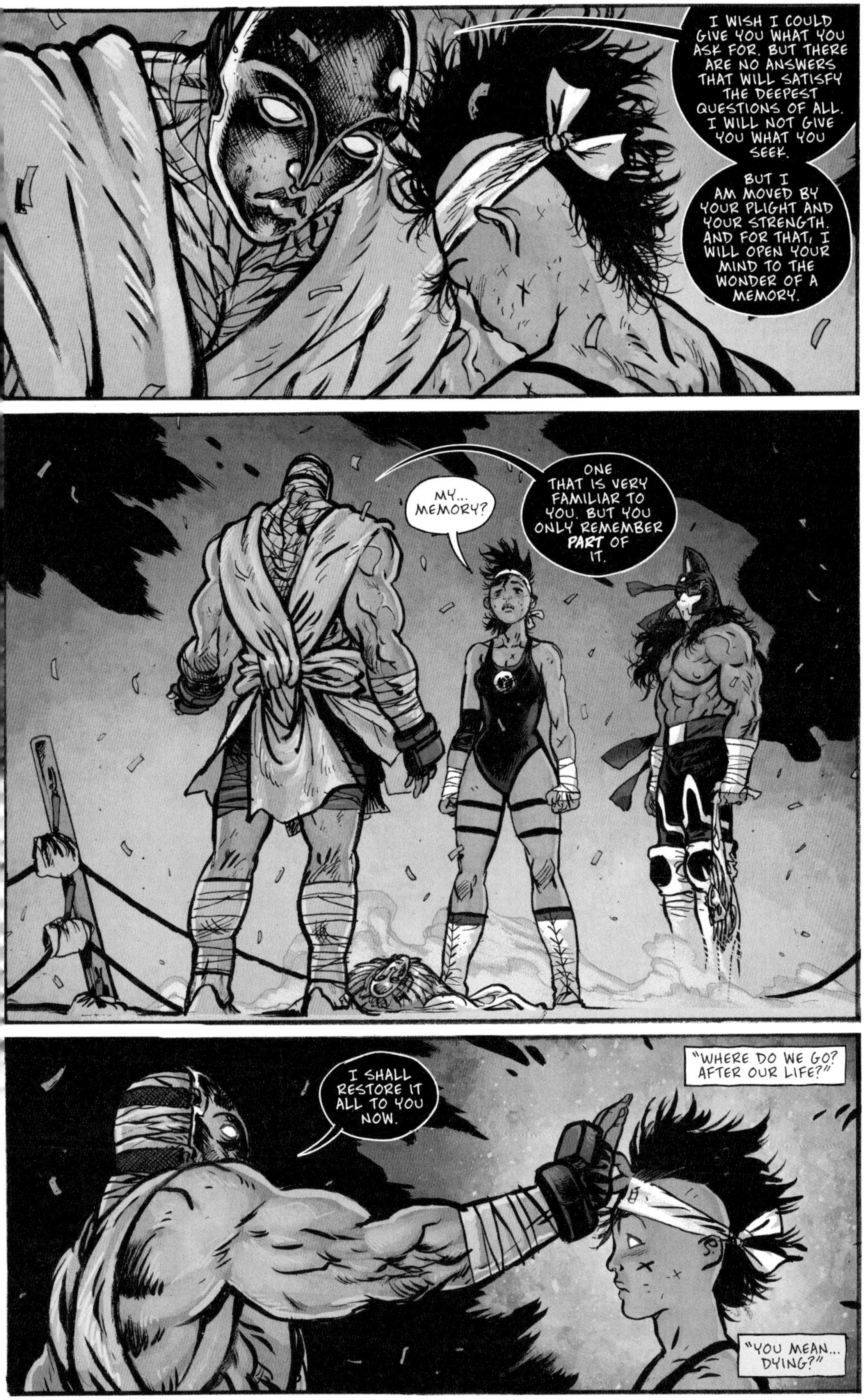
I WISH I COULD GIVE YOU WHAT YOU ASK FOR. BUT THERE ARE NO ANSWERS THAT WILL SATISFY THE DEEPEST QUESTIONS OF ALL. I WILL NOT GIVE YOU WHAT YOU SEEK.
BUT I AM MOVED BY YOUR PLIGHT AND YOUR STRENGTH. AND FOR THAT, I WILL OPEN YOUR MIND TO THE WONDER OF A MEMORY.
MY... MEMORY?
ONE THAT IS VERY FAMILIAR TO YOU. BUT YOU ONLY REMEMBER PART OF IT.
"WHERE DO WE GO? AFTER OUR LIFE?"
I SHALL RESTORE IT ALL TO YOU NOW.
"YOU MEAN... DYING?"

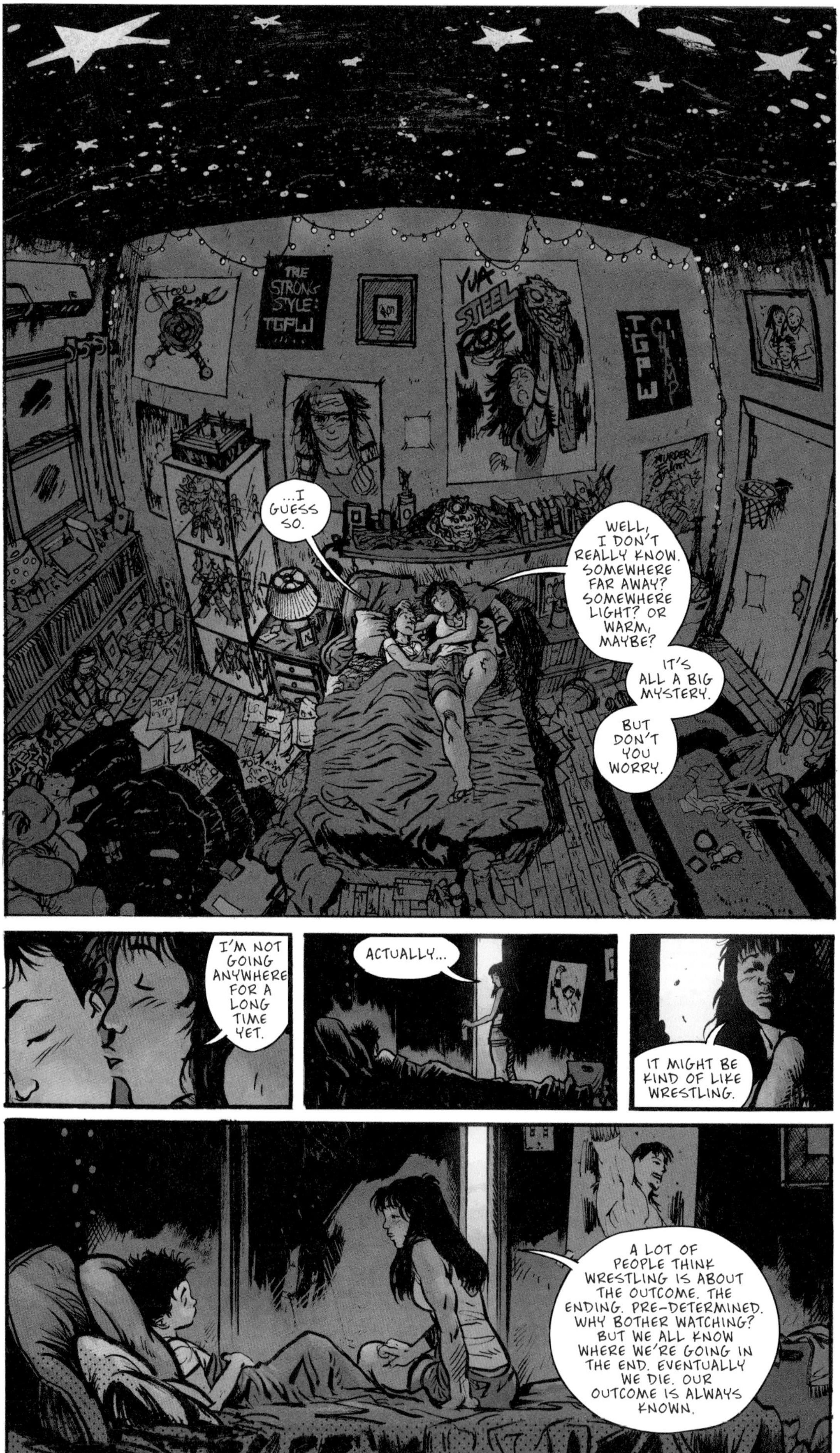
TRUE STRONG STYLE TGPW
YUA STEEL ROSE
TGPW CHAMP
...I GUESS SO.
WELL, I DON'T REALLY KNOW. SOMEWHERE FAR AWAY? SOMEWHERE LIGHT? OR WARM, MAYBE?
IT'S ALL A BIG MYSTERY.
BUT DON'T YOU WORRY.
I'M NOT GOING ANYWHERE FOR A LONG TIME YET.
ACTUALLY...
IT MIGHT BE KIND OF LIKE WRESTLING.
A LOT OF PEOPLE THINK WRESTLING IS ABOUT THE OUTCOME. THE ENDING. PRE-DETERMINED. WHY BOTHER WATCHING? BUT WE ALL KNOW WHERE WE'RE GOING IN THE END. EVENTUALLY WE DIE. OUR OUTCOME IS ALWAYS KNOWN.

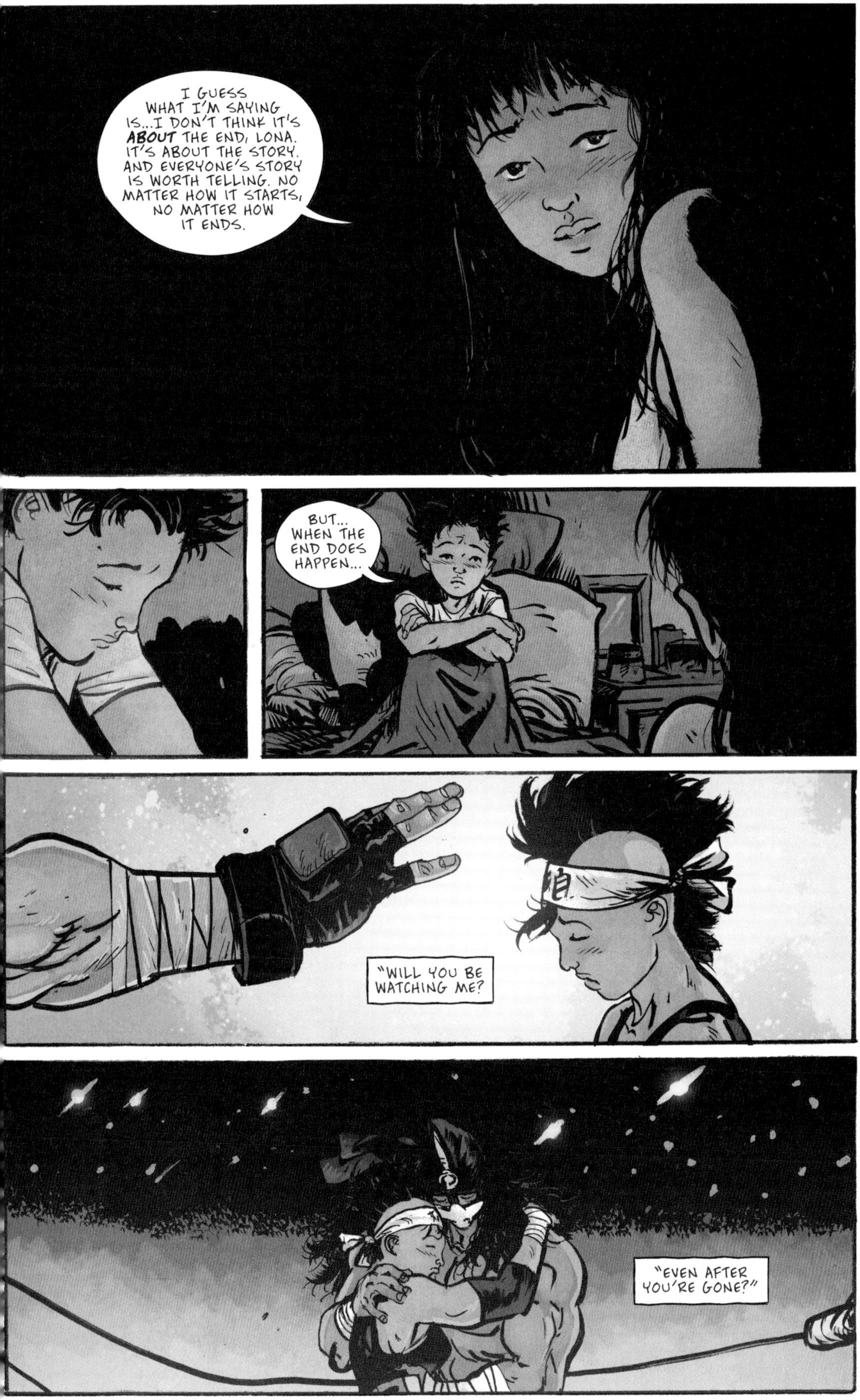
I GUESS WHAT I'M SAYING IS...I DON'T THINK IT'S **ABOUT** THE END, LONA. IT'S ABOUT THE STORY. AND EVERYONE'S STORY IS WORTH TELLING. NO MATTER HOW IT STARTS, NO MATTER HOW IT ENDS.
BUT... WHEN THE END DOES HAPPEN...
"WILL YOU BE WATCHING ME?
"EVEN AFTER YOU'RE GONE?"

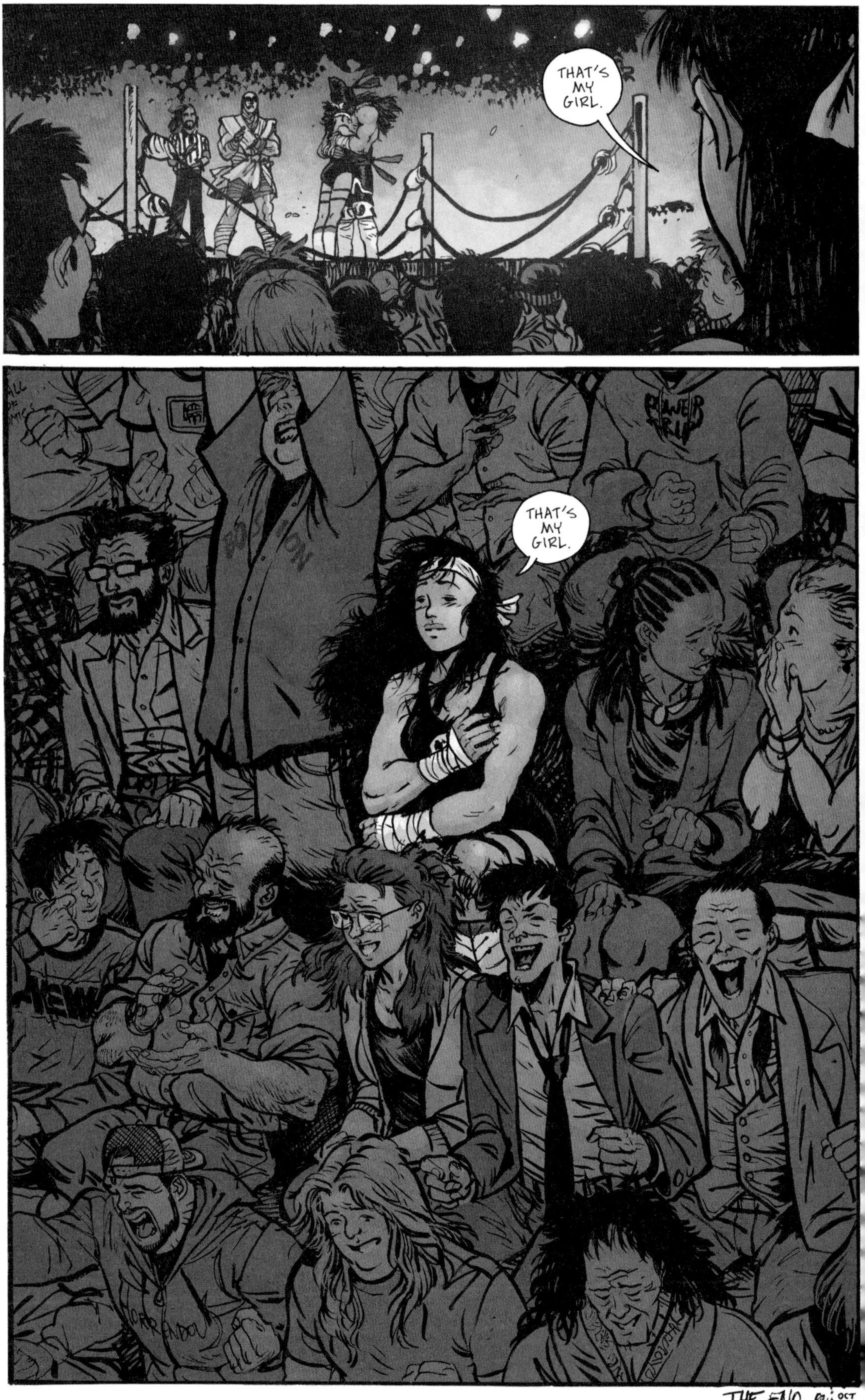
THAT'S MY GIRL.
THAT'S MY GIRL.

THE END OCT 2022

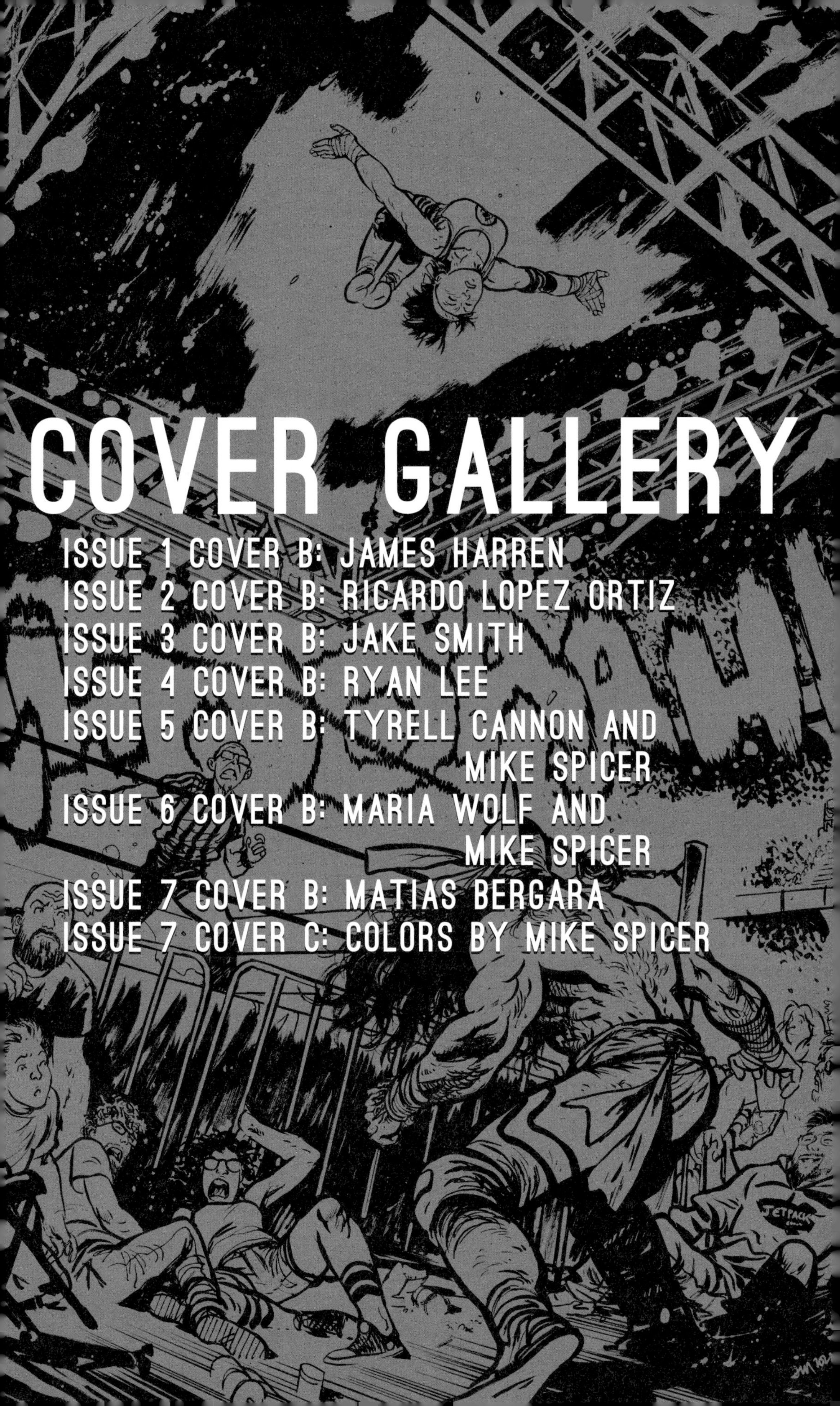

COVER GALLERY

ISSUE 1 COVER B: JAMES HARREN
ISSUE 2 COVER B: RICARDO LOPEZ ORTIZ
ISSUE 3 COVER B: JAKE SMITH
ISSUE 4 COVER B: RYAN LEE
ISSUE 5 COVER B: TYRELL CANNON AND MIKE SPICER
ISSUE 6 COVER B: MARIA WOLF AND MIKE SPICER
ISSUE 7 COVER B: MATIAS BERGARA
ISSUE 7 COVER C: COLORS BY MIKE SPICER

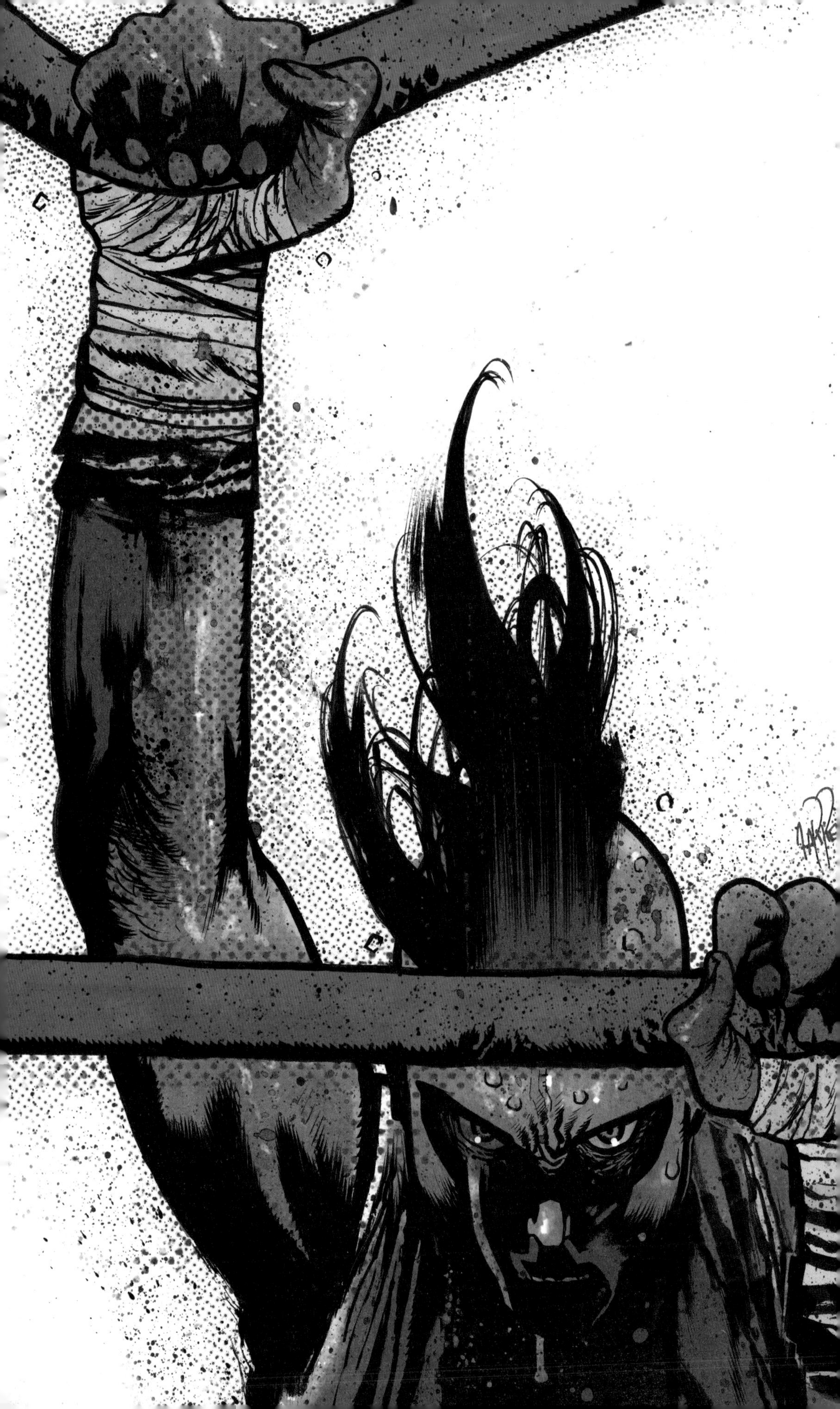

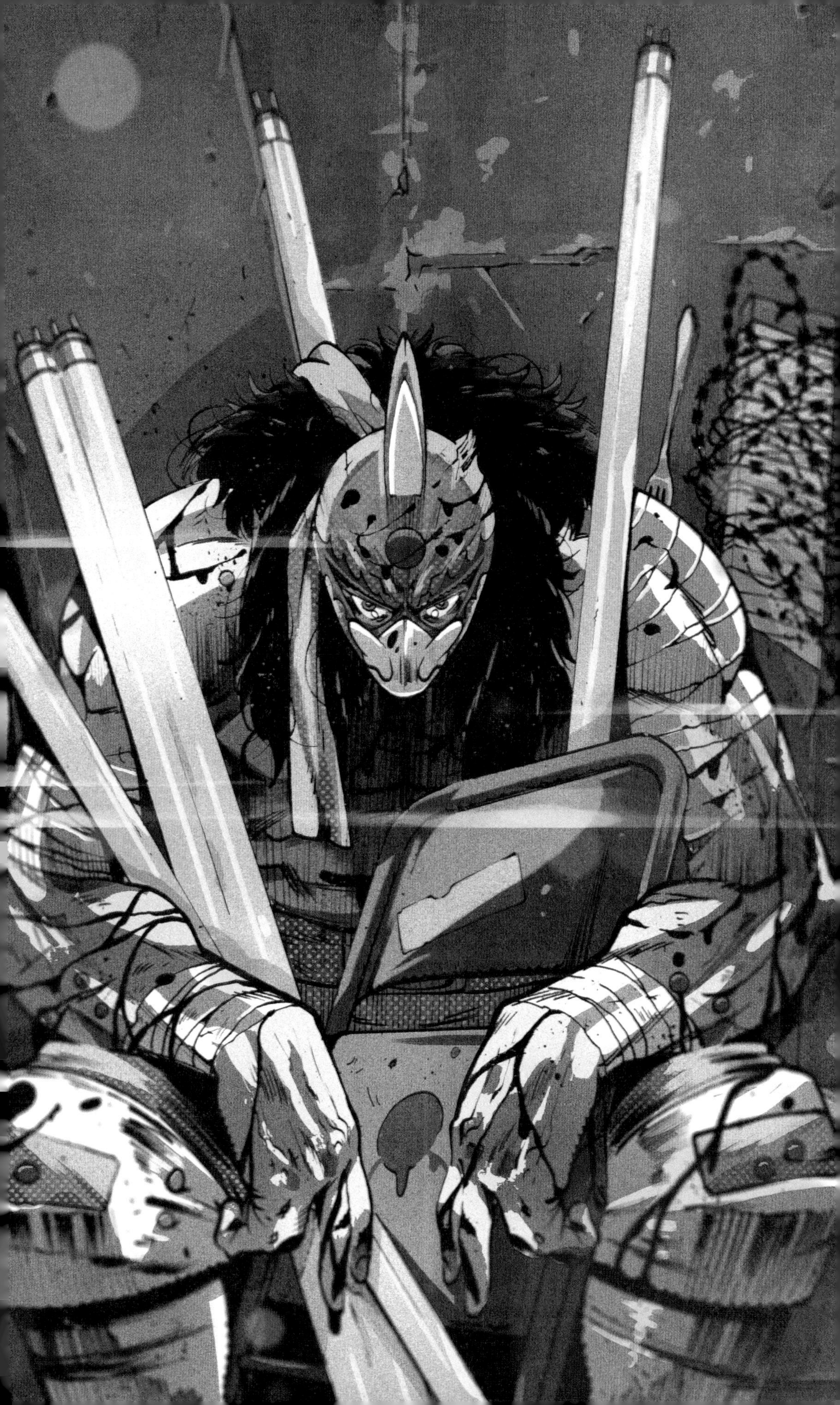

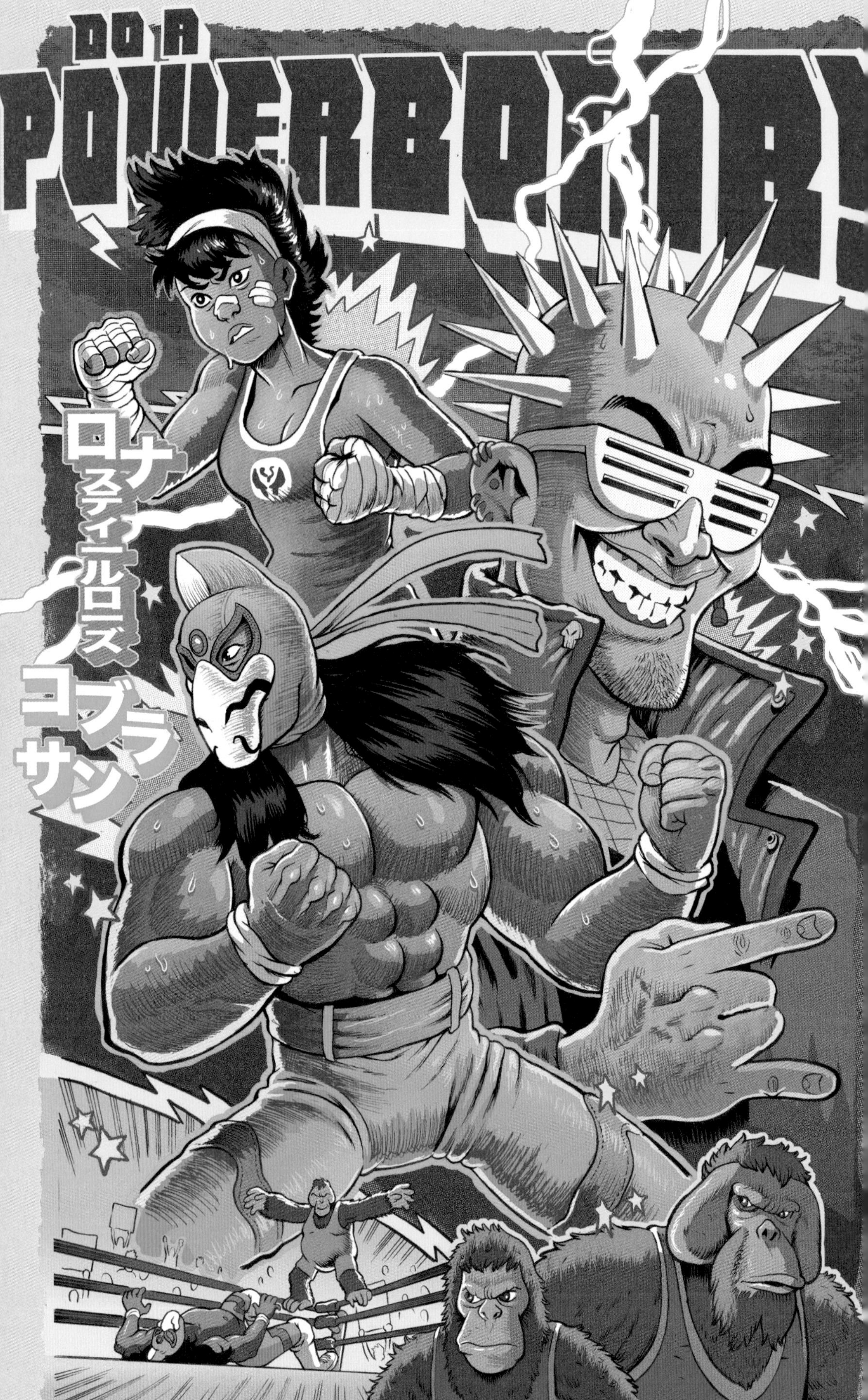
DO A POWERBOMB!
ロナスティールローズ
コブラサン

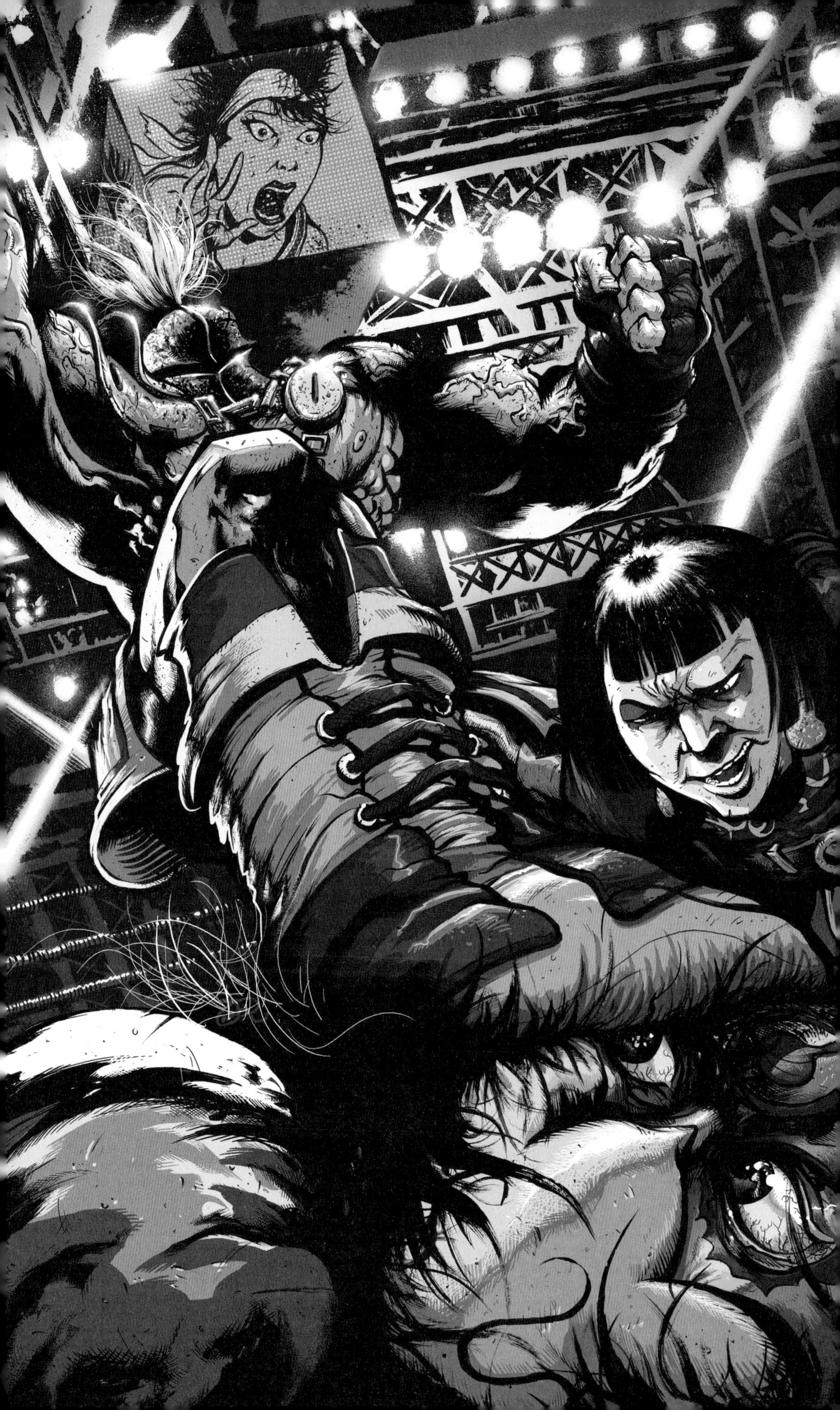

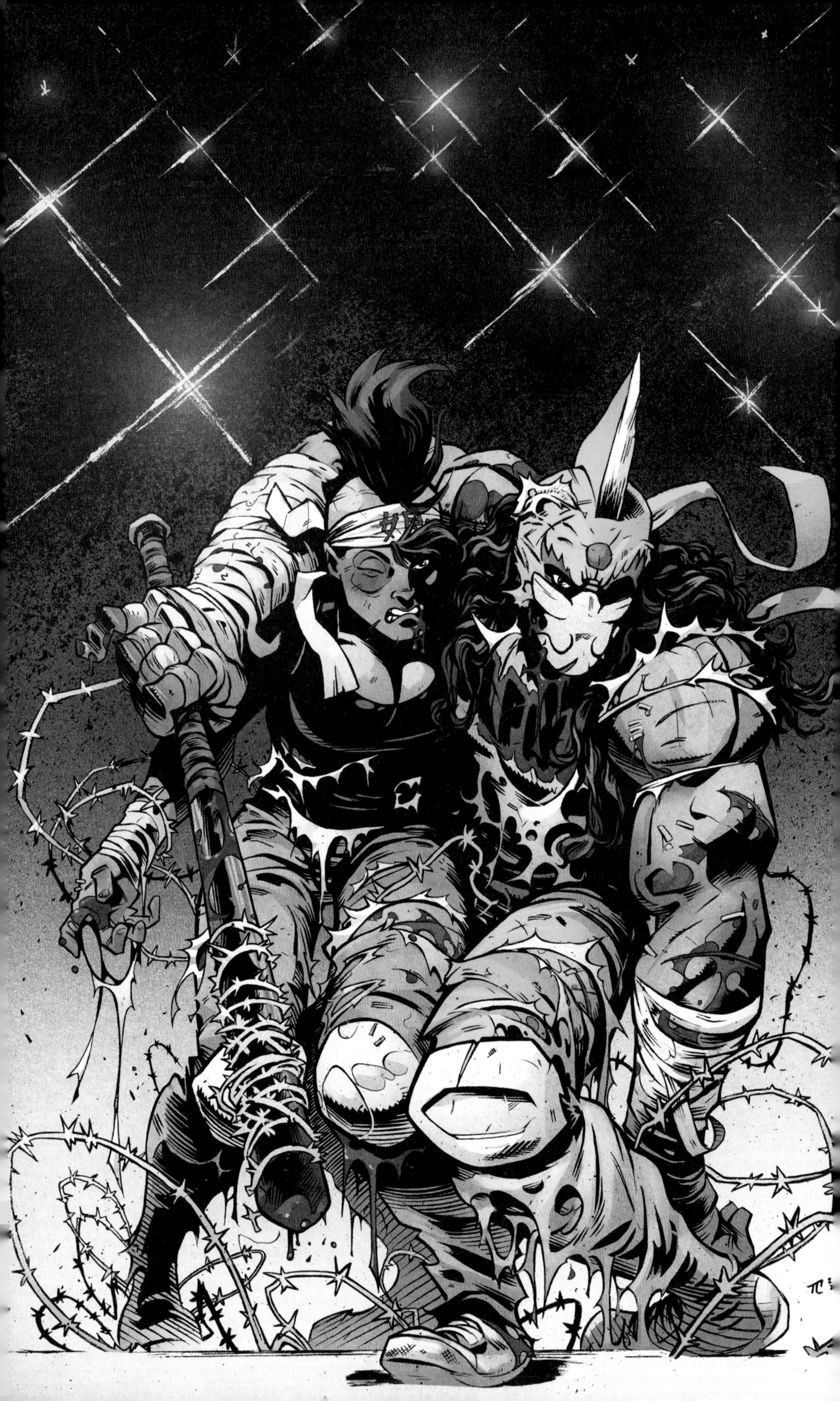

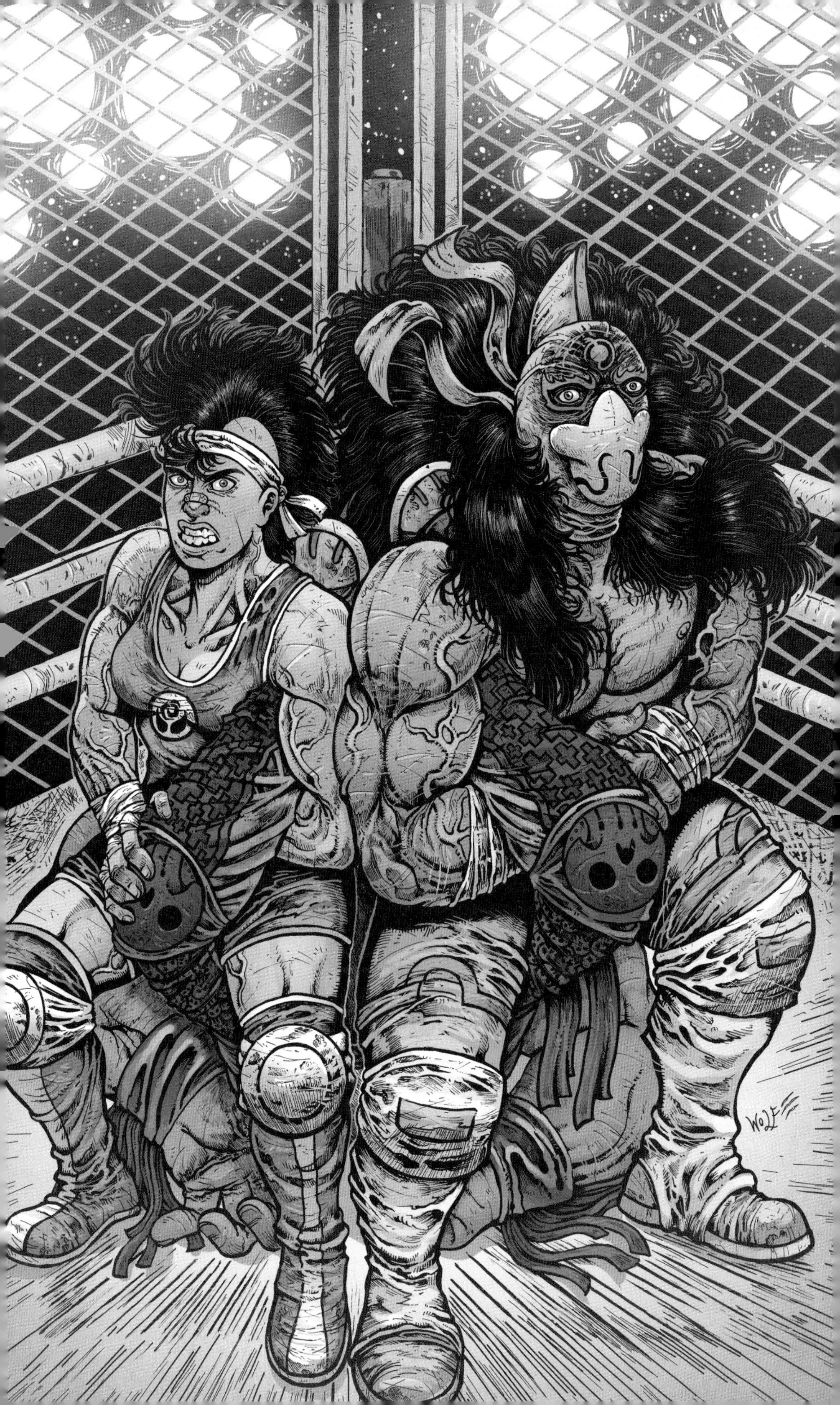

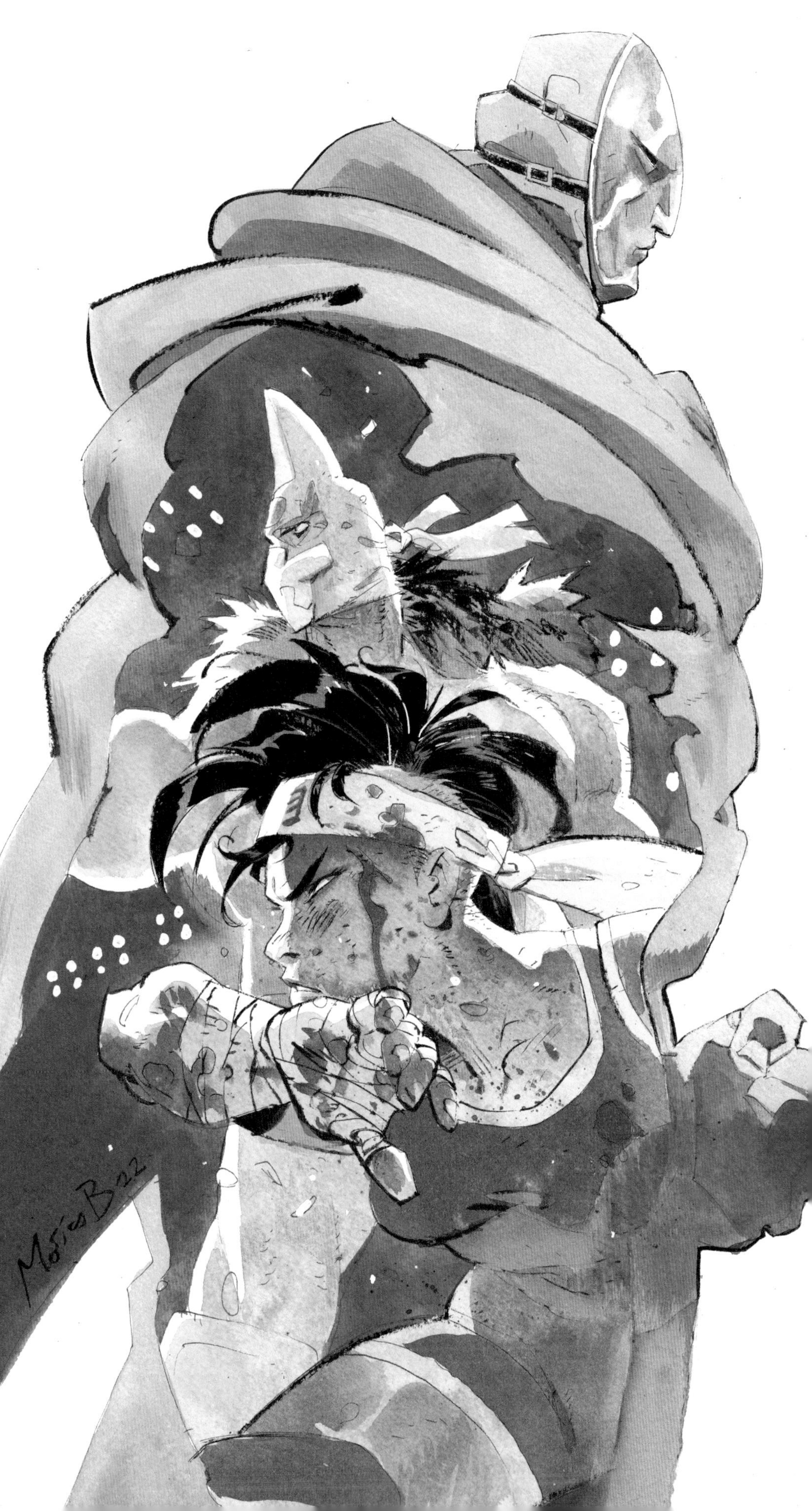

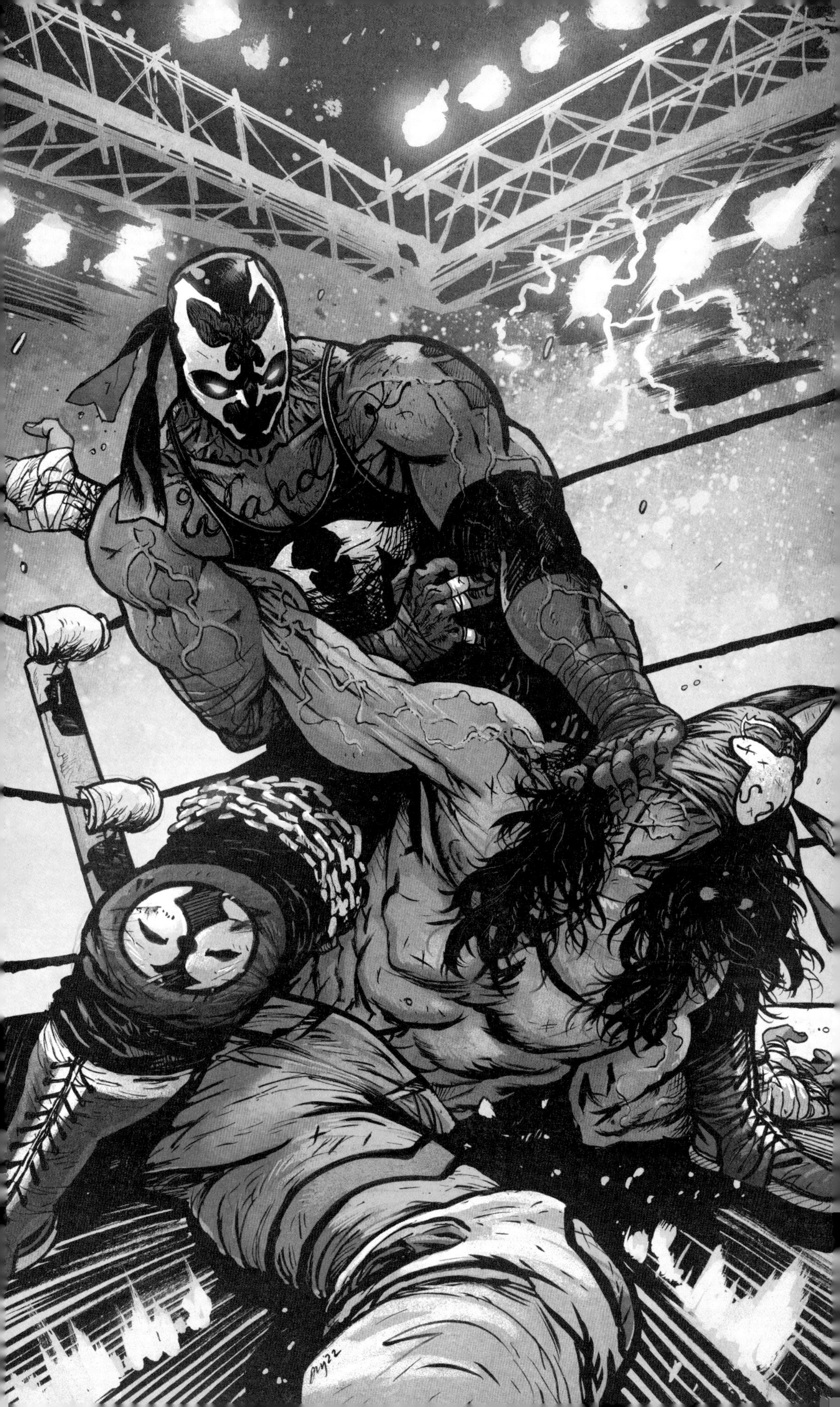

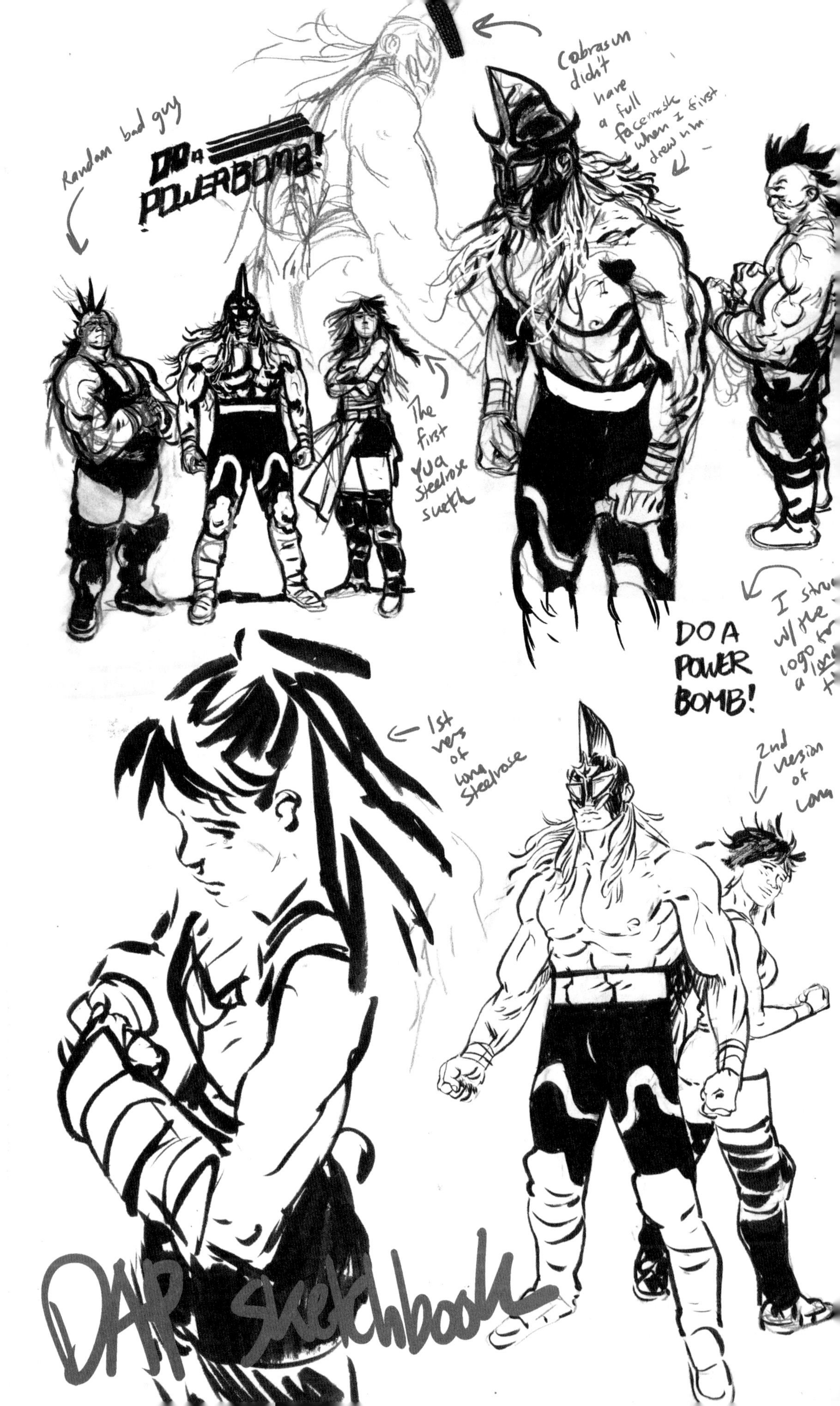
Randan bad guy
DO A POWERBOMB!
Cobrasun didn't have a full facemask when I first drew him
The first Yua Steelrose sketch
DO A POWER BOMB!
1st vers of Lona Steelrose
2nd version of Lona
DAP sketchbook

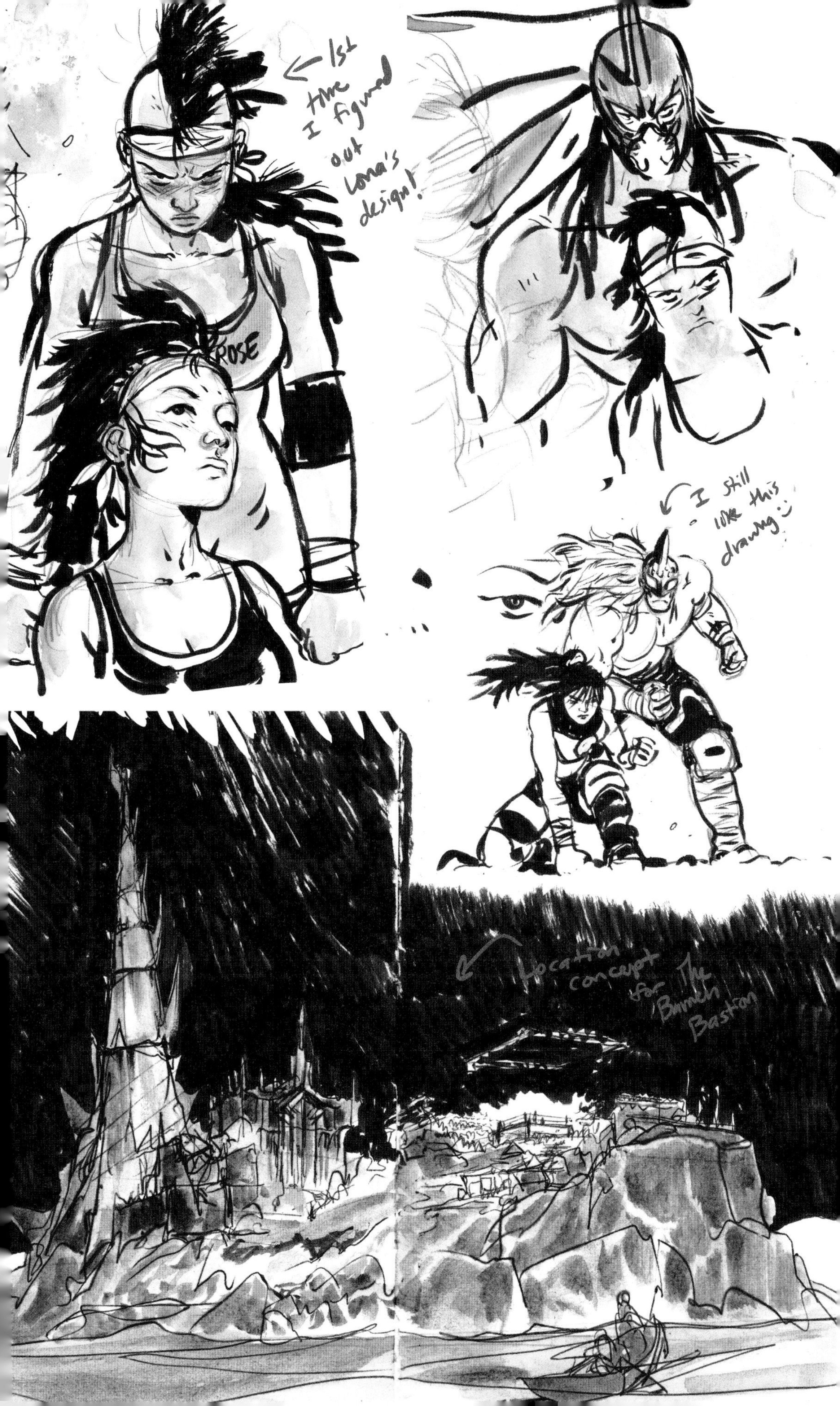
1st time I figured out Lona's design!
I still like this drawing :)
Location concept for The Burnch Bastion

MORE FROM THE WORLDS OF
DANIEL WARREN JOHNSON

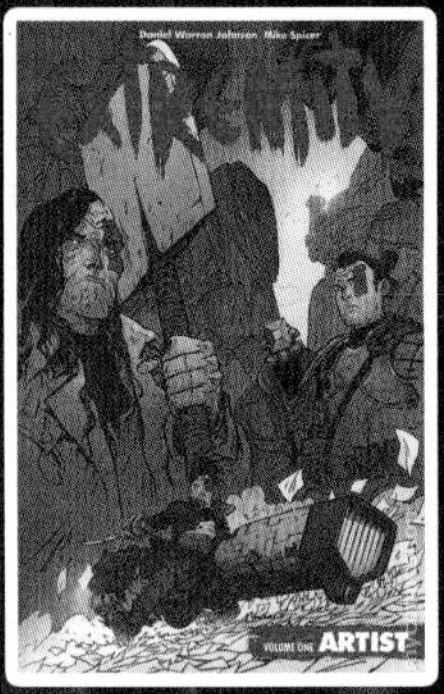
Daniel Warren Johnson Mike Spicer
EXTREMITY
VOLUME ONE ARTIST

EXTREMITY
978-1534302426
978-1534306493

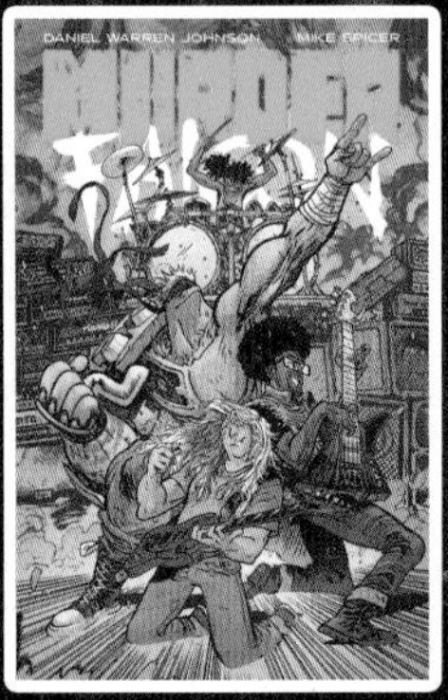
DANIEL WARREN JOHNSON MIKE SPICER
MURDER FALCON

MURDER FALCON
978-1534322134

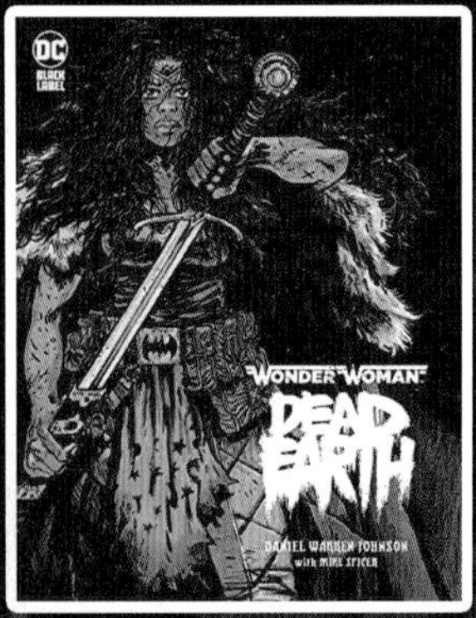
DC BLACK LABEL
WONDER WOMAN
DEAD EARTH
DANIEL WARREN JOHNSON
with MIKE SPICER

WONDER WOMAN: DEAD EARTH
978-1779502612

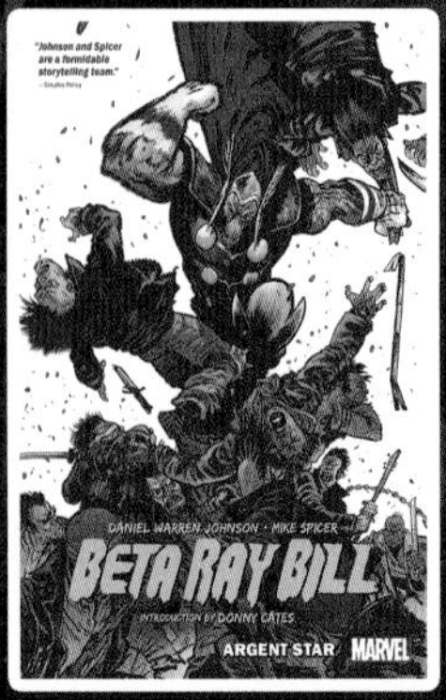
"Johnson and Spicer are a formidable storytelling team."
DANIEL WARREN JOHNSON · MIKE SPICER
BETA RAY BILL
INTRODUCTION BY DONNY CATES
ARGENT STAR
MARVEL

BETA RAY BILL
978-1302928124